Praise for
Shake Down the Stars

"Yes, I know you hear it all the time, but get ready for an absorbing story told with a unique and compelling voice. *Shake Down the Stars* is a treat. Renee Swindle's writing is funny, sharp, heartbreaking, and quirky, and her non–stock characters wonderfully memorable. . . . Enjoy the ride."

—Lalita Tademy, *New York Times* bestselling
author of *Cane River* and *Red River*

"Renee Swindle's *Shake Down the Stars* is a rich, savvy exploration of the many kinds of love, loss, and dysfunction that can unearth us or save us, bedevil us or deliver us . . . as complex and hilarious as it is surprising and lovely. *Shake Down the Stars* holds a mirror up to our best and worst selves, and Swindle writes with unflagging compassion and irresistible humor."

—ZZ Packer, author of *Drinking Coffee Elsewhere*

"I love, love, love Renee Swindle's *Shake Down the Stars*! It's fresh and unfamiliar—which is quite the trick these days! I love the protagonist and the very unlikely yet charming love interest. The novel manages to be both light and heavy all at the same time. I cannot tell you how much I like it. Well, I can. . . . *I loved it*. Seriously. One of my favorite reads of the past couple years."

—Nichelle D. Tramble, author of
The Dying Ground and *The Last King*

continued . . .

ALSO BY RENEE SWINDLE

Please Please Please

shake down the stars

Renee Swindle

 NEW AMERICAN LIBRARY

New American Library
Published by the Penguin Group
Penguin Group (USA) Inc., 375 Hudson Street,
New York, New York 10014, USA

USA | Canada | UK | Ireland | Australia | New Zealand | India | South Africa | China

Penguin Books Ltd., Registered Offices: 80 Strand, London WC2R 0RL, England
For more information about the Penguin Group visit penguin.com.

First published by New American Library,
a division of Penguin Group (USA) Inc.

First Printing, August 2013
10 9 8 7 6 5 4 3 2 1

 REGISTERED TRADEMARK—MARCA REGISTRADA

LIBRARY OF CONGRESS CATALOGING-IN-PUBLICATION DATA:

Swindle, Renee.
  Shake down the stars/Renee Swindle.
    p. cm
  ISBN 978-0-451-41664-3
  1. Divorced women—Fiction. 2. Self-realization in women—Fiction. 3. Daughters—
Death—Fiction. 4. Friendship—Fiction. I. Title.
  PS3569.W537S53 2013
  813'.54—dc23   2012043576

Set in Bell MT
Designed by Spring Hoteling

Printed in the United States of America

PUBLISHER'S NOTE
This is a work of fiction. Names, characters, places, and incidents either are the product of the
author's imagination or are used fictitiously, and any resemblance to actual persons, living or dead,
business establishments, events, or locales is entirely coincidental.
  The publisher does not have any control over and does not assume any responsibility for author
or third-party Web sites or their content.

For my parents, James Swindle and Lucille Swindle

For my agent, B. J. Robbins

And for Todd Foster

acknowledgments

For her constant support and encouragement, I'd like to thank my agent, B. J. Robbins. Thanks for standing by me over the years, B.J. Here's to many more.

For her keen eye and invaluable feedback, I'd like to thank my editor, Ellen Edwards. Every writer should be so lucky. I'd also like to thank everyone at NAL for helping make this book possible.

For their support and friendship, I thank the women of the Finish Party: Farai Chideya, Alyss Dixson, Jacqueline Luckett, ZZ Packer, Deborah Santana, Lalita Tademy, and Nichelle Tramble Spellman. I am so blessed to have you in my life.

Thank you to the writers I've worked with over the years, with a special thanks to: Heather Collins, Molly Thomas, Eric Pfieffer, Kelly Allgaier, Emily Morganti, Joseph Garrett, Cecily Sheppard, Beth Desmonti, Kelly Damian, Jonathan Seyfried, Kelly Tanner Jones, Emma Talbott, Elizabeth Nix, Max Delgado, Alex Dolan, Kay Spencer, and Miki Kashtan.

Further thanks to Jane Chandler for taking the time to speak with me; my beloved meditation instructor, John Osajima; and

Boniford Burnett, whom I look forward to seeing graduate from UC Berkeley. Thanks as well to all my students at Solano Community College and Diablo Valley College, San Ramon Campus.

For helping me stick with my initial idea and for their friendship, thanks to Chris Faber and Claudia Guerra. Thanks also to my longtime friends and early readers, Liz Gonzalez, Luna Calderon, and Susan Carpendale.

I'm grateful to everyone who contacted me on Facebook or sent an e-mail asking when the next book was coming out. Your messages kept me going.

Thanks to my parents for supporting me in my dream. One day I hope to pay you back!

Finally, thanks to Todd Foster and Grace Foster for opening their home and hearts. Love to you both.

shake down the stars

one

It's two in the afternoon, and I'm already nursing a bottle of scotch I took from the banquet hall where my sister's engagement party will take place. I've spent the last thirty-two hours with my family and figure if anyone deserves an early-afternoon drink, it's me.

Mostly I've been hanging out in one of two libraries. Margot's party is being held in an actual mansion: a now-defunct gentleman's club high up in the Oakland hills. The place is straight out of *The Great Gatsby* with its expansive lawns, indoor swimming pool, smoking room, the aforementioned libraries, and lookout tower covered in ivy. There are thirty rooms in all, two stadium-sized banquet halls, and a twenty-four-hour butler for VIP guests like my sister and her football player fiancé.

After filling my glass, I go to the window and spy my sister outside on the lawn, bitching at the gardener and his assistant. It's late September, and the sky is turning a foreboding gray; the wind is in a foul mood, lashing out at all the carefully placed freesias and gerbera daisies strung around the gazebo and attached to the back of every single chair on the lawn—all three hundred of them. Margot has it in her head that her guests will be distracted by the lopsided bushes just behind the gazebo, when, frankly, I suspect they're going to be more distracted by the rain that will surely fall on their heads if a storm breaks out.

Whatever.

I turn from the window and begin scanning the library's massive leather-bound collection until I decide on *The House of Mirth*. I'm about to sit at a small table near one of the stained-glass windows when a man the size of a troll walks inside. He steps directly up to me with an expectant grin on his face as though we know each other, but I've never seen him before in my life and have to assume he's with the wedding party that's rented the east wing of the estate. He's built like a wrestler and wears a silver suit that strains against his Popeye-like biceps; his chest bubbles out from his shirt like a growth. He looks, in fact, like a baby shark standing on its dorsal fins.

He runs his tongue over his upper lip while staring at me. "You. Are. Lovely."

"And you," I say, waving my hand at the alcohol-induced stench rising between us, "are. Shit. Faced."

"No shame in it. I'm here to celebrate, after all. I see you're not holding back either," he adds, nodding toward my scotch.

I raise my glass and take a sip. "Touché."

"Name's Selwyn. And you are?"

"About to read my book, if you don't mind."

He points at me with the same hand that's holding his glass. "You've got spunk. I like that."

"Spunk?"

"Yeah. Gotta little fire going on."

I look him over while taking another pull from my drink. He's not exactly troll-sized, probably five foot seven at best, but

I'm five foot nine and in heels, so from my vantage point he may as well be a Lilliputian. An Oompa Loompa. A hobbit. "How tall are you exactly?"

"Five-six-and-a-half and proud of it. Never let a man's height fool you. Height is never an indicator of a man's sexual prowess."

"I'll try to remember that."

He studies my face briefly. "I don't remember seeing you at the wedding rehearsal last night. You a friend of the bride or the groom?"

"Neither."

"Neither? You with the other wedding party?"

"Yeah. But it's an engagement party."

"Wooooo. Having an engagement party up here? Must be some engagement. So, you gonna tell me your name or what?"

"Why should I?"

"Because I'd like to get to know you better. Seriously, girl, I'm here all alone, and I have a feeling we'd hit it off. I'm the groom's cousin. I'm here for the wedding tonight, and I'll be on my way home tomorrow morning. I'm a good guy. I live in Livermore. I work for the mayor. No kids. No wife. What do you say we spend a little time together before I leave? Celebrate this weekend of . . . *amore* . . . with a private celebration of our own. You. Me. A bottle of Dom?"

I stare at his finger as it's making its way up and down the side of my arm. I can only hope that he's behaving like a throwback to 1970s bachelorhood because he's drunk. Otherwise, there's no excuse.

"We can take advantage of my room," he says. "The view is something to behold. Come on, baby. You look like you could use a little fun. And trust me: Selwyn P. Jones is a whole lotta fun. Ow!" He jumps back with a yelp.

Startled, I jump back, too. "How drunk are you?"

"You like James Brown?"

"I—"

"I *love* James Brown. Check this out." He kicks his leg and jumps into a furious spin. *"Ow!"* he yelps. "Hit me!"

I consider doing just that—hard over his head—but instead I look around the room for hidden cameras. Surely Margot is playing a joke on me. But no. No cameras. Just me and a drunk troll imitating James Brown.

I take two swigs from my drink as I watch him dance. It's probably the alcohol distorting my judgment, but from the little footage I've seen of James Brown, Selwyn's imitation seems pretty good. After another gulp, I'm smiling.

"Good gracious me," he says, "look at that smile. Baby, you've got a five-hundred-kilowatt smile." Seeing that he has me, he speeds up—pushing his pelvis out and back, swiveling his small hips this way and that. "Ow!" he yells. "Hit me two times." He kicks, but, suddenly winded, he bends over at the waist with one hand resting on his knee while clutching his stomach with the other.

"You okay?"

"I sure am feeling those crab cakes I had earlier." He pauses long enough to gaze up at me. "Come on, baby. What do you say? Let's spend some time together."

I kind of half shrug and half smile. "Okay. Sure."

"Really?"

"Yeah. Why not?"

"You're serious?"

"Yeah, I'm serious."

"Serious *serious*?"

"Is there another kind of serious?"

"Wow," he mutters. "I can't believe my luck. Hey, we don't have to stay here, you know. We can go into the city if you want.

Have a real night together. This is great. What time should I pick you up?"

"I think you misunderstand. I'm not interested in a date, but if you want to come up to my room, you're welcome to."

"Excuse me?"

"I'm in the Queen Anne. Give me ten minutes and you can come up."

"Hold on, now. Let me get this straight. You're inviting me . . . up to your room?"

"Yes."

"*Now?*"

"Yes. Now. Only thing, you have twenty minutes from the time you arrive. After that, I want you out." I go for the bottle of scotch on the table, leaving him with a dumbfounded expression hanging off his face. Four years ago, during my short stint in therapy, my therapist told me that my drinking and sleeping around served as nothing more than Band-Aids that would only cause deeper pain in the long run. She added that my wounds ran deep and were crying out for my attention. I dumped her soon after, telling myself that I couldn't take another second of her banal metaphors. Deep down, though, I know she must have been right on some level. I'm not an idiot, after all, and know perfectly well I'm acting out. What I don't know is how to make myself stop—or even if there's a point to stopping.

Selwyn claps loudly. "Goodness gracious. I am one lucky man. I have to tell you, though, twenty minutes isn't gonna be nearly enough. You're gonna want more soon as I—"

I hold up my hand. "Twenty minutes, and then I don't know you and you don't know me."

"Okay, okay. Fine, baby. But I should warn you: The ladies go crazy over Selwyn P. Jones, and you're gonna want way more than twenty."

I pick up the bottle and head toward the door. "Doubt it."

I change into a pair of short sweats and an old Cal T-shirt and take another look out the window. The sky is still storm gray, but the wind has died down. Margot stands on the lawn, talking to the manager of the club while staff members adjust the flowers laced around the gazebo. The gardener and his assistant work on trimming the bushes. *Margot: 1; Gentleman's club: 0.*

The football player sits in the last row of chairs doing his best to . . . teeeext aaaaa meeeeesssssssage, his massive fingers pounding Frankenstein-like against the tiny keyboard. The width of his back and small, peanut-sized head give him the shape of a walrus. Ask him a question about the meaning of life and the exchange goes something like the following:

> **Me:** So, tell me, Curtis, what's the meaning of life?
>
> **Curtis:** I don't know about any of that. I just try to stay focused on the game and my team. I'm a Christian, though, if that's what you mean.
>
> **Me:** Do you fear global warming will destroy life as we know it?
>
> **Curtis:** I don't know about any of that. I just try to stay focused on the game and my team. I believe in God, though, if that's what you mean.

Curtis is the Oakland Raiders' star quarterback and is slated to help them win the Super Bowl. If that's not enough, he made a chart-topping R and B album last year and earned a recent book contract; plus there are the countless endorsements coming out of his football player's ass. It's been a recurring dream that I can somehow get ahold of a mere quarter of his earnings and give it to the fledging school district where I teach.

I hear a cautious knock at the door, and assuming it's the troll, tell him to come in. When he sees me in my shorts and T-shirt, he gawks as though I'm wearing a negligee. "You look amazing."

"Could you do us both a favor and drop the gigolo act?"

"Who's acting? You look good, girl." He claps his hands together and steps farther inside. "Nice digs. I likes."

He wears a patterned silk robe and brown slippers; his calf muscles bulge beneath the black trim of his robe as he struts around. "I try to work out at least four times a week," he announces before disrobing. He flexes his muscles. He's naked except for the slippers and a pair of black silk boxers. "May I?" he asks, eyeing the various bottles of booze on top of the antique bar.

"Help yourself."

He pours a shot of bourbon and downs it with a quick shake of the head and smack of the lips. He then flicks off his shoes and leaps kiddie-style onto the bed, giving the empty space beside him a few pats. "We don't have much time, baby. I want you to experience what many have said is the best love they've ever had."

I take a sip of my own drink, and then another. "I'm sure I'm about to experience something."

I keep my eyes trained on the ceiling as he kisses me. He's a surprisingly good kisser, but I realize I'm not drunk enough to do what we're about to do, and all too soon his tongue feels more like a wet mass of wiggling flesh, and my own tongue, horrified, begins to retreat.

"What's wrong, baby? You seem a little tense."

"I think I need another drink."

"You don't need another drink; you need to relax. Why don't you smile for me? If I see that kilowatt smile of yours, I'll be able to turn on the magic and you'll feel good in no time." He snaps his fingers to a beat only he can hear. "You wanna have a good time, don't you?" he says, going into his James Brown. "I say, 'You wanna have a good time?'" When he juts his elbows out and starts bobbing his head, I smile. He actually has a sweet face. Nice long eyelashes. Big brown eyes. Soft lips.

"There's that smile." He grins. He stares down at me and touches my chin with his finger. This time when we kiss, I find myself thinking about a certain activity that would help me relax even more. I turn away so that he can no longer kiss my face. I then push his shoulders, nudging him southward.

It doesn't take him long to get the hint, and he begins to wiggle his way under the sheets like an excited seal. He stops just before his head is about to disappear. "I've been told I'm the best there is when it comes to certain oral delights."

"You certainly talk a lot."

He gives me a wink and disappears under the blankets. I'm feeling better and thinking that things just might work out, when there's a tap at the door followed by Margot bursting into the room without the prerequisite "Come in."

I immediately use my thighs as a vise, willing Selwyn not to budge. I then quickly tuck his robe behind my pillow and rearrange the blankets into a huge mound over my knees, clutching a second pillow to my chest for good measure.

"I can't believe this weather," she says. "Why me? Why today?"

One good thing about narcissism: Margot doesn't notice my erratic behavior for a second; nor does she notice the pile of blankets. Honestly, she's just that self-centered.

"Haven't you ever heard of waiting for permission before walking into someone's room?" I give my thighs a firm squeeze and speak loudly enough that Selwyn will get the point—*Do not move!* He responds by surreptitiously lying flat on the bed and shaping himself into a motionless blob.

Margot takes long, elegant steps across the room. She spent most of her childhood on the beauty pageant circuit and still moves as though balancing a book on her head. She soaked up every pretty feature from Mom and her father, and now serves as a perfect composite of the two: doe-eyed, high-cheek-boned, worthy of every double take she receives. I, on the other hand, took after my father: long-limbed and angular, with a wide mouth and deep-set eyes. No one has ever mistaken us for sisters—half or not.

She stands directly next to the bed and peers out the window. "I guess I shouldn't complain about the weather when I have so much to be grateful for. I must be one of the happiest women alive."

"Lucky for the rest of us, your humility remains intact."

"Seriously, P, I'm truly grateful. Last night Curtis was so sweet. After kissing me all over my face, he fell down to his knees and kissed my—"

"Too much information! I keep telling you, I don't need to know every detail of your sex life."

"I was going to say he fell to his knees and kissed my *hand*, stupid. He proposed all over again."

"How many times is the man going to propose?"

"As many times as he wants, thank you very much. I can't believe how God has blessed me. He's handsome. Rich. Kind. What more could a girl want?"

"Intelligence?"

She cuts her eyes.

I feel the troll give my ankle a shake. Message received, I ask, "So, what do you want, anyway? I was about to take a bath."

"I wanted to talk. I'm a little down, I guess. I wish Grampy were here is all."

She sits next to me on the bed. I worry briefly that she'll catch on to the fact that there's a man under the covers, but no surprise, she's completely oblivious.

"I keep imagining how happy Grampy would be if he knew I was marrying the one and only Curtis Randolph."

Margot's father raised me from the time I was eleven. His father, Grandpa Wright, or Grampy, died two years ago. My own father, the deadbeat, left when I was barely two months old. He sent Mom money from time to time, but never with a return address. By the time I turned three, he'd disappeared altogether, turning Mom and me into characters from a Dickens novel. Mom worked two jobs, as a waitress and a sales clerk, but money was as elusive as that person you've always had a crush on but who never notices you.

After years of life on the poverty line, Mom met Charles Wright, Margot's father. Charles was a banker at the time, and, like some kind of economic superhero, swooshed in, married Mom, and moved us three rungs up the socioeconomic ladder. Margot was born a year into the marriage, and suddenly Mom had the life she'd always wanted: a man, a home, a little girl she could afford to spoil rotten. I, meanwhile, gained a sister eleven years my junior. Then, sometime while I was in high school, Charles announced that he'd been called to serve God. He started a church in a small movie theater, and now that same church is some one thousand members strong.

"I know you miss Grampy, Margot," I say, "but you should be grateful that your father is alive and present in your life. Try to focus on that."

"You're right," she says, taking my hand. "You're right. I wish more than anything that someone else could be here, too."

I lower my gaze. "Margot."

"Dad is going to say a few words about Grampy, and I'd like him to say a few words about Hailey, too. I think it's important that they *both* be remembered tonight."

"*Margot—*"

"I want tonight to be about family. I think we should honor her."

I pull my hand away. "I don't think that's a good idea. Just leave her out of it, okay?"

"But it's a blessed event, and we need to have her presence here."

"Blessed event? What makes an engagement party a blessed event?"

"It's blessed to me. Curtis and I are making a holy promise to each other. Daddy agrees. I think it would be nice if he said a few words. Just a few, that's all. I want everything to feel spiritual, and I want my niece to be with us."

I shake my head in disbelief. "This isn't about Hailey, Margot; it's about you."

"Me?"

"Yes, you. Look at all the money you're throwing around, and it's not even your wedding yet. Everything is out of control."

"And so what if it is? Curtis and I have been through a lot, and now we're tighter than ever. I want this party to represent that."

"Been through a lot" meaning Curtis has *cheated* a lot. Only eight months ago he was caught messing around with a groupie. Margot forgave him, spurred by his tearful apology and the pair of diamond earrings he gave her. The marriage proposal followed soon after.

I feel the troll's breath on my thigh, slow and labored. I wonder if he's passed out under there, but there's nothing I can do. I need to make sure Margot doesn't sabotage me. "It's your engagement party," I say. "Your marriage, your life. Just whatever you do, please leave Hailey out of it."

"She was my niece, you know. I miss her, too. We all miss her. We will *always* miss her."

"I don't want her mentioned during your party, Margot. I don't."

"Why do you have to be so stubborn?"

"Why do you have to be so selfish? Just leave her out of it, okay?"

Resigned, she rises from the bed. She glances at the drink on the nightstand, then makes a point of staring at Selwyn's drink on the opposite table. "You need help, Piper. You really do."

"Okay," I say. "As soon as you leave, I'll get on it. Thanks. See you later."

She saunters to the mirror in response. "I just need one more thing."

"Why am I not surprised?"

"The girls aren't feeling well. Hélène says it's a mild fever. I just checked on them, and they seem fine. Anyway, she says she has some family thing she has to go to—a christening or something—and has to fly to LA. She says she told me, but I swear she didn't. Of course she gave me one of her voodoo stares. I'm certain she's put a curse on me. *That's* why it's so cloudy today."

"You really need to quit with the stereotypes."

"I wanted everyone to see the girls in their chiffon dresses, but now I'm not sure."

Margot's ten-year-old twins, Sophia and Little Margot, are the product of her relationship with the hockey player no one speaks of. Like my own father, the hockey player disappeared after he learned he was going to be a father. Unlike my dad, he's been sending monthly checks since the girls' birth—enough money that they attend one of the most expensive schools in the Bay Area, have a nanny who may as well be their surrogate mother, and are set through college.

"Just how sick are they?"

"Sophia's been throwing up, and Margot has a mild case of diarrhea."

"Margot!"

"Well."

"Did you call the doctor?"

"Of course I called the doctor. She said to watch them overnight, make sure they get their fluids, and if they're still under the weather, bring them in on Monday." She shrugs. "I think they're making a turn for the better, but I can't see forcing them to participate. And I can't ask Mom to watch them—*I need her.*"

"So you want me to watch them."

"Would you mind?"

"Of course not."

"Thanks. I knew you'd say yes. I just don't want you to be upset because you'll have to miss the ceremony. But I've already thought it out. You'll be able to watch the film version, and it'll be even better. You can pause and rewind."

I imagine fast-forwarding for long stretches.

I feel a weak hand squeeze my calf and think of all the brain cells Selwyn must have lost by now. "Sounds good. And if that's all you need, I think I'm going to take a bath now."

"We need you upstairs by four o'clock. If I'm not there, tell the voodoo priestess I want her back by Monday morning."

Satisfied, she gives a ta-ta wave—"Thanks, Sis!"—and is out the door.

I wait a few seconds. "All clear."

Hearing he's safe, Selwyn crawls out from beneath the covers like a man recently shipwrecked, clawing at sand and inhaling massive doses of air.

"Are you okay?"

His eyes roll upward as he offers a weak nod.

I get out of bed and lock the door. Selwyn, though, remains on his back, still trying to catch his breath.

"You sure you're okay?"

His chest rises up and down in great heaves. He covers his

forehead with his arm as he stares into the ceiling. It takes
him a while, but then he suddenly jerks his head in my direction. "Hold on now. Wait a second. Your sister is marrying *Curtis Randolph*?"

I nod.

"*The* Curtis Randolph?"

I nod again.

"Curtis Randolph of the Oakland Raiders Curtis Randolph?"

"Yes, Selwyn. Curtis Randolph of the Oakland Raiders."

"Curtis Randolph," he murmurs. "*Curtis Randolph*. That
man . . . That man is the top quarterback in the country! He's
going to take the Raiders all the way to the Super Bowl! Damn,
girl, I just might have to dump the wedding I'm going to and
check out your sister's engagement party. What time does it
start?"

"None of your business."

"But it might be fun to—"

"You're not invited."

"Damn," he mumbles. "Curtis Randolph. What if I just stop
by for a second?"

"You're *not* invited."

"Okay. All right. *Damn*. Curtis Randolph. That man is
a wizard with the ball. A genius." He eases himself up with a
grin and kisses my shoulder. "Lotta love between you and your
sister, huh? You two are like *this*." He crosses his fingers and
chuckles.

"Shut up."

I refuse to look at him but feel his stare and big goofy smile
all the same. He takes a finger and tucks a strand of hair behind
my ear. "Mmmmm. You sure are pretty when you're pissed," he
says. "Which is a good thing, 'cause I get the feeling you get
pissed a lot." He laughs to himself.

"Not funny," I say, giving him a playful slap near the shoulder.

"Aw, come here." He takes me in his arms and kisses my temple. "Shall we continue?"

"I don't think so."

"Why not, baby? We'll find our groove in no time. I have a feeling it's just around the corner."

"More like the next state."

"Aw, come on. Don't be like that." He smiles and lets his fingers do a little dance on my shoulder.

I push him away.

After giving his head a scratch, he sighs and falls back against the bed. "Curtis Randolph. Damn. Curtis Randolph." He sucks in a breath and adds, "Well, I should probably get ready for the ceremony anyhow. Would you like to be my date?"

"Can't. You heard—I'm watching my nieces."

"Well," he says, "can't say I didn't try. You're a lovely woman, Kilowatt."

"Thanks."

He pauses, eyes locked with mine. "May I ask what your sister was talking about? What you need to move on from?"

"Absolutely not."

He raises a hand in surrender. "I understand. I do. I just want to say, though, if you ever need anyone to talk to—well, I understand pain. Me and pain? We go *way* back."

I see how sincere he is and take his hand. "Thanks. I appreciate it."

He kisses my cheek and climbs out of the bed. After finding his slippers and robe, he goes to the door. "So I guess this is good-bye, huh?"

"Looks like it."

"Well, if you're ever in Livermore, promise to look me up."

"I will never be in Livermore." I'm not even sure where

Livermore is, actually. Not to mention the ugly sound of it—makes me think of various organs like kidneys and spleens.

"But if you are. I'm an attorney. I work in the mayor's office. City hall. Can't miss it. Now, what do you say you give me one more smile before I leave?"

I toss my shoulder up, as Margot might, and smile as if posing for a picture.

"Beautiful," he says, shaking his head. "Just beautiful."

two

I don't need to rely on my college French to understand that Hélène is pissed. I stand just inside the girls' room, watching her pick up clothes while cursing under her breath. Margot's twins are camped out on the Edwardian sofa, watching TV.

Hélène is Senegalese and arrived in the States via France. She has wide square teeth and small red eyes she lines heavily with black eyeliner. As usual, she wears her signature overalls and bright yellow sneakers. The front of her hair is braided into what looks like an upside-down basket with a fluffy synthetic ponytail shooting out the back, much like feathers on a rooster. The first sign that she was a nanny to be reckoned with was her absolute refusal to wear a dress or straighten her hair. Margot threatened to fire her over her appearance, but the girls instantly fell in love with her and begged their mother to keep her on. *Hélène: 2; Margot: 0!*

Hélène is the only nanny not afraid to stand up to Margot, and the only nanny who's lasted longer than a year. Margot keeps her around not only because Sophia and Margot adore her, but she considers it a bonus that she speaks only French to the girls and is willing to work on the cheap. We have no idea how old she is. An older-looking twenty? A younger-looking forty? No one dares ask.

She marches up to me. "Your *sis*tah," she says, pointing an inordinately long finger in my face. "Your *sis*tah is *no* good. I tell her my sister have a baby and I need to go to the christening, but she *no* care! The christening is in LA. I have to catch the plane, you know? I told her last month I no stay for this party because I have to be with my family." She thumps her chest. "*My* family. What she think? I have no family? I tell her I fly today, and she calls me a liar. A liar! Why would I lie about such things, eh?" She glances over at the twins, then lowers her voice conspiratorially. "Her girls are sick, and she don't care. All that woman cares about is her party."

She's right. Since Margot started dating the football player, the girls have been getting the short shrift.

I say, a little too late, "I'm sure she cares."

Hélène guffaws. "Care. What she know about care?"

"I'm sure after the wedding Margot will—"

"She have party tonight for engagement. She have party last weekend for engagement. How many parties does one person need, eh?"

Last weekend's party was with her closest friends—in-house manicures and pedicures followed by a catered tea, the event covered by a style magazine. She and the football player have also been featured in various magazines with the occasional spots on entertainment news programs. Since the engagement, they've also been followed by paparazzi, giving Margot the excuse to buy several pairs of expensive sunglasses.

"Last night I tell that woman—your *sis*tah—I tell her she needs to—" She glares hard as if she's suddenly had enough with me, too. "Eh. What good does it do to talk except I waste my breath. That woman—that woman, she never change." She finds her purse and rattles off to the girls in French as she kisses their cheeks. She then stares me down. "Sleep by eight, eh?" She juts her chin toward Sophia. "And don't let that one there eat no ice cream. I don't care how she beg."

She gives me one last hard stare before deciding it's okay to leave. After she closes the door, I walk over to the girls and join them on the couch. They have blankets up to their chins as they stare at the TV. They are identical down to their dusty-colored skin and elongated faces; their light brown curls and hazel eyes are remnants of the hockey player. "Should I order soup?"

"Yeah," they mumble simultaneously.

Sophia says blandly, "I want celery root with porcini."

Little Margot says, "I want the butternut squash with marjoram."

"When I was a kid, we had the choice of tomato, bean, or chicken noodle."

"Ew!"

I love the girls, of course, but they've grown up in a way that has afforded school lunch menus with choices like pan-seared tuna sandwiches and organic mashed potatoes. Even now, at ten years old, they carry the world-weary attitude of the rich, where only trips to Paris or Italy will suffice.

I call room service. On TV, a tween with an eighties-style blond do holds court in front of her locker. She's in a dither about—what else? A boy.

"What are you watching?"

"Dena Delaney," they reply in unison.

Margot says, "We own, like, the entire series."

"Seasons One through Six," Sophia adds.

"We're watching, like, every episode starting from Season One."

"It's our *Dena Delaney* marathon."

"We're, like, already halfway finished with Season Three," says Margot.

"So are you two upset that you can't go to the ceremony?"

"I am," Sophia says. "Margot isn't."

Margot says, "The wedding is, like, way more important— that's why. I'd rather be sick for this than the wedding. We can't miss the wedding for anything. We'll be pissed if we do."

"Yeah, pissed."

I start to watch TV along with them, but one minute in, I'm shocked at how everyone is behaving as if they're much older. And while the twins are in the habit of overusing the word *like*, this show, like, takes it, like, to a whole other, like, level.

"You guys wanna play a game of cards?"

"*No.*"

"Monopoly?"

"*No.*"

They don't bother looking my way. They're, *like*, transfixed.

I reach out and simultaneously touch their foreheads. "Are you feeling any better?"

"We are," Margot says. "It's Britney Bartles-Smith's fault we're sick in the first place. She had it, and now almost everyone in our class has it."

"Every. One," Sophia says. She's the quieter of the two, watchful and old-lady acting since birth. She says, "I'm feeling better. I think I'll have some ice cream after I finish my soup."

"You can't," Margot says. "We'll have ice cream tomorrow with some of Mom and Curtis's cake. Besides, if we have it tonight, we might throw it up."

"Yeah, we'll be like Ashley Burrows."

I gather from their high-pitched giggles that they're feeling better.

"Ashley throws up on purpose," Margot explains. "She doesn't want to get fat."

"How old is Ashley Burrows?"

"Ten."

Margot says, "She has a therapist she sees every week." She looks toward the television. "We'll have cake tomorrow when we're feeling better," she announces as though speaking aloud to herself.

Sophia says, "Yeah, when we're feeling better."

They perfected their relationship as zygotes swimming in Margot's uterus. I imagine when they're much older, they'll continue to function like a well-mechanized impenetrable team. At ninety, after long lives with their husbands and their own kids, they'll share a house, locked in a comfortable routine of TV watching and gossip. The only person missing, of course, will be Hailey.

I sigh quietly and reach for the phone. "Soup. Coming right up."

The sound of people applauding wakes me. I'd meant to sneak out and watch the ceremony from the beginning, but I must have fallen asleep. I check on Sophia and Margot. Seeing that they're sound asleep, I find my sweater and quietly make my way downstairs and outside.

I stand close to the main building, far enough away that I won't be noticed. Almost every single seat is filled, and all eyes are glued to the gazebo, which is lit up with soft pink trellis lights. The sun is setting, right on cue, the wind has died down, and the sky is magically clear of rain clouds. It's as if even the weather knows to obey my sister or else.

The football player takes Margot's hand and gazes into her

eyes. Both he and Margot are miked. "I want you to be my woman. I wanted you to be my woman from the second I saw you."

I wait to see if he might beat his chest and drag her off by the hair, but instead he bends to his knee. His suit strains against all his muscles. Applause breaks out as he takes Margot's newly de-ringed hand and he reaches into his pocket. A woman in the back yells, "Aw, right now!" and everyone laughs.

"Margot, I want you to be my woman for life." He opens the small velvet box, and Margot screams and covers her mouth in a way that signals Curtis has gone off script.

She goes for the ring, much like Curtis chases down a football, all hands and speed, and before Curtis pops the question (again), she's already put the ring on her finger and is waving it to the audience. "Can you all believe this? He got me a new ring!" There are a few chuckles in the back as Margot fans herself as though she might faint. She manages to settle down, though, and finally gazes at the football player who is still on his knee with a big dopey grin on his face. "Margot Marie Wright, will you marry me?"

In the silence that follows, Margot reaches down and takes the football player's chin between her fingers. "Curtis, I am your woman and you—you are my man. In front of God, in front of our family and friends assembled here today, I humbly accept your proposal of marriage." Curtis brings her to his knee, and they put their tongues through a kind of roping exercise.

Mom and the Reverend stand up in the front row and begin to applaud. Everyone joins in, and Margot and the football player finally come up for air. Margot grins and holds up an I'm-not-finished-here-yet finger. She then takes the football player's hand and stares deeply into his eyes. "I will love you till I'm old and gray. You are mine and I am yours, Curtis Francis Randolph, and I want everyone here to know how much I love you."

He looks at her adoringly. "Oh baby," he says with a sigh, going in for a deep kiss.

"Oh God," I moan. I can't take another second and sneak off to the side of the main building, past the front parking lot, and down the path that leads to one of the lookout benches surrounding the grounds. I sit near a pathway next to a secluded wooded area. The sky is clear enough that I can see Venus and Hercules to the south of Serpens. If I had my telescope, I'd focus on Jupiter and its three satellites—Callisto, Ganymede, and Io. It's a perfect night for Jupiter.

When I was young, I was called more than a few names for my obsession with astronomy, but I never cared. Looking at the stars has always been one of the few things in life that's given me a sense of calm. Mr. Hoffman, a man Mom dated for nearly three years, introduced me to astronomy. He taught science at an all-boys Catholic prep school in Manhattan and would dress fastidiously each morning in a suit and tie. It was weeks before I realized he was a teacher and not a banker or office employee.

He lived in a two-bedroom house one block from our apartment building, and while Mom worked her night job waitressing, Mr. Hoffman would babysit. He loved Mom with the kind of love that's painful to watch, even for a nine-year-old girl, but when I asked her one night when she was going to marry him, she laughed like I hadn't seen her laugh in months. "Now where did you go get that idea from? Me and David? Marriage? Child, you have gone and lost your natural-born mind." She'd just come home from her job at the department store. When I pressed her on the matter she said, "He's a nice man, Piper, I'll give you that, but nice doesn't pay the bills. I'm looking for someone who can help us out of this shitty situation we're in, and marrying a Jew who doesn't make good money makes no sense."

She laughed again and flipped off her shoes as she headed toward her bath.

But she continued to see Mr. Hoffman just the same. We spent most nights at his house, in fact. He'd have dinner waiting for her when she came home from work; he'd massage her feet while we watched TV, and he'd take her out whenever he could, usually dinner and a movie.

On the nights when Mom worked late, Mr. Hoffman would heat up TV dinners, and we'd watch our favorite sitcoms, followed by tapings of *Cosmos* or *Nova*. Mr. Hoffman always talked excitedly about space; he'd give me books on the solar system and astronomy and would tell me about the laws of planetary motion and measuring space through light. He'd often take out his telescope, too, a Meade TX with auto star, and we'd go into his backyard and spend hours stargazing. He'd often say he'd love for me to grow up to become an astronomer or astronaut, as easy as Mom would say she'd love for me to grow up and find a job in a nice office that paid good benefits.

When Mom started cheating on him, we both pretended nothing was going on. But I'd already met the other guy, Uncle Gerald, and when she'd call late and say she'd have to work, I knew she was lying. Eventually, while we watched TV one night, Mr. Hoffman admitted he knew what she was up to—"She's with the other guy, isn't she?"

I was devastated when they broke up. Not only was she dumping Mr. Hoffman, but we were moving to Maryland to live with her sister—our eighth move since my birth. On the day we were set to leave, I imagined things would play out as dramatically as they did on TV. I envisioned two different scenarios while Mom and I loaded the U-Haul. In scenario one, I waited patiently for Mr. Hoffman to show up, teary-eyed and begging us to stay. I imagined Mom recognizing how much she loved

him and announcing that we would always be together. To celebrate, he'd give me his old telescope after buying a new one for
himself. *Here, Piper, I want you to have this. I love you as much as if
you were my very own.* In the second scenario, the sadder of the
two, Mom would tell him we were moving no matter what, at
which point he'd get his telescope from his car and hand it over
to me. *Here, Piper, I want you to have this. I'll miss you.*

But Mr. Hoffman never showed up that day, and Mom and I
loaded the U-Haul and started the drive to Maryland without a
good-bye or a telescope. I wrote Mr. Hoffman within a week of
our arrival. The gist of my letter was *I hate it here and miss
you more than anything. Can I at least have your telescope?* His
reply arrived in less than a week, written on the prep school's
stationery. The gist of that letter, which was more than three
pages long, was *I miss your mother more than anything. Is she seeing
anyone?*

I'm half watching the news, half dozing, when I hear a knock
at the door. Danielle, Margot's event planner, greets me by
saying, "Tell them to serve the champagne right after the
second speech. Not a fucking second later. Got it?"

I'm tempted to nod yes, but then I notice she's speaking into
the phone clawed around her ear.

"And the waiters need to enter stage left. Just like we discussed. And tell Walter not to dim the lights until they've started
pouring. I'll have his fucking head if there's a single spill."

Danielle is all height thanks to the ten-inch stilts posing as
shoes she wears. Her form-fitting, shell-colored suit highlights
her red hair, swished tonight into a seashell-shaped pinwheel that
rests on the top of her head. She's the dame in a Raymond Chandler novel, the vamp in a 1940s thriller. She's also Margot's best
friend. Their friendship almost ended recently when Margot told

Danielle that she'd hired the one-name wonder Firth to oversee the wedding.

"We need you downstairs in exactly ten minutes flat."

It takes me a second to realize she's talking to me.

"Curtis has put together a video montage, and we need all family members present. That means you. Front table."

I look down at my sweats and socks. "I'm supposed to watch the girls."

"Not anymore. We're switching things up. I'll watch the twins while you're downstairs."

"Why don't I know anything about this?"

"It's a surprise. Curtis had it in the works for weeks but didn't want anyone to know. Piper—" She exhales a smile. "He's written a song for her, 'We Are a Family Built on Love.' He's going to sing it while showing the video he put together. It's so romantic. He's releasing the song as the first single from the new album. His people are already saying it's going to be a hit. Wait—hold a sec." She's suddenly all business again and begins pacing the room as she bosses around the unfortunate person on the other end of the phone.

Danielle and Margot met when they were cast together in the music video for the hit "Black Bitch/White Bitch: It Ain't No Thang." By the end of the video, Margot and Danielle were hosing each other down with water while the star rapper and his cronies sat on a fake stoop, pointing and laughing. But Margot and Danielle hit it off, despite the circumstances, and now go on annual Best Friends Forever vacations and talk and text incessantly. Seeing that her video and modeling days were numbered, Danielle used the money from her second divorce to start a catering business, which led to her gig as event stylist. No one would know from looking at her elegant hair and makeup that she's capable of doing the wide splits while hanging upside down from a pole, as seen in the heavy metal video "Five Licks of Your Cherry Pie."

Off the phone, she rests her hand on her hip with a straight-forward no-nonsense look in her eye. "Did Margot tell you why she didn't pick me?"

She means for the wedding. Luckily, I don't have to lie. Margot may have told Mom her reasons for choosing Firth over Danielle, but she said nothing to me—although it's easy to assume that she's going for name over friendship.

I reply with the oft-used "Well, you know Margot."

"Yeah," she mutters. "But I don't care what anyone says, damn it; I would've made her wedding as beautiful, if not more beautiful, than that fucking Firth. Fucking bigheaded twit. I'm her best friend, after all, and if anyone knows what she needs, it's me. Shit. Hold on." Her finger pops up, and the pacing resumes. "That is *not* acceptable. He was hired for his fucking expertise, so he should have a plan B. Everyone has a fucking plan B. Wait. Hold on. What are you waiting on? We've got to get you dressed and downstairs!" Even though she's looking right at me, it takes me a moment to realize she means me. "The song and video presentation should only take fifteen minutes tops. And please greet people, Piper. No one has seen you all day. And don't be too embarrassed to cry when Curtis sings. He wants it to be a moving experience." Before I can respond, she takes me by the shoulders and ushers me toward the door. "Go, go, go!" she gunfires. I wait to feel her five-hundred-dollar shoe in my ass before she shuts the door behind me.

The ballroom is decorated art deco style with miniature Chrysler buildings and Model Ts made from finely cut crystal on every table. The male waitstaff wears spats and coattails; the females, beaded flapper dress with feathered headbands. A quartet plays jazz tunes near one of two gurgling champagne fountains. The lighting is low enough that everyone has a warm, golden glow. The football player and his teammates huddle around one of two makeshift bars, their huge round bodies stuffed into their tuxedos until they look like steroid-pumped penguins huddling before a play. Girlfriends and wives cluster at tables. Their barely-there gowns show off their well-oiled skin and firm bodies shaped by personal trainers and silicone. There are enough weaves in the room that I imagine whole villages of Chinese and Indian girls running around newly bald.

I'm helping myself to a few hors d'oeuvres when Mom walks over, decked out in silk organza, cut to show off her bare shoulders and cleavage. Even now that she's a self-proclaimed child of Christ—or whatever—her old ways still tend to make themselves known: low neckline, a skirt above the knee, too-tight sweaters. She can't help herself. Mom has gotten by on her looks even more than Margot has. And I suppose it would be hard not to; she's always reminded me of those classic beauties—the Dorothy Dandridges and Sophia Lorens. Growing up, she'd wanted to be an actress, and she even starred in a few off-off-Broadway plays. Her first and only Broadway play, the short-lived *Cat's Cradle*, starred an up-and-coming actress named Piper Michaels. Mom loved Piper's acting and her name. Mom's career as an actress ended when she turned nineteen and met my dad, a wannabe playwright and all-around loser.

Her smile fades as she looks over my dress. "What's with the burka?"

I'll admit that I'm a tad underdressed, but what do people expect from a high school teacher? Besides, my dress is still nice, in a sixties-style, post-mod kind of way. "I like my dress just fine."

"That makes one of you," she quips. "How are the girls?"

"Fine. They were asleep when I left. Danielle is with them."

She leans in close to my ear. "Did you see the mother?"

I have no idea what she's talking about.

"Curtis's mother. To your left. Tacky silver dress? *Braids.*"

I spot her in no time, laughing with a group of women. Her dress is the silver and black of Curtis's team, and her tiny synthetic braids are cut into a bob.

"What about her?"

Mom lowers her voice. "She brought *collard greens.*" She points to the buffet table against the east wall. I notice three large gray pots that don't fit in with the buffet-style service platters and crystal glasses. "Collard greens," Mom repeats. "And corn bread."

"Oh my God," I say in mock horror, "collard greens and corn bread. What's next? Chit'lins?"

"You know what I mean," she retorts. "Ghet. Toe."

"Guess some of us have forgotten some of the crappy neighborhoods we lived in. Remember the place on Huds—"

She shushes me as if someone might overhear. "Let's leave the past where it belongs, shall we?"

No one in her congregation knows about her—*our*—past. More specifically, they don't know that for most of her adult life, Mom behaved far more like Mary Magdalene than Mary, Mother of Jesus. Since I look so much like my father, she can't separate me from the guy she blames for ending her acting career. And I didn't come up with this idea because we don't get along. Back when she drank and drank too much, she used to go on about all she could have been if she hadn't gotten pregnant. If Mom lives vicariously through Margot—and boy, does she ever—I'm the daughter who symbolizes all she'd rather forget.

The group of football players bursts into laughter, catching

Mom's attention. "I guess Danielle told you about Curtis's surprise. He's amazing, that man." She begins to seek out Mr. Amazing himself from the mass of laughing testosterone. One extra-large player steps off to the side and—*wait a second*. It's not Curtis holding court, as I'd thought, but *Selwyn*—standing next to Curtis in his silver suit, drink in hand—life of the party!

"That little bastard."

"What?" Mom says, looking around.

"Nothing." I swig back my sparkling water. "I'll be right back."

"Don't take too long," she calls from behind. "They're going to need us at the front table any minute now."

I march right up to Curtis, who stifles his laughter. "Oh hey, y'all. Look who's here—it's my future sister-in-law." And then he does this thing I hate: He hooks his arm around my neck and pulls me in for a quick kiss on the cheek. I have to fight off the urge to wipe my face.

Curtis is the male version of my sister—dimpled, doe-eyed, completely self-centered. "So, listen up, everybody. I have a big surprise I got goin' on, and I have to make sure everything is situated. You all should grab your girls, fellas, and find your seats. They're gonna love what's comin' up next." They all fall into some kind of fist maneuver that involves a series of punches and hand claps that end in a loud "Woop!"

I, meanwhile, shoot a mean glare at Selwyn, who only shrugs and sips his drink. As soon as Curtis leaves, I say, "Can I talk to you for a second?"

One of the Hulk-sized penguins looks from me to the troll. "You know this guy?"

I take Selwyn by the wrist. "Not exactly."

I march him over to the other side of the room where no one can hear us. He looks up at me sheepishly.

"I told you not to show up here!"

He raises his hands as if completely innocent. "That was Curtis Randolph! I couldn't resist. Besides, my cousin's wedding was weak." He sips his drink. "Wait until I tell everyone at work. Curtis Randolph!" He takes a step back as though suddenly surprised, then looks me up and down while letting loose a slow whistle. "You look good, Kilowatt. Nice dress. Kinda shaped like a sack, but I like it. Shows off your legs."

"You really need to leave."

"Hey," he says, "party's just getting started. You heard Curtis. We should find a seat, watch the surprise."

I motion up toward the long banquet table. Mom is already seated and chatting with the Reverend. Margot sits next to Curtis's mom and his four siblings. "I'm supposed to be up there," I say. "And you're not supposed to be here at all."

His eyes glisten in the low light. "Nice to see you again, Kil."

I take the drink from his hand and help myself. Ignoring the big grin on his face, I give the glass back and head up to the table. *"Leave."*

"Catch you later?" I hear him say.

I keep walking.

I sit next to Mom, who immediately leans over and whispers, "Who's the short guy?"

The lights dim as the musicians move into an R and B tune. It's not long before the football player walks in from a side entrance. He's changed from his tux into a new suit, striped and with tails, as if he's about to introduce the first circus act of the evening. He asks everyone to be seated. "I have a surprise for my lady." He waits as everyone takes his or her seat; then he walks over to Margot, who brings her hands to her cheeks in disbelief. "Baby, are you serious? What's going on?" Curtis grins and gives a nod. At this point, a large screen rolls down from the ceiling, and the lights dim. The sound of a keyboard is heard as images fade in and out: Margot as a baby; a group shot of the football player's sisters; the football player's mom; Margot and the Reverend. I can only assume that Danielle helped him find and sort all the pictures.

After the intro is played, the football player says, "I wrote this song for you, Margot. It's the first song they're releasing for my new album. The title of the album, y'all, is *We Are a Family Built on Love*, and that's the title of this song. You ready? Here it is." He begins to sing as the pictures continue to flash on-screen. Even I'll admit he has a nice voice, beautiful even, and I won't be surprised if his next album reaches number one as well.

I spot Selwyn sitting at a table with an older couple near the back of the hall. I try to catch his attention so I can mouth the word *Leave*, but he's oblivious.

The football player starts working the stage, grinning and pointing to family members as he sings. Mom takes the Reverend's hand when an image of their wedding flashes on-screen, followed by the twins as babies. There are more pictures of his side of the family, then back to Margot sitting on the couch in sweats and no makeup. She screams in embarrassment when the image appears but then laughs good-naturedly. Curtis gives her a kiss and dips into the chorus: "Our song soars like a dove, and we are a family built on love."

Next is a picture of me at my college graduation, followed by a picture of me at one family function or another. The football player is suddenly in my face with the microphone: "Love never ends even when some of us go to heaven." The music swells, and he rises to his feet and stands directly behind me. Feeding off the energy in the room, he half sings, half speaks: "We lose our children, we lose people too soon, but our song soars like a dove, and we are a family built on love."

Another image flashes. It takes me a second to realize I've never seen this particular photo. I thought I'd seen every last picture of my daughter, but this one is entirely new. Her hair is in two thick plaits, and she's laughing as she tries to bite into a slice of pizza that's too big. It's a close-up shot, but I can see that she's wearing her new dinosaur T-shirt, the same T-shirt I bought for her while we were at the natural history museum one week before she died. "Where is that picture from?" I hear myself ask.

Curtis raises his hand as he begins to improvise on the word *heaven*. I stare up at the photo again, and this time I yell, "Who took that picture? Where did it come from?"

Mom clasps my hand, willing me to calm down. The Reverend leans over and whispers, "Your mother and I were babysitting. We took Hailey out for pizza. I took that picture."

I look back toward the screen, but the picture is gone, replaced by a photo of the football player on the field.

I can feel a sweat coming on and my stomach dip and shrink. It's been four years, eight months, and I still don't know when I'll lose it. Sometimes I'll burst into tears while doing something as mundane as cleaning my apartment or picking up groceries. Even now I feel out-of-body with that picture, an image of my daughter I've never seen before, sending me into a tailspin.

My eyes well just as the football player tries to remedy the situation by raising my hand in a kind of "We Are the World" fashion and singing all the louder. "Love never ends even when some of us go to heaven." Then he adds, "Our loved ones are in a better place!"

I hate him more than ever now, and before I know what I'm doing, I rise from the table and shove him as hard as I can. I hear a collective "Whoa" from everyone in the room. "Leave me the fuck alone!"

When he tries to hug me, I push him again, but he's a wall of muscle and doesn't budge. "You are my sister," he croons. "I am your brother. I understand your loss. Take it to the cross."

"Shut the fuck up! You're a fucking idiot! You don't know a damn thing about me!" I catch sight of Margot just as her mouth falls open in shock. Mom takes her hand, her own expression a mixture of horror and worry.

I rush away from the table, my eyes blurry with tears. I hear Mom calling after me, but I'm practically running now. An older woman dressed in a sequined gown stands up from her table and opens her arms. I push past her. I move past all of them, doing my best not to trip and fall. I keep my eyes glued to the back of the room, locked on one person who might be able to help.

Selwyn is already on his feet by the time I reach him. Before he can say anything, I look at him hopefully. "Get me out of here?"

He tosses aside his napkin. "You got it, baby."

three

Selwyn handles the car with an ease that signals he's sober enough to drive. When he reaches for the stereo, I touch his hand and softly shake my head no.

The clock illuminates the time: 10:06.

It isn't until we reach the bottom of the first hill and have the choice of right or left that he says anything. "Which way?"

I point left.

We continue in silence until we reach another stop. I point left again, and we follow a curvy road down one hill and up another. We drive on in silence until he says, "Listen, about earlier today. I know how I came across, and I want you to know that wasn't me."

"Who was it, then?"

"I don't know. I had too much bourbon, but I really am a gentleman."

"Fine."

"I feel like I should explain, because I like you and don't want you to think I'm a nut."

"What do you care if I like you or not? You don't even know me."

"I feel like I do. Haven't you ever had a feeling about some-one? I like you."

"You must be really lonely," I grumble.

After a pause I hear him say, "I have a feelin' you are, too."

I turn and stare out the window. Whatever.

What I really want is a drink. At the same time, though, I'm not desperate enough to ask him to take me to a bar—that would feel too tacky, even for me. Still, some kind of cure-all sure would help right about now. I just want to shake the image of that picture.

I feel my eyes tear up, and I turn farther toward the window. The wind has picked up, and the trees along the road take on the shape of ten-foot-tall nebulae, elongated and eerie. I catch glimpses of San Francisco's skyline as the car begins to make an ascent up a steep hill.

It's not until we reach Bear Grove Lane that I realize where I've been leading Selwyn all along. Focused now, I sit up straight and start giving specific directions. Soon, we come to a parking lot at the end of a dirt road. The lot is empty and sits before a gravel pathway that looks as if it leads to nowhere.

Selwyn eases the car into a parking space and cuts the engine. "Where are we?"

"You'll see." I climb out of the car; he follows suit, pausing before he closes the door. "Kilowatt, what's going on? Where are we?"

"It's a surprise. Trust me."

He eyes me suspiciously, then goes to his trunk and takes out a flashlight and a blanket, followed by some kind of kit with the word EMERGENCY printed on the front.

"What the hell is all that?"

"Precautionary measures. Look around you. We're in the middle of nowhere. Who knows what'll happen. This kind of stuff comes in handy."

"A *blanket*?" I say. "What do you think we're going to do, take a nap?"

"You ever heard of Donner Pass?"

"What does Donner Pass have to do with anything? Trust me, Selwyn; nothing's going to happen. And if it does, I promise I will not eat you."

He remains dubious but returns the blanket and emergency kit. "I'm keeping this, though," he says, raising the flashlight.

"Fine." I feel the cold air on my bare arms and hug myself.

"You're going to freeze in that dress. If you don't want the blanket, at least take my jacket." He gives me his jacket, and I thank him. Due to his height, it hits right at my hips, and except for the length of the too-short sleeves, it fits perfectly.

We start down the gravel road with me doing my best in my heels not to topple over. It's perfectly quiet except for the sounds of our shoes. The light from the flashlight creates skeletal shadows.

"You know what this reminds me of?" he says. "One of those horror movies. With the teenagers. I feel like any minute somebody's going to jump out from behind a tree wearing a hockey mask, and he's going to strangle us and leave us out here for dead."

I stop, midwalk. It's not so dark that he can't see the irritated glare I give him.

"What?" He shrugs. "I'm just sayin'." We continue walking. He's quiet a beat, then says, "Why do you think hockey masks are so freaky?"

"Just—," I start. "Just be quiet, all right?"

We walk until we reach a chain-link fence. To the right, a

sign reads LEHMAN LABORATORIES: WHERE SPACE AND SCIENCE MEET.

"I get it," he says slowly. "This is some kind of *X-Files* madness. You're a secret agent fighting off aliens, and you want me to join the agency."

"Selwyn, if I worked for any agency at all, trust me, I would not ask you to join."

He chuckles. "Sure thing, Agent Scully."

I shake my head and walk up to the fence. Usually it's open and visitors walk right in, but now there's a lock at the entrance. "It's locked," I say, giving the lock a worthless tug. "I don't believe it."

"I do. Look." He points to the signs on the left: NO TRESPASSING! DANGER: KEEP OUT! I rebut by pointing to the small sign just to the right: SPACE LAB: OPEN TO THE PUBLIC TUESDAYS AND THURSDAYS. EVENING VIEWINGS SIX–MIDNIGHT.

"Kilowatt, today's Saturday."

"Crap. You're right. I don't know what I was thinking."

"Well. Can't say we didn't try. Let's get out of here."

"Don't you want to know what I was going to show you?" I point down the pathway that starts on the other side of the fence. In the distance, the top of a large dome peeks through the trees. "See there. That's where they keep the Betacam telescope. It's housed in the building past the science lab. The building with the dome. I was going to show it to you."

"A telescope, huh? What do you know." Not impressed in the least, he turns to leave.

"Wait a second. Have you ever looked at the stars through a telescope?"

"Can't say that I have."

I shake my head in a pitiful manner that says he's just proven my point. "I really want you to see this."

"It's closed."

I think for a second. "There are two standard telescopes set up around the entrance to the Betacam. We could use those. It won't be the same, but it's a start."

"Great. But the gate's locked, and the sign says 'No Trespassing.'"

"Yeah, but we didn't drive all the way out here only to turn back. And besides, no one's around." Without any warning, I take off my shoes, toss them over the fence, and start climbing.

"Kilowatt! What the hell are you doing, baby? You can't do that. It's illegal! You're trespassing!"

I stop climbing long enough to look back at the empty parking lot and quiet road. "Do you think anyone's gonna care?"

I continue my climb. I'm feeling good now. I'm a modern-day Spider-Woman. I'm queen of the world.

Selwyn calls up. "Where I come from, fences mean keep out. That sign right there says 'Keep Out.' So I'm thinking if a person wants to *avoid jail*, she should get back down here and *keep out*."

"Don't be a wimp," I say, glancing down. "This is fun."

"Wimp, huh?" he mutters. "Wimp?"

"Yeah. *Wimp*. Scare-dee-cat. Chicken!"

He makes a point of grumbling loudly before sticking the flashlight in his back pocket. "Call me a wimp . . ." He spits in each hand and rubs them together like a gymnast ready to take on the parallel bars. He's surprisingly lithe, and in no time at all catches up with me. "I climbed a few of these back in the day," he says, seeing how surprised I am by his agility. "I won't go into detail, but let's just say I had to make a few getaways back in my youth." I watch as he hoists himself up and over and starts making his way down, leaving me, meanwhile, stuck at the top. I can't figure out how to get my leg up and over without tearing my dress, falling, or both.

"Don't think too much," he advises, his feet already safely planted on the ground.

"Easy for you to say."

I hoist up my dress and lift one leg over the top, wondering briefly if I've given Selwyn a show. Not exactly sure how to go about my next move, I remain frozen with my left leg on one side of the fence and my right on the other.

"Take your time!" Selwyn teases. "We have all night."

"Let's see *you* do this in a dress," I retort.

I try to find footing but have trouble with my left leg, specifically, how to convince it to move.

"You're thinking too much, Kilowatt! You're gonna lose your nerve."

"You're talking too much, Selwyn. Shut up!"

I count to three and kick my leg over, but my dress catches and I lose my balance. I dangle for a second, too afraid to move, but then I hear the inevitable rip and down I go. I scream and try to grab at the fence in hopes of easing my fall, but I'm moving too fast. The only thing stopping me from landing on my ass entirely is that I fall against Selwyn, sending him stumbling backward until he hits the ground along with me.

I land on top of him, sideways with my arm across his face. We both lie there momentarily, quiet and in shock.

Eventually I hear him say, "She just had to see a telescope."

I slowly lift my head. "Sorry," I say, thoroughly embarrassed. "Are you okay?"

"Oh yeah, I'm fine. I'm *great*."

I roll off him, and we manage to stand. Selwyn brushes the dirt off his shirt while I check for signs of external bleeding, hemorrhaging, or at the very least a scratch.

"Are *you* okay?" he asks.

"I think so." I look down at my dress and see a rip, five or six inches long, running down the side of the seam. "Shit. Look at this."

I show him the tear, and he clicks his tongue. "We should just go back. All of this is a bad sign."

"No, let's keep going. It'll be worth it. You haven't seen anything until you've looked at the stars through a good telescope. Telescopes are incredible. They're building a five-million-dollar telescope in Chile right now that will allow us to see back in time, farther than man has ever seen."

"Huh?"

I find my shoes and start putting them on. "Light! Light takes a long time to travel, and the telescope they're making will have the ability to uncover up to a million galaxies seen as they were ten billion years ago. We'll be looking back at galaxies in the past."

"Galaxies in the past, huh? What do you say? Okay, let's leave."

I roll my eyes. "But I want you to see Saturn. Come on, please? You'll like it; and besides, we're already on the other side of that fucking fence, and I'll be damned if I'm climbing back over again."

He shakes his head with a sigh. "Saturn," he says, taking his flashlight from his back pocket. "Time travel. Great. Lead the way, Spock."

We follow the path past the science building to the space center. It takes three flights of stairs to reach the platform where the telescopes are set up. By the time we reach the third, we're both out of breath.

"This had better be good," Selwyn says, climbing the last step. Winded, he bends over and waits to catch his breath.

The two telescopes are housed in front of the main building. They're slightly more powerful than a basic Dobsonian-mounted Newtonian reflector and perfect for a first-time stargazer.

I lead Selwyn to the middle telescope and adjust the view-finder. I then take a moment to find Saturn with its golden rings. I see we're in luck, too, because its satellite Titan is just rounding the corner.

"Okay," I say. "Take a look."

Selwyn hunches down and stares through the viewfinder.

The first time I saw Saturn was with Mr. Hoffman in his backyard. I'd read about planets in school, seen mock-ups in movies, but to see a planet up close, right there in front of my own eyes, thousands and thousands of miles away but seemingly close enough that I could reach out and touch it, well, it was just like Mr. Hoffman told me it would be . . . *mind-blowing*. I felt infi-nitely small and insignificant; yet I also knew our own planet was floating around in all that great expanse, and I was part of its movement, part of a galaxy, and hence part of that infinite vastness and expanse, and that made my ten-year-old self feel magnificent. From then on, I became fascinated with the night sky. Mr. Hoffman called me a natural-born stargazer.

All too soon I hear a low "Kilowatt." Selwyn is quiet again until another murmur. "My God . . . Kilowatt."

"Yeah." I grin. "I know."

"It's beautiful. . . . I never . . . Oh my gosh."

"Yeah. I know."

"God, look at those rings. This is incredible."

"If you were to stretch Saturn's rings out, the distance would reach as far as Earth to the moon."

"Get outta here."

The stargazer in me grows more excited. "I have to show you Mars next. And you have to see the crevices on the moon. I swear you'll feel like you're standing right in front of it."

He turns and smiles up at me. "This is really somethin', Kilowatt."

I return his smile. "Let me show you Mars."

I'm about to reach for the telescope when I hear, "Freeze or I'll shoot!" I jump—we both do—but then I think, *Freeze? Do people still say that?*

Selwyn and I make a synchronized turn, hands raised, legs crossed at the ankles like backup singers performing a 1960s groove.

A cop stands in front of the steps, gun pointed our way. "Okay, you two. Hands in the air. Nice and high. That's the ticket."

I raise my hands even higher. I can tell the cop means business, but there's also something only mildly intimidating about a cop who talks as if he were part of a crime noir drama. Plus, I notice that what I thought was a gun is a Taser.

"Yeah, that's it. Steady now. Nice and slow."

He moves ninjalike on his tiptoes, his Taser raised with outstretched arms, as if at any minute Selwyn and I might pull something on him. He's of a brown-skinned variety that makes him appear all races at once, and he's dressed entirely in black with black combat boots and a heavy black jacket and black cap. A pencil-thin mustache floats between frog lips and a bubble nose.

He walks up to Selwyn as if after ten years on the job he's finally catching some action and wants to make the most of it.

"Stretch 'em," he says. He kicks Selwyn's feet apart and actually starts to frisk him.

"Hey, leave him alone!" I yell. "He hasn't done anything."

"Just let him do his job," Selwyn says as though trying to keep everyone cool.

"Yeah," the wanna-be cop says, "let a man do his job."

He takes out Selwyn's wallet, checks his driver's license, and, unimpressed, returns it to his pocket. He then gives Selwyn one last pat and takes a step back. "You're clean."

"I could've told you that myself." He jerks his arm away and immediately straightens his tie as he goes about gathering back any remote traces of lost dignity. "Look, Officer. We got lost. We were on our way home from a party and got turned around." He reaches for his back pocket.

Seeing him make a move, the cop leaps forward. "Watch it now!" he yells.

"Come on, man; you just frisked me. I'm clean, remember? I just want to give you my card." He takes out his wallet and hands the cop a business card. "Name's Selwyn. Selwyn Jones."

"He works for the mayor of Livermore," I add emphatically.

The cop turns on his flashlight and reads the card. "So if you work for the mayor, what the hell are you doing out here?"

"Like I said, we got lost, but my lady here wanted to see the telescopes. We're having a tough night. You know how it goes."

I shoot him a look. *"Your lady?"*

"I'd like you to be." He winks.

"You do realize we haven't known each other for a full twenty-four hours?"

"But think of it, Kil; it's been amazing. You just showed me Saturn. I knew there was something special about you, and I was right."

The cop lets out a loud whistle. "Both of you, quiet! Shut up!" He steps closer. "You two need to be more careful. Lotta nuts come out here."

"Yeah," I say, staring right at him. "What are you, anyway? You're not a cop, are you?"

"Never mind what I am. I protect this facility here, and that's all you need to know. They have top-secret stuff in those buildings that radicals and terrorists would love to get their hands on."

He starts toward the steps, leaving Selwyn and me to wonder what we're supposed to do. Once at the stairs, he pauses.
"What the hell are you waiting on? When I say nuts, I'm talking
about you. I want you two outta here!"

We do as we're told and rush over. He gives a satisfied
nod, and we start down the stairs and back toward the front
gate. We're back at the entrance in no time.

The cop unlocks the gate and waves us through. "All
right, you two. No more breaking and entering for the either
of yas."

"Thank you, Officer," Selwyn says.

When we have the courage to turn around, we see our cop
watching us closely, rocking on his heels, arms crossed.

"What a weirdo!" I mutter.

"Laurel without Hardy."

"Abbott without Costello."

"Stop being a wise guy," Selwyn mimics.

I laugh. "'No more breaking and entering for the either of
yas.'"

"Where do you think he was from?"

"I don't know. Some lost *X-Files* episode maybe." And this
time I wink.

Selwyn smiles and opens the car door for me. After we fasten
our seat belts, Selwyn turns. "Where to?"

I know it's time to head back to the party, but I can't say
I want to. I don't want to face Mom, or any of them for that matter. And Selwyn's right, in a way. It does feel like we have a connection, even if it's entirely imagined. "You really don't mind
playing chauffeur?"

"Not at all." He pauses as he thinks over what he wants to
say. "This has been good for me." He grins and rolls his head in
my direction. "Since I'm playing your driver, might be nice to

wake up in Mendocino tomorrow morning. Calistoga. I have all night and all day. Don't mind at all. We can make a trip out of it." He puts the key in the ignition, grinning happily at the thought of a little B and B and a day of sightseeing.

"Actually, I was wondering if you wouldn't mind taking me to Martin Luther King and Fifty-fifth."

"Martin Luther King Boulevard? In Oakland?'

"Yeah."

"That's where you wanna go?"

"Yep."

His entire body deflates as he lets go of any and all romantic notions of soaking tonight in a hot tub in Calistoga. He shakes his head wearily and turns the ignition. "Martin Luther King and Fifty-fifth it is."

Twenty minutes later we're standing in front of LaDonna Smith's altar. Candles are lit and burn quietly in the night. Nailed to the telephone pole is a laminated picture of Donna Hawks, LaDonna's mother, holding LaDonna in her lap. LaDonna was six years old when she died, two years older than Hailey. Above the picture someone has nailed poster board with the words WE LOVE YOU and WE'LL MISS YOU in bright pink glitter. Surrounding the candles are weighted balloons and teddy bears. I asked Selwyn to stop at the liquor store before we ended up here, and now I add a bag of gummy bears to the bowl filled with candy.

"Did you know her?" Selwyn asks.

"No."

"Do you know what happened?"

"Drive-by. They were going for someone else, and she got caught in the cross fire. She was in a coma for two days but didn't make it."

"Tragic. Just tragic." He stands and reaches for my hand, but I pull away.

There's another altar for Markus Money Burnett just at the end of the block. And on Fifty-sixth there's another for Anthony Tucker. Anthony, who was only fifteen, was shot by the police. He was a straight-A student, and just before his death, he had received a full scholarship to West Academy.

What Selwyn doesn't know is that I live only a couple of blocks away from where we stand. When I have insomnia, which is always, I sometimes leave the house at four or five in the morning and walk from one altar to another; there are at least four altars in a one-mile radius. Sometimes I leave gifts—flowers for Anthony, candy for Shawn on Sixtieth. I started a letter for LaDonna's mother once. *Our daughters would've liked each other*, the letter began, but I was crying too much after only a few sentences and never finished it.

Selwyn kneels down and relights a candle that's gone out.

He stands, and we look at LaDonna's picture in silence. This time when he reaches for my hand, I let him take it.

"Where to?"

We're back inside the car. I figure now that I've shown Selwyn LaDonna's altar, there is one last place I'd like to visit. I know it's odd at best to want to show a virtual stranger your daughter's grave site, but it's been an odd night to say the least, so I may as well go the distance.

"Drive up MLK and make a right on Sixty-fourth."

"You got it."

Minutes later, we pull up to a massive front gate with its two large pillars on either side. Selwyn brings the car to a halt. "What's this?"

I didn't tell him where we were going, specifically because of the look he's giving me right now. "I want to show you one last thing." I start to get out of the car, but he doesn't budge, keeping his gaze straight ahead as he stares at the gothic gates and black void just on the other side. His eyes widen, and his hands grip the steering wheel as if the car were careening down a hill. "That's a cemetery."

"I know; I can explain."

"No need to. I'm afraid this time you're on your own, Kil."

"Why?"

He looks at me as if I were crazy. "It's a cemetery, that's why!"

"Selwyn, come on. Don't be ridiculous. You've practically been arrested and possibly shot at, and now you're afraid?"

"Hell yeah, I'm afraid! You should be, too. My momma always taught me, never go into a cemetery after midnight."

"Your . . . *momma?*"

"Yeah, my *momma*. God rest her soul."

I think for a second. "Where are you from, anyway? Before Livermore, I mean."

"Alabama."

I roll my eyes in a manner that says, *That explains so much.*

"What?" he says. "You have something against Alabama?"

I hear banjos playing and envision broken-down porches. "No, not in particular."

"Ain't nothin' wrong with the South. Despite the way we met, I want you to know you're looking at a real Southern gentleman right here."

"Okay. Fine. So tell me why you're so afraid, *Rhett.*"

"All kinds of things come out in a cemetery at night. Ghosts, demons—"

"Goblins? Fairies?"

"Watch it," he says, crossing his arms.

"*Selwyn.*" I let my tone do the work for me.

"I'm not going. But if you want to, go right ahead. If you're not back in fifteen minutes, I'll dial 9-1-1. Go on. Nobody's stopping you." He waves a hand. "Bye."

I lean back in the seat. "If you believe in demons and ghosts, then you must believe in angels."

"And?"

"Well, if you believe in angels, then you know that angels are protectors and will protect us from demons."

I'm in uncharted territory here. But I also know that talk of angels always makes people go soft. After Hailey died, everyone kept talking about angels and how Hailey was now an angel, as if that was supposed to make her death okay. When I returned to work after my leave of absence, Beatrice Krackau (Mrs. Butt Crack to the students), a teacher I rarely talked to, walked into my room during my prep period and proceeded to stand behind me with her hand on my shoulder as though we were asked to pose for a painting. "She was needed in heaven, that's all. God needs his angels."

I glared up at her from my desk, but she only shrugged in a way that implied there was no fighting God's need for more angels. "Are you serious?" I asked. "I'm sorry, but if he's *God*, and assuming—*omnipotent*, why the fuck does he need angels in the first place?"

"She's helping our Lord."

"She was four years old! What would God need with a four-year-old child? Get out of here with that shit! I mean it—out!"

Poor Mrs. Krackau looked at me as though I'd gone insane, and maybe I had. The thought that Hailey died for some inexplicable "plan" made me livid, and thinking of her as an angel didn't help a bit. It felt like an insult, actually.

But tonight I'm determined, and if I have to speak of angels, so be it. "Don't be afraid, Selwyn. We'll be protected by angels, I'm sure. If there's evil out there, there's good, too, and good always wins." I realize how silly I sound and, embarrassed for myself, reach for the door. "Oh, fuck it. I'll go alone."

I start to climb out of the car but then hear him say, "I'm an idiot."

I turn and make a face that says, *Well, if you say so.*

Selwyn doesn't smile, though, and instead he shifts his gaze beyond the black gate.

"What?"

"It's taken me this long to realize why we're here." His face goes soft. "I'm sorry."

"There's no need to apologize. I should apologize. It's beyond strange to bring you here in the first place. But I feel like being here. I come here at night sometimes. I know it's weird, but it's what I need right now. I just thought I'd like to invite you, but if you don't want to, I understand. I do."

He takes a breath. "I'd be honored. Besides," he adds, taking the keys out of the ignition, "Momma also said a person should stand up to his fears."

"I love your momma," I say, my smile growing big and wide.

He looks at me a beat, his eyes round and shiny. "That smile. That smile."

Selwyn holds the flashlight as I guide us through the cemetery. In hopes of making him feel less afraid, I ramble on about how pretty the cemetery is during the day—how it's more like a park with all the great views, the duck pond and boysenberry bushes, the people who come here to walk their dogs, but he remains dubious at best and mutters a sarcastic "Oh yeah, it's *exactly* like a park."

To keep him focused, and because I don't know a thing about him, I ask him to tell me something about himself.

"Well," he says, ready to settle into a good story, "when I was a boy of about eight or nine and growing up in Alabama—"

I'm exhausted already. "Oh God, never mind."

"What?"

"I'm just not in the mood to hear about the South—those willow trees and june bugs, Southern witticisms." I shiver dramatically.

"Girl, you have more attitude than ten women dressed in too-tight shoes."

I give him a look that says, *See what I mean?*

We finally reach the top of the hill we've been climbing for what feels like several hours. We stare silently at land and sky spread out before us, the bright expanse of city lights, and the bay and both the Golden Gate and Bay Bridge far off in the distance.

We stand without saying a word until Selwyn murmurs, "My, my, what a beautiful view. It's so peaceful."

I turn and wave my hands in the air. *"Boo!"*

"Everybody's a comedian," he mutters.

After a few minutes of gazing at the view, we continue to walk until we reach a crest.

"There it is," I say, pointing to Hailey's tombstone.

I gaze down at her name and the words BELOVED DAUGHTER. I then find myself going down on my knees in the wet grass.

Selwyn soon joins me, resting an arm around my back. "Listen—"

I know exactly where he's headed—those strands of familiar platitudes—and interrupt him before he can start. "No, actually, I don't want to listen. I don't want to hear anything even remotely"—I make imaginary quotes in the air—"supportive or understanding. I don't want to hear how things will get better, or how time heals all wounds, and I don't want to hear about how God has a plan and how everything happens for a reason."

He holds me closer. "But I know you'll get through this."

"Or that," I say, pushing him away.

I pull at a swath of grass and look up at Venus. Beautiful star. Horrible planet. Almost the same size and weight as Earth but nine hundred degrees and full of noxious fumes.

Selwyn says, "But I do know you'll get through this. I understand your pain."

I suck my teeth.

"I haven't experienced what you've experienced, no. I won't try to compare, but I do know loss."

"Who?"

"My brother, Sylvester. We lost him years ago, but that doesn't matter much. Still feels like yesterday. He was only twenty-two. We were eleven months apart. More like twins when you get down to it. Everybody said so, too. You saw me around town, and you saw my brother. That's how tight we were. I mean, we did *everything* together—football team, baseball, all that. Sylvester and Selwyn. *S and S!* Everybody knew us." His voice drops. "Yeah. Cancer. Broke my heart when he died. He may as well have taken a part of my soul with him."

I reach over and take his hand.

"I just want you to know in some small way I understand. You'll get through this."

"No, I won't actually." I bury my head in my knees. I feel Selwyn gently run his hand up and down my back. He's smart enough to keep his mouth shut, and we stay like that, me with my head tucked and Selwyn stroking my back, for a good while. Several minutes pass before I feel him give me a good hard shake.

"What?"

"You hear that?"

I lift my head. "What?"

"Someone's coming."

He points the flashlight toward a grove of trees. Finally I hear it, what sounds like an army of footsteps coming our way.

"Who do you think it is?" he whispers.

"I don't know, but try to calm down. Other people are allowed to come here, too."

"Yeah, but not at this hour." He starts to move as though ready to take on a drove of zombies.

I touch his arm. "Calm down."

He sits but grabs my hand as if we'll have to flee in any minute.

All too soon, a pack of teens crests the hill. They wear long black trench coats, white powdered makeup, black boots and heavy eyeliner. As I suspected, we have nothing to fear. The group is made up of what I call the vampire kids, teens and twenty-somethings who come to the cemetery at night to celebrate vampires and all things goth.

Selwyn starts to stand as they approach, but I pull him back down. "It's okay. They're just a bunch of kids."

There are codes of behavior in the cemetery he knows nothing about, and except for the few times I've heard their laughter in the distance, the vampire kids have always been respectful.

There are nine kids in all tonight. When they reach us, Selwyn aims the flashlight on each of their faces one at a time, as if they're under criminal suspicion. He holds the light on one kid in particular, who wears white makeup and black lipstick. Piercings punctuate his cheek, nose, and eyebrows; his face is a mask in the stark glow of the light. He winces and starts to say something, but the guy in front, lanky and long-haired, who, I've assumed, is the lead vampire, recognizes me and lightly slaps his friend's arm. "No worries," he tells his friend, "she's cool." He tosses his pierced chin my way. "Hey."

"Hey," I return.

He offers a gentleman's nod before waving his friends on. A girl of about fifteen stops in front of us and offers a childlike wave before bursting into a fit of giggles. The guy next to her shushes her and drags her along.

The entire group is gone before Selwyn has a chance to take out his stake and cross. He exhales loudly. "What in heaven's name was *that*? 'Bout scared me silly."

"They're goths or whatever. They come out here to get away from their parents and act weird. No harm to it."

"Well, they scared the holy bejeezes out of me."

He aims the flashlight toward where they've walked off.

"They're gone, Selwyn. Everything's okay." I rest my chin on my knees and close my eyes. As far as I'm concerned, it would have been perfectly fine to watch Hailey grow up to be an unruly, weird teenager.

"You okay?"

"Yeah," I whisper. "We should probably get going."

I don't move, though. Instead, I draw Selwyn's jacket around my shoulders and continue staring at Hailey's tombstone. It's those dates edged above her name that do me in. When I feel Selwyn's hand on the back of my neck, I take in as much air as possible and slowly exhale. "It was a car accident, in case you're wondering. We were on our way to school."

What I don't say, though, what I've never told anyone, is that the accident was entirely my fault. I was like any other parent in a rush to get her child to school, but I was driving too fast and ran into a truck. There's no other way around it. She'd be here today if not for me.

I stand abruptly. "Anyway."

Selwyn begins to say something, but thinking better of it, remains silent. He stands and takes my hand. We hold hands briefly until I pull away. "Let's go."

• • •

We pull up to a quiet residential street in Berkeley. Elm trees and cedars line the sidewalk; every house is dark and quiet. I gesture toward a 1930s crafts-man in need of a paint job. "This is it."

Selwyn cuts the engine and looks out at the row of houses and trees. I've confounded him yet again. "I thought you wanted a drink."

"I do. My husband lives here. Full bar."

"Husband?"

"Ex," I say, slapping my hand against my forehead for effect. "Ex. I keep forgetting to add the ex part."

"How long have you been divorced?"

"Not long enough that I can remember the ex part."

He eyes the house guardedly. "So this ex of yours would be . . ."

"Spence. Spencer."

"You're just going to stop by—at this hour? It's one in the morning."

"We didn't have that kind of divorce."

He thinks this over while continuing to stare at the house. The porch light is on; then again, it's always on. Spence figures that by not turning it off, he won't have to remember to turn it back on. It's the same logic he used when he decided to replace our garden, once filled with flowers and succulents, with a blanket of flat green grass: No more flowers meant no need to worry about gardening.

"So you're saying he won't mind if I show up with you?"

Now I'm confused. "Selwyn, you're not showing up with me."

"I'm not?"

"Of course not."

"Why not? I'd like to meet him." He pulls his shoulders back and takes another look toward the empty porch as though Spence might step outside at any minute, strapped with two guns and ready for a duel. "I'd like to meet this ex of yours. We'll have a quick drink, and we'll say our good-byes."

"*We?* Selwyn, I don't think you understand. It's late. I think we should call it a night."

"What do you mean? Come on, Kilowatt. The night's young. We're just getting started."

"No, Selwyn. I've kept you long enough. I really appreciate everything you've done for me tonight. I do. You were a real hero, but we should probably say good-bye."

"All right," he says. "So when am I going to see you again?"

I force a halfhearted smile. "You're not, Selwyn. This is it."

"Kil," he says, looking genuinely surprised, "come on; you don't mean that."

"I thought you understood. I thought we were just hanging out for the night."

"Okay. Granted, the way we met was kind of strange, but this has turned into more. Think about it, Kil. All we've been through? We at least have to see each other again."

"I don't think so. Look at me. I'm not a together person. I had you take me to a cemetery, for goodness' sake. I'm fucked-up."

"So am I. Who isn't?"

I sigh. "Selwyn."

"Okay. That's fine. I get it. You're right. We don't have to see each other again right away, but this can't be good-bye. We get along. Might be nice to be friends at least. Keep in touch?"

"I'm sorry, but I'm not interested. In friendship or anything else." I reach for the door. By now, every nerve and cell in my body is screaming for a shot of scotch or three or four and a nice soft bed. "There's no point in dragging anything out, Selwyn. I really appreciate everything you've done for me tonight. I'll never forget it."

"Not even friendship, Kil? I needed tonight just as much as you did. Life doesn't give nights like this all too often."

I don't want to get sucked into his sad story, frankly, and don't bother asking what he means about needing tonight as much as I did. As nice as he's been, I've learned it's best—easier all around—to keep my distance from people. I'm damaged goods, as they used to say. I touch his hand. "I'm sorry, Selwyn. I'm just not looking to make new friends."

He eases back in his seat and stares at the roof of the car. I imagine he's thinking of what his mother would tell him to do right about now, something along the lines of *Never pressure a woman, baby. Pressure is like steam under the lid of an iron pot; sooner or later one of you will explode.*

After a moment he says, "Fine. If you're not interested, you're not interested. You know how to find me if you ever change your mind, though, right?"

"Yes," I tease. "Livermore. You work for the mayor."

"That's right. If you ever change your mind, I'd love to see you again. Hell, I'd be willing to have my heart broken ten times over by a woman like you."

I feel my entire body softening. "Like me?"

"You are who you are, Kilowatt. No pretenses. No games. I like that; that's hard to find in a person. I'd trust you over a million nuns."

I laugh. "I guess that's a compliment."

"Are you going to be all right?"

I gather he means in a bigger sense. "Probably not."

"There it is," he says, shaking his head. "Damn. That smile, that smile." I hadn't realized I was smiling, but I am. "You know, Kil, we probably never would've worked out anyway. That smile would've done me in every time."

I start to reach for his hand, but he's managed to find a modicum of determination by now and turns the key in the ignition.

"I'll wait here until you're inside." His eyes remain fixed on the road as if he's already driving away.

I get out of the car and walk to the front door. I use my key to open it and step inside. When I look back, he shifts the car into gear, leaving me with nothing to do but watch him drive away.

four

I follow the sound of the TV down the long hallway, past the bathroom and kitchen. I find Spence sitting on the couch, shrouded in darkness except for a beam of light shooting from his new TV. He wears a pair of cords and his favorite Harlem Skydivers T-shirt. The light illuminates his face and dome-shaped Afro so that he appears like a space creature in a Kubrick movie or a Byzantine saint.

He's watching one of his documentaries. He wasn't much of a television watcher before our divorce, but now he watches hours at a time, almost all documentaries: *The Civil War, World War I* and *II, Baseball, The Roosevelt Years.* Subject matter is of no importance; the only criterion seems to be that the film is at least four hours long.

The room itself is fairly neat except for the piles of empty boxes in two corners. Along with the TV, he's recently purchased a KitchenAid mixer he'll never use, a new laptop, and bundles of video games that he keeps in his office.

I help myself to his drink sitting on the coffee table—whisky with too much water, but whisky nonetheless. He looks me up and down as I sip—okay, gulp, his gaze landing on the tear at the side of my dress. "What the hell happened?"

"Oh, you know, the usual—a party, a troll, a fence. I'm fine."

He raises a brow. "Your dress tells a more sordid story."

I take several more gulps of whisky.

"Help yourself," he says sarcastically.

"Thanks." Feeling better, I join him on the couch. On TV a flock of flamingoes grazes while a camera pans from above. Spence takes a sip from his drink and hands me the glass; I sip and pass it back.

"Your mom called."

I keep my eyes on the flamingoes. I dread having to see Mom ever again.

"First two calls, she wanted to know if you were okay and if I knew where you were. Third call, she wanted to know why you hadn't called and said she feels bad about what happened, but that you ruined Margot's party. Margot called, too. She wants you to know that she'll have someone pack everything you left behind and bring it to your apartment. Oh, and she also says she's pissed that you ruined Curtis's song but forgives you."

I rest my head on his shoulder. I dread ever having to see either of them ever again.

"And Charles called."

"The Reverend, too?" I ask.

"Yeah, he said something about owing you an apology? He wants you to call."

I let out a long sigh.

"Sounds like the party was a success."

"Or something like that."

The camera appears to fall underwater, and we watch a

family of hippos swim as gracefully as a school of fish. Spence takes my hand and digs himself deeper into the couch.

I'm not sure what he thinks I've been up to tonight, but, thankfully, he's not one to ask, which saves me from having to explain my behavior. He has no clue about the men I've been with, and I don't intend for him to ever find out. He's an assistant professor at UC Berkeley. Philosophy. I sometimes think his devotion to his field is why nothing riles him. When the goal is the question, you're never concerned with answers.

After another minute of watching hippos, I say, "I'm going to need a ride home tomorrow."

"And your car is . . . ?"

"Back at the mansion. I used a cab to get here." I stand with a yawn while stretching my arms, then start toward the bathroom. From behind I hear him say, "The plot thickens."

I walk past the guest bedroom, past our—Spence's—bedroom. Once in the bathroom, I open the cabinet and pop one of his Ambien. Next, I head into the bedroom and take out a pair of sweats and a T-shirt. I've staked out the bottom drawer of his bureau for nights like this, which, since I'm here almost every night, are innumerable.

We haven't defined what we're doing. Even though we see each other almost every night and have sex as frequently, we're not officially back together. We're not officially anything, except in mourning.

Before Hailey died, Spence and I were experiencing one of those lulls married couples face from time to time. It was a longer lull than most, though, and I became increasingly jealous and insecure. Spencer comes from a long line of MDs and PhDs; a great-great-grandfather, his mother loves to brag, was president of a private liberal arts college.

I come from a long line of what? Men who leave women? Women who sleep around? My insecurities might explain why I became jealous of the philosophy department's new hire, Melinda Green, a Harvard-educated hotshot lured from Michigan State.

Not long after she came on board, Dr. Green approached Spence about writing a paper together on some obscure subject only a handful of academics would read. As they worked on the paper, the e-mail trails and coffee dates started piling up. The morning of the accident, Spence came into the bedroom, dressed and ready for work. It was his turn to take Hailey to school, but she was still in her pajamas watching TV. When I asked where he was going, he explained he had a meeting with Melinda. "Don't you remember? I told you about this last week. You said it would be fine." But I hadn't remembered saying any such thing, and I told him so.

Back and forth we went: "We were sitting right there on the bed and you told me it was fine that I meet her today."

"Why would I say it was fine when Thursdays are your day to take Hailey to school? Besides, you knew today was your day, but you chose instead to schedule a meeting with Melinda."

"I told you, this was the only time she could meet!"

"So what?!"

I shot out of bed, telling him it was his turn to take Hailey to school, like it or not. That was when he said Melinda was already at the café waiting for him. He then said something about how I always got my way, and this time he wasn't going to give in. I snapped back that if I always got my way, he wouldn't be e-mailing "Dr. Green" so often and going on so many "coffee dates"—the implication, along with the quotation marks that stayed suspended in the air, irreparably pitting us one side against the other.

That was when he carefully closed the bedroom door, signal-

ing that whatever he was about to tell me should not be overheard. I crossed my arms and waited.

"What the hell are you trying to say, Piper?"

"I'm not trying to say anything."

"Yes, you are. Are you implying something here? 'Cause if
you are, I think you should spit it out."

"I'm not implying anything, Spencer."

"The hell you're not. I can't believe that you would cheapen
us like this. Listen to yourself. Is this what you want us to turn
into? We're talking about you and me here, Piper. Is this the kind
of marriage you want? Huh? Is it?"

"Maybe you're innocent, but I bet she's not."

"She's *married*."

"I know she is, Spencer. That's why they call it *cheating*."

I'd never seen him look at me with such disdain. He locked
his eyes with mine, his breath labored with anger. "Maybe you
don't remember that I already told you because you had too much
wine that night."

"And what's that supposed to mean?"

"I had one glass. How many did you have?"

"What are you now, the wine police?"

He cut his gaze and walked to the door. "Stop thinking about
yourself for once and take our daughter to school. I'm not your
fucking servant."

And I did.

I took our daughter to school.

And it seemed for the duration of the morning, I could not
snap, yell, or pick on Hailey enough. She was doing some kind of
dance in the backseat as we drove to school, and I yelled and told
her to stop playing around and keep her butt still. I said this
right before we hit the truck.

After she died, I couldn't push Spence away far enough or

fast enough. I accused him of cheating on me daily; I told him if he hadn't been messing around with Melinda, writing some paper no one would ever read, our daughter's death could have been avoided.

Eventually, my rages became more acute, and I began demanding a divorce. Spence, entombed in despondency and depression, finally agreed.

I walk into the kitchen, pour a double scotch, and toss it back. After my body relaxes with a resounding "Thank-you," I make another double for myself and a shot of whisky and water for Spence, then join him on the couch. Since the divorce, almost two years ago now, we've become exactly like the Cosbys, except we have no children, drink too much, and lack a general optimistic outlook on life.

On TV a pack of hyenas watches a herd of grazing zebras. "Uh-oh," I say.

Sure enough, we watch as they chase down the zebras. A slower zebra is caught at the leg and down he goes. The shot cuts to three vultures overhead. They greedily eye the spectacle below with napkins tucked under their chins and knives and forks poised.

Soon, I feel the nice tug-of-war between the Ambien and the scotch, and I rest my head in Spencer's lap. We're divorced and we're fucked-up, but we're slowly making our way back to each other. Once, after we read Chekov's *The Lady with the Pet Dog* in class, one of my students said, "Anna and Dmitri are tight like that; you know what I'm sayin', Miss Nelson? Things are complicated, but they get each other. You know what I'm sayin'? Ain't nobody coming between those two. Anna is Dmitri's boo." That's how it is with Spence and me. No matter what has gone on between us. We get each other. He's my boo.

• • •

I feel a warm circular object pressing against my cheek. It's not hot enough to make me jump or scream, but it does get me to open my eyes. I wait for my brain to tell me what's going on. My clues: a framed poster of Hitchcock's *Vertigo* and a hideous red leather recliner, both purchased while Spence was on one of his buying splurges.

My hand dangles off the side of the bed, but as soon as the smell of coffee reaches my nose, I use what energy I have to reach up and blindly touch Spence's arm, then wrist, then fingers, and finally the mug of coffee.

"Here." He takes the mug from my cheek and places it in my hand.

"Hangover," I moan.

"Yeah," he says, giving me two aspirin.

He waits while I swallow the aspirin, then walks to the door-way and pauses. He wears a sweater over loose-fitting jeans. From what I can tell, he's already shaved. "Oatmeal is on the stove. You should get going after you eat."

"Where are we going?"

"Not us. *You.* You have school today."

"School? Today's Sunday." From the look on his face, I gather that I might be mistaken. *"Isn't it?"*

"P, it's Monday."

"Monday? What happened to Sunday?"

He doesn't bother responding and leaves.

"Is this some kind of joke?" I call after him. I wait for a response but only hear him knocking around in the kitchen. "Spence?! Are you serious?"

"As a heart attack," he calls out. "It's Monday."

I force myself to sit up. *Monday.* How can it be Monday

when—*What the hell happened to Sunday?* I sip my coffee and begin retracing my steps. Engagement party. Selwyn. Spence . . . *Sunday.* I try again. Engagement party. Selwyn. Spence . . . A blip of a memory flashes: jazz documentary and a tall bottle of Grey Goose. Followed by a second blip: William Churchill taking a picture with Roosevelt and Stalin. More Grey Goose.

Right. *Sunday.*

I call out: "I think I remember now. We watched documentaries on Louis Armstrong and Churchill yesterday. Vodka was involved?"

"You got it. You passed out before the Blitz."

I moan and make my way out of bed. It's six twenty. At least I have plenty of time to get ready. I start looking for the T-shirt I've been wearing for the last two days.

Spence says from the kitchen, "I forgot to mention that my mom called. She's on her way."

"Please tell me you're kidding and this is all a bad dream."

"I'm kidding and this is all a bad dream!"

I mutter more than a few curse words under my breath. Forgetting all else, I start looking for my purse and car keys so that I can get the hell out of the house before my former mother-in-law shows up. I start tossing clothes this way and that. Spence appears in the doorway, holding a wooden spoon, his hand devoured by an oven mitt made to look like a cow's head.

"What are you looking for?"

"Car keys."

"Stay and have some oatmeal. It'll make you strong."

"I don't want to be strong. I just wanna get the hell out of here." I start tossing clothes again. "Where are my keys?"

"I think you've forgotten—you have no car."

"Shit!" I slap my hand against my forehead and sit on the edge of the bed, defeated. "My car is back at the mansion."

"That's the story I was told."

"Would you give me a ride home?"

"Not now."

"Please?"

"Nope. Mom is on the way. I'll give you a ride after we eat."

"Pretty please?"

"P." He glances down at my bra and the pair of boxers I'm wearing—his. "Get dressed."

"But—"

Just then there's the distinct sound of the front door clicking open, followed by a bright and cheery "Hello! Anybody home?"

Spence's eyebrows shoot up. "What do you know, she's already here."

"I thought you said she just called!" I whisper through gritted teeth.

"She did. She was probably calling from around the corner."

"It's six fucking thirty in the morning. Why is she here so early?"

"You know Mom—rise and shine and all that. She wanted to surprise me with a good breakfast."

"Hello! Where's my handsome boy?"

Spence keeps his eyes locked with mine. "I'm in here, Mom. I'll be out in a minute."

"I can't believe this," I grumble. "First I have to find out it's Monday, and now your mom shows up?"

"Stop whining, P. She's my mother."

I switch tactics and wrap my arms around his waist. "Will you take me to get my car?"

"Out of the question."

"Drive me home, then. *Please?* Tell her I need to get to work and you'll be right back." I figure I'll take a taxi to my car later. The high school where I teach is only a twenty-minute walk from my apartment, and footing it won't be a problem, especially now that I know the ex-mother-in-law is here.

But my begging is of no use. "You have plenty of time," he says, unhooking my arms. He then points the oven mitt at my nose. "Get dressed."

The sunlight cuts through the kitchen blinds like a saber, forcing me to wince and duck as I make my way to the table. Elaine, the former mother-in-law, stands at the counter stirring gruel in a huge black cauldron. Her skin is a fine lime green and she wears her usual black pointy hat, black dress, and black pointy shoes. Her broom is just off to the left.

Thanks to my hangover, the bacon sizzling in the skillet sounds more like gunfire. I recognize fruit and bagels from the deli up the street. Spence's oatmeal has been relegated to the corner of the stove.

Spence greets me. "Morning," he says, his coffee mug poised at his lips, eyes glued to his laptop.

"Good morning," I mumble in return. I found a pair of jeans and a sweater to wear. I've washed my face and have managed a semblance of a ponytail but not much else. My head pounds.

Elaine glances over her shoulder as she whips eggs at top-notch speed. "Hello," she mutters, and goes straight back to whipping.

When Spencer introduced me to the family, Elaine told me that she looked forward to getting to know me better, but our relationship remained strained at best. We're too different. Elaine became a homemaker soon after graduating from Sarah Lawrence and marrying Spencer's father, a judge. She spent her life creating a perfect home for her elder son, Howard, and later for Spencer. I, on the other hand, tend to avoid the kitchen at all cost, and to Elaine's horror, went back to work after Hailey turned six months old. Our relationship was made none the better after the accident. I know she blames me for the loss of her youngest grandchild. I suppose this is the one thing we do agree on: I blame me for that, too.

Elaine gives the eggs a final beating, then dumps them into the hot skillet. She's found me here twice within the last month, and I can tell she's none too pleased.

"Can I help with anything?" I offer.

"I've got everything taken care of. You just sit and relax. Spencer, would you put out the butter?"

"Sure thing."

She adds, "And either pull your pants up or put on a belt."

"This is the style, Mom," Spence says, giving her a peck on the cheek. He tends to revert back to being her baby boy when she's around, and Elaine, naturally, relishes her role as Mother Supreme.

Once breakfast is served, she chats it up with Spence briefly, but after she has fired a couple of sharp glances my way, it's obvious that her mood has darkened. Passive-aggressive woman that she is, she won't spit it out and only grows increasingly silent. I'm sure Spence can tell her mood has changed, but he doesn't take the bait, and we all continue eating with the dark spell she's cast above our heads.

She clears her throat a couple of times, but we ignore her. Finally, not being able to stand that no one is asking her what's wrong, she folds her hands on the table and clears her throat in a way that says she's finally ready to speak up. "I have something I need to say, and I'm afraid I'll need your attention."

Spence stops squirting ketchup over his eggs and sets the bottle down. I place my spoon on the edge of my plate. I'm almost grateful that my hangover is keeping most of my thoughts in a fog.

She takes a breath and looks at Spence. "I didn't come here with the intention of starting anything, but seeing that you have company at this hour, I feel it's time I stop holding my tongue."

"Mom." Spence sighs.

"To be honest, Spencer, I'm worried about you."

"Mom," he moans. "Not now. Can we just eat?"

A perennial argument during our marriage was that Spence never stood up to Elaine as he should. I'd tell him time and again that it was his responsibility to put her in her place; but he never really said anything, leaving Elaine and me to battle it out over issues such as whether she should be allowed in the house when we weren't home or how she needed to keep her advice about the raising of our daughter to herself.

"Divorce means people go their separate ways; yet I keep having to find her here. It's not right, Spencer. You two are *divorced*."

"Yes, we are," Spencer says. "But Piper and I are adults, and what we do is our business, and you know that."

I raise my brows as I take a sip of coffee. "Hear, hear."

"But it's my business when you're being dragged into something that's doing you harm."

"Dragged?" I blurt. "It's not like I'm forcing myself on anybody. Spence wants to see me as much as I want to see him."

"But you can't say what you two are doing is emotionally healthy."

Spence says, "I appreciate the thought, Mom, but what P and I do together is our business."

Elaine turns her attention my way. "I know it's difficult to find a good man these days, but you need to let Spencer get on with his life. You've both proven that you're not good for each other, and frankly, *you* asked for the divorce, so *you* should be the one to move on."

"*Mom*," Spence warns.

"You have to get it together, Spencer. I'll be the first to admit that what has happened to you—to both of you—is the worst thing that can possibly happen, but Spencer, you have a lot going for you, professionally and otherwise, and I don't want you to lose ground. You could have your life back. It won't be the same, but you don't have to live like this." She looks over at me, her gaze moving down to the sweater I'm wearing—Spencer's sweater. She holds her gaze, then slowly looks up, her mouth drawn tight. "I don't understand. You wanted the divorce, but you won't let him go."

"He's a grown man," I say.

"That may be so, but he can't move on with you practically shacking up with him years later."

"Mom."

"I'm sorry, Spencer, but I'm tired of finding her here and tired of holding my opinion. I've had enough. What you both have faced is unimagin—" Her voice cracks and she stops. She appears startled, as though she's hiccupped or burped in polite company. She clears her throat and continues. "What happened to you both is unimaginable, but you can't continue to live like this. She's a bad influence on you, Spencer."

"Mom."

Elaine shoots me a look. "Well, she is. She doesn't even know how to mourn properly."

"What's that supposed to mean?" I ask.

"You know exactly what it means." She glares hard, as though she can see right through me. I know she's referring to the fact that I'm still sleeping with Spencer, but her stare is so incriminating, I briefly wonder if she knows about the other men as well.

Spencer says, "We all have our own ways of dealing with what happened."

"I know what's right," she says. Her hands are balled into fists, but she's already shaking at the shoulders and teary. "Don't you think I miss her? There's not a day that goes by that I don't remember something about her. I miss my grandbaby every single day." Embarrassed by a sudden flash of tears, she stands abruptly and goes to the sink.

Spence and I exchange glances before he joins her. "Mom."

It's true. While Elaine never liked me, she loved Hailey and doted on her. She constantly bought her presents and babysat more than we needed. And she made her Halloween costume by hand every year. When she was a one-year-old, for instance, Hailey went dressed as an heirloom tomato, Elaine stitching the word *heirloom* on her green felt hat, which served as the stem. Hailey loved her right back, too. I can still see her running down the hall to greet her. *"Granny!"*

Spence takes Elaine in his arms.

"I have every right to worry."

"I know," he says.

She sniffles a few times. Just when it seems she's calmed down, she breaks from Spencer's hug and goes for a napkin and blows her nose. She then looks at us both, determined again. "You two are still young, and you can't allow yourselves to self-destruct. Think of what you can do if you go your separate ways. You can focus on yourselves and rebuild your lives. You two are *divorced*."

When we don't respond, she finds her purse and sweater.

"You don't have to leave, Mom," Spence says gently. "Stay. Finish your breakfast."

"No, I can't say I feel comfortable staying. I prefer to leave."

"Stay, Elaine," I say.

"I don't think so. I'm not one to take on the role of hypocrite. Spencer, I'll visit again when I know you're alone."

Spence shoots me a look after she leaves and shrugs his shoulders. He then shakes his head sadly and follows. This is the story of our marriage.

When I can catch only the low murmur of their voices coming from the hall, I give up on trying to eavesdrop. As much as I want to hate Elaine, to be angry with her, I can't. I know she's right about me—and she doesn't even know the half of it. I pick up my fork and toss it across the table, watching as it clangs against Spence's plate. I then walk zombielike to the bedroom and climb into bed.

Minutes later, Spence appears in the doorway. "Hey." He walks over and climbs in next to me. We're perfectly quiet until he reaches under the covers and takes my hand. "You know, maybe she's right."

"About what?"

"You know, making some changes."

"So you don't want me to come over anymore? Is that what you're trying to say?"

"No, I'm not saying that at all, but I'm not sure we can go on like this either." He kisses the top of my forehead.

"I'm sorry I asked for the divorce."

"I know."

I press my head into his chest and inhale deeply. I think of my drinking and the nameless, faceless men I've been with. "Your mom is right about me," I say into his stomach. "I *don't* know how to mourn properly."

"Who does?"

He strokes my hair quietly. My guilt only intensifies, though. I'm not sure I've really thought of what I took away from Elaine—from *everyone*—who knew Hailey. She was a granddaughter, a niece, a cousin. I knew this, of course, but seeing how upset Elaine was makes me feel more culpable. I took her grandbaby away. I took Hailey away from everyone. I move to the other side of the bed and bury my head between my knees. Despite how hard I try not to, I soon start crying. "I'm sorry, Spencer."

"About what?"

I can't tell him about my driving that day, there's no point at all. A confession won't bring her back, and the guilt in the matter is my cross, no one else's.

He rubs my back. "Don't let my mom get to you, P. She's just upset."

"I know. I just—I don't know what I'm doing. I can't take this anymore. I'm fucked-up, Spencer."

He moves up besides me, touches my chin, and forces me to look at him. "Hey now. Let me tell you something. We are *both* fucked-up. You don't get a hold on crazy, girl."

I nod. After the funeral, the only thing that kept me from going and killing myself was the thought that I'd be leaving Spencer alone. Not to mention what my own suicide would do to the twins.

I feel Spence pull me in closer. "We just need to give it time, remember?"

This is our running joke; it seemed everyone told us all we needed was time. I force a fake smile while sniffling and wiping at my eyes. "Yeah, time. That's the answer."

"Time heals all wounds," he says.

I'm equally sarcastic: "Yep. We'll just wait it out and everything will be fine."

After wiping a stray tear from my cheek, he smiles. "Better?"

I nod, and he hunkers down next to me and takes my hand.

We soon find ourselves looking toward the doorway. Our fingers entwined, our heads touching, we stare at the doorway as if at any minute Hailey will come running into the bedroom. I know with everything I have that Spence is willing this along with me. We stare at the door, waiting for our little girl to show up, dressed in her jammies. She will be either still drowsy from sleep and complaining of a bad dream while holding her doll or teddy bear; or she will be wide-awake and running toward us, bounding into bed and asking Daddy to make her favorite chocolate chip and banana pancakes.

Spence wraps his arms around me, and we stare at that door with everything we have. We stare and stare. We stare and wait until we hear the sound of someone starting up his car and neighbors chatting. And that's when the spell is broken and Spencer pulls away. "Come on," he says. "I'll take you home."

five

"Hamlet was a pussy."

"Detrane, watch your language, please."

"Sorry, Miss Nelson. Hamlet was a fucking wimp."

"Detrane."

"But I'm stating the truth. How you gone watch your uncle kill your father and not do anything about it?"

A few students nod their heads in agreement; others raise their hands.

I survived the morning with Elaine and now sit on top of my desk discussing Hamlet with the sixteen students who decided to show up to seventh period. I call on Sharayray.

"But if you kill somebody, you gotta make sure your shit is right," she says.

"Language."

"Sorry, Miss Nelson. I'm just sayin' you have to make sure things are right, like, morally. Like when you have to kill, like going to war or something, 'cause otherwise you're as in the wrong as the other person."

Arthur says, "My uncle Perry says everybody involved in politics is going to hell. That's why I know Claudius was up to no good."

Every semester I force my juniors to make their way through *Hamlet*. Every semester it's the same: *Oh* hell *no! I can't read this shit*. But by the end, most recognize that Hamlet has been through as much as they have: death of a close relative by murder, backstabbing, cheating, parental abandonment, suicidal thoughts, incest, bad relationships—it's all there.

MacDowell High is one of the poorest schools in an already financially strapped school district. To the larger society, my students are merely statistics, their lives eagerly discussed during any given election season and soon thereafter forgotten. But we do our best here; well, most of us do. I couldn't imagine teaching anywhere else. The reward of watching a student from Mac-Dowell head off to the University of California or state college, hell, even community college, is far more gratifying than if I taught at a private school.

Michelle raises her hand. "Miss Nelson? Why you think Ophelia wanted to kill herself? Me and Sharayray think she was pregnant. Why else would she kill herself?"

I'm about to comment, when Gladys Edwards, the school's principal, enters the room. As soon as I see her, I hop off my desk and resume teaching as though I've been standing all along. She only smiles, though, as she moves to the side of the room, motioning to the students who look her way that they should pay attention. Gladys is another reason I continue to teach at MacDowell. Even with her whispery chipmunk of a voice, she keeps everyone in line. Students and teachers alike want to please her.

I check my watch. There are only three minutes left before the bell, so I tell my students to write about Ophelia for their

homework. Was her suicide a suicide at all? Is suicide ever jus-
tified?

Gladys asks Brandon how he did on his last math test as he
leaves, then asks Valerie to tell her mother hello. She wears her
usual skirt and jacket over a crisp white blouse, her packed round
body erect and all business.

I walk up to her after the class files out, prepping myself
for a lecture. I'm not sure exactly what I've done wrong, but as of
late I haven't done much right either. I hardly attend departmen-
tal meetings anymore, and I've been tardy a few times here,
absent a few times there. Before the accident, I was considered
one of the top teachers in the school, dedicated and hardworking,
but that was almost five years ago, long enough by now that
most people probably don't remember the old me.

I decide to make the first move. "I'm sorry for arriving late
this morning. It couldn't be—" But she surprises me; shocks me,
really, by taking me in her arms.

"Oh, Miss Nelson! Oh, Miss Nelson!" She pulls me down
several feet until my nose remains stuck somewhere in the crook
of her arm. "Oh, Miss Nelson!" She sways me like a wrestler
about to take down her opponent. "Oh, Miss Nelson!" she cries,
finally letting me go. "Thank you so much! God bless you!"

"You're welcome, but . . . *what did I do?*"

"Don't be modest." She grins conspiratorially as she pokes
her long fingernail into my chest. "I didn't know you had it in
you to keep something like this from me. I am your principal,
after all."

Her eyes go shiny as she takes from her pocket what can only
be a check. She unfolds it directly in front of me, long enough
that I see the number one followed by a series of zeros.

"Ten thousand dollars," I hear myself say.

"Yes! Ten thousand dollars! Ten thousand dollars in the

name of that beautiful little girl of yours. Oh, Miss Nelson, we will honor this gift at MacDowell High for many a year to come, and you know we will buy books for the English department *and* computers!"

She lightly taps the side of my cheek. When she removes her hand, I touch my cheek as well. I know of only one person who can write a check with that many zeros. "Curtis," I say.

She pulls an envelope from her pocket. "Here's the letter. He's so kind, Miss Nelson. I'm just so impressed with him, Miss Nelson. Oh, you know I'm including this in my collection! I'm going to have it framed. Oh yes."

Gladys is the only person at the school who knows I know the football player. I've never wanted people asking me to ask him for favors or looking at me differently. But Gladys is a huge Raiders fan, and for her birthday last year, I asked him to sign a shirt and football for her. Apparently this was a big deal. She practically cried when she saw her gifts and later told me she had them encased behind glass in her den.

She hands me the letter. I immediately recognize Margot's handwriting as I skim over the page.

"He says you convinced him he had to help our school. He's given a donation in your daughter's honor!"

I have never talked to Curtis about doing anything in Hailey's honor, and I have to assume his sudden generosity is to make amends for the weekend. Even so, the timing of everything doesn't compute. If the check is to somehow make up for his video presentation on Saturday, how did it get here so soon?

I hand the letter back. I don't want to lie, but I also don't see the point in telling Gladys I have nothing to do with the surprise check. "I guess I have to confess that I didn't know he was going give you the check today. I just saw him over the weekend, and he didn't say anything. When did you say the check arrived?"

"Not thirty minutes ago. A man straight out of a movie came into my office. Just as handsome as he could be. I thought he might be a detective and was about to inquire about one of our students, but then he greeted me politely as could be and handed me the envelope."

This sounds like Tru, Curtis's personal bodyguard and chauffeur.

I smile, and Gladys and I hug. Ten thousand dollars is no joke, as my students would say, but Curtis could have easily afforded fifty thousand.

"Miss Nelson, we will honor Hailey with this money. Starting with a computer lab in her honor, if it's okay with you."

"That would be great, Mrs. Edwards. Just—I don't want her name anywhere or anything. You understand?" I hope I won't need to explain why: I don't want to pass by her name every day, even if it's for something as terrific—and needed—as a computer lab.

She takes my hand. "I do, Miss Nelson."

"And if you don't mind, I'd appreciate it if we kept this private. I'd still prefer people didn't know I know Curtis or that I had anything to do with his gift."

"I understand. People might start thinking you're getting preferential treatment. I know how people gossip."

After a final hug, I pack up my things and head out. Besides having to figure out a way to get my car, I need to call Curtis and find out what's going on—and thank him.

I leave the main building, wondering if I should skip walking home and take the bus. When I reach the parking lot, I see a group of twenty or so students. My first thought is that a fight has broken out, but they're all too quiet and all staring at something or someone with such amazement that they appear, in what can only be described as an anomaly for our students, dumbstruck.

I make my way around a small cluster of kids. I recognize some of my own students, but no one pays me any attention. A Mercedes comes into view with blackened windows and a shiny exterior; parked nearby—*hold on a second*—is my own car, looking forlorn and sheepish next to such a sleek and fancy rival.

I hear his name before I see him.

"That's fucking Curtis Randolph," the kid next to me whispers. "I'm telling you, it's him. Gimme a pen, man. Hurry up."

Whispering, "Excuse me," I move through the crowd. I see him, then, bending over as he signs autographs.

As the texts and calls escalate, more kids start coming from all corners of the school. A few people watching from across the street make their way over.

Just then someone shouts, "It's Curtis fucking Randolph, y'all!" The gathering crowd starts screaming, too: "Curtis Randolph in da house! Yo yo! Over here!" More people start to rush over. They come out of nowhere, running toward us, pointing, screaming.

Tru gets out of the car. He's three times the size of the football player and tends to handle moments like these with a hard stare as his sole weapon. He calmly tells everyone to step back, then walks over to the football player who leans with his back against the Mercedes as he continues to sign pieces of scrap paper, notebooks, soccer balls, anything shoved in front of him. Tru leans in, and the footballer whispers something in his ear. He nods. "Okay. Form a single line. Everybody form a line and wait your turn."

I move to the front of the crowd just as the back door of

the Mercedes opens and Margot steps out, one mile-long leg at a time. She's done up in a kind of bodice-shaped jacket with a fur collar. There are fifty people standing around now, maybe more. They all crane their necks and stand on tiptoe to get a better view. She looks familiar enough, but they can't quite put their finger on who she is. Then, all at once, they seem to realize she's nobody, a beautiful nobody but a nobody just the same, and everyone's attention goes back to the football player, except for two boys up front who continue to stare.

She walks directly over to me. "P!" I quickly pull her away from the ever-growing crowd.

"What are you doing here?"

"We thought we'd bring your car," she explains. "The girls were curious about where you work, so here we are! Surprise!"

"The girls are here?"

"They're in the car. We had Tru drive your car. Which was a sight, let me tell you. He could hardly fit."

"So what's going on? What's up with the check?"

She pouts her lips. "Well, I was angry with you at first, but Daddy pointed out that you were upset and, anyway, we're both sorry for what happened, P. We didn't know those pictures would hurt your feelings. Curtis thought a donation to the school would be a nice way to make it up to you."

"Curtis or you?"

"Does it matter?"

"Guess not, but considering how much he's worth—he couldn't do fifty?"

"Piper! You ruined his performance!"

"So what? I was upset! He had no right. I told you I wanted Hailey left out of it." I feel my stomach tighten at the thought of the picture and Curtis's dreadful song.

Margot makes a point of gazing disapprovingly at the school's main building and trailers next to the track field. "Well, ten thou' or five, I'd be grateful, 'cause it sure looks like you all could use it." She looks at me now. "Are you okay?"

I nod.

"Where did you go, anyway? Who was the short guy you left with?"

Selwyn already feels like years ago, frankly, but I'm defensive just the same. "He's not that short. I had on heels. And even if he is short, who cares?"

"Well, who was he?"

I pause long enough to shake away the image of the look on his face when I told him good-bye. "Nobody—a friend."

"Well, as long as you're all right."

"I'm fine."

I look over at Curtis grinning at his fans. It strikes me that I'm being played. Their reasons for showing up here are all too odd, too—*generous*. They bring my car and make a donation to the school and expect nothing in return? Uh, not in this particular universe.

"What's *really* going on?"

"What do you mean? I told you, we wanted to give you the check and bring your car."

"And what else, Margot?"

"You always think I'm up to something."

"That's because you are. Now what do you want?"

She rolls her eyes. "A tiny favor, that's all. Curtis and I need to get away."

"From what?"

"Curtis has so much on his plate right now, and then when things didn't go well at the party—" She gives me an accusatory look.

"I know you're not blaming me. I was upset."

"I know, but you hurt his feelings. You called him an idiot in front of his family."

I widen my eyes. *What can I say? I call 'em as I see 'em.*

Margot clicks her tongue. "Curtis wants to drive to Tahoe for a few days and get some R and R. Mom says she can watch the girls, but she can't get them until tonight. Can you watch them for a few hours until she can pick them up?"

I try to make sense of it all. "You two are going to Tahoe . . . *right now?*"

"Well, yeah. I told you, he needs to de-stress. I don't think people appreciate all that man has on his plate—the album, the wedding, the book deal, and let's not forget he does play football. He really needs this. He had our bags packed this morning. I'm supposed to figure out what to do with the twins."

"That's a nice way to talk about your children."

"You know what I mean. It's not like I didn't warn them that I'd be busy until the wedding."

"And what was your excuse before the wedding?"

"Look, I didn't come here to be judged. Can you watch them or not? We wouldn't have to ask if not for the African sorceress; now she says she won't be back from LA until tomorrow. So if it's not you, it's Danielle."

Danielle: possibly more selfish than Margot. The girls often complain how she stays on the phone the entire time they're with her.

"Of course I'll watch them."

"Great. Mom will pick them up around ten."

She checks her watch, then checks on the football player who's now posing with a group of gangbangers, all flashing their signs. The crowd has easily tripled in size, but Curtis shows no sign of fatigue. He's a star for a reason, I'll admit, all stellar looks and style. Too bad he has the brainpower of a gnat.

We make our way through the crowd. Curtis catches sight of us and says something to Tru, who starts telling the throngs to back away. Everyone is clearly disappointed but does as instructed; some take last-second pictures with their phones.

Curtis walks over and hooks his arm around my neck while rubbing a fist against my chin. "Sister-in-law!"

"Not quite." I grimace.

He lets me out of his vise grip and takes Margot's arm. "So, did you get the check?"

"Yes, thanks. I really appreciate it."

"My pleasure, Sis, my pleasure. I always want to give a little somethin' back. Next, I want to buy you a car. No offense, but that piece of shit you're driving now is a piece of shit." He sticks a toothpick in his mouth and works his back teeth. "My bad about the other night, by the way. I was trying to make you feel better, but I understand how my gift was taken the wrong way. It's a sensitive subject."

Margot beams as she takes his hand. "We all make mistakes." He turns and runs his finger along her jaw, then begins kissing her. I try not to look as their cheeks bulge like those of two squirrels carrying nuts. I clear my throat, and Curtis gives Margot's ass a pat. "Why don't you get the girls, baby?"

"Sure thing." Margot walks to the car. Having absolutely nothing to say to the football player, I tell him I'm going to help. Margot gives the back window a few taps, and it rolls down.

"Hey," I say, taking a peek inside. The girls hardly pay attention; they're too fixated on whatever they're texting. "Hello, Aunt P."

Tru gets their bags while the football player gets into the front seat of the Mercedes and takes out his cell. Sophia and Margot climb out of the Mercedes, wearing their private school uniforms and impassive faces. "We're hungry," Sophia says.

"We'll order a pizza," I say.

"Chez Panisse doesn't have pizza," Little Margot says.

"The café but not the restaurant," Sophia explains.

"They're expecting Chez Panisse for dinner," says Margot.

Chez Panisse is easily one of the more expensive restaurants in the East Bay. The only time I can afford to eat there is when I'm with Margot or babysitting. I wait while she gets her bag and takes out a few bills—four one-hundred-dollar bills to be exact.

"Great," I say, taking the money. "Chez Panisse it is."

The girls climb into my Honda. Tru gets behind the wheel of the Mercedes while Curtis continues to talk on the phone.

Margot gives me one last hug. "I *am* sorry about that picture."

"I know."

"Girl," Curtis says, interrupting us, "you need to hurry it up. Traffic is gonna be a bitch as it is."

"Coming, baby!"

She gives one last air kiss to the girls and rushes over to the Mercedes.

I actually don't blame Margot for her alarming amounts of narcissism and airheadedness; I blame Mom, and to a certain extent the Reverend. The entire time Margot was growing up, they rarely disciplined her; they never taught her to be grateful for all she was given—which was everything she wanted. And then there was Mom going on about her looks and how she was going to be a big star. It never mattered to her how many times I made the honor roll or did well in a difficult class; any accomplishment was forgotten within minutes. So it's no wonder Margot's a spinning supernova in her own vast universe. I just worry about the girls, whom she is ignoring more and more, just like Mom ignored me when she was single. She had no trouble dropping me off with various sitters in pursuit of her own selfish needs. I was only lucky in that my main sitter—father figure, really—was Mr. Hoffman.

I climb inside my car and start the engine.

Little Margot looks out from the back window. "That's where you teach, Aunt P?"

"Yep. That's it."

Margot looks at Sophia. "See, told you."

"Looks like a prison," Sophia says. "Where's the lawn?"

"There is no lawn."

"So, like, where's the driveway where the nannies and assistants drop off the kids?"

"In a land far, far away, my darlings," I say, backing out of the parking lot. "A place where tax dollars are spread evenly, and separate but equal is truly a thing of the past."

After eating a prix fixe meal at Chez Panisse, the twins and I head back to the apartment, where I remind them what a broom looks like and demonstrate how it's used. "See, isn't it incredible? Next time you're here, I'll show you the vacuum!"

We make popcorn once they've finished their homework and watch the movie they've chosen that involves a teenage star from one of their favorite TV shows. After they go to bed, I take out *The Lady in the Lake.* I put on water for tea and Mozart's Symphony no. 38. Another way Mr. Hoffman ruined me for all things hip or cool was to introduce me to classical music. Once, while listening to Beethoven's Concerto no. 1 in C, he said, "I don't believe in God, Piper, but I do believe in Mozart and Beethoven, Caravaggio and Van Gogh, the genealogy of Mars and the expansion of the universe. That's my religion."

Mom shows up long after the girls have fallen asleep. She's been counseling the women's group she leads and looks as tired as when she'd come home from her second job at the coffee shop. After asking about the girls, she sighs and starts unpinning her hair, rolled in a tight French twist. Mr. Hoffman also once said he was a believer in Mom's hair. He'd had a little too much red wine and said, "I am a believer in your mother's hair, Piper. Its texture and its smell."

She removes the last bobby pin and her hair collapses past her shoulders. "I understand Curtis gave a donation to your school."

"He did."

"You could sound a little more grateful, Piper. That was a lot of money."

"Not for him."

She glowers.

"I'm grateful! I'm grateful." Admittedly, I'm also hurt that she hasn't asked how I'm doing. The last time she saw me, I was rushing out of Margot's party, after all. I offer to get her some tea, then head to the kitchen, separated from the living room by a small bar. When I asked for the divorce, I told Spencer he could have everything, and I meant it. He bought me out of my share of the house, and I moved to a neighborhood that most people would consider borderline dangerous, but my apartment is also within walking distance of the school, and I wanted it on the spot when the manager said I could have access to the roof.

Mom removes her shoes and begins massaging her feet. I doubt the congregation realizes how much she helps the Reverend with the church. She not only takes care of hiring staff, but she's always spearheading at least two committees, plus she's involved with the scholastic boosters and women's council.

"I thought you'd be more excited, Piper. Curtis didn't have to give you a cent, you know."

"I know."

"Especially after the way you behaved. You do realize you pushed him."

"I know; I know. I was upset. I think he'll live."

"Well, we were all very sorry about that photo. But this is exactly what I've been talking about—you can't keep acting out. Somehow or other you have to get it together. You could be doing so much more by now."

I think back to Elaine this morning and her harping on how Spencer and I could be doing more with our lives. And now Mom is on the same rant. She has a rather deep voice but sounds like she's squealing right about now, and my brain and body rattle with every word. I never ever drink more than a glass of wine when I'm watching the girls, but now that she's here to pick them up, I go to the shelf where I keep the scotch, just out of her view, and pour two shots into my mug and toss them back. After taking a breath, I pour another shot, then add my tea bag and hot water. Much. Better.

I take our tea to the living room. Mom is quiet as she sips. I think of telling her about seeing Elaine earlier. One of the few places where we do come together is over our hatred for Spencer's mother. If Mom thinks Curtis's mom is "ghetto," she considers Elaine uppity. At the dress rehearsal for our wedding, Mom leaned over and whispered, "I wish whatever crawled up that woman's butt would find its way out."

"It's becoming clear to all of us that you're not doing as well as you think you are, Piper, and we're all worried sick." She pauses. "Charles would like to perform a laying of hands on you."

I arch a brow. "Excuse me?"

"He wants to pray with you."

"I'm not going to church, Mom. And he's certainly not laying his hands on me."

"But he wants to help. You wouldn't have to go to church if

you didn't want to—although goodness knows it wouldn't hurt. He could come here."

Sometimes I want to shake this brainwashed Christian in front of me and plead for my old mom to come back, but then, what good was the old mom? Having Hailey in my life gave me a sense of purpose and fulfilled me in so many ways that I didn't have to deal with any issues I had with Mom, but now everything seems to be in my face, sans filter. I study her briefly.

"Do you ever think about Mr. Hoffman?"

Now it's her turn to be frustrated. "What? Who? Good gracious. Why on earth are you bringing him up?"

"I don't know. I've been thinking about him lately."

"Well, stop it."

"Do you?"

"Hardly."

"Don't you ever think about how things would've been if you hadn't dumped him?"

"I don't need to. I can tell you right now how they would've been. Boring. Dull. I don't know what kind of spell he put on you, Piper, but you need to forget about him. I most certainly have."

"He was the only man you stayed with long enough for me to get to know."

She brings her hand to her forehead as though taken over by a migraine. "Not this again."

"Remember how he'd make those incredible meals for us? How we'd go to the movies together? Why did you break up with him?"

She looks up from under her hand as if I've gone mad. "He was *Jewish*!"

"And *so*? Jesus Christ was Jewish, and you don't have a problem fawning all over him."

She waves my comment away with a smirk.

"Why were you so awful to him?"

"I will not let you point a finger at me, Piper. As soon as I met George—"

"Gerald—"

"George, Gerald, whoever. As soon as I met him, I told David he wasn't the only person I was seeing. It was up to him to stay or leave. I swear, I wish you'd drop this odd fascination you have with that man."

She finishes her tea. "If you want change, Piper, God can help. You see what he's done in my life, what he does in your sister's life. He can do the same for you. I serve a living God. Just as the trees die in winter, praise God, they rise in spring. Let your stepfather lay hands on you. It can't hurt."

"What is this? The Middle Ages? No, thank you."

"But—"

"No. Thank you."

"Fine." She stands and reaches for her purse. "Why don't you help me wake up the girls so I can get out of here."

Ironically, the fact that I lost Hailey has only worsened my relationship with Mom. What I've come to realize is that death highlights problems that have existed all along.

"Fine."

I pour another double after Mom and the girls leave. I think about taking a walk around the altars but instead go to the hallway closest, unlock all four bolted locks, and take out my Meade 1x. I pay extra for access to the roof, but it's worth it.

After putting on a sweater and jacket, I climb all six flights and set up my telescope. The sky is dark enough that I aim toward the Pleiades, an open cluster of stars, with the hope of seeing nebular gas. I'm in luck, and I gaze as the gases swirl in blues and greens. The Pleiades lie four hundred light-years away; the stars are just babes, really, only fifty million years old, newborns when you compare them to the sun, and so young their gas clouds still linger.

I stare at the Pleiades until I feel the day falling away, until I feel my entire being disappearing into stars and gas, wispy and ethereal. If only.

six

Two weeks later, I'm listening to the wind pounding against my bedroom window. It's early October, and the weather is already getting cooler. Even though it's two a.m., I can't sleep and climb out of bed. I know I'm making a mistake even as I go to the closet and take down the box where I keep Hailey's things, but I walk to the closet just the same. I keep the box on the top shelf, pushed deep into the corner and hidden behind several shoe boxes. After taking it down, I sit on the floor and carefully open the flaps. I take out one item at a time. A coloring book. A necklace made of plastic hearts. Her favorite doll. A pair of baby shoes. I'm not sure why I saved these items over any of the others, but they're what I chose to keep.

I find her favorite T-shirt near the bottom. I bought the shirt on one of our many mommy-and-daughter visits to the Chabot Space and Science Center. The shirt is blue with a gold comet shooting off into space, the words CELEBRATE HALLEY'S COMET! written in gold glitter.

I close my eyes as I think of combing her hair; wrapping her in a towel after her bath. Bedtime stories. Her voice from the hall—*"Come here, Mommy! I wanna show you something."* My body rocks back and forth as tears come. I bring her shirt to my nose and mine for her smell. But it's pointless, and I'm soon crying so much that my throat and head begin to throb. I'm a supermassive black hole, feeding off my own grief and longing.

The room tilts as I make my way outside. I have it in my head that I'll feel better if I get some fresh air, maybe do some stargazing. It's still dark, after all, and even though the sidewalk shifts every time I take a step, I'm undeterred. I take a swallow from the bottle of scotch I've wrapped in a paper bag. I try to stare at the stars, but each time I look up, I lose my balance and tip off to one side. Since stargazing isn't going to happen, I decide to visit a few altars and continue up Fifty-sixth Street. I walk for what feels like hours, but Money's altar is nowhere in sight, and I'm beginning to wonder if I've made a wrong turn. *Hmph*—lost in my own neighborhood.

A cop pulls up alongside me just as the sidewalk turns into an escalator. I feel myself being lowered down to the first floor but manage to stay steady.

The cop rolls down his window—he's mustached, unibrowed. "I don't need to ask what's in that paper bag you're holding. Where're you headed?"

I point west, then change my mind and point east.

He waves me over to his car. I'm transfixed by the unibrow floating above his eyes, thick and turdlike. I imagine that it was passed down hundreds of generations, starting with some long-ago matriarch who sprouted downy hairs on her chin, the Original Brow flat-lined over her guppy-shaped brown eyes.

"You workin' tonight?"

"Work?"

"You're a ways from the avenue." He glances back toward San Pablo Avenue, a main drag typically dotted with prostitutes.

He looks me up and down. I'm confused at first but then follow his gaze, starting with my shoes—I'm only in my house slippers—on up to my cardigan and spaghetti-strapped top underneath. I'm drunk, but not so drunk that I don't know how I must look.

I move closer to the car. "I'm not working, Officer. My only crime is insomnia." The ground refuses to stop moving and my feet slip back in a kind of Sammy Davis Jr., Mr. Bojangles two-step. I study his brow after finding my balance. I hear myself say, "Tweezers," before bursting into a fit of giggles.

He narrows his eyes while I take a long pull from my brown paper bag. My jacket has fallen open and he makes no pretense about what he's staring at. "It's unsafe, you know, to walk this area at night."

I take another pull. "Why don't you give me a ride in your big fat car, then? Keep me safe."

I've indulged in my own fantasies involving illicit sex with handsome men, but when you're slurring things like "Why don't you give me a ride in your big fat car," and hearing a response like "My car isn't the only thing that's big," the moment is no longer fantasy come to life; it's just plain stupid.

But this is what happens, and all too soon, we're parked beneath a highway overpass. After cutting the engine, the cop pulls my chin toward his face. I keep my eyes open as he shoves his tongue in my mouth and gropes at my breasts. After a minute or two of this, he places his hand on the back of my head and begins pushing my face toward his lap. That's when I grimace and say, "Not very subtle, are you?"

• • •

The next morning I'm sitting on my bathroom floor with my head suspended above the toilet. Ironically, the song "Oh, What a Beautiful Morning" plays from the TV in the living room. I'm waiting to puke, but my stomach is empty by now and nothing comes but dry heaves. I splash cold water on my face and return to the living room. A clip from *West Side Story* has replaced *Oklahoma!* I gather from the narration that the show on TV is about the American musical.

When my stomach growls, I vaguely remember a piece of toast for lunch and go to the fridge. Limp celery. A half container of yogurt. Days-old Chinese takeout. I find a spoon and eat peanut butter from the jar, then mumble, "Fuck it," and toss the spoon into the sink. Why eat peanut butter when Elaine always makes sure her darling son's fridge is stocked? I find my purse and keys. It's when I'm at the door that I hear the distinct sound of an unclasping buckle and see my fingers laced around a gold zipper. My stomach tightens, and I'm forced to go back to the couch and sit down. I press my hands to my temples and close my eyes. I see my fingers pulling the zipper, followed by the reveal of stark white briefs. I feel the cop's hand pushing the back of my head. I hear his voice: *"Yeah, that's it."*

My stomach surges, and I cover my mouth as I rush toward the bathroom. This time I manage to throw up more than just air.

I'm surprised when I open the door to the Berkeley house and find Spence in the hallway, putting on his jacket.

"Where have you been? I've been calling all day," he says.

I think of how only a few minutes ago I was sitting beside my toilet. "I had a little too much last night. I guess I've been sleeping most of the day."

"You *guess?*" He smirks as he grabs his knit scarf and hat.

"Where are you going?"

"You didn't bother listening to any of my messages?"

I stand there, trying to remember the last time I used my cell phone, let alone where it might be. I snap my fingers and start patting down my jacket. After I find it, I hold the phone in the air and give it a little shake. "Should I listen now?"

Spence says, "I've been going to these meetings. I've gone twice now. Roland told me about them."

"Roland?"

"Our old neighbor. The widower."

Five houses over. Nice man. Always alone except for his dog.

"He's been trying for a while now to get me to visit this group he belongs to."

He's just evasive enough that I understand he would have preferred to tell me about this mysterious group over the phone. I can't imagine what kind of meeting Spence would be too embarrassed to tell me about except—"You didn't join AA, did you?"

"Of course not. The meetings"—he drops his gaze as he wraps his scarf around his neck—"are for people who've lost loved ones."

His answer catches me completely off guard, and I find myself quietly repeating what he's said.

"Roland has been going for a few months, and every time he saw me, he asked me to come along. I finally joined him."

"Who's Roland mourning? His wife died twenty years ago."

"Sadie."

I draw a blank.

"His Lab."

"He joined a group of people who lost loved ones because of a dog?"

"Piper."

I feel a pang of guilt. Roland and Sadie were inseparable, and Roland was one of those pet owners who treated his dog with the kind of care that bordered on pathology.

"Sadie died, huh?"

"Yeah. A few months ago, but the old guy is still having a hard time with it. He said the meetings help. I finally joined him, and I like it."

"Why didn't you tell me?"

"I wasn't sure you'd be into it, but then I changed my mind and left you a message."

He's right. I'm not into it. We both hated when people suggested we join certain groups, usually with names like Morning Mourners or Spirits and Humans Reuniting. Even the more straightforward groups didn't appeal. We didn't like the idea of broadcasting our problems or exposing our grief. Just thinking about it now makes me want to convince Spencer that he shouldn't go, that we should keep things as they are—safe and just the two of us. *No other mourners allowed.*

"They're a nice group, P. It's good for me right now. I need to start getting out more."

I think of Elaine's rant a couple of weeks ago and the countless lectures she's probably given him since. "Are you doing this for yourself or your *mommy?*"

"I'm just giving it a try, Piper. It doesn't have to be a big deal." He zips his jacket. "You can stay here if you want. I'll be back in a couple of hours."

"I'm starving," I whine. "What do you say you go to the meeting next time, and we order a pizza and watch a movie or that documentary on FDR you've been wanting to watch."

"I already saw it. Last night. While you were ignoring my calls."

"But I didn't realize my phone was off."

He starts toward the door. "I should get going. There's plenty of food. Have at it."

"Wait." I'm not sure it's possible to feel jealous of a meeting, but I'm ready to tell him anything to keep our little routine going. "In the spirit of going out more, what if we chuck the pizza idea and go to an actual movie theater and get actual popcorn and the whole bit."

He feigns thinking it over. "Nah. I'm in charge of bringing the cookies, and I don't want to let the group down." He snaps his fingers. "Almost forgot the cookies!"

I start to follow him to the kitchen but stop short when I catch my reflection in the hallway mirror. I look jaundiced, and my eyes are bloodshot. I take off my hat and use the compact from my purse to do what I can. I plop a couple of eye drops in each eye and comb my hair into a ponytail. If Spence is determined to get out more, I certainly don't want him doing so without me. I'm just adding lip gloss when he returns with the cookies. I can tell from the gold label on the box that the cookies are from Lulu's, our favorite bakery. "So I'll see you in a couple of hours?" he asks.

"Can I join you?"

"Really?"

"Yeah. I'm in mourning, too, you know."

A smile starts at the corner of his mouth. "I know. I just know how you feel about these things."

"Don't be silly. I'd love to go." I take the box of cookies so he can open the door. "I was just thinking that I need to get out more myself."

He reaches up and gives my nose a pinch. "Liar."

Friends of Friends in Mourning is held in Elmwood. Our hosts' house sits at the end of a street so dense with elm trees, a canopy of branches hangs above us. The house itself, a large two-story craftsman with a wraparound porch, takes up an entire corner.

Diane and Mitch Montgomery, our hosts, greet us with hugs. Diane is dressed in a kind of Moroccan-styled tunic that falls past her knees, loose slacks, and Indian slippers that turn up at the tip. She wears her graying brown hair in a long ponytail held together by a brass clip. Mitch, also long-haired and ponytailed, wears a silk patterned shirt, beaded necklace, and bracelets on either wrist. I have to stop myself from rolling my eyes.

After Spence makes introductions, Diane tells him to put the cookies in the kitchen and make himself at home. Mitch joins Spencer, his arm gingerly on his back as he leads him to the kitchen.

The house is filled with fifteen or so guests, who chat by the fireplace or in the kitchen or as part of the group gathered around the spread of food set on the dining room table. Extra chairs have been put in the living room for the meeting. Diane links her arm through mine as she begins to pull me toward the fireplace. She explains that she and Mitch started the group six years ago, after losing their college-aged son when he was walking through campus and was struck by another student speeding by on his moped. She points to a picture on the mantel. Her son stands on a rocky hill, holding a wooden mask next to his face. "That was taken while we were offering service to a small indigenous tribe off the Caymans. He was fifteen at the time, and before we left, the leader of the tribe gave him the mask he's holding. Mitch and I have been traveling since we were kids. We saw no reason to stop after Chandler was born. When he died, we immediately signed up for the Peace Corps and spent two years in Ghana and later, two more in Antigua." She holds my arm tighter, her gray eyes shiny. "It never gets easier, but you learn ways to cope. How about a tour of the house?"

I'm pulled along as she points out various pieces of artwork from her and Mitch's jaunts around the world. The tour
ends with what she refers to as her "pièce de résistance." We
walk down a long hallway that leads to the opposite end of the
house, then come to an abrupt stop. I stare at a seven-foot-tall
wooden statue of a man with requisite hoop rings in his ears
and nose and what has to be a two-foot-long penis. "I know,"
Diane says in reference to my staring and utter silence. "He's
gorgeous, isn't he? He's direct from Papua New Guinea. Mitch
and I bought him for a steal while we were there. Pretty impressive, huh?"

I keep my gaze trained on his massive-sized shlong. "I'll say."

For the life of me, I can't make out why Spence wants to be
here. So far, Diane and Mitch are just the kind of couple we find
obnoxious. They're conspicuously moneyed but not doing anything with their money except bargain hunting across the globe,
collecting culture just so they can give tours in their home and
talk of their adventures with the "natives." They are all things
PC but only as much as it suits them. I know I'm being bratty
and judgmental, but I don't get it. Spence wants to bail on a night
of drinking and watching TV—for *this*?

Diane and I turn a corner, and I hear his laughter. It's
been a long time since I've heard him laugh like this—light
and easy. But the sound of his laughter also makes me suspi-
cious, and I instinctively narrow my eyes. We round another
corner, and I see him standing in the dining room with a young
woman. They're both laughing so hard, their heads fall back in
unison.

I hear Diane at my side: "Shall I get you some wine? We
have another ten minutes before the meeting starts."

"Yes, please," I say, my eyes trained on my ex. "Make it a
double."

She gives me a curious look and heads for the kitchen. I walk slowly toward Spencer and the woman as though dragging my feet through mud. She's of the happy variety with round cheeks and big brown eyes that are currently locked on my husband— *ex*-husband—all topped off with a mop of soft brown curls. And she's young. No more than twenty-five, if that.

They take deep breaths as their laughter subsides: postcoitus breathing with dreamy smiles on their faces. Knowing Spence as well as I do, I'm sure he doesn't realize he's here because of this girl. But I know she's exactly the reason he's here. I walk directly up to him and stand by his side.

"Oh, hey," he says. "Tisa, this is my wife—" He laughs, embarrassed. "Ex-wife. *Ex*. Piper."

Tisa smiles warmly. "It's so nice to meet you. I've heard so much about you."

I steal a peek at Spence: *How is it that she's heard so much about me?*

"We went out for coffee," he explains.

I raise my brows. *Coffee?*

"Spencer told me you teach at MacDowell," Tisa says. "I think that's amazing. Teachers have the most important jobs of all. I think if we followed our authentic paths, there would be more teachers and artists and fewer lawyers and politicians. I truly honor what you do."

I have to stop myself from gagging. *I truly honor what you do?* Ugh. "And what do you do?" I ask.

Spence answers for her. "Tisa is just back from Senegal."

She shares a smile with him that indicates his reply is an inside joke. "That's the polite way of saying I'm unemployed at the moment. I finished courses at Cal for my master's in social work and needed a break. My aunt left me money when she passed, and so I used it to live abroad for a year."

"Lucky you."

"Yeah, the time away was just what I needed. The Universe definitely provides."

"Isn't it too busy imploding on itself?" I chuckle lightly, but neither she nor Spencer joins in. Whatever. I hate the way people talk about *the Universe* as if it were a person or something. "So, is your aunt the reason you're here?" I ask.

"Yeah. She died last year." She leans in. "These meetings do help; you'll see."

"But it's not the same," I murmur.

"Sorry?"

"It's not the same. Losing an aunt or a pet is not the same as losing a child."

"*Piper.*"

"I'm sorry, but it's not."

"My aunt and I were very close. She was like a mother to me."

"It's still not the same."

Spence gives me a look: *Can't you be nice?*

I return the look and then some: *No, I can't. Losing your aunt is not the same as losing your child. It's not!*

Diane interrupts our silent eye wrestle. "Here's your wine, Piper. Sorry it took so long. Mitch had to get more bottles from the cellar."

I thank her, forcing myself not to chug it all back at once. I'm grateful for my empty stomach; the wine goes straight to my head without a single detour.

"Everyone okay?" she asks. "Refills?"

Spence shakes his head no. Tisa holds up her mineral water and says she's fine.

When Diane leaves, Tisa gazes at the floor. "I'm so sorry. I didn't mean to compare."

Spence bumps my arm ever so slightly.

"It's okay," I say, but my voice is tight and unforgiving.

Spence, ever the diplomat, fills the awkward silence: "It's

fine, Tisa, really. We're all friends here." He extends a hand toward the living room. "Shall we find a seat?" Tisa offers an apologetic smile as she walks past me. I pretend not to notice and gulp back more wine. Spence pauses as he reaches my side and presses his mouth close to my ear. "Easy now," he whispers.

The meeting is reminiscent of AA meetings I've seen on TV, except no one here looks remotely down on his or her luck; most of us are drinking our hosts' expensive wine while our plates brim with gourmet appetizers. We sit in a circle around the living room. I sit two people over from Spence; Tisa sits away from him, too, closer to Mitch. There are two newcomers besides me, so Diane explains a ritual the group uses involving the Native American talking stick. Instead of raising a hand, if you want to speak, you ask for the stick and have at it. Living in Oakland now, I forget how annoying rich people of this ilk can be. I don't have to wonder how multiculturally "hip" or PC they'd be if Detrane showed up with me, or Sharayray.

A young blond woman asks for the stick. Dead husband. She says she finally gave his clothes to Goodwill. People nod in support. Next is Roland. He's silver haired and soft spoken. At six foot four, he dwarfs the chair he sits in. He's nice enough to say how happy he is to see me here tonight and falls into memories of his time with Sadie at Tilden Park. I close my eyes briefly and wish upon him the courage to go to the pound and get another dog.

I feel my heart rise to my throat when Spence asks Roland for the stick. I try to beg him with my thoughts not to say anything, but he's already holding the stick and looking around the room.

He takes a moment before speaking. "I—I just wanted to say a few things about—" His voice cracks, and he pauses long enough to clear his throat. "I just want to say a few things about my little girl."

I let my gaze shift toward the floor and hold my breath. I don't dare look at him. If I do, I'll burst into tears; I know it.

He's quiet as he tries to gather the strength to continue. When I finally look up, he's staring right at me. "That's her mother over there. Piper. We lost her almost five years ago now. I know everyone talks about how special their children are, but my little girl really was special." He laughs to himself. "Sometimes I'd come home tired, and Hailey would wrap her arms around my neck—" His shoulders buckle as the tears start. We hardly talk about Hailey, and when I see just how much he's been carrying inside, I start to cry, too. Why don't we talk about her more? He pulls himself together. More deliberate now, he sniffles and says, "She would wrap her arms around my neck and kiss me. And she'd say, 'Daddy, no one expects you to be perfect.'" He coughs and takes a deep breath. "I mean, how does a kid learn something like that? My daughter, thanks to her mother over there, knew the names of the planets and a few constellations." He chokes back any more tears that want to come and takes a long, deep breath. "Anyway," he says, after a second breath, "she was something else. And I miss her. That's all. And I want to say thank you for having me here. This has been good for me."

Tears continue to stream down my face as people pat Spence on the back and offer hugs. The woman next to me tries to put her arm around me, but I shake my head no and go about wiping my face and pulling myself together as quickly as I can. When I'm finally calm, I cross my legs and grip my chair. I don't look up.

"That ex of yours is one fine specimen."

I look over at the woman who's just sat down next to me. I'm sitting on the Montgomerys' backyard porch with a small plate of cookies resting on top of my knees.

The meeting has ended, and everyone is milling about inside the house over dessert and coffee.

"Excuse me?"

The woman turns and stares over her shoulder. I follow her gaze and see Spence through the kitchen window yukking it up with a few other guests; my stomach drops when I see Tisa at his side.

"Your ex," she repeats. "He's a cutie." She hands me a glass of wine. "Here you are, sweetheart. I saw you from the window sitting out here by your lonesome self and thought, 'I bet that girl could use a refill.'"

I thank her. I did want a refill, but I didn't want to go back inside. For a group of mourners, everyone sure is cheerful; plus, I couldn't take a second longer of watching Tisa and Spence.

"I'm Clementine, but call me Clem. I've always hated my full name."

"Piper."

"Piper? And I thought my name was odd. How on earth did you get a name like Piper?"

"My mother."

"Fair enough. My mother and grandmother shared the genteel name of June. I get Clementine. Go figure." She takes a long pull from her wine. She's busty with small features and a pout of a mouth. Auburn hair. Late fifties I'd guess, with a light Southern drawl. She was one of the few guests, like me, who didn't say a word during the meeting, which is a surprise since she comes across as a motor mouth. "Bet you got teased an awful lot with a name like Piper. Let's hear it."

I grin. "Let's see. . . . Piper Diaper. Pipeline. Piper the Sniper. Pipe Head, or there was the abbreviated version of Pipe. My sister's name is Margot," I add. "And my mom is Margaret. Go figure."

"My turn. I didn't get teased because of my name so much as my boobs. There was Twin Peaks, Double Trouble. Silicone Valley. Lactation Station."

"Lactation Station? Whew. That's harsh."

She makes a loud smack after polishing off the contents of her glass. "One thing's for sure—Mitch and Diane know their wines." She sets her empty glass down and wraps her arms around her knees. "Anyway, real sorry for your loss."

"Thanks."

"Was it illness?"

"Car accident."

"Those buggers will get a person every time."

"How about you? If you don't mind my asking?"

"I'll tell you what, Piper Diaper; if they were giving a prize for the biggest loss in this here group, I'd win hands down. Lost my son, my husband, and my big brother all in one shot. Plane crash. Everybody gone."

"Sorry."

"They were on their way to Vegas. My husband was flying the plane. Just a fun trip for the boys, you know."

There is absolutely nothing to say that she hasn't already heard, so I scoot closer and hold up my plate of cookies.

"Don't mind if I do." She chooses a chocolate-mint macaroon. After a couple of bites her chewing slows and her eyes widen. "My Lord, this is delicious."

"Yeah. They're from our favorite bakery."

Favorite, not only because Lulu's bakes the best cookies and cakes around, but also because it's where Spence and I met. We were sitting table to table when we noticed we were both grading papers. He was working on his doctorate at the time and teaching Intro to Philosophy. We struck up a conversation that led to a walk along College Avenue.

Clem finishes a cookie in no time. "Hold on a sec." She disappears into the house and comes back with an entire bottle of wine. "Now this is what I call a meetin'." She fills both our glasses, and we clink. "Cheers."

"Cheers."

We don't talk for a while, just eat and drink, the mix of cookies and wine our reward for putting up with the meeting.

Clem finishes another cookie and polishes off her wine. I don't judge. What else are you supposed to do after losing your entire family if not drink?

"How long?" I ask.

"Almost nine years ago now. My boy was only twenty-six. My husband was the love of my life. My brother, Billy, was my parents' only son. Momma took it so hard; she passed not long after. How's that for tragedy?"

"Not bad," I say softly.

"Told you, sweetheart, biggest mourner here."

"How long have you been coming to the meetings?"

"Off and on for three years. I've slept with half of the widowers here. Diane and Mitch may as well be running a high-class singles bar." She chuckles.

"Do you think you'll ever marry again?"

"Wrong question, sweetheart. Question is, do I think I'll ever *feel* again."

"I've wondered the same thing myself."

I watch as she pours more wine. As different as we are, I'm struck by the fact that I may as well be looking at my future self: drunk night after night and sleeping with widowers.

I think of Spence and glance back at the house, but there's no sign of either him or Tisa. I can't imagine losing Hailey and Spencer in one fell swoop, and I feel an onslaught of panic and dread at the thought of living my life without him. All of these years in limbo and I've never considered that I could actually lose him. In truth, I've been waiting until we get back together; officially back together, that is, with a second wedding and the whole bit. And then, only then would we think of having another child. But what if I have things wrong and we need to get back together now? What are we waiting for, anyway? Why are we playing at pretend marriage when we still love each other? I sip my wine while thinking that I need to talk to him. I love him and can't lose him.

I start to stand, but I don't want to leave Clem behind so abruptly. I have virtually no friends, and I already like her. After Hailey died, I pretty much secluded myself in hopes of never having to deal with anyone's pity ever again. And there were also those who shunned me, as though by virtue of our friendship my bad luck would rub off on them. But Clem's frankness and ability to relate are not lost on me. "I should get going," I tell her. "I'm not sure I'll be coming back to any of these meetings, but if you ever want to meet for coffee or lunch, I'd love to talk more."

"I'd be delighted. We can go to the bakery you told me about and stuff ourselves with cookies."

"That's a deal." I take pen and paper from my bag and jot down my phone number. "Promise you'll call?"

"Scout's honor." Her head gives an imperceptible bobble.

"Clem, are you okay to drive? Spence and I can give you a ride home if you want."

"Oh, don't worry about me. I live up the street. One reason I haven't given up on these meetings is that I can drink as much of this fine wine as I want, then walk my drunk ass home."

She laughs, but then as if distracted, leans back on her hands and lifts her face toward the night sky. I follow her gaze and see she's staring at Sirius and Centauri, their double helixes shining as brightly as ever. I say good-bye, but she doesn't turn; she just keeps her eyes focused skyward.

My stomach shrinks when I see Spence and Tisa in the living room saying good-bye to Roland as though they're a couple. Tisa smiles her happy nitwit smile when I walk up. "How did you like the meeting?" she asks.

"Fun!" I say.

Spence narrows his eyes. *Be nice.*

Roland gives me a hug and says he hopes to see me again. He shakes Spence's hand. "Day by day." I manage not to roll my eyes when Spence and Tisa repeat the mantra.

Tisa gives Spencer a hug. "I should get going, too." She hugs me next as though we're long-lost friends. "It's so nice to meet you, Piper." She waves good-bye, but then she says, "Thursday? Same place?"

Spence practically blushes. Although I'm just not sure if it's because he knows I'm looking at him or what. "Yeah, see you then."

He helps me with my coat after she leaves. His silence says he knows good and well I'm waiting for him to explain. He doesn't, though, leaving me to ask, *"Thursday?"*

"We're meeting for coffee. It's nothing." He waves good-bye to Diane. "See you next week!" he says, and starts ushering me out the door.

"What did she mean by 'same place'?"

"We've had coffee a couple of times, same café. It's nothing."

"Yeah, you keep saying that. But if it's nothing, then why didn't you tell me about it? We tell each other everything."

He doesn't respond until we're at the car. "There was nothing to tell, okay?" He opens my door and motions for me to get inside. He remains silent until we're safely driving away.

"But if everything is on the up-and-up and innocent—"

He hits the brakes a little too hard when we reach the stop sign at the corner. "Tisa and I aren't up to anything. This is what Mom meant about moving on, Piper. You need to remember we're no longer married."

I think of Clem and my decision to talk to him. If ever there was a time to talk about getting back together, it's now. "But what if I don't want to move on? What if I want more?"

Curious, he glances over at me.

"I was talking to someone tonight. She lost her husband, son, and brother in a plane crash."

"Damn."

"I know. But talking to her, Spence, I realized how much I don't want to lose you. I mean, I know we're there for each other, but I want us to make things more official. I love you, Spencer. I want us to get back together. Really back together. Maybe I could even move back in. I'm practically living there anyway."

We drive quietly. I know better than to press him. As much as we love each other, for me to actually verbalize what I hope we're both feeling must come as a surprise. But someone had to say it; someone has to help us out of our perpetual limbo, and I don't mind at all that someone being me. Seeing him with the nitwit has helped me realize that we need to get back together. I need to stop sleeping around, and I could do with drinking less, too. I reach over and take his hand. "Your mom is right about moving on, but I want to move on together."

We're at the house by now, and he cuts the engine. He then gives my hand a kiss and returns it to my lap.

"Listen, P. I have to tell you something."

"What?"

"I asked Tisa out."

"To coffee, you mean."

"No. When we meet for coffee, it's more like the meetings. We talk about things. You know, she talks about her aunt, and I talk about Hailey."

"You talk about Hailey with her?" I don't mean to sound so shrill, but it's too late.

"And you," he adds, as though this will help. "We talk about everything. But next time is more like a date *date*. You know, dinner . . . a movie."

I bite hard on the inside of my lip as I try to steady my breathing.

"I'm curious, that's all," he says. "Like I said, I want to get out more. Tisa is nice. Doesn't mean I'm marrying the girl; it's just a casual night out."

"What's so casual about dinner and a movie? You said it yourself—it's a date."

"P," he says, taking my hand again, "come on. Support me on this."

I snatch my hand away. "Support you? I can't believe you're going out with her after what I've just told you."

He takes the key out of the ignition and clicks the doors open, his way of signaling that I'm getting out of hand. He always clams up when our talks become too heated.

"I refuse to feel guilty about this, P. I'm not doing anything wrong here. And if you think about it, it might be good for you to get out, too. Wouldn't hurt for you to lie low on the alcohol either."

"You're one to talk."

He leans back against his seat and stares at the roof of the car. "It's just one date." He turns slowly. "You know I love you, Piper. I will always love you. We were a family. We still are. I just—I feel dragged down."

"By me?"

"No. Not you. By everything. I feel like I'm wasting away. I don't want to spend the rest of my life like this."

"We could try to help each other. It's *me* you're talking to. No one knows you better, Spencer. No one can love you more than I do."

"I know." His eyes meet mine, and when he doesn't look away, I lean in and close my eyes. I open my mouth just enough, but then, not a second later, I feel nothing except a peck on the cheek. I shoot my eyes open and see he's already on the other side of the car.

"Friends?"

I'm not sure if I'm more angry or embarrassed. Before I say something I might regret, I get out of the car, slamming the door behind me. I rush up to the front porch and start digging in my purse for my keys.

He walks up and watches me closely. "Piper, did you hear what I said? Can we be friends?"

"Why should I be your friend while you're fucking that nitwit?"

"I keep telling you, we're not doing anything."

"Not yet," I say. I find my keys and start to let myself inside the house, but then he moves in front of me with his arm blocking the door.

"No, Piper. That's what I'm trying to tell you. We can't keep doing this. I need a break. I want to be alone."

When he refuses to move, I take a step back. All these years of walking through that door, and now he won't let me inside. *"Spencer."*

He lowers his head. "Some other time, okay?"

My throat is tight, my tongue dry. I start for my car. "I hope you have a nice time with Tisa!" I yell. "I hope you two have fun fucking in our home!"

"P?" he says. "P! It's not like that. It's just for a little while, okay? I'll call you."

I ignore him, though. I get inside my car and drive away as quickly as I can. Naturally, the last thing I want is for him to see that I'm crying.

seven

Margot is dazzling in white silk crepe. She turns in front of one of the long mirrors at Rebecca Rankoff's studio, and we ooh and aah at the creped back and matte crepe finishes of the gown she wears and the veil woven with hints of gold. Already teary, Mom clasps her hands in adoration. "Oh baby, you look stunning. Absolutely stunning."

Danielle stands beside Mom and bursts into teary applause. "Margot! Oh my God! Curtis is going to flip when he sees you."

I join in, too. It's hard not to. The dress is sexy yet sophisticated, modern yet timeless.

Last week, a couple of days after Halloween, Margot and Curtis signed a deal for a new reality TV show called *Margot and Me*. I knew the show was a possibility what with all the meetings and phone calls taking place long before their engagement party, but since nothing came to fruition, I assumed the idea was merely that. But apparently TV has become so bad, someone out there believes a vapid football player and his vain girlfriend are interesting enough to garner an audience. Who knew? The show will focus on Margot more than Curtis, with the plot revolving around what it's like to be married to a football star. The producers also think they can gain a Christian audience since Margot and Curtis are involved in the church. Moreover, there's her attempt at starting an acting career and their plan to have a baby. Combine this with guest appearances from people in the entertainment and sports industry, and everyone is predicting a hit. Cameras have already started following Margot. The only reason they aren't here now is that Rebecca Rankoff, the wedding gown designer, refuses to allow cameras inside her place of business, and everyone agrees the wedding dress should be a surprise, anyway.

In order for the wedding to air during sweeps, Margot and Curtis changed their initial date from March of the year after next to July, only eight months away. It's been a nightmare as far as changing venues, but she and Curtis are willing to do what it takes, and bribe whomever necessary, to get what they want. The only person they couldn't bribe is Firth, who was booked solid, which means boon times for Danielle, of course, who ecstatically agreed to take over the planning.

Mom gives Margot a hug. "I'm so proud of you, baby."

"Oh, Mommy," Margot says with a sniffle. "Isn't it perfect?"

We're all being fitted today by Rebecca herself, an elfin-like creature who speaks in hushed tones as though her vocal cords sit on reeds blown by a gentle breeze. She whispers now to one of her assistants who rushes up to Margot and wraps measuring tape around her waist before typing something into her tablet.

I walk over to the walled mirror and gaze at my reflection. The Greek-inspired bridesmaids' dresses are made from silk chiffon with taffeta trim. Going against the typical edict whereby the sister serves as maid of honor, Margot gave Danielle the

number one position ("You don't mind do you? I know the wedding means a lot to you, but Danni was around more when I was
single, so she really gets what this means!"). I'm actually perfectly fine with being a lowly bridesmaid. I'd have no idea what
to say for a toast, otherwise.

Rebecca steps up and fluffs the bow on top of my shoulder. "It
should sit high like a flower. Like so." I have to lean in closely to
hear her. Danielle, on the other hand, is another story. "Offer him
fucking seventy, then!" she barks into her cell. "I don't give a rat's
ass. We need him in July. He should be grateful we're asking at
all. Tell him this is the kind of publicity he fucking needs if he
wants to play with adults."

Rebecca winces. I doubt many of her clients have dropped
the F-bomb in her studio.

Danielle gives a satisfied nod before clicking off. "Baxter is a
yes," she tells Margot. She continues pacing the studio while
typing a text. Baxter is a rap artist Curtis wants for the reception, even though it means paying double to get him to cancel a
tour date so that he can be there to rap his three most popular
songs.

Mom stands next to me and looks at her reflection, while
Rebecca, Margot, and Danielle confer about the dress. Mom's
off-the-shoulder dress highlights her figure and long legs. Unable
to get enough of her reflection, she moves and sways while hum-
ming to herself. While she claims she hopes Margot's TV show
becomes a vehicle for God's Word, I'm sure the former actress
in her is thrilled about the face time she'll be getting on the
tube.

She lifts the hem of her dress and watches the chiffon billow
around her knees. She smiles rather demurely when she remembers I'm there. "You look beautiful, Piper. Who knows? Maybe
you'll meet someone at the wedding. You never know. Lots of

single men will be there. Lots of athletes and actors—the sky's the limit!"

"Not interested. I'm bringing Spencer as my date."

She goes back to her reflection with a wave of the hand. "What is going on with you two, I'll never understand. I will say this, though. If a man wants you, he marries you. Or in your case, remarries you."

What Mom knows about my relationship with Spence pretty much adds up to nothing. It's been a little more than a month since he told me about the nitwit, and after a fierce meltdown that involved impressive amounts of scotch, I've come to realize the best way to deal with the situation is to wait things out. He initially kept calling, but I made it clear that I didn't want any communication between us until he stopped seeing her. I suppose I understand why he needs a break, but my hunch tells me that losing all contact with me will speed the process along. I figure another month or so, tops, and he'll realize how much he misses me. No one understands him like I do. We have a deep and abiding bond, and if it takes dating an airhead for him to realize it, so be it.

Margot comes over and kisses Mom on the cheek, and they fall into yet another mother-daughter embrace. "Oh, Mommy, can you believe it? I'm so happy."

I look away awkwardly; except for perfunctory hello and good-bye hugs, Mom and I don't touch much. But then Margot clasps my hand—"Group hug!" She pulls me in next to Mom and forces us into an embrace. I feel self-conscious at first but then wrap my arm around Mom and close my eyes. I think about string theory as I press my face close to hers. I think about my other self existing in a dimension where I share a heartfelt hug with my mother and sister, and we three have the kind of genuine fondness healthy families share, and after I leave Rebecca's studio, this other self goes home to Spencer and Hailey and I tell them about my day. If the theory is correct, somewhere light-years away it's highly possible I have everything I've ever wanted.

Our table at Aqua is located next to one of several floor-to-ceiling windows that overlook the shimmering blue bay. While everyone discusses wedding details, I look over the drink menu and debate the joys of a dry martini or vodka on the rocks. I haven't been drinking as much since I last saw Spencer; I want to prove to him, and myself, that I can cut back, but I've also spent the last two hours with these three and still have to get through lunch, and there's only so much a person can take. So when the waiter comes to our table, I figure *desperate times* and all that and order a double martini.

I can't help but notice how quiet everyone is after he leaves. They all stare with such solemnity, I begin to wonder if I've sprouted horns. "What?" No one says a word. Margot looks down at her hands. Danielle smirks ever so slightly.

"What?"

"We're concerned," Margot says.

"About?"

Mom reaches for her water. "You know."

"I have no idea. What's going on?"

"The drinking?" she says.

"I'm not the only one drinking. Margot ordered sake. And you just ordered an apple martini," I say to Danielle.

"Yeah," Danielle replies, "but I don't have a drinking problem."

"Excuse me?"

"You already had champagne at Rebecca's."

"So. Rebecca offered everyone champagne. Who in her right mind turns down free champagne?"

"We need you to have it together by the wedding," she says firmly. "No drinking!"

Margot, who has remained perfectly doelike and passive while her friend berates me, finally pipes up. "What she means is, we're concerned, P, and we want the wedding to be perfect."

"The wedding is in *my* hands now," Danielle continues, "and I need everything to be just right."

"I'm sorry; I thought the wedding was about Margot."

"Of course it's about Margot. I want the wedding to be perfect for her." She takes Margot's hand. "But the wedding is also going to be a televised event, which is why it has to be perfect. The show is about how Margot maintains her impeccable sense of style as much as anything else."

"Thank you, Danni," Margot says, patting Danielle's hand.

"You're welcome, Mags." They beam at each other before she trains her icy greens back on me. "We're talking about a TV show! Margot is going to be a big star. A scandal at the wedding would fucking ruin that for her."

"Danielle, watch your language."

"Apologies, Mrs. Wright."

I look at them all. "Scandal? Outburst? You're making me sound crazy."

Silence.

"When you drink, you get emotional. In a *very bad way*," Margot says, continuing with the Bambi act.

"And when you talk as if you were two years old, you're *very annoying*." I look around for the waiter. My drink can't come soon enough. "Is this about the engagement party?"

"It's about your life," Mom says, sounding both snide and weary.

"Cameras will be there," Danielle gripes. "We can't have anything go wrong."

"So you've said."

"We've noticed you're drinking more and more," Margot

says. "I want to see my big sister happy and pretty. Alcohol won't help."

"You could be doing so much better in life," Mom says.

I look from Mom to Danielle to Margot and back to Mom again. Slowly I start to get it. Something about the moment seems suspiciously rehearsed or at the very least discussed.

"Is this supposed to be some kind of intervention?" I start to laugh. "An intervention at Aqua! An intervention over drinks and sushi!" I look around the restaurant as if people are watching. "Family intervention taking place at table four!"

"Lower your voice, Piper," Mom says under her breath. "This is no laughing matter."

"I'm sorry." I giggle. "I just never heard of an intervention at a sushi restaurant."

"We're not using the word 'intervention,'" Margot says. "We just wanted to talk to you. We're worried."

"Let's get real, *Mags*. You're far more concerned about your wedding than about me. I get it."

"That's not true."

"It's not?"

Mom says, "You're making terrible choices, Piper." She stiffens noticeably, her mouth taut. "Drinking and hanging around with your ex-husband aren't going to bring her back."

"I know that. Don't you think I know that?"

"We all miss her, and none of us will get over the loss, but if you don't want to pray or go to church, we're not going to watch you self-destruct."

"Thanks for the love and support, Mom."

"I'm willing to pay for therapy," Margot chimes in. "The best you can get. Cost is not an issue."

"Show her," Danielle whispers.

Margot jumps. "Oh, right."

She takes out a pamphlet and slides it across the table. There's a picture of a white farmhouse sitting in the center of a green field and the name of a rehabilitation center at the top.

"Have you all lost your minds?" I practically shout. "I'm not an alcoholic!" I slide the pamphlet back across the table. "I'm fine!"

Danielle hands the pamphlet back to Margot. "I knew she wouldn't listen."

"Not to you," I snap. "Not all that long ago you were doing the wide splits on a pole. Why should I listen to you?"

As if he's heard my cries, the waiter mercifully arrives with our drinks. "God bless you." I make a show of chugging back my martini without pause and slamming down the glass. The waiter does his best not to react as he continues serving the table. Before he has a chance to leave, I ask for another.

I then look at Danielle. "Here's something you'll understand, Danni. Go fuck yourself. Why Margot doesn't see how selfish you are is beyond me. Oh wait. She wouldn't see it because she's as selfish as you are."

"At least she's not a cold bi—"

"Girls!" Mom says.

Margot says, "I wish you'd pray. God can help you through *anything*, P, but you have to let him help you. Look at all that he's done for me. You can have the same thing."

Mom mutters a "Praise God," then adds, "How you're living now certainly isn't working."

I glare hard. I'm tempted to point out her hypocrisy: *With all the sleeping around and drinking you did? You judge me?* But she's practically scowling at me, and I back down as I always do.

"Don't you want to be on TV?" Margot says, looking confused.

"No, I don't want to be on TV. In fact, I want a contract written up that says they are not to tape me—ever!"

She falls back against her chair, dumbfounded by the notion that someone might pass on the opportunity to be followed by cameras 24/7. "But why, Piper? Everyone wants to be on TV!"

"God, Margot, you're like your generation's Andy Warhol."

"Who?"

"Never mind." I sigh. "Thanks for the concern, everyone, but I don't have a drinking problem. I'm fine. I haven't had a drink in weeks. So just stop worrying about me. I'm fine."

"How many times are you going to say you're fine?" Danielle says offhandedly. "You sound defensive if you ask me."

"But I didn't ask you."

I toss my napkin on the table. I'm hoping to come off as confident, but by now I'm starting to think I have the word *Loser* emblazoned on my forehead. "I don't understand why I have to be the bad seed and the one who has to get picked on instead of supported." I rise from the table. "I have to use the restroom."

"No one's picking on you," Mom says.

"We love you," says Margot.

I march off, though, before they can see they've gotten to me. I need a minute alone and only wish I'd grabbed my phone so I could call Spencer. I know I've imposed a moratorium on talking, but it would be so nice to hear his voice now, to have him make the perfect sarcastic comment about my crazy family.

I walk past the restroom and directly outside where I hug myself against a strong wind. I walk toward the bay. I wish for the gazillionth time that Hailey was with me and that I could go back to those four years when everything felt normal, when I didn't need anyone but my nucleus of a family—me, Spencer, Hailey.

Not knowing what to do with myself, I walk a little farther. I'm nearing a cross street when I hear someone say, *"Kilowatt?"*

I turn and squint my eyes. *It can't be.*

"Selwyn?"

He walks up in a suit and tie, face beaming. "Is it really *you*?"

"Is it really you?"

We laugh and share a long hug.

When my smile broadens, he clutches at his chest as though he might faint. "Oh lawd! There it is! You're killin' me, baby!"

"Stop acting crazy," I tease.

"It's so nice to see you. I can't believe it."

"I can't either. What are you doing here?"

He glances at a gray-haired man standing off to the side. "I'm here on business. Dave, this is Piper." He pauses and smiles. "An old friend."

Dave and I shake hands before he turns his attention back to Selwyn. "Listen, Selwyn; I should take off. Call me next week, and we'll set up that meeting."

"Sure thing." They say good-bye, and Selwyn quickly grips both my arms as though I might be an apparition. "Am I dreaming?"

"Stop being silly." I laugh.

"What are you doing in the city?"

As soon as I think of my intervention, it's as if someone has raised an it's-okay-to-cry lever, and I well up.

"Kil? Hey now. What is it?"

"Nothing. Everything. My family. We're having lunch and I hate them. And they hate me. I don't know why they hate me, but they do. Actually I do know why. I'm a fuckup. And why do I always feel like I have to tell you *everything*?" I manage to smile. I don't know what it is about Selwyn that makes me divulge so, but here I am telling him everything, admitting things I wouldn't admit to anyone.

"Hey now, stop putting yourself down. Is there anything I can do?"

I think of asking him to whisk me away as he did at the engagement party, but that would only prove them right—that I can't handle awkward situations, like family interventions, without freaking out or disappearing. "No. I'm fine. I'll be all right."

"It's so good to see you, Kil. I think about you—a lot, if you want to know the truth. Are you busy? Can I take you out for coffee?"

"That would be nice, but I'm having lunch with my family."

"Right. Of course. Well, when can I see you? I have to see you again. This is kismet. Serendipity. If today doesn't work, when? I've wanted to contact you, but you made things so clear last time, I thought I should leave you alone. But now here you are! This is fate, what we're dealing with right here."

I feel excited myself. It's not lost on me that we're having one of those serendipitous moments in life, too difficult to explain. I mean, who knows why all that matter and energy decided to collide one day, and—*boom*—the big bang? Or who knows what events led Selwyn here, right at this moment. The point, it seems, is that he's here. And what's more, I honestly can't believe how good it is to see him. And he looks *good*, too. I realize now, in the light of day, how he gives off the impression of a man who likes himself and who lives well. He seems like a guy who's . . . What's that word again? *Happy.* Yes, that's it. He's that rare thing in my circle of family and no-friends-to-speak-of: a genuinely happy person.

"You know," he says. "I've been wanting to thank you."

"Thank me?"

"Yep. Thanks to you, I am now the proud owner of a Meade 280."

"A Meade 280? Are you serious?!" Now I *am* tempted to run

away with him. My telescope is of good quality and nothing to be embarrassed about, but the Meade 280x is a gorgeous telescope, top of the line, and used primarily by professionals who can afford its high-end price tag.

"I told you that our night together meant something to me. Seeing Saturn that night? That changed me. I bought the Meade a couple of weeks after we met. I was hoping you'd call and I'd be able to show it to you."

"I'm sorry about that."

"No need to apologize. Now is what matters. So when can I take you to dinner?"

I find myself shaking my head no. It's great seeing him, but my sense of excitement is mixed with an underlying anxiety, partially due to a gnawing sense that Selwyn and I aren't good for each other. No, strike that. I'm not good for Selwyn. It's obvious he's a nice man, but his crush, or whatever, is unnerving. I don't deserve it. And then there's an even more important factor.

"I can't, Selwyn. I'm trying to work things out with my ex-husband, and I can't deal with any other complications. He's my focus right now. I'm sorry. My husband and I . . ." I try to think of the words. "We just have this history."

"Ex-husband," he says. "You keep forgetting that."

"Right. See what I mean?"

"Yeah, I do. That's fine. But we ran into each other like this for a reason. Hey, I know how to do friendship. I know it's hard to believe I can contain all this powerful love energy, but I know how to hold back."

"You are so crazy," I say with a laugh.

"But it's true. Seriously, I respect whatever it is you have going with your ex, but I would like to be friends. Can I at least get your number?"

I feel my head shaking back and forth as if the decision has been made deep in my bones. I wouldn't know how to fit Selwyn into my life, regardless. How would I even introduce him to Spencer once we're back together? *By the way, here's a guy I almost slept with at my sister's engagement party.* No. We should leave things as they are.

"I don't think so, Selwyn. It was really nice seeing you, though. You're good?"

"I'm good." He studies me while letting out a long, hard sigh. "You don't want to try friendship, Kil? I'm telling you, this is fate."

"Let's just be happy we saw each other, okay?"

"Damn, girl, you're as stubborn as a hungry mule with a bale of hay."

I glance toward Aqua. "I should get back. If I don't hurry, I might miss my intervention."

"Intervention?"

"Never mind. It's nothing."

"You're gonna regret this day, Kil. Passin' up a good man like me—*twice*. You know you like me."

"I do like you," I admit, my tone serious. "But—" I lower my gaze. "Things are complicated. My life is . . ." *A fucking mess*, I think. I don't know any happy people. I wouldn't know what to do with someone like Selwyn.

"Hey, let me stop pressuring you. It's okay. Always good to trust your instincts." He reaches up and kisses my cheek. Oddly enough, it's not until then that I remember he's shorter than I am, our difference in height made more pointed, again, by the fact that I'm in heels. "You stay well, Kilowatt. Try not to let people bring you down. You're a thin-skinned girl. Feisty, but thin-skinned."

We hug as people make their way around us. I wish I had

something to offer him besides conflicted feelings and rejection. I feel him staring as I walk back to the restaurant. It's sad to see him only to say good-bye, but I do feel infinitely better as I walk back to Aqua. There's nothing like seeing a friend before having to face family.

eight

I t's past ten p.m., and I've been on the roof stargazing for the last half hour. It's been a good night. I have a nice view of Pollux, a first-magnitude star thirty-five times the sun's luminosity, and Castor, which some refer to as Pollux's twin, is almost as bright. I'm still gazing when I hear several people talking down below. When I lean over the rooftop, I see a group of ten or so people passing, some carrying glass votive candles. Christmas is less than a month away, and I wonder if they're conducting some kind of holiday ritual—except, we're not a holiday ritual kind of neighborhood. Hardly anyone puts up Christmas lights, for instance; if anything, around here you worry about your Christmas bounty getting stolen.

Mrs. Mathews leans out of her window. She lives in the complex across the street and serves as the block's cable news network. She knows everyone and is known for shouting the day's events from her window. She wears a Christmas hat and munches from a bag of chips. When I ask what's going on, she yells, "Tank died! Everybody's going over to Gaskill!" She tends to shout, even on a quiet night like this. "You know Tank!" she adds, when I don't respond. "Big guy! Always on that bicycle! Yeah! He dead!" She begins fanning herself. "You hot?"

It's actually cold out, and I'm wearing a down jacket. "Can't say that I am."

"I'm hot as hell. I think I'm gettin' them hot flashes. You know Delores got that menopause. I think she gave it to me."

"I don't think you get menopause through contact."

"You up there looking through that telescope?" she says, ignoring my comment. "If you see any aliens, you let me know!" This has been her running joke since I moved here. Before I know it, she slams the window shut.

I don't remember Tank, but I've never been around when people are actually making an altar, so I quickly put my telescope away and join them.

The procession ends at Fiftieth and Gaskill where there's a larger crowd of thirty or so people. Lit candles are spread out in front of an apartment complex's carport, along with empty bottles of Hennessy, flowers, and teddy bears. Several balloons are tied to a stop sign.

Hennessy is being passed around, and everyone talks and laughs loudly while drinking from plastic cups. If not for the poster board lining the carport with *RIP Tank* spray-painted in large letters, no one would suspect people have gathered to mourn and pay their respects. There are as many young women as men, their ages ranging from teens to midthirties. A few girls sit on the hood of a car, holding balloons and kicking their legs and laughing. Others write messages on the poster board or the garage wall itself. I walk closer and watch a woman draw a heart on the wall and write Tank's name in the center. Her heart joins messages such as *Tank, I miss you, bro*; *Gaskill MB Mob Forever*; and *We Have 2 Stop the Violence Fareals!* A young man taps my arm and hands over a bottle of Hennessy. It's been almost five weeks since my "intervention," and except for an occasional night-cap, I haven't been drinking at all. Figuring what the hell, though, I raise the bottle—"To Tank"—and take a long, hard pull.

"Don't hold back," the man says, watching me.

"I never do." I take another swig and return the bottle. "How did he die?"

"What else? Over some nonsense. He used to be in a gang. He got out several years ago. Some fool popped him over in West Oakland over some fight they had long long time ago. You know how these gangbangers be." His voice sounds as if he's been smoking since the age of three. But he has a soft beard and soft eyes that contradict all his muscle and girth. He looks to be in his early thirties and wears a bomber jacket and construction boots. "Did you know him?" he asks.

"I don't think so. I live around here, but I don't remember seeing him."

"If you live around here, you saw him. Everybody knew Tank. Big dude. Got them light green eyes. Always on his bike."

"How did you know him?"

"We worked together out near Fruitvale, building them new town houses. Name's Jeremy, by the way." He extends his hand, and we shake.

"Piper."

"Piper? What kind of name is that?"

"The kind my mother gave me."

He grins and gives me the bottle. We pass it back and forth until I feel a warm buzzing in the back of my brain.

"Tank and me volunteer with Youth Construction, helping the young brothers and sisters learn construction skills. Tank was a mentor to a lot of these kids out here tonight. He was just coming home from a job when that fool up and shot him."

"I'm sorry for your loss. It's all so damn tragic."

"Yes, it is."

Two boys, both in their late teens, approach. They wear matching T-shirts with a picture of another boy their age on the front with RIP ANTHONY GREEN at the top. T-shirts like these are worn at funerals and kept as keepsakes. My students wear them frequently at school. Jeremy cups each boy's hand and claps them on the back. As they exchange condolences, I make my way to the carport just as a woman finishes taping up more poster board. I watch as she takes out a marker and begins writing. *Thank you, Tank, for teaching me to believe in myself.* She hands the marker to me.

"I didn't know him."

She smiles with a shrug as if this is of no importance and walks away.

I start to write in the center of the poster board, taking up more space than I need to. The poem I write was included in the program at Hailey's funeral, and I know every word by heart. I take my time, writing slowly in big cursive letters.

When I'm finished, I hear Jeremy behind me. "That some kind of Shakespeare?"

"You're close. John Donne. 'Death Be Not Proud.'"

He reads the last lines in his throaty baritone: "'One short sleep past, we wake eternally, and death shall be no more; death, thou shalt die.'

"I likes," he says, handing me the bottle. "I likes."

Spencer is telling me that he loves me, but the sun is shining in his face and I can't see him clearly. I try to move out of the bright glare, but every time I do, the light only brightens. "I want you back, Piper. I never should have left you in the first place."

A loud ringing noise starts. "Do you hear that?" I ask him. "What is it?"

"Someone's calling." He takes me in his arms and we begin to kiss, but the ringing phone distracts me. "Is that your phone or mine?"

I open my eyes and try to look around, but I have to shield my face from the sunlight streaming through the window. I blink a few times as I sit up and slowly shift from the dream I was having to what appears to be reality: me in my bedroom, a throbbing headache, and no Spencer.

But I do see someone else.

"Mornin'." Jeremy sits in the chair in the corner of my room, tying his construction boots, dressed in his jeans and jacket.

"Morning." I feel around under the covers to see if I'm dressed and exactly how much I'm dressed. T-shirt. Underwear. I sit up while drawing the blanket to my chest.

Jeremy walks over and kisses the top of my forehead. "I gotta bounce."

"Okay."

I look around my bedroom for clues and catch sight of Scrabble pieces strewn about the floor. I point. "What's that about?"

Jeremy strokes his beard with the tip of his fingers. "You don't remember? I beat your ass at Scrabble and you started throwing your pieces at me."

I stare at the Scrabble pieces until our night together slowly surfaces. While at Tank's altar, I told him I was a teacher, and that somehow led to a shared love of Scrabble. We played all night while drinking Hennessy. I was drunk-pissed when I lost and chased him around the apartment until we landed in bed.

"You only beat me because I was drunk."

"Girl, you need to quit. I won fair and square."

He gives me another kiss before starting toward the door. "Listen, like I told you last night, if it weren't for Amy, I would

see you again, but even just the little foolin' around we did last
night can't happen again."

I latch onto "little foolin' around." I have to ask. "So did
we . . . ?"

He catches on and blinks hard. "Naw, we didn't do anything.
Nothing worth writing home about, anyway. Don't worry, girl. I
didn't take advantage. I don't play like that. It was because of
Tank I ended up here anyhow. 'Sides, Amy is one of them psycho
bitches, if you wanna know the truth, and messin' around on her
would likely get you and me both killed."

"No need to explain." Truly. He does not know the depths of
my disinterest. "It was just the night. No problem. I'm seeing
someone, too."

He gives the wall a pat. "You be good."

"You, too."

I hear the door close and try to recount the details of our
"foolin' around." I lie back in bed and close my eyes. Jeremy's
probing fingers slowly come to mind. His gravelly voice: "I can't
do much else, girl. Amy would kill me." I doze for a little while,
but then I remember the ringing sound in my dream and check
my phone. I expect to see Mom's or Margot's name on my caller
ID, but I'm wrong. Happily wrong. It's Spencer. *Spencer!*

"Hey, it's me. It's been too long. I miss you, P, and I can't stop
thinking about you. I was wondering if we could see each other.
I'd like to talk."

After I replay the message a second time, I run for the
shower. My headache, Tank, my night with Jeremy; all of them
are forgotten.

The house has a kind of Sunday-morning quaintness to
it. There's a wreath on the door and while the lawn hasn't
changed, there are potted flowers on the porch and a

potted bougainvillea, its bright fuchsia-colored flowers already beginning to frame the side of the house.

I give an excited knock. On my way here, I picked up a coffee cake from Lulu's. Spence and I always liked Sunday mornings—reading the *Times* in bed with coffee and a favorite baked good from Lulu's. I'm hoping my gift, in its own small way, will show him how much I'm willing to go back to who we were.

When I hear the latch at the door, I pull my shoulders back and hold up the cake with a big smile. I'm all set to announce *Surprise!* when Tisa of all people opens the door. "Piper?" She opens the door farther, her robe and pj's, her messy curls and dewy face signaling that she's just woken up. "What a surprise."

I try my best to appear unshaken, but I can't help wonder what the hell is going on. Spencer misses me, and can't stop thinking about me—and yet the nitwit is here?

"I hope I didn't wake you. I know it's early. I thought I'd pop by with some of Spencer's favorite coffee cake. But I could just leave it and talk to him another time."

"Don't be silly. We're in the kitchen reading the paper—Spence is reading the paper." She suddenly wraps her arms around me. "I'm so happy to see you."

I remain frozen with the coffee cake in midair.

"You wouldn't know this, but my hope has been that we can all be friends. I just think that the Universe is constantly providing us with ways to connect. Love is made with small steps. That's what I wrote in my journal yesterday. And now, you're here."

I watch the butterflies swirling around her head; a group of fairies and nymphs soon join in. I'm sickened by the thought that I'm being invited into what was once my own home by a twenty-year-old ninny, but pride wins out and I politely follow her inside.

I try to peek into each room for evidence that she's moved in, but it's been only a few months, and I talk myself down from the notion.

She leads me to the kitchen where Spence sits at the table in an old Stanford sweatshirt and pajama bottoms. He has his laptop out and a coffee mug in his hand.

"Honey," Tisa says, "look who's here."

Spencer practically jumps from his seat when he sees me. "Oh. Wow. Whoa. What a surprise. Hey, you." He collects himself and rises from his seat. "What are you doing up so early?"

I choose a lie—of the white variety. "You called and I had a few errands to run, so I thought I'd stop by. I brought you coffee cake." I hold up the box. "From Lulu's."

"We love that place," Tisa says, reaching for the box. "Why don't I help you with that. Coffee?"

"Sure."

I watch her take a mug from the kitchen cabinet and pour coffee as if she owned the place. I have to keep myself from staring. Only a few months ago I was spending almost every night here, and now I'm suddenly a guest. Who does she think she is? Spence and I bought this place together, I want to tell her. We raised a child here. *Get out! Get the hell out!*

I find a seat at the table where I once served breakfast to my family. The same table where Hailey once ate her cereal and Spencer and I would sometimes have candlelight dinners. I sit. I keep my mouth shut.

"Excuse my mess," she says, setting down my coffee and taking the second laptop to the counter. "I was shopping online while Spencer read the paper," she explains. "I was telling him about bargains I'm finding while he was keeping me current on the news." She moves her computer to the counter, takes out the coffee cake, and sets it on the table along with forks and knives. All I can think is that she doesn't know that Spencer told me he misses me. Knowing Spence as I do, he probably doesn't want to tell her anything until he talks to me.

"So, how's school?" he asks. "How are things?"

"Everything is great."

Tisa starts to leave with her laptop and a slice of a cake. "Babe, I'm going to finish in the other room. Give you two some privacy."

"You sure?"

"Yeah, you two go ahead. I'll join you later. Why don't you show Piper the backyard. You guys can sit out there and enjoy the sun. You can use one of the heat lamps if it's cold."

"Heat lamps?" I ask.

"Wait until you see what he's done with the backyard, Piper."

It appears Spencer's compulsive shopping has led to the greater good of the backyard. There are two large heat lamps and new patio furniture on the deck; the barbecue has been cleaned and the entire yard replanted with native plants and flowers.

"Nice."

"Yeah. I've been working around the house more." He points out various plants and tells me that the patio furniture is made entirely from bamboo and organic fabrics.

"You've done a good job. It's nice."

"Yeah? You like it?"

"I do."

We sit at the table and smile warmly at each other. "It's really good to see you, P," he says finally. "I've missed you."

"I've missed you, too, Spencer."

We eat and drink coffee and fall into our natural rhythm of conversation. I catch him up on my sister's antics and he tells me about the book he's been working on and that he's been writing regularly.

Eventually, he gazes out at the yard, then looks at me rather sheepishly. I decide to help him along. "You said in your message you wanted to talk?"

"Yeah. I actually have some news." He digs his hands into his hair in that way he does when the last thing he wants to do is talk.

"What is it?"

"Tisa wanted us to tell you together—have you over for dinner one night—but I thought it would be better if I told you first. I was going to ask you to coffee, but now that you're here, I guess I should go on and tell you." He sighs and pushes himself back into his chair and crosses his leg; he then decides to uncross his leg and fold his hands into his lap. Squirming, I believe it's called.

"What is it?"

He clears his throat and gazes out across the lawn.

"Spencer."

"Tisa's pregnant."

I knock over my mug of coffee and watch as it splatters across the deck. I feel as if I've been pushed under water and I'm forced to gasp for air. In fact, I do. I inhale as deeply as I can, while making a loud throaty sound.

"Shit," Spencer says, shooting up from his chair. "Are you okay?"

"Does it look like I'm okay?" I gasp.

"I'll get some paper towels."

"Fuck the paper towels. *Pregnant?*"

He starts to leave. "I'll be right back."

"No," I command. "Stay." I bend over and continue trying to catch my breath. "Pregnant, Spencer? You're kidding, right?"

I glance up as he lowers his head.

"You've only been dating for a minute."

"It's been since September; that's almost four months."

"That's exactly my point. You hardly know her, and you're making a baby with her? Haven't you heard of using protection? What are you? Teenagers?"

"But I'm happy about it, P. We're both very excited. We think it's still too early to tell people, but Mom and Dad know, and I thought it was important that you heard the news from me first."

I take a deep breath just as my lungs constrict again. I move my gaze back to the ground. *Pregnant.*

"I think I'm going to be sick."

"P, I want your support."

"How far along is she?"

"Two months."

"Great. So basically you started fucking her the first night you went out."

"Hey, I'm sorry you're upset, but let's not get ugly."

"Fuck you."

I throw my head all the way back and stare into the sky. "You said you weren't sleeping with her."

"It was an accident. The first time we did it, I mean. So I wasn't lying necessarily."

"You're a bastard. A lying bastard."

"*P.*"

"I thought I was coming here so that we could get back together."

"Back together?"

"Your message said you missed me, and you couldn't stop thinking about me."

"Well, yeah, but—"

"You haven't known her six months! How can you two be doing this? It's so foolish!"

"We love each other. Sometimes you just know."

"You don't know shit, Spencer. You don't know shit! She's fucking three years old!"

"Will you lower your voice?"

"*No!*"

"She's a great girl, Piper. We're going to have a baby. Can you be happy for me?"

"No, I can't. I hate you." I'm on my feet, pacing the parameters of the deck. Not only does he not want me back—fucking Tisa is fucking having Spencer's baby. They're having a baby. He's making a family with her.

"What about Hailey?" I say.

"What about her?"

"What do you mean *what about her*? How can you forget her like this! You're betraying her!"

"What? How am I betraying her?"

"You're having another baby, that's how."

"Piper, you're making absolutely no sense. I'll always love my little girl; you know that." He steps closer and tries to touch my arm, but I won't let him. "P, this doesn't have to be bad news. I'm proof that we can move forward in our lives. Nothing is stopping you from meeting someone, too, you know. You can meet someone and have a family."

"But I don't want to meet anyone! I don't want any more children!"

"Don't say that."

"But I don't." I feel my lungs tightening again and begin patting my hand against my chest as if this will somehow help my heart rate slow down. "I don't want any more children," I say to myself. "I don't. I want Hailey back. I want Hailey." I drop my head into my chest and whisper fervently, "I want Hailey back. I want my baby." Hugging myself, I whisper again and again as if reciting an incantation: "I want my baby, I want my baby back." I can't make myself stop. A part of me thinks if I say it enough, she might just appear. "I want my baby. I want Hailey. I want Hailey back."

When I feel Spencer's arms around me, I bury my face into

his chest and burst into tears. He runs his hand over my hair and rocks me while I sob. We stand together until eventually my tears turn to an occasional hiccup. "I miss her so much."

"I know, baby. I do, too." He kisses me near my temple and holds me tighter at the waist. I snuggle my face against his sweatshirt and close my eyes. I know everything there is to know about Spencer. Except for this separation, we've never spent more than two days apart. I've seen him at his happiest, Hailey's birth, and at his lowest, her death. *How in the world can he leave me?*

"Everything is going to be okay, Piper. A baby is a good thing. Can you be happy for us? Please?"

"No. I can't. I can't." I pull away.

"Okay," he says. "Okay." He leans down so that he can meet my gaze. "I'll always love you, P. You and Hailey have a special place right here." He points to his heart.

I know the gesture is meant to be kind, but right now it's nothing more than trite and beneath him. Its underlying message: He's locked Hailey and me away in the recesses of his heart so that he can make room for Tisa and his new baby.

His new baby.

"I should go."

"No, I can't let you leave like this. Stay, finish your cake."

"No, thank you. I really should leave."

"You're going to be okay, P."

I bite down on my lower lip to keep from crying. "No, I'm not." I open the patio door and walk through the kitchen and into the hallway. I pause when I reach the den.

Tisa sits on the couch with her back turned as she types on her laptop.

I hear Spencer coming from behind. "Babe?"

I turn but immediately feel myself blush when I realize he's talking to Tisa. "Piper's leaving. We should say good-bye."

She looks over her shoulder and sees me in the hall. "Leaving? Already?" The laptop rises on her knees, and I catch the sight of baby cribs on the screen. The floor shifts from under my feet, and again my lungs collapse and my windpipe shuts down.

I inhale through my nose. "I have to go."

She rises from the couch. "No, stay. I was hoping we could all talk. Did you tell her our news, babe?"

"Yeah," Spencer says. "P, stay and talk. You'll feel better if you do."

I'm near frantic by now and rush toward the front door. "That's okay," I call out.

I open the door and run to my car. I tell myself not to look back as I hear them call after me. I start the engine and peel out of the driveway. It's not until I have some distance between us that I glimpse them in the rearview mirror, standing on the porch hand in hand.

"Miss Nelson?"

I'm currently floating past the Cat's Eye Nebula, as red as a rose. I just can't figure out how it's possible that I'm hearing Gladys's voice right now. How did she manage to find me in outer space? Shouldn't she be running things back at the school?

"*Miss Nelson.*"

I feel someone's hand on my shoulder and watch as the beautiful nebula begins to expand.

"*Miss Nelson.*"

Another shake.

"Miss Nelson, we need you to wake up now."

Gladys's voice is right next to my ear, so close it strikes me that the nebula may not be real after all.

I feel my slumped-over body sitting on a chair, the left side of my face pressed into wood. I probably wasn't floating through space either.

I open my eyes and stare directly into Gladys's gold belt, loud and gaudy and with some kind of bird at the buckle. I roll my eyes upward and catch sight of a plastic Santa pinned to her blouse, followed by her stubbly chin and sad, disappointed mouth. "Miss Nelson, we need you to wake up."

I slowly sit up, even as the room shifts under my feet. I wait as the blur of faces staring at me comes into focus. My students eye me with their mouths agape. Some whisper; others giggle. The clock on the wall lets me know it's only first period.

Gladys clamps her hand down on my shoulder. "Everyone, get back to work. Miss Nelson isn't feeling very well today. Mr. Young will watch you until the end of the period. Miss Nelson?"

She gives my shoulder a tight squeeze, and I rise like a student who knows she's in deep shit. I feel spittle on the side of my mouth and wipe. I try to fix my hair, which is a lopsided mess, but give up. "Sorry," I mumble to the group of students on my right. Theresa cuts her eyes at me. I look to the other side of the room and offer another apology. "I'm not feeling very well," I explain. "Sick all night. Probably shouldn't have come in today."

Theresa says, "It's okay, Miss Nelson."

Tranica adds with a laugh, "Yeah, Miss Nelson. We all know what it's like to have a hangover!"

Several students burst into laughter; some high-five one another.

"Enough!" Gladys snaps. She uses her walkie-talkie to call Mr. Young, the vice principal, who arrives in no time.

Gladys doesn't say a word as we trudge down the hallway and only keeps her arm linked in mine, much like a nurse helping a patient.

We're halfway down the hall when I feel my stomach surge. "Gladys?" I whimper.

She studies my face closely. "Miss Nelson, you're not about to be sick, are you?"

My head swirls along with everything around me. When my stomach takes another dive and I feel the bile coming, I clasp my hand over my mouth and nod.

Gladys turns up her nose in disgust. Not waiting until she dismisses me, I run for the girls' bathroom. I have to push a student aside as I rush toward a stall. I make it on time at least, and I remain bowed over the toilet until my stomach is empty.

I avoid looking in the mirror while washing my hands and rinsing out my mouth. What's the point? I can tell how awful I look from Gladys's reproachful glare.

She's gone when I reach the hall. I take my time walking to her office and try to piece together what happened. I remember the scotch I opened last night. Since hearing about Spencer and the nitwit, even I'll admit I've been drinking more heavily. I remember rushing to work this morning and the grammar exercises I passed out at the start of class while I breathed through my hangover. "Work on this. Keep quiet," I had told them. But that's it. I have no idea how long I was asleep before Gladys came to wake me.

My things are already in her office. She motions to the seat on the opposite side of the desk. I've never been called to the principal's office and can't seem to meet her gaze. I don't need to see her face to feel her rebuke, though. Gone, the sweet smile and airy voice, the offer of candy and a pat on the back.

When I get the courage to look up, she stares back with the same severity that's known to get a stone-cold gangbanger to give up his gun. No wonder the kids respond to her as they do.

"I understand your loss, Miss Nelson. I understand that

you've had your world turned upside down and that you have experienced the kind of loss no one should have to suffer. But we cannot accept this kind of behavior. I prefer to return every cent of that money you and Mr. Randolph gave the school than to have one of my teachers showing up here drunk out of her mind."

I start to speak.

"Don't you dare try to deny it—and falling asleep during class? Your behavior is completely reprehensible."

"I'm sorry," I mutter.

"Are you? Do you know the effect you're having on your students? Poor Alexandra Clark came in here, thinking you'd passed out. She thought you were dying! She came running in here, begging me to dial 9-1-1. Miss Nelson, you know what our kids see in their homes. We can't let them see that kind of dysfunction here at school. I won't have it. As you know, many of our kids have experienced their own share of loss, too, and they need role models, not teachers showing up here and behaving like you did today. School should be their haven."

"I'm so sorry. You're right, Mrs. Edwards. I'm sorry." I hang my head farther. I have never felt more ashamed than I do right now. "It'll never ever happen again, Mrs. Edwards. I swear."

"You bet it won't. You're going home—without pay. Use the rest of this week and Christmas break to do what you need to do. That gives you sixteen full days to get your act together. But when you return from break, Miss Nelson, I want all of you back. No more absences, no more missed meetings. If you mess up a single time, I'll do whatever I have to do to have you suspended. I'll do whatever it takes and will fill out every bit of paperwork. I do not care about your donation to the school; I care about our kids, and the only reason I'm not suspending you now is that I know you care about our kids, too. I know you're a good teacher because of what you've accomplished with your students in the past. I want *that* Miss Nelson to return two weeks from now. If I can't get one hundred percent of her, I'll settle for ninety-five, but no less. Miss Nelson, do we have an understanding?"

"Yes, ma'am."

"Good. Now please go home and take the weekend and your vacation to figure out whatever it is you need to figure out so that I won't have to fire you."

"Yes, ma'am."

I get my purse and briefcase and slink out of the office toward the exit doors, my head hanging low in shame.

nine

I knew the Reverend's church had quadrupled in size since I last attended as a teenager, but seeing the three interconnecting buildings and immense stained-glass windows help me fully appreciate what a one-thousand-member church actually means.

I'm here out of desperation. After Gladys sent me home yesterday, I'm ready to try anything to get my life back on track. Hence, the "miracle," as Mom is calling it—my visit to tonight's Friday evening service.

Mom called last night while I was stargazing. There's currently a storm taking place on Saturn, large enough for amateur stargazers to see. Gigantic plumes of smoke rise from Saturn's lower region as if being discharged from a locomotive, billowy and caterpillar-like in shape. Because of the storm's location and length, astronomers are calling it Storm Alley. I listened to Mom as she went on about what a great speaker Bishop Thomas is and how he uses science as part of his sermons. He's so popular, she told me, the Reverend was lucky to get him on the Friday before Christmas.

I hadn't had a drink all day (I'm going to sober up or else), and her voice was grating on my nerves, but I managed to offer the appropriate uh-huhs and listen as she sang rhapsodically about the bishop. When I told her I'd go, making sure to leave out the info that I was almost fired that day and much in need of a miracle, she went on about God having a plan for me—"Praise Jesus! You won't regret it, Piper. I promise you!"

So here I am.

From the droves of sheep flocking to tonight's program, it appears that the entire congregation skipped catching a Friday night movie so they can hear tonight's guest speaker, Bishop Ron Thomas of Atlanta. I follow one of the men wearing a T-shirt that says PARKING as he leads me to an empty space. After cutting the engine, I find the pack of cigarettes I bought on the way here. I'm sure it's bad form to smoke in a church parking lot, but I'm craving a drink so badly, it's either light up before going inside or not go at all.

The air is filled with the kind of excitement that makes it seem as if we're attending a rock concert. I'm in no rush, though, and watch the hordes make their way to the building while quietly smoking my cigarette. It's not until I reach the nub that I smash it underfoot and join the gridlocked crowd at the front of the church.

Ushers lead us inside. There are two elevators against the back wall and ushers handing out programs at various entrances. After taking the elevator to the second floor, I find a seat in the front row of the balcony. There are so many people, I half expect peanut vendors to walk up and down the aisle. One thing's for sure: The Reverend has come a long way since preaching in the movie theater where I was forced to hear his sermons every Sunday.

Down below, there's a massive Christmas tree decorated in

white lights and silver and white ornaments. A four-piece band plays while two young men wearing microphones jump and run back and forth in front of the stage and up and down the aisles, clapping their hands above their heads and pointing at people as they call out cheers.

"Do you love Jesus?"

The crowd responds, *"We love Jesus!"*

"Do you love God?"

"We love God!"

"I can't hearrrrrr yooooooou!"

"We love God!"

On and on until I'm praying for an aspirin.

Once the church is full, the organist shifts into a quiet hymn. The screen behind the podium rolls down as one of the cheerleaders steps on stage and asks everyone to close their eyes. He then leads the congregation in prayer. I close my eyes but feel like a charlatan. I don't think of God so much as the image of Storm Alley lining the underbelly of Saturn. I know I've been here only five minutes, but watching a storm take place thousands and thousands of miles away already feels more holy than this.

The band switches into a different song as the choir starts to enter. The two women on either side of me, the entire congregation, in fact, are on their feet at once and start clapping and raising their hands toward the ceiling. The choir enters from two different entrances, one person after another as if there's no end. It's a mixed choir and a relatively mixed crowd, which is no small feat when one considers how segregated churches can be. They follow one another up to the stage, clapping and walking on beat, all dressed in bright yellow robes decorated with purple and gold Kente cloth. Once they're on stage, Mom and the Reverend walk out hand in hand, waving to the congregation like politicians. The Reverend kisses Mom's cheek, and she finds her seat in the front-row pew. After a minute or two she turns and begins searching the church. When our eyes meet she blows a kiss and waves. I honestly don't remember the last time I've seen her this happy to see me, and I smile and wave back.

The music dies, and the Reverend nods his head solemnly. He's handsome with slicked-back hair and big white teeth. "Good evening, saints."

"Good evening."

"I don't know about you, but I serve a mighty God. I say, I don't know about *you*, but I serve a mighty God!"

People suddenly stand on their feet and start whooping it up.

I listen passively, meanwhile. Everyone has always fallen for the Reverend because he's handsome and charming, but for all these years, he and I have never exchanged a meaningful conversation. I was grounded on a regular basis for "disrupting" Sunday school or Bible class because I dared to ask questions I thought were perfectly reasonable: Why did Mary have to be a virgin? Did she remain a virgin while she was pregnant? Or, how can anyone possibly believe humans were created in a day when it's been proven it took billions of years for humans to evolve from bacteria?

Charles never said anything to me directly; punishment came through Mom. "Just shut your mouth during Sunday school. It's all based on faith; that's how we know."

I could sometimes hear her and Charles arguing about me, too. "You have to get her to behave appropriately, Margaret. She's the child of a minister now. I can't have her sneaking off when she's supposed to be in Sunday school."

"I'm feeling good today, saints!" he says now. "Hallelujah! I'm feeling sanctified!"

I clutch my stomach. I wish I felt something even remotely close to sanctified, but I feel more akin to a veteran experiencing post-traumatic stress and have to fight the urge to run out. I watch Mom nod in agreement with whatever the Reverend is going on about. I suppose she could honestly believe everything he preaches, but she sure did a three-sixty once he showed interest in her and told her he was a child of God. She abruptly stopped going out on dates, stopped drinking, and stopped bringing men home. To this day I'm not sure if she truly accepted Christ in her heart or Charles; maybe it's both. I'm not sure, but whatever the case, she's not the most loving Christian in the world. At least my unsaved mom had a sense of humor.

The ushers open the doors, and the last of the stragglers walk in. I lock my gaze on a young couple. The guy isn't as tall as Spencer, but he may as well be his doppelganger with his goatee and globe-shaped Afro. He has his arm around a woman carrying a toddler. I drop my head at the thought of my husband—*ex*-husband—with his new baby. It still hits me hard: Spencer being a father to someone other than Hailey. I can't get my head around it.

The choir finishes its song, and the Reverend goes on again about how sanctified he is and how he's not of the earth. "I am only visiting this place! My real home is the heavenly realm! We are only passing through, saints! One day we will return to the arms of our heavenly Father! Amen?"

I feel myself growing increasingly irritated. Why do Christians hate Earth so much? It's a perfectly fine planet. What would they prefer? Uranus? Four hundred degrees Celsius on a good day? Or Neptune? A beautiful sky blue but more than two hundred degrees below. They should be grateful to be here. We have the sun and plants and animals. Water. Insects. Everything here is a miracle, and I can't imagine their mythical heaven being any better—not as beautiful, anyway. I mean, gold streets and harps? Yawn.

I stare at the Reverend, feeling fifteen all over again, forced to sit through three-hour services *plus* Sunday school. And the Reverend always played up the false modesty once we were home: "I think they understood the Lord's message today, Margaret. He was speaking through me, and I was surely his vessel and servant."

I turn my gaze to the couple with the baby. Spencer's doppelganger holds the baby while his wife wipes the baby's nose. I quickly look away. I'm starting not to feel so hot, frankly. I want a drink. I want a drink real bad. I try to focus, but it's as if the Reverend's head has turned into a bottle of scotch. I remember my cigarettes in the car, and all too quickly I'm telling myself that I'll go out for a quick smoke and then return to hear the guest speaker. Knowing how the Reverend likes to hear himself talk, I'll have a good twenty minutes before he even introduces the bishop.

I excuse myself as I step over people and practically race down the stairs and make my way outside. I head straight to my car and find the cigarettes. I stare at the few stars that are visible, exhaling my first drag with a deep sense of freedom and relief.

"Smoking will kill you."

I turn and see a man walking toward me. He wears a yellow suit that makes him look as if he belongs in a jazz quartet circa 1930, and he's skinny enough that the suit makes him look like an elongated banana. Matters aren't helped by his odd doo-wop-looking hairstyle. He does the dopey-man chuckle. "You're one of them bad women. Smoking like that when you should be inside the church, hearing the Word."

"You're one to talk. You're at least thirty minutes late."

He steps closer. "I got caught in traffic; but as they say, better late than never." Chuckle chuckle. He raises his Bible, which has to be as heavy as he is. "I made it, though, praise God. I'm just in time to convince you to put out the poison stick and come inside with me."

I think of Eve and how bored she must have been stuck in paradise with a mindless man who was too busy naming animals to converse. No wonder she was more interested in the snake. Which reminds me of another problem I had back when I was forced to go to church: Why was Eve the bad guy? What's so wrong with curiosity?

"I'll pass." I take a drag of my cigarette. "I want to finish my poison stick," I tell him. "Besides, I get the gist. You Christians are adored and special, while the rest of us are going to hell where we'll burn for eternity. Yee haw!"

He laughs nervously. "What's your name?"

"Jezebel."

He brings his Bible to his chest like armor. "I should get inside. I'm late as it is."

"Why don't you stay out here and keep me company?" I lean back and give the hood of my car a pat. I then take a puff of my cigarette and cross my legs.

"Keep you company?" His voice practically breaks.

I stare into his eyes, feigning to put him under my spell. He laughs nervously and shrinks back while clutching his Bible. "You afraid of me?"

"No."

"Then what's the problem?"

"There's no problem."

He's a cheap form of distraction, but it's kind of fun making him nervous. I figure I'll fool around a little, have another cig, and give church another try. I take a step closer and move his jacket aside with my fingertip. "Don't be afraid," I whisper. "I won't hurt you."

I get the feeling it's been a long time since Henry or Harry or whatever the hell he said his name is has had sex. His hands race against each other as though if he's quick enough, God won't catch us making out in the backseat of my car, but he can't figure out what he's doing and, thanks to his clumsy skills, minutes in and we're both still fully dressed. He grabs at my thigh. "Easy now."

"Sorry." He then starts to unbutton my sweater but can't get past the first button. Frustrated, I begin to help him. When my sweater finally opens, his eyes practically fall out of their sockets, much like the old cartoons where the cartoon dog sees a bone or cute poodle and loses it on the spot. I lean back and wait—*and wait*—while he tries to unfasten my bra. Total amateur, this one. It's as if he were still a virgin. Then again, considering I'm in a church parking lot, he just might be.

"You're not a virgin, are you?" I ask.

"No, ma'am!"

Ma'am?

I'm about to tell him to never use that word again when I hear a noise outside. I try to see if someone's there, but every time I move one way, Harry or Henry's elongated head blocks my view. I hear what sounds like a cough and tap him on the shoulder. "Hey, did you hear that?" He's too busy trying to unhook my bra to pay attention. Whoever is outside tries to open the door, but it's locked and the person begins pounding on the window instead.

Harry or Henry turns enough that I see a face peep through the window. Mom's face.

"Piper Michelle Nelson, you'd better get your ass out of that damn car before I drag you out!"

She starts pulling at the door so hard the car rocks back and forth as though we're caught in turbulent seas. "Get out, I said! I know you hear me in there, you heathen! Get the hell outta that car!"

Harry and I rock this way and that. He struggles to fasten his belt. "Oh, dear Lord! Jesus, help me. Please, Lord."

Mom gives up rocking the car and starts pounding her fists on the roof instead. "Get out of the damn car!"

Harry turns and sees whom we're dealing with. "Oh Lord! That's Sister Wright! Oh help me, Jesus!"

"Open the door," I tell him.

"There's no way I'm opening that door, ma'am!"

"*Stop calling me ma'am!*"

Mom puts her face in the window. "Harold Roberson? Is that you?"

"No, Sister Wright! My name is Justin."

"Stop lying and get out of the car!"

Harold sighs and buttons the collar of his shirt. "Dear Jesus, please help me," he whispers. "I am in so much trouble."

He gets out of the car with his head hung low as though prepared to take his rightful place at the guillotine. Mom, meanwhile, is already waving her hands and pacing. "Harold Roberson, you'd better get inside that church right now! You are supposed to be a youth leader, and you're out here acting as if you've lost your mind. Your duties are hereby suspended. You hear me? Suspended. And you *will* have a talk with Reverend Wright about this."

"It's not my fault!" he says, pointing my way. "That woman tempted me!"

"*What?*"

"It's her fault!"

Mom steps closer with her hand on her hip and says through gritted teeth, "Unless she dragged you into that car by force, you had something to do with this, too. Now get inside the church before anyone sees you."

"Yes, ma'am."

He rushes off while I put on my sweater and climb out of the car. I start to open my mouth to speak, but then I'm staring at asphalt and there's a ringing in my ears. I raise my head slowly and bring my hand to my burning cheek. *I've just been slapped. Mom slapped me.*

As soon as I lower my hand, Mom slaps me again—and again. She then starts pummeling me with her fists. My body doesn't understand that it should protect itself, because my mother of all people is the source of every blow. "Mom, stop it! Quit!"

Finally, I raise my arm to defend myself against the next onslaught of fists.

When she raises her hand again, my instincts kick in and I swing back. My aim is off, but I manage to hit her on the arm.

"Don't you raise your hand to me! Who the hell do you think you are? How dare you come here behaving like this! What is wrong with you?" She shoves me, but I push back, hard enough that she falters.

She looks around at the empty parking lot as though making sure no one is around and then cuts loose. "What the hell is wrong with you? I can't believe I find you out here—at your father's church—having sex!"

"We weren't having sex. He barely touched me!" I probe the side of my cheek as though realizing what just happened. "You hit me!"

"Damn straight I hit you. You deserved it, too! I should hit you again!"

When she lunges toward me, I quickly get in my car and slam the door. "Piper Michelle, I am talking to you!"

After fumbling with my keys, I start the engine and roll down the window. "You don't have a right to say a word to me. Not a single fucking word! How dare *you* hit me! I should call the cops on you!"

She grits her teeth and pulls at the door handle. "Open the goddamn door!"

"No!"

She continues to hold on to the handle even as I start to pull away. "Open the damn door, Piper. Right now!" She doesn't let go until I boost speed and head toward the street.

I watch as her reflection diminishes in the rearview mirror. A man runs up to her, ready to help.

I look out toward the road. My face burns hot as I speed away.

I press my head deeper into my pillow, but I can't drown out the rock music someone is playing. I close my eyes and pull my blanket over my ears, but it doesn't help. When a man with a high-pitched voice screams over a tortured guitar solo, I give up and roll onto my side and open my eyes. It takes me a good minute before I realize I'm not at home and not in my bed.

I blink a few times and wait for my brain to tell me where I am. My hungover synapses creepy-crawl to their final destinations while the rock music continues to blast. I follow the noise until I see a speaker hanging in one corner of the room. I then catch the sound of running water and assume whoever lives here is taking a shower.

Gathering my nerve, I take a cautious peek under the covers. A man's T-shirt. No underwear. I sit up and try to take in more clues. My purse is on top of a dresser next to two half-empty bottles of scotch. Just above the dresser hangs an eight-by-ten glossy of a silver race car. On the opposite wall hangs a signed picture of a bodybuilder—*To Kurt, Stay strong!—Walt*. Next to it hangs a picture of a boxer, also signed—*To Kurt, From Antonio "The Brute" Chavez, Middle Weight Champ '06*.

I look around the room for more of my things. When I see my pants and sweater, I stop trying to figure out where I am and start putting on my clothes as quickly as I can. I'm reaching for my purse so I can get the hell out, when a man steps inside the room. He's naked but for a ratty blue towel wrapped around his waist. Trails of steam float off his lobster red skin. He's massive, all muscle and bulk, and stands with his legs apart and hands on his hips à la Yul Brynner in *The King and I*.

"Dressed already?" He walks over and kisses my cheek. Wet gray curls frame an angular face that's all jawline. His hair is misleading, though. He can't be more than thirty-five. "You're not trying to sneak out, are you? I thought we'd get breakfast. I know a place up the street makes a mushroom spinach omelet that's to die for."

"I . . ." I take a step toward the bedroom door. I have no idea who he is. "No, thanks. I think I should get going."

He taps my nose with the tip of his finger. "Not acceptable. 'Sides, it's my treat. Your body needs fuel after such a long night."

He bends down and kisses the tip of my nose. I think about string theory, except in this alternate universe I'm dating a bodybuilding Neanderthal.

I look at the photos on the wall in hopes of kick-starting my memory. The race car catches my attention again, its sleek silver body and the number twenty-six painted on the door. I stare hard until a flash of speeding down the highway with the sound of my own penetrating scream in my ear comes to mind.

The Neanderthal follows my gaze. "We can take her out again after breakfast. We can even go down to the track. Let me put my clothes on and we're outta here."

Something about the word *track* brings more specific images to mind: a wood sign advertising Liberties Pub; the Neanderthal in a bowler hat and leather jacket—"You're gorgeous"; lots of talk about the race car he built from nothing; how he loves to go to the track at the end of the month and "show her off."

Riiiiiight.

Race car guy.

I remember now how he walked into the bar—the I'm-the-shit swagger. I knew right off he was the worst kind of man, vain and boring, but I was already plastered by then and upset about what had happened with Mom. He walked right up to me and set his bowler hat next to my shot. "You're gorgeous."

"That hat," I said by way of response. "Very *Unbearable Lightness of Being.*"

"What?"

He leans in now and touches his nose to mine. I shudder when I feel the wet tendrils from his hair on my cheek. Something about this one gives me the creeps. "Actually, I really should get going. Rain check?"

I rush to the bedroom door, but just as I open it, he says, "I don't think so," and slowly closes the door with a sly grin. "How about one more time?"

"I can't. I'll leave my number." I haven't had a chance to put on my shoes but try to open the door again. When I do, he immediately closes it shut.

"You were incredible last night. Kurt wants more."

"Look, I'll be honest. I'm seeing someone. Last night was a mistake. I have a boyfriend."

"Boyfriend? You a two-timer, gorgeous? You a bad girl?" He grins in a way that says the fact that I have a "boyfriend" means absolutely nothing and is only getting him off. He presses his lips down on mine, then startles me by prying my mouth open with his tongue. I squirm and try to push him away, but when he doesn't notice or care, I drop my things and use both hands to push hard at his wall of a chest until he gets the message and steps aside.

I pick up my shoes and purse. "I really have to go." I'm too quick for him this time, and I slip through the door and start down the hallway.

"Wait a sec."

I do nothing of the sort and move faster. I see the front door, but then he catches me by the wrist and pulls me back.

"You should dump him and be with me. You gotta be with me one more time at least."

The towel drops and he grabs me around the waist. "Kurt wants to be with you. You turn me on." I try to knee him, but he's all brute force and stupidity. There's enough fear surging through me by now that I know this isn't a joke, and he's serious, but he's all muscle and as much as I try to fight him off, I know there's no winning. Physically there is no fight. Physically he's twice my weight, twice my body mass. But mentally, mentally I'm sure I can think of something.

His breathing slows as he begins kissing my neck. "I like you a lot, Samantha."

Samantha?

"I like you, too, but like I said, I have a boyfriend."

I try to push him away again. All the while I'm thinking . . . *thinking.* I need to get out of here. Of course, I knew something like this could happen, sleeping around like I've been, but now that it's happening, I feel oddly out-of-body—heady, cerebral, but not in a way that's of any help. When I feel his hand reaching under my sweater, I hear Sharayray's voice—see her in the back of the class talking to Kristine and Michelle. Was this last year? Two years ago? The girls were having lunch in my room, and I remember eavesdropping, smiling to myself at Sharayray's hubris, proud of her for always being so tough. *"It's exactly like they be saying. No means no. I don't care how horny the motherfucker is. So when that fool wouldn't listen, you know what I did? I pulled a Mike Tyson on that motherfucker. Girl, I bit down so hard on that fool's ear, I had that motherfucker screamin' like the bitch he is. I was like, motherfucker, don't you ever ever keep foolin' with me when I tell you no. Who you think you playin' with, bitch? Bitch was holdin' his ear and cryin' and shit. I'm tellin' you, girl, I had that motherfucker in pain."*

So I wait. And wait. And when the Neanderthal turns his head just to the left, I take Sharayray's blessed advice and pull a Mike Tyson on the motherfucker. Before he realizes what I'm doing, I'm biting through cartilage and flesh, clamping down hard until I hear the motherfucker screaming like the bitch he is.

He cups his ear and whines. *"Owwwww!* My ear! Holy shit! My ear! Sammy, I thought you were kidding!" He holds his ear and whines like a petulant child. "I'm sorry, Sammy. Don't leave."

"You're a fucking idiot."

"I wouldn't hurt you, Sammy. Kurt really likes you!" He clasps at his ear. "You hurt me! Why'd you hurt me, Sammy?"

I can hear all of his blubbering even as I slam the door and escape. I run down the apartment corridor and take the stairs that lead outside two at a time. When I'm at least three blocks away, I sit on someone's stoop and put on my shoes.

The setting sun throws me. I had assumed it was morning. I look up and down the street. Back and forth.

I have absolutely no idea where I am.

Shit.

I stand and try to get my bearings. It's when I'm at the corner that I realize I'm not in Oakland but San Francisco.

The Mission District.

Fuck.

I head toward the nearest BART station. As I walk, the whats and hows start to pour in. Church. Harold. Mom slapping me more than once in the face. My drive through Oakland until I wound up in Rockridge where I had several drinks at a high-end restaurant with a bar. And then . . . then . . . I couldn't drive, so I thought I'd take BART home, but I took the wrong train and thought it was funny that I was headed into the city. Once here, I didn't bother taking a return train back home. Instead, I ended up taking a walk. And that was when I found a pub called Liberties.

I find a seat on the train and close my eyes. I expect to feel a sense of relief for getting away from the Neanderthal, but honestly? All I feel is deep and abiding shame. I think of the guy in the church parking lot. I think about what a lousy teacher I've been to my students. I think of Mom slapping me and the disgusted look in her eyes.

I can't go on like this. *What would Hailey think of my behavior?* I feel tears coming. Except for a few people, the car is practically empty, so I don't bother trying to hold them back. It's as if my heart has become too weak, too drained from trying to keep things together.

No, I absolutely cannot continue like this. What's more, I know I need help. I feel the Neanderthal's hands on me and bring my feet up on the seat. I hear myself say through my tears, "I need help." A man three rows up turns and scowls. I'm sure I must look mentally ill or like a drug addict. I don't care, though. "I need help," I whimper. "Somebody, please. I need help." I curl up into a ball on my seat and let the tears come. I cry through several stops and through the tunnel leading back to Oakland. I cry and cry and cry.

ten

I crawl into bed once I'm home and stay there well into the next morning. I spend most of the day throwing up, sleeping, and crying. When I finally get the strength to get out of bed, I go straight to the bottles of scotch in my kitchen cabinet and start pouring them out. As I watch the liquor run down the drain, I admit that I have a problem. I've been trying to trick myself into believing that because I have a respectable job and a fair number of smarts, I can handle my liquor, but I can't. What's more, I need to stop using Hailey's death as an excuse to drink. What happened with the Neanderthal scared the shit out of me. I have to quit. I have to.

After emptying four bottles, I take down an as-yet-unopened lovely fifteen-year-old Glenlivet, an oak-based scotch with a hint of citrus. It's a sad sad thing to see the golden liquid pouring into the drain, and it's not long before the aroma overwhelms me, and somewhere near the base of my cortex, my brain begins its rebellion— *Drink! Drink!*—sending preliminary signals to my nerves and cells that they must stand together at all cost and break my will—*Drink!*

Even as I set the empty bottle next to the others, I know my brain and my body will eventually win. Sure, the kitchen is free of alcohol now, but what happens tomorrow? Hell, what happens *tonight?* Frustrated, I put all of the empty bottles in a bag, quickly dress, and take them to the recycling bin downstairs. I then start walking up the block with the hope that a tour of the altars will help clear my head.

I visit Tank's altar first. The candles and teddy bears are still there; someone has added a bowl of uncooked yams and fresh flowers; the poster boards are still in place, as is Donne's poem. Just next to the poem someone has written: *I miss you, Tank. Your turn to look after me now.*

I walk up to Sixty-fifth and visit Dexter Allen's altar. Dexter's altar is on his parents' front lawn. There are a row of vodka bottles and candy bars spread in front of a small trickling fountain. At the foot of the fountain is a plaque: DEXTER ALLEN, SON, FATHER, BEST FRIEND. IF MY TEARS COULD BUILD A STAIRWAY TO REACH YOU, I'D CRY FOR ETERNITY.

As I come up to the corner of Fifty-fifth, I notice a ten-speed bicycle chained to a stop sign and painted entirely white. Plastic flowers have been tied all around the bike and candles placed on the sidewalk. The front tire, also painted white, is smashed and juts off at a crooked angle. A large flyer with a photo is taped to the pole: PLEASE DRIVE CAREFULLY AND WITH RESPECT TO EVERYONE AROUND YOU. In the photo a young man is playing outdoors with a girl of eight or nine. Beneath that are the words MICHAEL, WE WILL MISS YOU AND LOVE YOU ALWAYS. I close my eyes and do my best to send supportive thoughts to Michael's daughter and family. I then think: *I have to stop drinking. I have to stop drinking.*

Finally, I make my way to the corner of Fifty-fifth and Market where I light a candle for Lil' Sonny. Sonny was shot next

door to a liquor store. Two balloons are tied to the chain-link
fence, separating the store from the house next door. Someone
has made a poster that has pictures of Sonny. Sonny dancing.
Sonny holding who I guess is his little boy. People have written
things like *Save a place for me!* and *I love you, baby, Always and forever. Lil' C.*

Next to the poster board is a bright yellow flyer.

> Prayer and support for those who have lost
> beloved family members and friends due to ill-
> ness, police brutality, gang violence or drugs or
> any unforeseen circumstance or act of God.
> Please join us. First Congregational Church
> AME. 122 43rd. Seven p.m. Second and fourth
> Sundays. Rec Room. Punch and cookies pro-
> vided.

I check my watch. Six forty-five.

The mourners' group at First AME is the antithesis of
Friends of Friends in Mourning. The walls are covered
with yellow and pink wallpaper, fading and peeling in
spots. A sign that reads NO SMOKING is inexplicably burned crisp
at the edges. As promised, there's a table set up with cookies and
punch next to a two-foot-high Christmas tree that droops under
the weight of too many ornaments. Two people help themselves;
the others, six in total, sit in a circle in the center of the room. I
join them, returning polite smiles while promising myself that if
I start to feel remotely like I did while at the Reverend's church
two nights ago, I'm outta here.

A man who looks to be in his early seventies, mustached and
bald, introduces himself as Deacon Morris. He then claps his

hands and says, "All right, let's all get started." He's slack in body, and the top of his pants reach into his chest. But his muscular arms tell another story, hinting that he was strong back in the day; his booming voice adds to my hunch. "Sister Arlene, will you lead us in prayer?"

Everyone bows his or her head on cue except for me. Instead, I look around at our ragtag bunch. One guy's face sags in on itself thanks to his missing teeth. The woman next to him wears a red wig that looks more like a crooked hat. I think briefly that if I leave now, no one will notice, but Arlene begins her prayer, and I can't get up the courage to sneak out.

"Dear Lord, we thank you for this meeting and this time to come together to worship you in your glory and to share our pain and losses, and our successes, too."

"Amen."

"We thank you for your son who had to lose his life in order for us to know life."

"Yes, Lord."

"Thank ya, Lord."

"You yourself, God, know what it's like to lose a loved one, and we thank you that you understand our grief and heal us in the name of Jesus."

I can't help but think, it's not the same. God, if you buy into the myth, didn't *lose* his son at all. His son rose from the dead. Big difference. Our loved ones aren't rising from anything.

I start to reach for my bag so I can leave. I want to kick myself for thinking that a mourners' group in a church rec room would be of any help, but just as I grab my bag, the prayer ends, and Deacon Morris asks each of us to give our names. When we're finished he says, "Now, we are assembled here to share our grief and our pain, but we are also here to share love, as our loved ones would want us to do. Who would like to start?"

A young man in his twenties, who introduced himself as Marcus, raises his hand. He sits hunched down in his chair; his jacket sports the name of a hip-hop artist. "I lost my cousin Greg last March. His name was Greg, but everybody called him G-love. He wasn't even doing anything except going to the store to buy a soda and some Cheetos, and he got robbed and beat up so bad he went into a coma and died. Died over, like, five dollars he had left in his pocket. They don't even know who did it. But if I ever find out whoever beat him like that, because I swear I think it was Cornelius, they is going to pay." He bounces his leg rapidly as he looks around the room. "Oh, you best believe that." He nods firmly. "I will find whoever it is and show them what's what."

Deacon Morris says, "Careful now, son. Eye for an eye leaves everybody blind. Why don't you tell us what you liked about your cousin. What made you all close?"

Marcus looks at him as though it's a trick question, but then he thinks to himself and chuckles. "G-love—G-love was called G-love for a reason. That dog had all the ladies, round the way and then some. But he was a gentleman—don't misunderstand. G-love was a *real* gentleman, like, all old-school about it. He knew how to treat a lady well, and that's why they all loved him. Everybody loved G-love. He never had nothin' negative to say about nobody, and ain't nobody had nothin' negative to say about G-love. We all just loved him." He takes his hat from his knee and hides his face.

The man next to him reaches over and gives his shoulder a firm squeeze. "No shame in showin' your grief, son."

Deacon Morris says, "G-love, in his own way, has reminded us all here tonight about the importance of kindness and love and of being a gentleman. We all thank him for that. We thank Marcus for sharing. You are welcome here tonight, son."

Several in the group say, "Amen."

The woman to my right, Coco, begins rocking back and

forth. She wears a pink T-shirt with plastic rhinestones made into the shape of a cross. She's a large, heavyset woman with short braids that frame her round face. She holds her purse in her lap as though waiting at a bus stop. "Yes, Jesus." She rocks. "Yes, Lord." She rocks and calls out Jesus's name a few more times, then takes a breath. "I just wanna thank you all for having me here tonight. *Yes, Jesus.* I needed to come here and be with you all. I really did." She takes a handkerchief from her purse and dabs at her eyes. She then pulls her skirt past her knees and crosses her weighty calves at the ankles. "Brothers and sisters in Christ, I lost my son Reginald Michael Jeffries due to gang-related violence. Yes, Jesus," she whispers. "Help me through it, Lord."

The woman next to her pats her back as she rocks. We all wait.

"Yesterday," she continues, "my son would have turned eighteen. He would've been eighteen years old. How long had I been waiting to see my boy turn eighteen?" She looks at each of us as if we know the answer.

"Long time," a man to my left says. "You were waiting to see your boy become a man."

"That's right." She nods. "That's exactly right. A woman raises her boy so she can see him into adulthood. Ain't natural to have it go any other way. He was turning into a good man, too. He was just graduating from high school." She digs in her purse and takes out a pocket-sized photo and hands it to the woman next to her. We all take turns looking at the picture. I fear that I might recognize him from MacDowell, but I don't. He's skinny and all teeth, and he's obviously proud of the trophy he's holding. I pass the picture on.

Coco looks at us all. "So tell me this: Why they have to go and kill my son? What did he do to anybody?" Her rocking starts again. "I feel like if I could understand why, I could feel better; but I'm just as lost, y'all, I really am." The picture is returned, and she stares down at it as if she's never seen it before. Then, without any warning whatsoever, she bursts into tears.

Like a trained professional caregiver, the woman next to her rises from her seat and begins using her hands to make small comforting circles on her back. Coco cries without any inhibition, and she is soon wailing loudly like a dying animal. It's so heartbreaking, I lower my head and begin to cry softly.

Eventually a woman goes over and hugs her, then another. Deacon Morris begins praying, while Coco rocks and cries until her body is nothing more than a trembling mass.

Deacon Morris says, "That's right, can't nothing you do but sit with that pain and let it carry you over. Just be with it."

I feel as though he's talking to me. Coco has calmed down by now, but I'm crying harder. "I want my baby," I hear myself say. "I want my baby back." I begin choking on my tears and hiccupping wildly. I try to tell them: "I can't live without her. I need her back!" I let out my own wail and cry with everything I have. I cry for Marcus. I cry for Coco. I cry for everyone in the room. I cry for every parent who's lost a child and every child who's lost a parent. Our loss is too much to bear, and I cry because it *is* too much to bear.

I hear Deacon Morris. "Go ahead and cry, young lady. Let it all out!"

I cry all the harder.

"Let it out!" he shouts.

I realize he's standing right next to me, pressing his hand into my back as if loosening a cancer lodged deep inside my body. A new level of grief that not even I, dowser of grief, knew existed slowly begins to seep out of my body. I cry and moan as my voice rises and falls, and my body shakes and convulses like a fish caught on a line, flinging itself to and fro.

"Let it out!" Deacon Morris shouts. I wail and moan all the louder. I'm not sure if I'll ever stop. I cry because of my horrible fight with Mom. I cry because I've lost Spencer. I cry because I can't forgive him for having another child. I cry because I can't forgive myself for driving so fast that day.

"That's right. Brothers and sisters, you can take that pain and you can turn it into a source of love. Let it soften you, weaken you, humble you. That is how you can turn it into good!"

I hear someone cry out, "Amen." Soon someone else is touching my shoulder, while another holds my hand. My convulsing has turned to rhythmic rocking, much like Coco's rocking earlier. I don't fight my body or my tears, nor do I fight the words that come back: "Please help me. I can't do this anymore. I need help."

I hear Deacon Morris say, "Your loved one is here saying you can go on. Let that pain take over you. It's a wave that'll crash you down, but you'll be standing tall in the end. You are strong enough to hold on to it. You are a beautiful child of God. He's letting you know you can go on." He sounds jubilant. People clap and sing out.

When I feel someone taking my hands in theirs, I open my eyes and stare directly into Coco's tear-streaked face. I feel as though I've never seen a kinder, more compassionate face. She doesn't say a word as we gaze into each other's eyes, one mourning mother to another. Everyone, I see now, is standing around me, touching me in one way or another. Someone from behind smiles and says, "That's real good. You doin' real good."

I feel myself coming back to my body. My breath slows. Coco takes me in her arms, and we hug tightly. I inhale the smell of baby oil deep in the crevices of her neck, the perfume dabbed behind her ear. I feel her arms hold me close, and I hold her. We don't dare separate.

"Angels all around," I hear Deacon Morris say. "Our pain, our great pain gives us the capacity to have compassion for others. That's a blessing." He touches my arm, and Coco and I slowly separate.

"We know what it's like for that woman in the Motherland who lost her children to AIDS. *We* feel the pain of that sister who's lost her friend to drugs."

Someone says, "Amen."

"We don't have to keep our walls up. We don't have to become bitter. We're strong enough. We're strong enough to get through. These two grieving women have so much to offer. We can all take our pain and turn it to good. I say, we can all take our pain and turn it to good!"

"Amen!"

"Yes, Lord!"

"Teach, Deacon Morris."

"Our pain has crushed our walls, and we go out with open hearts. Love is here with us tonight and every day of our lives just as surely as our loss and our grief. Let us let love make us strong. Let us allow love to make us formidable opponents to hatred and self-loathing. Let us let love carry us."

Coco takes my hand and gives it a firm squeeze. I squeeze back.

Deacon Morris says, "Can I hear an *amen*?"

We all say amen together.

eleven

By the next morning, my once-beloved relationship with scotch has been replaced by a codependent relationship with my toilet, whereby anytime I want to stand and leave, I'm back on my knees heaving into its porcelain belly whatever contents I'm trying to keep down. My skin is cold and clammy, and the grim reaper has been going at my head with his scythe much like a Russian serf harvesting a field of wheat.

My only saving grace is that I don't have to go to work for two whole weeks and have time to hold out in my apartment, rid my body of alcohol, and get clean and sober once and for all. Margot has been calling and texting since yesterday:

What happened?! What did you do?!

Call Mom!

Call me!

Are you okay?

I texted her to leave me alone, I'm fine, but by early after-noon, I'm curled up on the bathroom floor, exhausted, with my head resting against the cool tile. What's funny, or not so funny,

I'm already thinking about the scotch I tossed and how it would ease the pain in my joints and what feels like a swelling of my skull. I close my eyes and think of all the alcohol I'm going to have to give up if I quit, not only scotch, but all alcohol: merlots and chardonnays; pinots and Rieslings; margaritas on a hot summer's day. I'll have to say good-bye to a group of old reliable friends, and I'm not sure I want to.

I roll onto my back and hold my stomach as it surges and swells. I ride a wave of nausea and cramps as they fight out which will torture me more.

An hour later I'm in the bathroom again, my head suspended above the toilet as I wait to puke. Dry heaves come a few times, and I tear up as my stomach clenches again. I still haven't had a single drink, but hours spent at the toilet, and the feeling that I surely must have swine flu or some other exotic disease, have finally taught me there's no way I'm going to beat this alone.

I close my eyes and will myself to stand. So when my stomach finally relaxes, I drudge over to my laptop and look up AA. Meetings are everywhere, it appears, with the closest being today at three. Whoopee!

I drive up Mandela Parkway until I reach the address I've written down, a recreational center located next to a small park. Luckily the snack I had earlier is staying put in my stomach, but I'm already doubtful. I mean, *AA*? I'm not that bad off. I just need a break from drinking, that's all. Surely in a few months I'll be capable of having a glass of wine now and then. And what about holidays? One drink of wine at Christmas or New Year's isn't going to hurt anyone.

But then I shake my head wearily at the entrance to the rec

center. Knowing that I'm already thinking of Christmas, only days away, says everything. *Crap.*

A group of fifteen or so people sits in a haphazard circle in the center of the rec room. I hum a few bars to "Is That All There Is?" to myself as I find a seat. Here I am again: another meeting, another circle, another Christmas tree, this one covered with paper decorations and a very confused Star of David on top.

A woman with thick black hair braided into two plaits is speaking. Her hair and tight jeans suggest she's in her late twenties, but the bags under her eyes and leathery skin reveal she's much older.

I steal surreptitious glances around the room to listen. Just about every race is represented. Some look like the stereotypes I've seen in movies; others surprise me, like the blond woman who looks like any child's soccer mom.

The woman with the braids says something about blow jobs, and I snap to. Apparently she used to turn tricks in the bathrooms at MacArthur Park, but thanks to God and the meetings, she's been sober going on six years. She thanks everyone for listening. There's a sputter of applause, and then several hands shoot up.

I stay through the entire meeting without saying a word. I'm not feeling this group, frankly. One guy talked about his meth addiction and another spent time in San Quentin. I felt moved by the mourners' group, but here I feel distant. *Prison? Meth addiction?* These aren't my people. I'm all too happy when the last person speaks and everyone begins to recite the prayer I've heard off and on over the years: "God give us the power to change the things we can and accept what we—"

As if on cue, my stomach surges as they're finishing, and I make a beeline in search of a bathroom. I find one at the end of a hallway and throw up crackers and orange juice before I have a chance to close the stall door.

A woman stares with an impassive look on her face as I wash my hands. When I'm finished, she hands me a plastic cup filled with water. She was one of the few people who didn't speak during the meeting, just sat while nodding her head, her arm resting on the back of a chair. I take the water and thank her.

"Detox is a bitch."

"You won't get an argument from me."

She smiles at this, her mouth full of gapped teeth. She's a woman who belongs in a Toulouse-Lautrec painting, round and plump with lacquered black hair that bursts from a tightly wound ponytail into a pom-pom of shiny curls. I wait for her to laugh gaily and do the cancan.

"Sherry," she says.

"Piper."

"You okay to go back inside?"

As I follow her back to the main room, I explain that I'm not sure AA is for me. "I've only smoked pot a handful of times, and as far as drugs, I've never tried anything stronger than Ambien. I'm not, you know—giving blow jobs in a park."

"So what brought you here? Stopping by for cookies and punch?"

I start to say something about the mourners' group, how the last thing I want are more cookies and punch, but her hard stare gives me pause. She may look like she's ready for wire-rimmed skirts and bloomers, but I get the feeling she's like the best teachers at MacDowell, able to detect bull in a single bound. "People don't just show up to meetings. So why . . . *are you here*?"

"I don't know."

"Yes, you do."

I throw my head back. "I don't." I want to leave. I want to go home, crawl into bed, and forget everything. I know, however, that it's now or never. I need to tell the truth for once. I gnaw on my lower lip and tap my foot. "I'm afraid."

She cups her hand around her ear. "What was that?"

"I'm afraid I'll start drinking again if I don't get help."

She nods as if I've done good work and we can now get down to business. "You like soup?"

Not what I was expecting.

"There's a place that serves good soup up the street. Let's see if you can keep it down. You're a bag of bones, Miss Lady, and trust me, if you're ready to wrestle with the demons, you're gonna need your strength."

Dan's American Diner is anything but. It's pure Americana with its red booths, black-and-white checkered floor, and chrome countertops, but the menu is Vietnamese and soul food, of all things. Sherry explains that the Vietnamese couple who bought the place hail from Mississippi and decided to create a menu with the foods they love; hence, side orders like spring rolls and cucumber salad alongside collard greens and candied yams. Sherry orders two bowls of pho, but not before chatting with our waitress; she's also already said hello to an older man sitting at the counter, after giving him a hug and checking up on his family. She's gregarious and warm, and I doubt anyone here would suspect she just left an AA meeting.

While we wait for our soup, she tells me she's been sober for twelve years after three failed attempts. She worked as a nurse at Alta Bates, but once her drinking took over, she found herself stealing pills from the hospital. She managed to get away with her pill popping and thievery for years before she was caught. "Little pill here, little pill there and nobody notices." But she was also one of the best nurses at the hospital, so instead of firing her, they offered rehab. She completed the program only to start up again once she went back to work. Her rock bottom was when her children disowned her.

"I can't blame them. Whenever I was high, my entire personality took a nosedive. I'd go from depressed to piss-fire angry. My dad was a drunk, and even though I swore I'd never be like him . . ." She slaps her hands on the table with a shake of her curls. "My son takes a phone call now and then—Christmas and his birthday usually, but my daughter? I haven't talked to Tianna in more than eight years. *Ocho años*," she repeats slowly. She works at Berkeley's Public Health Clinic now and is studying Spanish at Laney College.

"You've changed, though. You're sober. They can't see that?"

"My kids only know the me that was an alcoholic and an abuser. That's who they grew up with."

"But you seem so happy."

"Day by day."

The line doesn't seem like such a worn-out cliché when she says it.

The owner of the diner comes with our soups and says hello. I get the feeling that Sherry's popular not only at the restaurant but everywhere she goes. It's the way she looks directly into people's eyes and smiles her Toulouse-Lautrec smile. She makes me think of bubbles, actually, *bubbles rising in a flute of champagne*—but that's another story.

I watch her, imagining how full her life must be—days filled with people and friends and good times. If I'm point A, Sherry's point Z, as far as Venus to Uranus, an unimaginable and unattainable distance.

I blow on my soup and begin slurping the hot broth and noodles. I want to try, I do, but I know this will mean telling the truth, not just that I lost my little girl, but also how I lost her. The guilt has been crushing me for years, and even though I know I'll never forgive myself, something tells me if I'm going to stay sober—really sober, *Sherry Sober*—I need to be honest.

I set my spoon down and carefully run my hands over my napkin. "Sherry, can I tell you something?"

I take the long route, starting with my drinking in college and continuing with my relationship with Spencer. I tell her about Mom and what happened at the church Friday night. I tell her about the men, about the Neanderthal.

Every topic hovers around my secret. I look out the window while waiting for my confidence to build. The sun hangs low, and I think briefly of how long it's remained at its perfect distance from Earth—not too close that we burn a fiery death, and not too far away that we freeze.

I feel Sherry's gaze, willing me to come back. "I'm right here, Piper, and I'm not going anywhere. I'm not going to judge you either, if that's what you're thinking."

"I know," I say. "I know."

I return to Hailey and the morning she died. "I was pissed because of the fight with Spencer and how he was flirting with Melinda. How I *thought* he was flirting with her. I put Hailey in her booster seat, and I remember feeling so angry. I kept yelling at her to be quiet when all she was doing was being four. I was yelling at her when she died. My last words to my daughter were 'Stop playing around back there and keep your damn butt still.' I was probably going ten miles over the speed limit when I hit that truck. If I hadn't been speeding, she would still be here. It was my fault."

My hands are shaking, so I have to hold on to my teacup to get them to stop. "I don't know what to do. I don't know what to do with this guilt I feel. The drinking is the only thing that helps, but it's not helping anymore. I don't know what to do, but at the same time I deserve the shame and guilt." I use my napkin to wipe the tears from my face. Crying has become such an old habit by now, I don't care if anyone notices me.

Sherry strokes my hand while I cry. When I finally have the courage to look at her, she says, "Sounds to me like an accident."

I shake my head and sniffle. "I was speeding. It was my fault."

"Nothing was intentional. That to me, sweetheart, means accident. A terrible, tragic accident, but an *accident.*"

"I don't know how to get on with my life when it was my fault for ending hers."

"Let me tell you something. You're never going to 'get on' with life. You have this moment. You have the next. And then you have the next. And every one of those moments is different. That's why you gotta surrender. You think life is algebra? One plus one is two? *Psssht.* It's crazy messed-up life that we're dealing with, not an algebra quiz. You surrender, Piper. You forgive yourself for being a human being, and you surrender to a power greater than yourself."

I practically roll my eyes—Oh, wait, I *do* roll my eyes. "I don't believe in any of that."

"Any of what?"

"God. Jesus. Any of it."

"Did I mention God? Did anyone here say God? A higher power is whatever you define as a higher power. But you need to turn your pain and confusion over to something. Addicts have a way of making everything about *me.* Good, bad, whatever, it all comes back to us. Our joy. Our hurt. Our anger. Our guilt. We make it all about ourselves as if no one else has any problems, as if we were the first person to ever experience a negative emotion. Drunks and addicts have a highly specialized skill at lying and manipulation, and if we don't surrender to something, we'll continue lying and manipulating and leading self-centered, self-destructive lives without anything ever changing. You can trust me on that one. Giving up booze is giving up what you think is your safety net, and for once in your life, Miss Lady, you just might let something bigger take over. Personally, I had to learn the hard way about the importance of getting down on my knees every night and every morning. I was too tired to try anymore. It felt good to say, 'I give up.'"

I turn my attention back to my soup to keep from saying anything smart-alecky. Getting on my knees and praying? I'd rather have a lobotomy, which for me is what prayer amounts to.

I return my attention to the setting sun, turning everything in its path a fiery orange-red. Mr. Hoffman would often wonder why more people didn't make science their religion. "Why turn to fables when directly above our heads we have the entire galaxies to worship and study. Why can't that be enough?" he'd ask. "We should all be walking around amazed that we exist. Amazed by the sun and moon and the stars. Why do humans have to make things so small, Piper?"

When he'd get like this, the night would usually end with a glass of red wine for him, hot cocoa for me, along with a concerto by one of his favorite composers. Music was part of his religion, too, and we'd often listen to Mozart or Beethoven. He'd close his eyes, showing me, I later realized, how to listen properly. "Notice the French horns here. Ah, see how the cello does its best to keep up with the piano? It's like a dance."

I smile and bring my finger to the windowpane. "I just realized that I do revere something. I revere the sun."

"The sun?"

"Here we are warmed and kept alive by a big ball of hydrogen fuel and gas. Someone close to me used to say he worshipped the universe—the *actual* universe started by the big bang, not the New Agey kind. That's what I believe in—all that out there: nebulae and planets, satellites, and galaxies."

She frowns as if I'm not only an alcoholic but also a wacko; yet I'm buoyed by my thought. As long as I've studied the universe, stared directly into its magnificent mind-blowing existence, I've never really considered how it has saved me over the years, calmed me, given me perspective.

Mr. Hoffman would also say that we humans take our place in the universe far too seriously. "What do we know about anything?" he'd ask, chuckling. "We're nothing more than odd beings on a planet, formed from amoeba!"

I'm finally seeing what he meant. For good or bad, I'm an "odd being" living on a planet, muddling my way through. I close my eyes briefly and envision some early human taking a quick piss in the woods, only to have her child attacked by a lion or any other predator. My example is extreme, sure, but it helps. We've been here a million years—that's enough time for a lot of mistakes, and tragedies, and accidents. I mean, I'm not alone in this. We are all kind of crying out to the people we've hurt. We are all human for what it's worth, living our odd human existence with all the glory and loss a human's life entails.

Sherry says, "I don't get it. You say you worship the sun? Is that some kind of African thing?"

"No, it's a science thing, I guess. I'm interested in astronomy. I'm starting to realize it's the one thing that's been keeping me sane. Think about it. All the key elements in the universe started from a dying star. Carbon, iron, gas. What the stars leave behind are the exact chemicals that we're made from. It's beautiful." I point toward the sun and sky. "We're part of that. Made from the exact same stuff. It's pretty amazing."

From the way Sherry shrugs off the view, I have a feeling she doesn't see my point. "Your higher power is your higher power. Just make sure you rely on it."

I feel good until the waitress appears with our bill and it's time to leave and a particular what-the-hell-am-I-going-to-do-once-I'm-home kind of panic sets in. For the first time in years I won't be going back to my apartment and having a drink. I won't be going home to anything except myself. Suddenly, all my talk about the universe and what it means to be human sounds like nothing but babble.

"You okay?"

"Not really. I don't think I can go home."

She keeps an eye on me while tearing the bottom portion of the bill and taking out a pen. "Listen, I want you to take my number, and if you feel that urge, feel that bottle taunting you, I want you to call me. It doesn't matter how late it is or how early. It doesn't matter if it's five minutes from now." She presses the thin slip of paper into my hand. "Call when you feel guilt coming at your throat. Call if you feel depressed or alone or depressed *and* alone. Call me anytime, you understand?"

I can't remember the last time someone was this kind to me, and I stare down at the table in as much embarrassment as gratitude. "Thank you."

"No need to thank me. Just call if you need to; that's all I ask."

She stands from the table and motions for me to stand as well. "Come here." She pulls me in for a hug. After a moment I hear her voice next to my ear. "It was an accident, Piper. Start there. It was a tragic accident. Keep telling yourself that, because it's the truth."

twelve

"Next up, our Spring Fling dance. Any volunteers?"

My hand shoots up.

"Are you sure, Miss Nelson?" Gladys asks, glancing down at her notes. "You already chaperoned at the Valentine's Day dance and are helping with this weekend's car wash."

"I know. It's fine. Count me in."

The few teachers present look at me askance. Everyone is wondering what is going on with me of late; usually during faculty meetings I'm in the back trying to stay awake if I bother to show up at all. But I returned after winter break with a vengeance. There is no function I'm not willing to help with, no faculty meeting I've yet to miss. I smile weakly at Joe, one of three science teachers here at MacDowell. The number of teachers who attend meetings this late in the semester is up and down; today there are sixteen of us, a paltry representation of the forty-member staff.

The dynamics in any given meeting are exactly the same as in our classrooms: We have our dominators, wisecrackers, shy lotus blossoms, and my former clique—the apathetic group that sits in the back, everyone checking his or her watch and sneaking in text messages.

I glance down at my ever-growing list of things to do. Along with helping out with this weekend's car wash, I'm also substituting for Beatrice during my prep period next week and helping with a fundraiser for seniors who can't afford a yearbook or senior class photos.

It's been two months since I started AA, and while I now know the importance of remaining humble and taking things day by day, I have to confess I'm pretty proud of my sobriety. I'm eight weeks, four days sober, to be exact, and I have two sobriety chips to prove it. The chips look like poker chips and are nothing special—unless you've been an alcoholic most of your life; then they're golden. I keep mine in the box where I keep Hailey's things. Staying sober can be challenging at times. I had Christmas dinner at the rec center with a handful of other addicts; New Year's Eve I was alone with a bottle of sparkling apple juice. But I'm also seeing what life as a sober person has to offer—the peace that comes from staying home and watching a movie or reading a book with a cup of *tea*, for instance. Not to mention the joys of waking up and knowing exactly where I am, or spending time with the girls and not counting the hours until they leave so that I can have something stronger than a glass of wine.

I attend meetings every single night and on weekends. I keep in close contact with Sherry, too, and I'm following the Twelve Steps; not nearly as religiously as some, but I am trying to be more thoughtful and kind, to others and myself. As soon as I returned from winter break, I spoke to Gladys and apologized for my behavior at school. What's more, I apologized to my first-period class for passing out as I had. I know some would have left it alone—why apologize?—but I wanted my students to know my behavior was reprehensible and that I hoped to make amends by doing my best from here on out. Some students stared back with the typically bored expressions, while others looked on with skepticism, but most were dumbfounded that a teacher would apologize to her class. As Pernell Clark said, "I ain't never forgetting this day in all my life. A teacher saying she's sorry? To me? That's crazy. That's just crazy."

I even contacted Selwyn. I didn't have his address, so I sent a card to Livermore's city hall. I apologized for blowing him off—twice—and thanked him for being so kind and supportive. I still haven't heard from him and don't think I will, frankly. I mean, how often can you reject a person and expect him to keep taking it? But it's about the actions we put out, as Sherry says, not the response.

Sherry also pushes me to take responsibility for my own actions and has helped me to see how my alcoholic me-ness stopped me from having a more expansive, empathetic view of life. Now when I think of that night at the Reverend's church, for instance, I at least understand how horrified Mom must have been at finding me in my car with that guy, and how my choice to seduce a man in front of her church was totally out of line. Hell, I can't even use being a drunk as an excuse. What I can't let go of, can't forgive, however, is that she slapped me—more than once. Not to mention the disgusted look in her eyes when she called me a heathen. Last Sunday at the mourners' group, a woman named Janet talked about her close relationship with her mother. At one point she said, "Mom was everything to me. Our mothers tell us who we are." If she's right, it's no wonder I'm so messed up. As a young girl, I saw Mom go through man after man, so why should I be surprised that I acted out sexually when I drank? Sherry and I both agree she's my biggest hurdle, but I'm still too angry to deal with her right now, and since I haven't heard from her, I have to assume she feels the same.

Gladys mentions next year's budget, and there's a collective moan. "Less money, more students," she laments. "I know we're up to the challenge. Meeting adjourned."

"Glad I won't be here next year," I overhear Sarah half whisper to Tina. Sarah and Tina are in the math department. Sarah has been here only two years, but like many of our newly hired, she burned out as quickly as a supernova and is leaving at the end of the school year. Turnover is one of the main problems at MacDowell, along with a lack of funds, low wages, apathy, high dropout rate, school fights. . . .

I glance up at the banner behind Gladys's head as I gather my things—CHILDREN ARE OUR FUTURE! And I read the words added by a disgruntled teacher in bright red Sharpie: *As long as they can afford private schooling!*

I head to the trailer where we hold after-school study hall. Supervising study hall once a week is another task I signed up for. Mrs. Fitch started study hall last year as a way to give students a safe and quiet place to study after the school closes. So many of our kids go home to parents who don't enforce homework, or their homes are too noisy for them to focus. She came up with the idea to open one of the trailers next to the science building from three o'clock to six thirty. The trailer is even more dilapidated than the rest of the school, with a droopy ceiling stained brown from water damage, and missing tiles. I say hello to Sylvia, the teacher I'm replacing, and take out the papers I need to grade after she leaves. A boy and girl sit up front working intently from thick history books. The only other students here are Sharayray, who sits on a desk in the back combing

Martina's hair, and Jesse, who's so busy texting that he doesn't bother looking up.

I look around the empty room with feigned drama. "It's so crowded in here, it's a wonder you can get anything done. So many students taking advantage of study hall. I'm amazed." The two students up front take their eyes off their books long enough to determine whether I'm joking or not. I don't recognize them and assume they're enrolled in one of our four AP classes. Sharayray, who's had me for English for two years now, ignores me.

The two brainiacs return to their studies, hunched over and as intent as monks grappling with an ancient text. I carry a tinge of resentment toward our AP students, grouped together from the start after achieving a high test score in early elementary school and from then on placed in higher-level classes with stricter standards, tracked from their early years to succeed. In other words, they have a chance.

Sharayray trades her brush for a comb. Martina leans back and pops her gum. "Ladies—gentleman," I say to Jesse. "This is study hall, not a beauty salon. Let's stop combing hair and focus. Jesse, take your phone outside if you don't plan on working."

"We're hella studying," Sharayray quips. "We're just taking a break." She takes a wad of Martina's hair and uses a comb to make a fine part scissor across the back of Martina's scalp. Supposedly Sharayray has a gift for "designing" hair, and she makes money on the side by styling hair at her house and during lunch breaks at schools. What students don't know is how smart she is. Sharayray has always been embarrassed by her high marks and tends to hide her achievements from other students or blow them off. "I just be guessin' the right answers," she says.

"Miss Erin lets me do hair up in here. She don't care what we do."

"Do I look like Miss Erin?"

She sighs loudly as she climbs down from the desk and sits next to Martina in a loud huff, leaving Martina's hair looking as if it's suffering from a personality disorder with one side neatly braided while the other side shoots out in wild strands.

"What about my hair?" Martine whines. "I can't go outside like this. She looks to Sharayray for help, but Sharayray only shrugs in my direction. I've been tempted to tell her how her words of wisdom inadvertently saved me from the Neanderthal. Of course I won't, but it was her voice I heard before clamping down on that idiot's ear (*"I pulled a Mike Tyson on that mother-fucker"*) and escaping his apartment.

"Well, okay. Hurry up and finish."

Jesse exchanges his phone for a game. Martina slaps his arm. "What?" he says.

"Miss Nelson wants you to study, not play around."

"I am studying! I'm studying this game."

Blond and blue-eyed, despite his baggy jeans and ratty plaid shorts, Jesse has the solidly Waspy looks of someone who belongs at Park Royce Preparatory, one of the top schools in the Bay Area. But he lives in a foster home and grew up in the hood, as they say. He's been dating Martina since they were freshmen, a lifetime in teen years. His foster mother, Eula, dotes on him, and his foster brother, Angelo, a senior, makes sure he's treated just like everyone else.

He and Martina continue to bicker like the old married couple they've already become. I tell them to quiet down. "Why are you all here, anyway? People are trying to study," I say.

They look up at the brainiacs as if they've never seen people study before, then answer at once: "We are studying!" "There's nothin' to do outside!" "It's chill in here!"

"Well, if you're staying, please find something productive to do. I know at least two of you have English homework."

Martina smiles her I'm-so-cute smile and takes out *Long Day's Journey into Night*, our final play of the year. When she slaps Jesse again, he takes out a math book.

Everyone finally quiets down, and I'm in solid grading mode, one essay after another, until I hear Sharayray: "Miss Nelson, is you a alcoholic?"

I look up and all eyes are on me. I buy time saying, "The question is '*Are* you an alcoholic?'"

"Well, *are* you?"

Since we alcoholics are masters at lying, honesty is a huge focus of AA meetings, but I'm not sure that admitting my addiction to a group of teens is the right thing to do. Even so, most of the faculty knows about Jesse's mother's drug addiction, which is why he was put into foster care in the first place, and the brainiacs must be here instead of at home for a reason. Which is my way of saying these kids have seen it all.

They continue to stare.

Oh, fuck it.

"Everyone has struggles in life, and I've struggled with alcohol, but I'm trying my best do better. We all have challenges, but as long as we're alive, we're capable of change. I've made mistakes, but I'm here for you and I don't plan on giving up on any of you."

Martina chomps on her gum. "Do you have a boyfriend?"

Hearing her question, Sharayray and Jesse throw up their hands as if she's gone too far. "You can't be asking her shit like that!"

"That's none of your business!"

"You asked her if she was an alcoholic!"

"That's different!" Sharayray says.

"How?"

"It just is!"

"I ask all my teachers if they have boyfriends!"

"But it's beside the point," says Jesse. "We were talking about something serious, and then you have to get up in her business."

"I wasn't in her business any more than you were, fool."

The matter of my alcoholism is soon lost in their bickering, and after another minute I tell them to go back to their reading. Martina has a mouth, and I'm sure she'll spread what she heard here today, but I'm not worried. I have a feeling most won't care. Besides, I'm doing my best now, today, this hour, this minute; that has to be enough.

Thirty minutes later, Jesse and Martina have decided they've studied as long as they can handle it and start to leave the trailer hand in hand. "Use protection," I tell them as they walk past my desk.

"Miss Nelson! Dang!"

"I'm just sayin'."

Jesse adds, "Don't worry, Miss Nelson; the last thing I want is a baby."

"And you think I do!" Martina shrieks.

"No. I was talking about me."

"If you're talking about making a baby, you're talking about *us*! Unless you're making babies with somebody else!"

"I'm not making babies with anybody; that's my point!"

They continue their back-and-forth as they head out the door.

When it's quiet again, Sharayray raises her hand. "Miss Nelson, you remember how you gave me that list of books to read summer before last?" She'd just finished her freshman year and hadn't earned a grade lower than a B+. But I was onto her and wanted to keep her love of reading alive, so I gave her a list of fifteen books, everything from *Their Eyes Were Watching God* to *The Hunger Games.* She read them all. But by her sophomore year . . . with all my drinking, I dropped the ball and stopped paying her or any of my students much attention outside the bare minimum.

"Yes, I remember."

"Can I have another list for this summer?"

"Of course."

"I was thinking maybe if you can help me with my writing a little, I could work on that, because I already like to read, Miss Nelson. I'm good at it. I understand all the themes. I've just been thinking, if you give me another list, I can read and work on my writing. I'm thinking I want to go to Berkeley. You know. I can go there if I want to."

As soon as she says Berkeley, the male brainiac turns to look at her, and she immediately gives him the finger. "Whatchu lookin' at? You think I can't go to college? You the only one think he can go to Berkeley? Yeah, I'll see you there. You little—"

"Sharayray."

"Sorry."

The boy turns in his seat, and Sharayray sticks out her tongue.

"Sharayray."

"Sorry."

"Of course you can go to Berkeley," I say.

The brainiac frowns at me as if I'm the purveyor of false dreams, then shakes his head and returns to his book. When I know he's not looking, I stick my tongue out at him, then look over at Sharayray, who is already focused intently on reading the play in her hand.

I place my bet on Sharayray.

A week later, I'm standing on Clem's porch with a box of cookies from Lulu's. I spoke with Sherry about how lonely I sometimes feel, and she recommended something I already intuitively knew: I need more friends. Hence, Clem. I've thought of her from time to time since Friends of Friends in Mourning. She was the only person who seemed as lost as I was that night, and that her husband, child, and brother all died at once still seems unimaginable. When I told Deacon Morris about her, he suggested in his own way that instead of merely thinking about her, I should put some action behind the thought and see how she's doing. Kindness, he reminded me, is a verb.

I had to stop by Diane Montgomery's to find out where she lives. I remembered Clem telling me she was within walking distance of the Montgomerys', but I had no way of knowing which house. Diane was nice enough to point out her place, a two-story craftsman with the blinds drawn tight—"just up the street"—then invited me in for coffee. When I declined, she made me promise I'd return to a meeting sometime soon. "It's important we go through a thorough mourning process. You must come back." I responded by telling her I had enough meetings to attend as it was and left it at that.

After the third ring I begin to wonder if Clem is home, but then the door creeps open and she pokes out her head. It's almost eleven, but from the way she winces at the sunlight and clutches the top of her robe, I have a strong feeling I've forced her out of bed. I smile, ready to say, *Surprise!* but as I stare into her perfectly blank face, I think better of it. Why the hell did I think she'd remember me? I haven't seen her in months. I'm here, however, and figure—"Clem, it's me . . . Piper? We met at the Friends of Friends in Mourning meeting about . . . five months ago? I was thinking of you and thought I'd stop by. I haven't forgotten you." I hold up the box of cookies as a hopeful reminder. "These are for you. You really liked them when we met. Remember?"

She opens the door but only so wide. Her tousled auburn hair, heavy bags under her eyes, and wan coloring all suggest she's suffering from one hell of a hangover, and it's best I make a quick exit. I speak rapidly. "I would've called, but I never got your phone number. Diane pointed out your house. I was thinking about you and wanted to say hello, that's all. I'll just leave now. Just—here—I'd like you to have the cookies. I don't know if you ever made it to Lulu's, but I remembered how much you liked them."

She takes the box as though there might be a bomb planted inside. I feel my face grow warm with embarrassment and start to leave, but just as I do, I catch a gleam of recognition in her eye as if *her* hungover synapses are kicking in and she's finally remembering the whos and whats.

She opens the door farther but then suddenly cups her mouth with her hand and shoves the box of cookies into my chest. *"Shit."* With this she turns and runs back inside, leaving the door wide-open.

"Clem?" I step inside, only to be greeted by a dark, quiet house. "Clem? You okay?" I walk farther inside. The rooms are spacious and well kept, but the curtains are drawn, giving the whole place a haunted-house feel.

"Clem?"

I hear a toilet flush and follow the sound down a second hallway that leads to a bathroom. I find her on the floor in ye

olde familiar pose: on her knees, head suspended above the toilet. When she looks up, her head makes a wide arc until it falls
back. "You might want to close that door less you want to
see me—"

Too late. She pukes again.

I take a facecloth from the towel rack, run warm water over
it, and hand it to her. She thanks me, wipes her mouth, and
flushes. She then stares up at me, eyes bright with recognition.
"Piper Diaper. Piper the Sniper."

"Lactation Station."

She laughs and chucks her head toward the toilet. "Sorry you
had to see that. Had a little too much last night."

She goes to the sink and washes her hands. She looks three
times older than when I saw her last, and she wears men's pj's
beneath her lopsided robe that looks a size too big. She's got two
pairs of socks on each foot.

She notices me staring. "I must look like glorified shit."

"Hangover'll do that to you."

She gazes into the mirror and starts rapidly pinching her
cheeks but then gives up. "How about a cup of coffee?"

"Sounds good."

I follow her down another hallway. My pace slows as I
take in the framed family photos lining the wall. There's a photo
of a young Clem holding a little boy; Clem and her husband on
their wedding day; a teenager, who I guess is her son, giving the
peace sign on a beach; father and son standing on a boat. I'm so
busy staring at them all, I'm half startled when I hear Clem clear
her throat. I turn and see her waiting for me at the end of the
hall, hand on hip. "Kitchen's this way."

The kitchen is the only room so far with the curtains open.
There are several casement windows and two French doors leading out to the backyard. Inside, there's an oak table with six

chairs, and an island with a second sink and wine refrigerator; the refrigerator is the size of a vault.

"Nice place you have, Clem."

"I probably should've moved years ago, the place is so big, but I've been here too long and can't get myself to do it." She takes a hair band from a drawer and puts her hair in a ponytail. "Lotta memories here, too."

I set the cookies on the counter and sit at the large table. She doesn't exaggerate. I can feel the ghosts: Tommy leaving for school and Frank sitting where I sit right now reading the morning paper. Clem at the sink telling Tommy he's not too big to give his mother a kiss before he leaves the house. My throat clutches at the thought of everyone lost.

Clem opens a cabinet and then another. "Now where is the coffee? I swear, every time the cleaning lady comes, she moves everything around."

It's the way she does a backward two-step before closing each cabinet that makes me wonder if she's still buzzed. "Hmph, guess I'm out. What do you say to mimosas instead?" Before I can say AA, she sets champagne and orange juice on the table. I stare at the champagne while feeling my pulse quicken. It's not that I want to drink, but I do feel anxious, anxious enough that I think it might be best if I leave.

"You know, I feel like I'm intruding. I should probably take off. I don't want to be a bother."

"Don't be silly; you just got here."

"I know but—"

"You stay put. I know how to treat company—don't come here saying I don't. You showin' up here is a surprise is all." She opens a cabinet and takes out a bottle of aspirin and a coffee mug, then pours champagne into the mug and tosses back the aspirin. "That's better." She finds two flutes next and puts them on the table. "We'll have us a nice brunch is what we'll have." She pours far more champagne than orange juice in each flute and holds up her glass. "Cheers."

I move my hands to my lap.

"Well, come on," she says, wiggling her glass. "Cheers."

"I think I'll pass on the champagne."

Her gaze becomes instantly sharp and focused. "What gives, Piper Sniper? My champagne isn't good enough for you?" She frowns when I remain silent. "Oh, I get it. You didn't come for a visit. You came to judge me. You didn't want company. You're like all the rest of 'em who think I'm a charity project. I'll tell you what, though—I'm perfectly fine." She crosses her legs and takes a dainty sip of champagne as if she were sitting at a Southern cotillion. It's all for effect, of course, gestures she hopes will prove she's not drunk that work to the contrary. I rise from the table. If I'm of the ilk that drinks to pass out, she's the angry drunk everyone had best avoid.

"Where do you think you're going? You do judge me. You came here to judge me!"

"I told you why I'm here, Clem. I know it was a few months ago, but I thought you were nice and we had a nice conversation. I thought maybe we could be friends, and I brought you the cookies because I was thinking about you." I start to leave. Problem is, the house is a maze, and I can't find the front door.

"Piper!"

"Where's the door?" I yell back.

"Not tellin' you!"

I turn and see her standing a few feet away. She clutches tightly at her robe, her mouth slack. "I apologize. You surprised me, showin' up here. I had no business being accusatory, though. I'm not used to people being nice, wanna know the truth; people tend to pity me, and it turns my stomach. I hate pity."

"Trust me, I don't pity you. I know what that's like myself, remember?"

"Come on back to the kitchen. I'm ashamed of being so foolish. It was nice of you to stop by. I do apologize."

We return to the kitchen, and she sets out the cookies and plates. We both take a cookie as though they'll magically make us feel better, and they do. "My Lord," Clem says, chewing her macaroon. "These are as delicious as I remember. Who is the woman who bakes these things? I'll tell you what, Piper—we should kidnap her and make her bake on demand." We continue eating, giddy with sugar. She mentions "that fine ex of yours" and tells me Spencer and "that girl who snapped him up" no longer attend meetings.

"They're no longer in mourning," I tell her. "They're expecting."

"Expectin' what?"

I look at her for a beat.

"No."

"Yep. She's knocked up."

I tell her the entire story while we eat and she drinks. When she refills her glass, heavy on champagne again, she asks, "So what gives? You don't strike me as the type to pass up champagne. Way I remember it, you enjoyed your wine."

"I sure did. A little too much."

"You quit drinking?"

"I had to. Everything was getting out of control—to put it mildly."

"Everything is always out of control, honey. That's the one thing you can count on."

"Yeah, but I was losing control of my life. I joined AA."

"AA, huh? I never understood why people would want to sit around telling everybody their troubles. Seems like a waste of time, you ask me."

"It helps to be around people who get what you're going through."

"Nobody gets what we've been through. It's bullshit if they say they do."

"We don't get a license on pain because we've lost people we love," I say, channeling my inner Sherry. "Everybody gets his or her share in one way or another."

"You try to come here and preach to me, you'd better have a better sermon than that."

"I'm not trying to preach. No one gets exactly what anyone is going through, but AA is a particular kind of support you can't find anywhere else. I couldn't, anyway."

She lifts the bottle of champagne. "This is all the support I need." I watch her make a point of taking a large gulp.

"What you starin' at?"

"You come off like you're strong, but it's okay to be afraid."

"Who says I'm afraid? What would I be afraid of? I had the worst thing happen. I have nothing to fear anymore."

"But you are afraid. You're hiding, Clem." I think of the pictures in the hallway, how active she once was. "You could be doing so much more with your life. What would your husband say?"

She's suddenly cold and steely eyed. "Leave my husband out of this, you hear me?"

I think of how people used Hailey against me, or so I thought, and let it go. "Apologies."

I wait until I decide on another tactic, my humans-bumbling-through-life theory. I don't feel at all that I can get through to her, but I'm here and may as well try. I think of Deacon Morris.

"Life is hard, but we don't have to face it alone, Clem. Just the other day I read about a mother of three who fell asleep behind the wheel of her minivan, sending herself and her kids plunging into the Ohio River. Only one child survived."

"That's inspiring."

"I'm trying to say we're not alone in our grief. Mothers have been losing children since the beginning of time, and I'm sure every mother who's ever lost a child feels as if she's the only mother to suffer such tragedy. And she has every right, too. But we're not alone in it. All we can do is live for those who can't be with us, and help one another out as best we can. I mean, do we really know what any of this is about? We abuse one another, die from illness, fight, make love, but this is it. We're just floating through space on a relatively small planet, not knowing what we're doing or why we're here. As far as I can tell, what else is life about except helping one another out?"

She stiffens, then turns and looks toward her backyard. "I know Frank wouldn't be pleased with how I've given up, but it's hard. Eight years ago, when I lost them, it was like everything stopped for me."

"I know."

She keeps her face turned as she sniffles and wipes at her tears. "Oh, you," she admonishes, while grabbing a napkin and tugging at her robe. "You have some nerve coming here and getting me all upset. Look at me blubbering and carrying on."

I reach over and take her hand.

She turns and continues dabbing at her face. "It's not like I've never thought of any of this. It's just that I get tired like everybody else." She gives my hand a firm pat and pulls back as she looks at me. "I can't believe you're here, Diaper."

I push the plate toward her, and she nods and takes a cookie.

I wait a moment before I ask, "What are you doing in the next few hours?"

She makes a face. "Not going to AA with you, I'll tell you that much."

"I wasn't going to invite you to a meeting, Twin Peaks. I was actually wondering if you'd want to catch a movie."

"A movie?" she says, as though I've invited her to a whorehouse.

"Yeah. You know, the place where you sit in the dark and stare at a big screen while you eat popcorn? What do you say? We'll drown our sorrows in bonbons and overproduced schlock."

"I don't know, Piper Sniper."

"Oh, come on. It's just a movie."

"I usually hang around here on Sundays."

"Yeah, I'm guessing you hang around here every day; that's the point."

She clutches her robe. She looks increasingly irritated, but then her expression softens and she all but smiles. "You know what? Damn it all, a movie sounds like fun. I haven't been to a movie theater in a lifetime. I'll take a quick shower and we'll see what's playin'."

"Great."

I can tell even she's surprised by how quickly she gets up from the table. "I won't be a minute. Help yourself to tea if you want."

She's already in the hall when she barks loudly, "Did you hear me offer you tea?"

"Yes, Clem."

"Well, put some on. No sense sittin' there with nothing to do. It's in the top cabinet on your left. And don't eat all those cookies. We'll take the rest to the theater."

"Yes, Clem."

I listen as she climbs the stairs, mumbling to herself about what she should wear and how she needs to find her wallet, which has to be somewhere in the house; she knows it.

thirteen

It's Saturday and I've been spending the morning working on next week's lesson plans. My juniors and seniors are still studying *Long Days Journey into Night*, while my freshmen will be starting *Of Mice and Men*, their last novel of the semester. April will be here in a couple of weeks, and the kids are already anticipating summer.

After the movie on Sunday, Clem and I had dinner together two nights in a row, and I managed to convince her to join me at the mourners' group. I don't know what it is about Deacon Morris and the people in that church rec room, but Clem found herself telling her story and has been attending the meetings with me ever since. We're becoming fast friends, Clem and I, and it feels—*good*. I still call Sherry on the occasion that I feel an urge to drink, but the calls are becoming less frequent. I'm not sure if I'll get Clem to come with me to an AA meeting, but she never drinks around me and says she's cutting back to a couple of glasses of wine a night. Thing is, I believe her. Not everyone who drinks heavily is an alcoholic, and even as bad off as she was, Clem may never have crossed over into the territory of good old-fashioned, I-can't-stop-drinking-despite-the-fact-that-I'm-destroying-my-life alcoholism.

I'm still working when I hear a sharp, rather mean-sounding knock at my door. I turn down my stereo and open the door to Hélène's pissed-off face. "Hélène?"

"Your *sis*tah promise me the day off, but what does she do? She goes to New York with that man, that Cur*tice*. I have no idea where your mother is, and I don't care what your sistah say; they are *not* Mrs. Calloway's responsibility. Her job is to clean the house, not look after the girls. They are not Tru's responsibility either. They are *her* responsibility. They need their mother."

"I'm sorry," I say, scratching my head. *"What?"*

She rolls her eyes in a huff. "The girls are downstairs with Tru. Your sistah—she promise me the day off. She say she be back from New York this morning. But is she back? Of course she not back. She tell me to take them to your mother, but your mother is not home, so I bring them here. Those girls know I care. They know I will shed my own blood for them. But they need to know someone in their *family* cares." She points her finger at me.

I hold up my hands. "Hey, I'm on your side." With the wedding growing closer, Margot is proving to be more selfish than ever. I'm thankful I get to see the girls more often, but I also agree with Hélène: They need their mother.

Hélène says, "I know you already had them last week, but I need time off. What your sister think? I'm her slave? No! I'm going to LA. If you can't keep them, I leave them with Tru. That woman? Your *sis*tah? She crazy. She think of no one but herself."

"It's fine if you leave them here. I'd love to have them."

She looks me suspiciously up and down. "Good. I get them."

I gaze around my apartment. I was planning on cleaning later, but now that the girls are staying with me, I can use their help. They need to learn that they don't exist to be waited on hand and foot.

They walk inside with Tru, whose height and girth always makes my apartment feel half its size. He excuses himself as he continues to talk on the phone. I give the girls a hug. When Margot tries to pull away, I refuse to let her go. "It's been so long!" I tease. "I've missed you! Never leave me again!"

"It's been four days," she says. "You've got problems."

They head straight to the couch and whip out their phones like synchronized gun slayers.

"Uh-uh-uh. No phones today."

"But it's important!"

"I don't care how impor—"

Tru taps my arm. "'Scuse me. Need to give you this." He hands me a fat envelope.

"Thanks," I say, feeling the weight of the bills and already thinking about lunch at Table Eight and dinner at Osenta. "What time are you picking them up?"

He holds up a finger and brings his phone to his ear. "Actually, Curtis would like to speak to you. She's right here, Boss." He hands me the phone.

"Sister-in-law!"

"Not quite."

Curtis chuckles in that way of his. I already know where this is headed but decide to wait it out. "So listen. Have you seen Margot's tweet?"

Margot is *so busy* lately she typically communicates through the twins—"Mom says hello"; "Mom says call her later"—or texts. Often she simply refers me to her blog or Twitter feed.

"Believe it or not, I also have a life, so no, I have not seen her new tweet."

"We're gonna be a part of this cooking show. The best cake these chefs come up with will be one of the cakes at the wedding. We fly to SoCal tonight and tape tomorrow, so since you have the girls already, how about keeping them for—"

"Is my sister there?"

"She's on the phone."

"Tell her I want to speak to her."

I glance over at the girls, who are busy texting. I then look up at Tru while twirling my finger next to my ear. He grins before looking down at his feet. "Will you watch them a sec?" I whisper. "I'm going to step outside for a little privacy."

"Absolutely."

I step into the hall, closing the door behind me. "Put my sister on the phone!" I say through gritted teeth.

"Simmer down, Sis. You experiencing your monthly business or something?"

"Put her on the phone, Curtis."

A second later: "Isn't it exciting? *Best Chef* wants us on their show!"

"It's great, Margot, but if you don't stop neglecting the girls, you're going to end up on a show about lousy mothers."

"I thought you said you like keeping them."

"I do. Of course I do, but don't *you* like them?"

"They know everything will return to normal after the wedding. Anyway, it would help so so so much if you could keep them for a couple of days. Please?"

"Curtis said you were picking them up tomorrow."

"What's one more day? Mom is flying with us, or I'd give them to her."

I feel my stomach drop when she mentions Mom. We're

working on three months since we haven't spoken. Margot knows what happened and tried to lecture me on getting help, but I basically told her what happens with Mom and me is none of her business. She hasn't mentioned it since. Why would she? As long as Margot is happy, so goes the world.

"I have to work on Monday, you know," I say. "I have this thing called a *job*?"

"I know that. Tru will pick them up on Monday and take them to school. Not a problem. Do you even know how big *Best Chef* is? This is all part of pumping my name before my show starts. I need to do this, P. It's very very important to me."

I hear Curtis in the background.

"I gotta go, P. You can watch them, right?"

Watching them will mean missing AA tonight and tomorrow, but I'm not leaving them with Tru. "Yes, of course."

"Thanks, Sis. I knew you'd come through. Love you, bye."

I go back inside and return Tru's phone. "My sistah, my sistah," I say, giving my best Hélène impression.

He smiles. "I'll get their bags."

I walk to the couch and sit directly between the girls, who continue their texting without missing a beat.

"I guess you two know you're staying here a couple of days?"

No response.

"Are you two listening to me?"

"I'm listening," Sophia says, eyes on her phone.

Margot continues moving her thumbs at breakneck speed. "I am, too." I try to grab the phone, but she's too quick and pulls away. "Stop, Auntie P. You can be, like, so immature."

"So, who are you texting? What could possibly be so important?"

"Nicole Liu," says Margot.

"And Ashley Mulligan-Peete. Nicole heard that Ashley kissed Brendan Richards, but it's, like, so not true."

"Brendan is dating Nicole," Margot offers.

"You guys are ten! What do you mean by dating?"

"Boyfriend and girlfriend. Now we have to tell her that Brendan didn't cheat on her; we know Brendan, and he's not like that."

"He's one of our best friends."

"And he told us he's been, like, so faithful."

"Isn't that a lot of drama for fifth grade?"

I watch their thumbs whiz across the keypads as they go about brokering peace accords between their posh friends. Tired of waiting, I snatch their phones and hold them high in the air.

"Hey! You can't do that!"

"I just did. No phones today."

They start to protest, but ignoring them, I put the phones in my purse, go into the kitchen, and take out a broom and a cleaning rag. They stare up at me as though planning twin curses. "Time for a quiz. Sophia, do you remember what this is?" I hold up the broom and watch as she rolls her eyes. "Margot? Do you recognize this?" She crosses her arms dismissively. "If you haven't figured it out, you two are helping me clean my apartment today. The entire apartment. Top to bottom."

They look at each other before returning to shooting their twin-powered glares on me.

"Like, why don't you have a house cleaner, anyway?" Margot asks.

"Yeah, why don't you just have somebody else clean this place?" Sophia adds.

"Are you two going to *pay* someone to come and clean?" I ask, hand on hip.

They look at each other: *"We could!"*

"This isn't about me, you two. It's about you learning responsibility and how to take care of yourselves."

"Seems to me we're taking care of you," Margot says.

I give Sophia the rag. She takes it apprehensively with her face turned away as though I've handed over a dead skunk.

"Get up. We're cleaning. This'll be fun. I'll even put on some Beethoven."

"Oh God," Margot says. "It gets worse."

My apartment is now officially spotless except for two full trash bags sitting in front of the door, waiting to be taken downstairs. We head for the bins out back. Mrs. Mathews calls down from her apartment window when she sees us, "Hey, you twins! How you *durin'*?"

"Fine."

"You helpin' your auntie with the trash?"

"Yes."

"Ain't that nice. You two sho 'nuff look alike. You ever get confused by who you is?"

The girls stare up at her curiously.

She eases herself farther out the window. "You know, Mrs. Sanders broke her hip. Yeah. Fell down, and it done broke something good. And you know Patrick got that new car. He's leasin' it. Gotta pay for it every month. Uh-huh." We wait as she continues telling us the day's news. All she needs is a ticker beneath her window announcing the stock market averages and Dow Jones returns. Her attention is diverted when her downstairs neighbor, Deborah, appears on the stoop. "Deborah, I know you hear your phone ringing in that apartment of yours. I know you hear it, 'cause I can hear it ringing myself! Why haven't you picked it up?"

"I knew I'd see you in a minute! What did you want?"

"You coming over for dinner tonight?! Anthony is bringing the steaks!"

Deborah and Mrs. Mathews continue shouting their conversation, and the twins and I are forgotten. I'm ready to suggest we go back inside, when two men pass pulling shopping carts filled with trash bags, each bag stuffed to capacity with cans and bottles. The carts are so full, the men use all their strength to make their way down the street. The taller one wears a towel around his head to keep the sun off his face. He could be a nameless drudge in any period stretching back to ancient days.

"Why are people always pulling shopping carts around here?" Sophia asks.

"Yeah. What's in them?" Margot asks.

"They collect empty bottles and cans and take them to the recycling center."

"Why?" Sophia asks.

"They get money for each can. That's how a lot of people get money."

"Really?"

They silently watch the men trudge up the street as if seeing ghosts.

While I sometimes bemoan their upbringing, I can't blame them for the limitations of their ivory-tower existence. I rest my hands on their shoulders. "We should get back inside and wash up. You two hungry yet?"

"I am," Sophia says. "What about Osento?"

"I'm tired of Osento," Margot says. "Let's go somewhere else."

I think of the wad of cash upstairs but then realize I don't want anything more than a burrito and chips. "You know," I say, "there's a perfectly good taqueria up the street. Why don't we just go there?"

"What's a taqueria?" they say in unison.

Oh. My. God.

• • •

Hours later, we're having dessert at Benoit, a French restaurant in the city. The taqueria went over surprisingly well for lunch, but after spending the day at the
Academy of Arts and Sciences and Golden Gate Park, the girls
wanted their typical four-star prix fixe meal for dinner. They
each order dessert in perfect French. San Francisco Stargazers
meets the third Saturday of every month at Pacific Point, and
since we're already in the city, I'm thinking that it would be nice
to stargaze with someone other than myself. Only problem, the
girls have never warmed to stargazing no matter how many lessons I've given, and I can't imagine them jumping up and down
with glee if I suggest spending an hour staring at the stars before
heading home.

I wait until half of their dessert is finished and the sugar has
kicked in before broaching the subject. "Hey, you two, I just
thought of something fun we could do."

"No," Margot says.

"We are not watching *Star Trek* again," adds Sophia.

"I wasn't going to ask you to watch *Star Trek*, smarty pants.
I realized something."

They exchange dubious glances.

"SF Stargazers meets tonight. Isn't that great?"

"No," Margot says, continuing to eat.

"We don't want to go."

"Oh, come on. They meet at the beach and they always have
hot chocolate, and they tell great stories. You don't even need to
bring a telescope! People just show up! Doesn't that sound
like fun?"

"No."

Margot says, "If I had my phone back, now *that* would be fun."

"But it's a full moon tonight and with the fancy scopes they have, we'll be able to see every crater and nook."

"No, thank you."

"No, thank you. Hailey liked telescopes, not us."

Margot shoots Sophia a look, and she immediately gazes down at the table. "Sorry."

I'm not sure how much the girls remember about Hailey; since I stopped talking about her long ago, I know I haven't helped matters. Now I worry that all that's left of her memory is a mystery cousin they hardly remember and a tragedy surrounding their aunt.

Deacon Morris said once that when you hide pain, it only shows up later in one form or another, just more virulent. He says it's best to deal with it straight on and with honesty. I think of this as I look at them.

"It's okay that we talk about her, you know. It's my fault for making you think otherwise."

"It won't make you sad?" Sophia asks.

"To some degree, I'm sure. But it's important. I don't want you to forget her."

"She looks cute in her pictures."

"Yeah, she was. She was really smart, too. Like you two."

"Do you think you'll have more kids?"

Margot bumps Sophia's elbow and glares.

"It's okay, Margot. I want you both to feel free to ask me anything—about anything. I'm always here for you, okay?"

They nod. I look at Sophia. "I can't imagine having another child."

"Maybe one day you will," Margot says.

"You shouldn't, like, be so alone," Sophia adds. "Sometimes you seem lonely."

"I'm working on that." I smile. "Which is another reason it would be *great* to see my old friends at SF Stargazers."

"Ha-ha," Sophia says. "*Not* going to happen."

Margot continues staring at me.

"You want to ask something else, sweetie?" I say.

"Yes."

"Go ahead. Like I said, you can ask anything you want."

"Can we, like, have our phones back now? It's been, like, *forever.*"

I use Mark Warner's homemade telescope to gaze at the moon. He made the telescope himself over a period of three years and even made his own equatorial mount. The girls and I came to the agreement that I could stargaze for one full hour if I returned their phones. They now sit on the beach next to a fire someone has made, roasting marshmallows and talking with another girl their age and her younger brother. We adults go about stargazing. There are roughly ten of us out tonight. I recognized most of them when we arrived, and I was greeted as though I'd been gone for only a couple meetings instead of nearly five years.

SF Stargazers isn't a social group in the usual sense. Even when I attended regularly, we rarely discussed our personal lives and tended to stick with those topics we couldn't talk about with non-stargazers—topics we were hungry to discuss, such as trips to various observatories, certain star findings, or telescope modifications and additions. That's what makes the group so special. We know absolutely nothing about one another, yet we feel grateful for friends who speak the same language.

I'm especially happy to see Mark tonight. A regular Carl Sagan, Mark has always been able to answer any question I've thrown at him. He has every right to be proud of his telescope, a DS 3 with ultra light and lots of power. It's no wonder it took him three years to build. His telescope has such a long range I should probably seek out clusters and constellations, but Mark seems to understand my fascination with the moon tonight and tells me to take as long as I want. Which I do. It's a perfectly clear sky and nice to be able to inhale the smell of the ocean as I stare at the moon's craters and shadows, ridges and crooks and hills. "It's gorgeous," I murmur.

"She sure is," I hear Mark say. "Can't beat Earth's satellite for beauty. Her face is bruised from the meteoroids that banged her up after the original big bang, but she looks just fine to me."

I pause long enough to smile up at him. He holds a cup of cocoa in his hands and wears a fleece jacket and his trusty binoculars around his neck. His silver hair blows in the wind. "Glad you're back," he says, which for a nerdy stargazer like himself may as well be a confession of complete love and adoration.

"Glad to be back," I say with a smile.

He looks up through his binoculars. "My biggest dream is to go to the moon and set up my telescope and look at Earth. I want to see how she'd look through my viewfinder."

"I like that idea."

I gaze through the telescope again. I'd always thought I'd bring Hailey to one of the meetings with me when she was old enough. I would have loved for her to meet Mark and to have shown her off. She would have liked Mark's idea of going to the moon with a telescope.

I imagine her now, older even—twenty, thirty—her shoes covered in moon dust as she sets up her telescope and stares down at Earth. And hell, since it's my fantasy, I imagine she finds me through her viewfinder, and I find her through mine. We smile at each other and laugh and wave. The thought that she might find me here, some two hundred fifty thousand miles away, makes me feel less lonely, more appreciative even. I know

Hailey would want me to enjoy my time here on Earth, to make the most of it. Earth is a lovely little planet, after all, with its perfect mix of air and water, gravity and sky, spinning forever and ever eastward on its axis, tiny as a pebble, suspended in a sea of black.

fourteen

Coco, all three hundred–plus pounds of her, takes two steps forward. Her buttocks undulate beneath her cotton top; her calf muscles quicken and relax. What are clunky, ugly shoes for the rest of us may as well be ballet slippers for her, as she extends a dainty, pointed foot before each step. The noise of the bowling alley recedes as one of Tchaikovsky's drippingly romantic violin concertos swells behind her. She then swings her arm back, and we watch the ball catapult down the lane and hit the pins in an explosion of white and black.

Another strike.

Clem and I don't bother applauding. Coco's strikes are now legend and all but expected.

"I think we've been duped," Clem says.

Coco walks back and takes a slow, meditative pull from her root beer. She was chatty and gregarious before walking through the doors of Albany Lanes, but as soon as she took her personal ball—gold and pink and engraved with her initials—from her personal bag—also gold and pink with *Hot Coco* embroidered at the top—she was all business, leaving Clem and me regretting the ten-dollar bet to the first-place winner.

She checks the monitor now. Her score so far is 130. Clem has forty points; I have thirty-two. Since we three started to bond over punch at the mourners' group, Clem and I have been trying to convince Coco to spend time with us. For weeks, we suggested dinner or lunch or even tea and cookies, but Coco always said no. That was until last week when Clem asked, "Isn't there anything you'd want to do? I know for myself it's no good staying in the house all the time. Piper and I are up for anything. You'll have a lot of fun." Clem looked at me expectedly and I gave a firm nod. "Yeah, just last night Clem convinced me to watch *The Notebook* for the first time. Let me tell you, nonstop excitement." I pretended to put my finger down my throat.

Clem gave me a look. "We'd love to see you outside of this here rec room, Coco. Isn't there anything you'd like to do?"

And that was when Coco said slowly, "Let's go bowling."

Coco sits next to me and wipes her hands with her special towel while Clem stands and readies herself. "Remember to keep your eye on the center line in that floor," Coco advises.

"I am tryin'!"

Clem brings her ball to the tip of her nose and gives her ass a wiggle. She wears tight white pants and a tight pink shirt. She's wearing makeup now, and her hair, dyed to resemble the dark red of her youth, is pulled back by a floral scarf. Clem, it turns out, is a babe.

Our neighbor has certainly taken a liking to her. George is a potbellied man the next lane over, and he can't help but stare with his bottom lip hanging open every time she takes a turn. His friend, Leonard, apologized for his behavior, explaining that George is recently divorced. But George, who's in his late fifties and roughly the same age as Clem, seems to think that because, like Clem, he's also from South Carolina and lived in a town only ten miles from where she grew up—("You grew up in Jarvis? You don't say! Do you know a fellow by the name of Randy Truss?" And Clem's cool response, "Can't say that I do")—he has every right to ogle and flirt.

"You need help with that ball, girl?" he says, watching her.

"I never needed no help with balls," Clem retorts.

"I bet you don't." He grins at Leonard who, embarrassed, goes for the fries he's eating.

"Let her alone now," Coco admonishes. "You know better than to break a bowler's concentration."

"Hell, she's breaking mine in those tight pants of hers."

Clem shakes her ass again and trots down the lane. We watch the ball fly straight up in the air and crash-land on the seamless wood floor before it rolls into the gutter.

George says, "Impressive."

"Oh shut up, you," Clem snaps.

He laughs, heaves himself up from his chair, and gets his ball. A few steps and—*strike*. He turns and smiles at Clem. "Why don't you let me give you a lesson or two?"

Clem holds her ball near the tip of her nose as she waits to take her second turn. "I doubt there's anything of relevance that *you* can teach *me*."

"Wanna make a bet?"

"Try to throw with more force," Coco offers.

Clem straightens her shoulders and back. She takes concentrated steps toward the pins, but as soon as she releases the ball, it shoots backward, flying straight toward me. I hear Coco shout, "Duck!" and cross my arms in front of my face, hoping I come out alive. When I hear a loud thud, I slowly open my eyes and watch Clem's ball roll past my foot.

"Sorry 'bout that," she says with a scowl.

"Pins are in the opposite direction!" George laughs.

"If you'd shut your trap, I'd be able to concentrate!"

"Ever think of joining a league, girl?" he says as Clem retrieves her ball. "You got talent!"

"I sure wish you'd hush up!"

Coco and I exchange looks. "Go on," she says to me. "Show 'em what you got."

I manage to knock down eight pins between my two turns. Then Coco's up—all grace and beauty on a bowling alley floor. Even George is mesmerized.

Strike.

Coco and her son, Reginald, were regular bowlers. They'd go as far as Vallejo to join weekend leagues. Coco was proud to tell us she keeps his room exactly as it was; it's still filled with all of his bowling trophies and ribbons. She hasn't bowled since his death and says her game is off, but Clem and I sure as hell can't tell.

After another game, we go to the pizzeria next door. It's spring break, and I've done nothing much except sleep, read, and hang out with Clem. Mostly we watch the bad movies she picks and eat ourselves silly at restaurants we've never tried before. Yesterday we went to a day spa in the Claremont Hotel—her treat. She says I'm too pretty not to keep myself up, and she talked me into a pedicure, manicure, and even getting my eyebrows shaped. And now here I am sitting in a booth with my two perfectly arched brows and two new friends, laughing and eating pizza. *Who would have thought?*

Before we left the bowling alley, George repeatedly asked Clem for her number, and now Coco and I tease her.

"You should have given him your number," says Coco. "When a man has a puppy-dog crush, you know he'll treat you right."

"*Pishaw!* Did you see that gut? Looked nine months pregnant and ready to deliver any second."

"Pishaw?" I say. "Did you just say pishaw?"

Coco says, "I'd rather have a man with some meat on his bones than somebody I fear I'll break soon as I get on top of him. Ain't nothin' sexy about going to bed with a man you think you might crush. You know what I'm sayin'? I like a man who can bring it! I like a man who makes me *feeeeel* like a woman." Clem and I watch, eyebrows raised, as she runs her hands over her body while rolling out her chest and undulating her hips.

"I'll say." Clem nods.

"You should get back on the horse, Clem," Coco tells her. "We are all sad women at this here table, but the body has needs, plain and simple. Nobody is saying you have to marry the man, but if he's willing and you're in a dry spell, you gotta make it happen. I'm just sayin'. Coco don't go too long without a little somethin' somethin'. I don't think it's good for a woman's overall attitude."

Clem says, "And I don't think it's good for a woman to sleep with men with big guts. I don't like 'em skinny; I ain't sayin' that. But you know Frank was active, and I'm used to a man who likes to get outdoors and who's in good shape. Frank and I played tennis and golf. We sailed. There were trips to wineries. Oh we had a good ol' time."

Coco stares at Clem as if she's just described trips to Neptune with layovers on Mercury. I gather that she can't fathom living the kind of life Clem shared with Frank, who made a huge profit off stocks and flew his own plane. Coco and I live a mere ten minutes from Clem, but I doubt Coco has ever been to Elmwood, and to Coco, Clem's life is probably more like what she sees on TV. But that's the point Deacon Morris always makes: If we allow it, loss can bring us together, break down our walls, and make us more caring—if we have the courage to let it happen.

"You should see this one here's ex-husband, Coco," says Clem, motioning to me. "He showed up one night at the meeting I used to go to, as handsome as hell. I wasn't surprised at all when this young thing snatched him right up."

"A young thing, huh?" Coco says, ready for a story.

I help myself to another slice of pizza and tell her the entire   Spence-once-loved-Piper-then-dumped-her-for-a-nitwit story, start to finish. I end circling back to the beginning of our conversation. "I guess you could say Spencer is my type. Smart. Tall. That's what I like."

"Well, he can't be too smart, dumping you the way he did," Clem says.

"Thanks."

"I always hoped that Reginald would be *honest* with whoever he ended up with. I hate men who lie to you. Why they think we can't tell they lyin', I'll never understand. I brought him up in the church and on the Bible and taught him from day one, respect women and show respect to whoever you're dating."

"I told my Tommy not to bring any mousy women home," Coco says. "I have no time for women who don't have a spine."

"Were you ever married, Coco?" I ask.

"Twice. By the time I found out I was pregnant with Reginald, I was finished with men." She shakes her head. "They some strange, you know what I'm sayin'?"

Clem and I nod.

"But when Reginald was born, you know how you do, I fell in love with him."

"I wanted a boy," Clem says. "I love how they dote on their mommas. My Tommy always doted on me. And I loved being the lady of the house looking after my boys."

We all fall silent as if her comment has induced us to go back to those days when we were mothers and caregivers. The moment doesn't last very long, though, because in walks George just then, belly and all. I nudge Clem with my elbow and gesture toward the entrance. When they make eye contact, George doesn't have sense enough to leave her alone and struts right up to our table.

Clem glowers. "You stalkin' me?"

"Naw, I ain't stalkin' you. This is America, and I have an inalienable right to eat. Free country, last I heard."

Clem glances at his belly, currently hovering above our table, round as Jupiter. "Looks to me like you're taking good advantage of your inalienable right to eat. What happened to your friend? *Annoy* him to death?"

"You sure don't hold nothin' back." He glances at Coco and me while chucking his thumb. "She always so sharp-tongued?"

"*Yes,*" we say together.

"Leonard's gone on to his family. I'm here by myself." His demeanor changes as he runs a hand over his hair. When Clem doesn't say anything, he tips an imaginary hat. "I don't mean to bother you ladies. You all have a good day now."

He starts toward a table in the back. I glance over at Coco, and we fix our eyes on Clem.

She gives her head a firm shake. "No."

Coco says, "It's just pizza. He means no harm."

"Look at him, Clem," I add. "He's all alone."

She looks over. George sits in a wide booth all by his lonesome self while he studies the menu. He wears long tube socks and corduroy shorts, and he has tucked his napkin in the top of his shirt. Clem shivers dramatically.

"What does Deacon Morris say?" I ask.

"Gotta pass on kindness; otherwise it doesn't get passed around," Coco replies.

"Oh, you two," Clem gripes. "You all want the company of a fool, so who am I to stop you?" She tosses her napkin on the table and struts over to George. From the back, in her tight pants and top, tennis shoes, and bouncing ponytail, she looks like a young woman from the 1950s.

Coco and I grin as we watch the silent film they put on: George's face lighting up when he sees her; Clem thrusting her hand toward our table and practically scowling as she invites him over; George clapping his hands and rising from his table before she can say, *Come join us.*

To make room, I move next to Coco. George squishes in next to Clem, who scoots as far away from him as she can. "Happy?" she says in a huff.

Coco and I smile. "Welcome, George," I say brightly. "Pizza?"

fifteen

"I am tired of all your complainin', woman. Like I said, the past is the past. Let it go!" Detrane is standing in front of my desk, pointing at Sharayray, who flutters her hands this way and that. She wears a blond wig and an old shawl I bought at Goodwill.

"But I miss what I had! I was, like, so beautiful when I was a girl. I was, like, all virginal and sweet."

Laughter.

It's early May, and now that my students have finished reading *Long Day's Journey into Night*, I've asked them to contemporize a scene and act it out. We have roughly fifteen minutes left until the end of the school day, but no one watches the clock because everyone is focused on Detrane and Sharayray's performance.

Detrane falls to his knee and clutches his hand to his heart. "Baby, of course I remember how beautiful you were. I wanna be there for you, but you got to give up the crack! I can't stand . . ."

Sharayray flutters her hands and waits for him to continue, but he starts gazing out the window as if *he's* become dreamy-eyed, drug-addicted Mary Tyrone. Sharayray half whispers, half barks, "Finish your line!"

Detrane points his finger and leans toward the window. "Is that . . . Isn't that . . . ?"

We all turn to see. The class is silent for a second before Tranica lets out a full-throttle squeal, "It's *Curtis Randolph!*"

The entire class stampedes toward the windows.

"Everybody, back to your seats! Back to your seats!" But I'm ignored, and giving in, look out the window to see for myself. Sure enough. In a linen suit and loafers, Curtis stands next to a long, black limo. He's talking on the phone while Tru makes his way around the car and opens the door for Margot, who's also talking on the phone, clad in a barely-there minidress. The TV crew from her reality show hustles for the best shot of the school.

My students start shouting Curtis's name. I can hear the classes on either side of us clamoring for his attention as well. I shout over the din of excitement and misplaced celebrity obsession as best I can. "Sit down this instant! I mean it!"

"But, Miss Nelson, it's Curtis Randolph!"

"Ohhhh, he's so fine!"

"Girl, I can't believe this!"

I threaten to keep them after school if they don't sit down, and reluctantly they go back to their seats, looking pitiful and pouty. I tap my hand nervously on my desk, wondering if something has happened to the girls or even Mom. Why else would they show up like this? Did something so horrible happen that they couldn't phone? Then again, why the cameras? And if there was something serious to deal with, wouldn't Margot have had the decency to wear something that reached midthigh at least? *Eh, probably not.* At any rate, it's still my intention to keep my relationship with the football player a secret, and I figure I should stop them at the pass—so to speak.

I go to the classroom door and peek out the window. "Everybody, stay put. I'll be right back."

There's already a commotion outside. Next door, Mr. Kirsner has lost control of his class, and his students are now rushing Curtis with torn pieces of paper and notebooks, anything he might sign. Mr. Kirsner yells at everyone to get back inside the classroom while Curtis laughs and signs his autograph. Margot stands to the side, the phone still pressed to her ear. The cameramen and the guy with the enormous mic, or what I've learned is called a "boom," try to film the chaos while Tru does his best to push students back so Curtis can have some space. Then, John Jones, part of the school's security team and always called by his full name, rushes past. "What the hell is going on in here?!" But when he sees what the commotion is about, he only goes for his walkie-talkie. "Gonzo, man, get over here right now! You won't believe who I'm looking at! Stat, man! You gotta see this!" He then raises his phone in the air and starts snapping pictures.

Hearing all the noise, my students beg to be excused, but I stay put in front of the door. "Hold on a second!"

The director of the shoot asks John Jones something, and John Jones points to my classroom. The director then says something to Tru, who leads Curtis through the crowd and right to—
"Sis!"

Curtis takes me by the neck and pulls me into his massive chest. He grips me so tightly I can't see what's going on and can only hear the hysteria breaking out. "Miss Nelson is Curtis Randolph's sister!" "Oh my God, it's Curtis Randolph! I'm going to faint!" He finally releases me, and I see all of my students on their feet and the boom above my head.

Margot makes her entrance next. "Surprise!"

Tru blocks the classroom door so no one can get in or out.

I pat my now-messed-up hair down and straighten the collar of my blouse. "What are you guys doing here?"

Curtis turns and faces his audience with a canned smile. "I am here to support MacDowell High. Thank you, youth of today!" He puts his arm around my shoulder and finds the camera guy, who's made his way to the back of the room, and grins. "I believe in our youth! I believe in our schools!"

The director begins to clap, and the students follow suit.

Meanwhile, I try to push Curtis off, but he holds on tight. "I don't want to be filmed," I say through gritted teeth.

"This will only take a second," he whispers back.

Margot takes my hand. She's so close, several strands of her hair stray into my face, and the director has to motion for her to stand aside a little. She does and delivers her line: "It is my good fortune to be engaged to such a generous man." She pauses and sends Curtis an air kiss. Strands of her hair land on my mouth, and I have to blow them off. She continues. "Curtis and I talked, and we both knew we wanted to give back to the schools. We want to help in whatever way we can."

The director holds up an actual cue card, and Curtis begins to read robotically: "That's right, Margot. Children, I want to tell you to stay in school. You want to be like me? You have to study hard. You are our future, and I am counting on you!" He and Margot let me go, and I step out of the frame. Curtis then starts shaking students' hands and signing autographs. Several students take his picture. Jessica and Maddie try to yuk it up in front of the camera until Tru asks them to step aside.

"What the hell is going on?" I ask Margot. "Why are you guys here?"

She's texting by now and hardly pays attention. "We're here to help your school."

"Right. Sure you are. What's the real reason?"

"Can you give me a second?"

"Margot!" I'm ready to grab her phone, but then the director shouts, "Cut!" and Tru begins moving everyone back. "Time's up! Give the man some space!"

Detrane comes over, jumping straight up in the air like a spawning salmon. "I got his autograph *and* his picture!" He then hugs me. "Why didn't you tell us you know Curtis Randolph? That's mad respect, Miss Nelson."

Margot pauses her texting long enough to look at him. "She didn't tell you?"

"You his girlfriend?" Detrane asks.

"Fiancée. I'm going to have my own TV show. My name's Margot. The show is called *Margot and Me*. Tell your friends." She offers a hand as though expecting Detrane to bow. They shake just as the bell rings.

I throw my head back in relief. *Saved by the bell*. "Out! Everybody out! Class is over! Go home!" Tru and I work together as we force them out of the classroom.

Once they're all gone, the director closes the door. "Good work, Bart," he says to the cameraman. "Now how about standing next to her desk for a wide-angle."

"No, Bart," I say. "Let's not. Put me on film and I'll sue. And you can't show the kids either. Isn't that illegal?"

"Their faces will be blurred. We're here for Curtis and Margot. Actually, it would help us out if we could get a little more interaction between you and your sister. How about a hug?"

"*Please, P?*"

"I don't think so."

There's a loud slapping sound at the window. Gladys is practically smashing her face in the pane as she peers inside. "Hello!" She waves. "Miss Nelson?"

"Tru, will you let her in, please?"

There are so many people outside the door by now that even Gladys has trouble making her way into the room. "Get back," Tru tells the onlookers. "Stay back."

"John Jones told me what was going on," Gladys says, her eyes locked on Curtis. She walks toward him while straightening her suit and running her hands over her stiffly coifed hair. "Hello," she chirps.

"Curtis, this is Mrs. Edwards, our principal."

"How do you do, Mr. Randolph. It is such an honor. And thank you so much for your donation. We are so grateful."

"You're welcome." Curtis takes her hand, and she does something I never would have guessed her capable of doing—Gladys giggles! She stands there and giggles as gaily as a schoolgirl. "It's such a pleasure, Mr. Randolph. Heeheehee!"

"Call me Curtis."

"Heeheehee!"

I tap her on the shoulder to get her attention. "Mrs. Edwards?"

"Oh yes," she says, taking note of Margot.

"This is my sister, Margot."

"How do you do."

Margot finishes a text long enough to look up. "Fine, thank you. All of this is for my TV show, *Margot and Me*. It starts next fall."

"Oh, how exciting!"

Margot turns to the director. "Should we go to her office to finish shooting?"

"Let's do it here. We should capture how sorely in need of funds this place is. Bart, get that water stain up there." Bart aims the camera toward the stain in the back of the room, then pans to the row of blackened windows in the back and down to the corner of the floor where the tile is coming up.

I suddenly see my room in a new light, through the eyes of

strangers. Coming here day in and day out, I forget how much repair my room needs. "Hey, Bart, why don't you at least get a shot of the artwork on the wall. There's more here than dilapidation." I point toward the pictures my students drew for last week's unit. To appease me, Bart reluctantly holds the camera on a poster or two.

"What's going on?" I ask.

Margot goes back to texting. "We need footage for the show."

"Don't worry, Sis. It's all good." Curtis turns back to Gladys and brings her hand to his chest.

"Heeheehee!"

"Mrs. Edwards—," he begins.

"*Gladys*. Heehee!"

"Gladys. I'm here today to award your school some more money. I believe in student success, and I know this school needs some money. I want to give you money for scholarships and books." He turns toward the camera and smiles.

"Oh, Mr. Randolph—*Curtis*, are you serious? You already gave us money, and we were so thankful. I just can't believe this!"

She hugs him now as he continues to grin into the camera.

The director says, "Got it," and Curtis immediately steps out of Gladys's clutches.

"How are we ever going to thank you?" She beams.

"Don't you worry about it. I'm here to help."

She stares up at him as if he's come down from on high. "I am such a fan, Curtis. You just don't know. I love your album. It's so nice to be able to listen to good music without all that cursing and carrying on. You're such a good role model for our youth. And thank you for taking such good care of our Raiders, too."

"It's what I'm here for, ma'am. My book drops this time next year. I hope you read it."

"I most certainly will!"

He gives Gladys a wink and starts to make various muscles in his arms and chest dance about, sending her into a frenzy. "Oh my!"

Show over, he says, "Now if y'all don't mind, Margot and I need a word with my sister-in-law in private. Gladys, I'll meet you in your office and tell you more about the money. First time I'll be going to the principal's office without being forced to!" He laughs.

Gladys pumps her fist into the air as she walks by me. "See you shortly, Curtis!"

Tru and the TV crew follow her out.

Curtis rests his hands on his hips and takes in the dry-erase board and all the posters and artwork.

"This is a *classroom*," I explain. "Those things over there are *books*."

He shakes his head and points at me. "Funny, Sis."

"So what are you two up to?"

Margot slaps her phone shut. "Why do we have to be up to something? And why are you keeping Curtis a secret? Seems to me you'd want everyone to know you know him."

"I want people to like me for me."

She considers my response and decides it makes sense.

I try yet again. "So why are you two here?"

Curtis says, "The producers think it would be nice if the audience saw my more intrinsic side, and I thought of this school."

I sigh. "You mean *altruistic* side."

"That's what I said."

"It's not. You said intrinsic."

"Did not."

"Did so."

"Whatever. They wanna show me being nice to people."

He tugs at his linen jacket; the diamond stud in his ear shines as bright as Venus.

"We're also here to discuss Mom," says Margot. "P, it's been four months! You two need to start talking again."

Curtis says, "The wedding is coming up fast, and we need you and your mother on speaking terms. We're creating a Christian TV show, and we need all hands on deck. We can't have you two fightin' and all that at the wedding."

"We want everyone to get along," adds Margot. "The show is about how to be a good family and how to have style and good taste."

"That's right. That's why we don't want any trouble. We don't want nobody sneaking off in the parking lot to hook up with men. You're gonna be related to me now."

Based on what Margot told me, news of the "parking lot incident" spread like all good gossip does in a church—like a California wildfire fanned by high winds. Since she has yet to mention Mom's slapping me, I'm under the impression she doesn't know just how bad our fight was, however. Regardless, I hate that the football player can use my transgression against me. I'll admit that I owe Mom an apology, but I owe him nothing. "I appreciate your stopping by and any donations you might have for the school, but what goes on in my life is my business. TV show or no TV show."

"You foolin' around in your stepfather's church parking lot is a family matter," Curtis insists. "I didn't know you liked 'em so young, Sis."

"What's that supposed to mean?"

"The guy in the parking lot. What were you guys doing out there, anyhow? That's just nasty. You couldn't go to a hotel?"

"You would know. Isn't that where you take all your groupies?"

"Piper!" Margot says.

Curtis practically growls with clenched jaws. "You're over the line, Sis."

Margot soothes him by stroking his jacket. "Let me talk to her, baby. Give me a second."

He keeps his evil eyes on me as he takes out his phone. Seeing that her ignoramus of a fiancé has calmed down, she takes me by the arm and walks me toward my desk.

"I had a long conversation with Mom, and she's ready to talk, P. She says she's ready to forgive and move on."

"She is?"

"Yeah. She would have called you, but you know how stubborn she is. Can't you please make the first move? Call her, P. This has been going on too long. I want my family back. Don't you miss her?"

I do, but I'm almost afraid to see her. Not that I think she'll hit me again, or anything like that, but I've been feeling so good lately and I have to wonder if part of my newfound happiness has to do with my time apart from her. Sherry has said family can be so toxic at times that we need a break, and I suppose that's what I've allowed myself to do—take a break. Hearing there's an opening, though, gives me pause. Maybe it's time I "face what frightens me," as they say in AA.

I search Margot's big baby browns. I want to believe what she's told me, but I've also known her all my life. "Are you telling the truth, Margot? Or is this some kind of ploy?"

"Ploy," she huffs. "I don't *ploy*. Mom wants things to go smoothly at my wedding as much as I do. She just thinks you owe her more of an apology, and that's the only reason she hasn't called first. Mommy loves you, Piper. She forgives you."

"And considering you were making out in the church parking lot, that says a lot." Curtis grins. I glare at him, but he's already texting again.

I turn back to Margot. I feel myself wanting to tear up at hearing Mom still loves me. A part of me does miss her after all. I'm just afraid. My new life feels both solid and tenuous. I settle on saying, "I'll think about it."

Margot takes me in her arms. "Oh good. That's all we ask. It's been so stressful with you two on the outs."

Curtis stares at a poster I made at home one weekend. Little mice wear clothes that match the characters from *Of Mice and Men* while exchanging dialogue from the book. He stares a beat, then chimes, "Baby, did you see how those kids reacted to me? Feels good to be a role model for the youth."

"I'm sure it does, baby. Lord knows they need role models like you."

"I wish they had role models that told them there are other things to do besides rap and throw a ball," I grumble. "Just because they're poor and working class doesn't mean their dreams have to be limited to music and sports."

Margot locks her eyes on mine. "They love you, baby. And they should. Anyway, let's get out of Piper's hair and go see the principal." She starts to urge Curtis to the door leading to the interior of the school. "We're donating another five-K to your school, P. That should do something for their dreams."

Thinking of what five thousand dollars can do for us, I hold my tongue. "Thank you. Thanks, Curtis."

"Any time, Sis. Shall we?" He offers Margot his elbow, and she kisses him; then they walk out to greet the fans who were willing to wait. I listen to the bedlam outside as I sit down behind my desk and bury my face in my arms.

I'm four months sober but sometimes . . . *sometimes* . . . I'm convinced just one drink, one itsy-bitsy sip, would solve all my problems. Hearing that Mom misses me has made me feel more anxious than I would have guessed. And then there are Margot and Curtis—I can't relate to them at all. I stare up at the water stain and think of all the other public schools in Oakland and beyond that also sorely need five thousand dollars and so much more. Where are our priorities when someone like Curtis garners all that adoration for . . . *what*? Meanwhile, almost half the staff members at MacDowell take on part-time jobs to support their families and children.

I take a breath and wait for the urge to drink to subside. When it doesn't, I reach for my phone. AA has taught me the rewards of humility, and I have no problem asking for help anymore. I haven't called Sherry in a good three weeks, but I need to hear her voice.

sixteen

I decide to go see Mom that weekend. She and the Reverend live near Lake Merritt, so I stop by their local farmers' market first. Mom loves the empanadas they sell here, and my plan is to buy her a half dozen. The crowd is larger than usual, thanks to the warm, sunny weather and clear blue skies. I buy the empanadas and load up on various vegetables and fruits that catch my eye. I visit the flower stall last. Mom doesn't know I'm stopping by. If she's not home, I'll leave the flowers and empanadas along with a note that says I'm thinking of her. If she is home, my hope is that the gifts will thaw any tension between us.

I've picked out a beautiful bouquet of pink and lavender peonies when I catch sight of a certain someone's globe-shaped hair. I tell myself not to turn, but I can't help myself; Spencer is walking through the crowd with—crap!——the nitwit.

Crap! Crap, crap! Shit!

I immediately duck for cover behind the flower stall.

The attendant selling me the flowers looks this way and that as I bend behind her merchandise. "Excuse me, lady. You still want?"

"Yes. Just give me a minute, please."

"Lady, no hiding back here!"

"I know. I'm sorry. Ex-husband!" I point, hoping the word is universal enough that she'll get it. I wait until I think enough time has passed before standing. "Sorry about that." I take my wallet from my purse and give her a hefty tip. I'm making a fast exit when I see Spencer coming toward me. *Crap! Crap! Shit!* There's no time to duck. When we see each other, we both try to avert our gazes, but then the nitwit, who's too dumb to realize she should pretend she hasn't seen me as would any normal new girlfriend when seeing her man's ex, calls out my name. "Piper! Oh my God, honey, it's Piper!" She walks toward me with her arms outstretched, a toddler running toward a parent. She has a waddle, too, thanks to her pregnant belly.

She tries to give me a hug, but on instinct I pull away so that I can avoid her stomach.

Spencer and I look sheepishly at each other.

"Hey."

"Hey."

"It's so nice to see you, P. How ya been?"

"Fine."

"Those flowers are lovely," the nitwit says. She wears a flowy dress that balloons outward when caught in the breeze. Her curly hair is pulled back, and she's young and pretty and really and truly pregnant.

She sees me staring and pats her belly. "We're so excited." She looks up at Spencer, who scratches the back of his head nervously. "We're having a boy." She rubs her belly as though she's the first woman ever to be pregnant. "Just a few months away!"

"Well, congratulations. I should get going. I have an appointment I can't miss. Good luck!"

I'm walking fast when I feel a tap on my shoulder. I know it's Spencer, but I don't stop.

"P. Hey, why are you rushing off?"

I turn and fix my eyes on his. *Are you serious?*

"I know. Sorry about that. She's excited. She means well."

I peek behind his shoulder and see her showing off her belly to the woman at the flower stall. "So, a son. Congrats."

"Yeah." He grins. "I can teach him about Mass Effect and Kant."

He smiles, and I can't help but smile back. Mortal Mission is one of his favorite video games. He always teased that I'd never understand his obsession with video games because I was a girl.

Our smiles broaden. "It's good to see you, P."

"You, too."

And it is. It's been six months—six *long* months—without a word between us. It's almost unimaginable that he doesn't know a thing about what I've been going through. He looks good, unnervingly so, in his Super Geek T-shirt and jeans. He's put on muscle and has shaved his goatee, which only highlights his full lips and dark brown eyes. But the time apart has given me some needed perspective and has helped me see how much I tended to romanticize our relationship, how I often forfeited reality for the romantic story I liked to tell myself. Even before we lost Hailey, somewhere along the way we lost each other. Spencer retreated behind work and video games and a constant need to research or distract himself on the Internet. I hid behind alcohol, a problem we never dealt with.

He checks over his shoulder for the nitwit, but she's nowhere in sight. "I miss talking to you," he says.

I start to make a snide remark about choice, and how he

made his. But I'm tired; not literally, just . . . I'm no longer in the
mood for high drama. I don't want to start pining for him again
based on some remark he throws me while his girlfriend is only
a few feet away. These past few months have felt precious.

I smile. "I don't think so."

"Seriously, it would be nice to catch up. Coffee?"

"Seriously, I don't think so. You have someone else to talk
to now."

I realize I say this without an ounce of bite. We'll always
have our memories of Hailey, and he'll always be the only person
who will ever *ever* understand what losing her felt like. I can be
grateful for that and let it be enough.

"Are you sure? There are plenty of people who divorce and
remain friends. Hell, I thought we'd always be friends. I know
Tisa would be fine if we kept in touch. She knows what you mean
to me."

"Tisa probably wouldn't mind if I showed up at the birth."

He starts to chuckle but then sighs and fixes his eyes on
mine. We stand together, feeling the weight of our past and our
daughter and what was our love. People pass. Time slows. Oakland isn't the biggest city in the world, and I'll probably run into
him again at some point, but this is our good-bye.

He holds my gaze until tears shine in his eyes. "She was
beautiful, huh?"

When he takes my hand, my own tears come. I nod. "She
was perfect."

We smile and sniffle, and then it's the nitwit calling his name
and walking toward us with a large avocado in her hand. "Babe,
you should see these. . . ."

"Coming, babe." He smiles and gives my hand a squeeze
before turning to join her.

I wipe my eyes and join the crowd of shoppers. I'm struck by the notion that even though I just saw my ex and his pregnant girlfriend, I don't feel the need to call Sherry.

Finding parking in Mom and the Reverend's neighborhood is a nightmare, so I pull into the first open spot, more than a half block away. After Mom married the Reverend, we moved from a one-bedroom apartment into a three-bedroom house that felt like a mansion. There were two more moves over the years until United in Christ Church became the behemoth it is now and they purchased the two-story, five-bedroom stucco with sweeping views of the bay.

When I'm close to the house, I spot Mom on the front porch chatting with a woman, but neither one notices me as I approach. Mom wears a velour jumpsuit with her hair pulled back and her bifocals atop her head. The woman she talks to is big boned with hammy arms and thighs. She wears all lavender with lavender shoes. I notice two large boxes at her feet before homing in on her lavender-painted toenails.

"Hey, Mom."

"Well, hello. This is a surprise," she sings. I notice a moment of irritation crossing her face, but she pushes any annoyances aside for the sake of appearances.

Rash behavior is the MO of many alcoholics, and I'm already second-guessing my decision to show up unannounced. I offer her the flowers. "These are for you. And I brought you the empanadas you like."

The woman looks from me to Mom and back again. "Sister Wright, is this your daughter? Well, praise Jesus. It is so nice to meet you." From a distance, she looked to be older, but I see now that she's in her late thirties, early forties tops. "What kind of flowers are those? They sure are pretty."

"Peonies," I say.

She waits for Mom to make introductions, as do I. Mom finally says, "Sister Carol, this is Piper; Piper, Sister Carol. Carol has been helping me with invitations for the Booster's Ball."

Carol taps a box with her foot. "Takes all day, but there's nothing like a signed invitation sent in the mail."

An annual affair put on to raise scholarship money for college-bound youth, the Booster's Ball has long been one of Mom's pet projects, which is rather ironic since she had no higher hopes for me than to find a job with benefits. But I don't begrudge the ball; it raises many thousands of dollars every year and is attended by council members and city officials who covet votes from United in Christ members.

Carol stares hard as she gives my hand a prolonged shake. I'm the mysterious daughter who never attends her own stepfather's church and was also caught making out in the parking lot; she must be curious. She places her hand over mine while I stare right back. Her false eyelashes are the same texture as her weave and long enough to be carried off as pets. I'm mesmerized.

"I've heard about you. You're a teacher."

"Yes, I teach at MacDowell."

"We have to get you to volunteer with the Carpenter's Kids. Anyone can volunteer with the Carpenter's Kids as long as they have a passion to help our youth."

Mom says, "Piper is busy teaching as it is, but I will do what I can to press upon her how her skill would be valued. I want to thank you again for all your help today, Sister Carol. I know you need to get going, so we won't keep you."

I imagine Carol can't leave quickly enough as far as Mom is concerned. Me showing up unannounced, with a church member here to boot, is not the best of occurrences.

"How do you like MacDowell? Those kids must be a handful."

"They are a handful, Carol," Mom interjects, "but Piper

knows how to set them straight. Did you need help with the boxes? I could—" She starts to step down from the porch, but Carol takes no notice.

"That would be nice. Piper, my car is at the corner. Would you help me with these?"

Carol catches me, and I'm guessing Mom, too, off guard. For starters, I'm sure she can carry the boxes herself. And second, why *me*? I shrug, though, and pick up a box. What's there to say—no?

I tell Mom I'll be right back and follow Carol to her car. After we put the boxes inside the trunk, she slams it shut and gazes at me with an odd look on her face that says she's either going to pronounce her undying love or eat me. I take a step back.

"Piper Wright—"

"Nelson."

"I'm sorry, that's right. Forgive me. Piper Nelson, let me tell you, I think God has given us this moment, Piper, and I want to tell you that God is a forgiving God. I want you to know that. I want you to know that the doors of United in Christ Church are always open for you. We all fall short of the glory of God, and whatever happened with Harry, I want you to know I forgive you, and more important, he forgives you, and most important of all, your heavenly Father forgives you. Thank you, *Jee*sus! Hallelujah!"

I'm stuck. *"Harry?"*

"Oh look at me. I'm so excited to meet you, I'm getting ahead of myself. Harry is my cousin's son, and, yes, he forgives you. He said you didn't know how young he was. I don't condone your behavior or his, but as I said, we all fall short."

I certainly remember now. *Harry. Harold.* The guy from the parking lot.

"Sometimes I think that you must feel so bad about what you did, and now here you are so that I can tell you personally that Harry is okay."

"I'm glad to hear it, but why wouldn't he be?"

"He backslid something horrible that night. He felt so bad."

I fight the urge to roll my eyes. This Harry person and I didn't do anything except kiss. But then I remember, rather resentfully, the importance of taking responsibility for my actions. I suck in a bit of air through my nostrils and remind myself that taking responsibility is why I'm visiting Mom in the first place. "I apologize for any harm to your cousin, Carol. Thank you for your concern and your forgiveness. I have no excuse for my behavior, but I'm sorry."

"As I said, we all fall short. Your stepfather is big on teaching the congregation forgiveness, and I take his sermons to heart. We would love you to come home, Piper. There is no love like God's love. I know. I had a drinking problem, too, but I was healed through Christ."

Whoa. Whoa. Hey. "Uh . . . drinking problem?"

"Your mom told my family you've been having a hard time." She wraps her hand around my wrist. "But the drinking doesn't help. You only end up in bad situations, like with Harry. You know what I mean? But you see, whenever I feel lonely or afraid, I can go to him. I don't need the bottle. I know he has my back, like no one else." Her voice rises, as her grip tightens. "Jesus is my man. I don't need drink; I don't need drugs. He's my man until I get a man! Oh, thank you, Jesus! I can do all things in him who strengthens me. Hallelujah!"

I ignore this one-woman praise service. I'm pissed at Mom for telling her my business. I'm not surprised she told her, but it's still annoying.

"I'm working on my problems, Carol," I say, wanting to end the conversation. "But thanks again for your concern. Please tell Harry I apologize."

She reaches into her handbag and takes out her cell phone. "Can I get your number? It's a miracle that I'm here and you're here. Would you allow me to speak with you one day about his Word and his healing power of forgiveness?"

"No, thank you, Carol." I don't want to ask what I'm about to ask, but I know it's the right thing to do. Damn it. "Do you have Harry's number? I'd like to call and apologize if you think it would help."

"That would be nice of you, Piper, but I'll go ahead and tell him I saw you, and if he needs anything, I'll contact you through Sister Wright. Harry will only grow stronger in his faith after this, I'm sure." She starts toward her car door. "We'll be praying for you, Piper. If you ever change your mind, get my number from your mother."

"Will do."

Mom is still on the porch when I return to the house. "Your timing couldn't have been worse. Of all the days for you to show up."

"Carol says it was a miracle. Maybe she's right. I was able to apologize."

"That might be so, but now the entire mess is going to come back up again. She's going to tell everybody she met you."

"And so?"

"And so . . . it's embarrassing."

Carol passes in her car, then, with a toot of the horn and a wave. Mom's face goes instantly from sour to happy, as does mine, and we both wave good-bye. As soon as her car is out of sight, Mom heads directly into the house. I'm half surprised she doesn't slam the door in my face when I follow.

"Mom. I'm sorry for what happened, okay? Can we talk?"

"I just wish you had called."

"I was in the neighborhood. Is Charles here?"

"He's at the church." Making no move to invite me into the kitchen or to sit down, she just stands before the living room window with her face pinched.

I take my cue from her silence and look out the window as well. Jupiter and Venus can be seen during daylight hours, and I wish momentarily that I was home on my rooftop.

"I'm sorry, okay? Margot told me you wanted to talk. That's why I came."

"Margot told you I wanted to talk? Margot? And you believed her?"

I suck in a breath. Stupid, stupid me. Of course Margot was lying.

Mom says, "If I wanted to talk to you, I would have called you myself. You know that."

"Fine. But I'm here now. I want to apologize. I can't imagine how awful it was for you to find me in that parking lot the way you did."

Refusing to look at me, she raises a brow.

"It's not an excuse, but I had found out Spencer is having a baby and I freaked out." I decide to leave out that I just ran into him. *What kind of day is this, anyway?*

She finally turns to face me. "He was bound to meet someone, Piper. What did you think? Still gives you no excuse for the way you behaved."

"I know. I know. I'm sorry."

"Are you? Because I don't think you understand the position you put me in. I'm the pastor's wife. What does it say about me that my daughter is molesting a child in a parking lot? Do you even understand what you did?"

"*Molesting children?* That's a strong accusation."

"If the accusation fits! You took advantage of a child— in front of a church! In front of my husband's church!" She remembers the flowers in her hands. "I'm going to put these in water."

Something Curtis said while visiting the school comes to mind—"You like 'em young" or some such inane comment. I then remember Harry's bone-sized frame and that god-awful suit. I follow Mom into the kitchen. *How old is he?*

"Barely twenty!" she snaps. She pours water into a vase, puts the flowers into it, and sets them on the counter.

I feel a strong sense of guilt. Twenty isn't much older than my students. "I'm sorry, Mom. I swear I had no idea."

"He had to go to counseling."

This revelation, actually, seems a bit much. "Counseling? We hardly did anything except kiss. And it's not like I attacked him either. Trust me, he was willing and able."

She waves her hand vigorously in hopes of wiping out details she'd prefer not to hear. "Fact remains, you're a grown woman, a grown woman who should know better. I had to find you in a car. In the church parking lot of all places. Why you're so hell-bent on embarrassing me, I don't know."

"Carol said you told everyone I was drinking."

"How else to explain your behavior?"

My first reaction is to tell her I hadn't been drinking, but this useless fact is pointless by now. "I didn't mean to embarrass you. That night was my rock bottom, Mom. I swear. I've made so many changes since that night. I even joined AA."

"AA?" she says, as if I said I've joined the Klan. "You mean to tell me you're that bad off?"

"Well, yeah. I'm an alcoholic. You and Margot were right—I have a problem. But I go to meetings, and I'm doing better."

She shakes her head as if I've completely confounded her.

"Mom, I want us to get along. I do. I'm sorry. I've been learning a lot about myself. I think some of my behavior might come from things that happened to me during childhood."

"I don't appreciate your talking about all of that. For the millionth time, Piper, let the past stay in the damn past. It wasn't like you were abused, for goodness' sake."

"I know, but if we could have an honest dialogue for once, we might stand a chance of having a better relationship."

She sighs and says nothing.

"Can we sit down and talk? That's all I want. I want you in my life, you know?"

I watch her move about the kitchen. She puts the empanadas away and sets aside the flowers in the vase that's too small. She then opens a cabinet and takes down a glass, then goes to the refrigerator for ice. "Mom?" Still ignoring me, she puts her glass down and rests her hand against the counter while placing the other on her hip.

"Piper, you have me in your life. You're the one who tries to ruin everything. Even now you're doing your best to break up my marriage."

This strikes me as an outrageous statement. "Break up your marriage? What are you talking about?"

"You know exactly what I'm talking about. Charles was nothing but good to us, and even back then you tried to ruin things. You never tried to get along with him. You want to talk about the past? Let's talk about the past. All the man wanted for us was to pray together, and you wouldn't pray, you wouldn't go to church, and whenever you did go, you acted up. Just like you did in that car with that boy! Charles is the pastor of the church, and he had to find out about you in that car!"

"I know, Mom, but—"

"Even after I married him you wouldn't let up. You had a decent stepfather, yet there you were, always going on about David and putting him in Charles's face. Like David was better. David this, David that. How was that supposed to make Charles feel?"

At the mention of Mr. Hoffman, I toss aside any idea of humility or contrition. It's obvious that my mom and I have completely different versions of the past, and she's on the side of nuts.

"This is exactly my point, Mom. *His* feelings. What about *my* feelings? You always put other men's feelings over your own daughter's. You always put Mr. Hoffman down, but you dated him for three years, and you didn't have a problem leaving me with him half the time either. Luckily he was an upstanding individual, or who knows what could have happened."

"What's that supposed to mean?"

"Think about it. You let your boyfriends *babysit* your child? What kind of mother were you?"

"I knew I could trust David. Why do you think I let him look after you?"

"Mr. Hoffman was great, but what about all those other men?"

"You act like I was never around."

"You weren't."

"I was working!"

"Bull. Not all the time. Half the time you were going out."

"Goddamn it, Piper. All you know how to do is whine and complain. No wonder Spencer is with someone else. I'd be, too, if I were in his shoes."

Her retort leaves me feeling as winded as if I'd been punched. She narrows her eyes as if she just might hit me but then goes to the cabinet above the refrigerator and takes down a bottle of bourbon. If we're competing for who can hurt the other more, she's just won. A part of me hopes she simply doesn't believe I've quit and that's why she can do something so heartless as to have a drink.

"Mom, I said I'm in AA; I'm trying to quit."

"I'm not offering you any."

"Can't you have a drink after I'm gone?"

"Charles will be back soon, and I don't like to drink in front of him." She swishes the alcohol in her glass before tossing it back.

"Unbelievable."

"I wasn't thinking about drinking before you got here. Now I'm tense and I want a drink. *And* it's my house."

I watch her pour another, knowing all the while that if I stay a second longer, I'll end up downing the bottle and hitting her upside the head. "I didn't try to destroy your marriage, Mom. I was young, and you were suddenly acting like a different person. Whore to Christian. I didn't know who you were anymore. I wanted the mother I knew to come back."

"Did you just call me a *whore*?"

"No! Well, yes, but I was trying to make a point."

We hear the front door close and both turn as if caught arguing by a parent. *"Margaret?"*

Mom quickly puts the bourbon away and her glass in the sink. The Reverend looks at me curiously before going to the table and setting down his briefcase. He then goes to Mom who raises her cheek while keeping her arms crossed tightly as he gives her a kiss. "What's going on?" he asks.

"Piper just called me a whore. In my own home."

"She misunderstood," I say.

The Reverend gives Mom a hug and asks if she's okay. She nods briskly.

"I think you should leave, Piper. Your mother is obviously upset."

"Mom, I didn't call you a whore. I was trying to say—"

She flashes a look. *Close your mouth right this instant.*

I do as I'm told.

The Reverend pulls himself up as if behind the podium at his church. "I'm sure our tempers have gotten the best of us. We can talk about whatever happened when we're all clearheaded."

"I came to apologize," I try to explain.

"I'm sure your mother appreciates your apology, as do I. Now, however, I think you should leave."

I glare at them, standing shoulder to shoulder like a team
holding their ground against Satan, or whoever they think I am.
Fuck 'em. To hell with both of them.

"I was leaving anyway."

I get as far as the aptly named 24-Hour Liquor. I can taste
the scotch already.

To hell with family, to hell with AA. I deserve a drink after
a day like this. I mean, Spencer? Followed by Mom? It's too
much. One tiny sip and I'll throw the bottle away and never
drink again.

As if in reverie, I go inside and stand in front of the liquor
selection. I search for a scotch I like but have to settle for a
cheaper brand. I buy a pack of cigarettes, too, and cradle the
bottle of scotch in my arms as I carry it back to my car.

I climb into the front seat and stare at the sky as I press the
bottle into my chest and blow smoke rings. As much as I want a
drink, I also fear losing the little ground I've reclaimed over the
past four months.

I catch a glimmer of the half crescent moon and tell myself
to call Sherry. But I'm also feeling whiny and pissy, and I'm sick
of having to call a stupid sponsor every time I feel weak. Hell,
even Sherry's name makes me think of alcohol. How crazy is it
that my sponsor is named after a fortified wine? She may as well
be named Vodka, or Ripple.

I take a deep breath and stare at the bottle I'm still holding.
I'm only a twist cap away from a drink. I tell myself that if I want
a drink after I talk to Sherry I'm allowed, but first, I need to call.

I'm so relieved to hear her voice I burst into tears. She waits
patiently until I pull myself together. I tell her everything as I
smoke, every detail about my argument with Mom.

"I just feel like I'm better now and I can handle a drink.
Just one."

"Hold on now. Sometimes it's one second at a time. Listen. Listen, sweetheart. Can you tell me what would happen if you have that one drink? Be honest, now. What would happen if you opened that bottle?"

I look down at the bottle stuck between my legs, then lean back in my seat and gaze out the window. "I'd have a drink and then three or four. Knowing my luck, I'd get pulled over on my way home and thrown in jail for drinking and driving. Or I'd get home and drink through the weekend, and I'd show up late to work on Monday. Or I'd wake up in a stranger's room. That would make me want to drink more. I wouldn't be able to stop."

"And tell me, sweetheart, what would happen if you don't take that drink?"

I think for a second. I don't see myself making up with my mom any time soon. I'm still all alone. "I don't know."

"Sure you do. Let's say you don't take that drink. What would you do tonight?"

"I guess I'd go to a meeting and maybe talk about what happened. I have papers to grade, and I'm watching the twins tomorrow. Coco and Clem and I are going bowling next Friday night. Graduation is coming up. It would be nice to see my seniors graduate. I haven't gone to the ceremony in at least three years. I always find a reason to skip it."

"See there. You have a lot going on. What do you say you start by going to your meeting tonight? See how you feel after that."

I stare down at the bottle.

"Piper?"

"Yes."

"Is the bottle still in your lap?"

"You read minds now?"

"Put it away."

I sigh loudly and toss it in the backseat.

"Are you there?"

"It's in the backseat."

"That's good. Is there a place where we can meet other than a liquor store parking lot?"

"There's a Thai restaurant at the corner."

"Okay, we'll meet there."

"You don't have to meet me, Sherry. It's the middle of the day. You must have things to do. Talking on the phone is more than enough."

"Piper, you're sitting in a liquor store parking lot and thinking about having a drink. I'm coming. Now the only thing is . . . where did I put my keys?" I listen as she moves around her house in search of her keys. She lives alone near Piedmont, roughly ten minutes away, but when I called, I didn't expect for her to leave her house. Knowing Sherry, she's been out volunteering or doing any number of things that don't involve relaxation.

"Sherry, really. I'll be fine."

"This is what I want you to do. Are you listening?"

I nod.

"Hello?"

"I'm here."

"I want you to go to the Thai place. Get us a table and order a few things."

"I'm not hungry."

"Even better. More food for me. I haven't eaten lunch and I'm starving. Get one of those Thai iced teas for me, too."

"Sherry, I promise I feel better. I'll figure things out."

"I have no doubt that you will, baby, but I'm not getting off this phone until you are in my presence." I hear a car door slam. "Give me the cross street. And order a soup for me, too."

I nod again. I'm too busy crying to respond. Suddenly I don't want a drink at all.

"Piper?"

"I'm here. Thank you for coming, Sherry."

"One day you'll do the same for someone else."

"My mother hates me."

"Your mother is caught up in her own stuff. You have to stop asking her for what she can't give you. She's not there yet. She might not ever get there. You have to stay on your side of the court."

Stay on your own side of the court. Meaning, when dealing with relationships, you can't play both sides. Meaning, worry about yourself. I understood the saying on one level, but after this last fight with Mom, I understand it even better.

I say quietly, "I need to take care of myself and stop looking to her for approval. She can't give it to me. I have to give it to myself."

"That's right. And all that anger you feel toward her is hurting no one—"

"Except me. I know. I have to let her go." I pause and stare out the window.

"You have to forgive her just like you're learning—"

"To forgive myself." There's another saying in AA I'm starting to understand: *See everything.* Widen your view to *everything* around you, not just the negative. Mom was awful, for instance, but what about Sherry?

I get out of the car and take the bottle from the backseat, walk it over to the trash bin, and toss it inside. I stare up at the sky again, thinking of Jupiter and its sixty-six moons.

"Piper? Are you there?"

"I'm here. I just threw the bottle in the trash. I think I'm going to be okay."

"Good. Maybe you'll have an appetite by the time I get there. Food is better with company."

I head back to my car and pop the trunk. I take out my binoculars, the best tool for stargazing when a telescope isn't available. I hold the phone to my ear while I tilt my head back and search for Jupiter. It takes a minute, and I probably look crazy to anyone who happens to pass by, but I eventually find it. "Sherry?"

"Yeah, sweetheart. I should be there any minute now; I'm already on Grand."

"Come to the liquor store first. I'm still here."

"You okay?"

"I'm fine. I have something to show you when you get here, and then we'll eat." I keep my binoculars aimed at Jupiter, a stunning bright diamond floating in a blue sky.

seventeen

My arms ache from working on the curve of the mirror blank for the Newtonian telescope I'm making. Mark's homemade telescope inspired me, and since school ended last week, and I'm officially on summer break, I've added yet another meeting to my roster. Every Friday I come to the Chabot Space and Science Center for the workshop on building a personal telescope. Participants pay for all the materials, a mirror blank, a grinding tool and the like, but Chabot provides the lessons and any device or instrument we need to help put it all together.

The room is the size of a small warehouse with six large worktables. There are fifteen of us in all, our ages ranging from as young as the high school kids who share a table near the back, to the twentysomething hipster couple listening to depressing industrial-sounding music, to the old man near the front who works in a kind of meditative trance.

"Hey, Diaper, look how buff I'm getting." Clem flexes her arms, which look as thin and freckled as ever, but I go with it.

She decided to take lessons with me. She's not all that interested in astronomy but is in a try-anything-once mode of late. Next weekend, for example, she will start taking a belly dancing class.

Mr. Yamamoto, a retired astronomer and lead volunteer, walks up to my table. "Very good, Miss Nelson. We'll have to discuss building your Dobsonian mount soon." He gives my shoulder a pat that says, "Well done," and moves on to Clem's table. He studies her mirror blank, which is half the size of everyone else's and lopsided. The class is more of an excuse to socialize for Clem, and she spends most of her time talking. Mr. Yamamoto stares as though he's going to say something, but he settles with, "Carry on, Miss Collier."

Clem purses her lips when he moves to the next table. "He doesn't like me."

"He doesn't like your mirror. Maybe if you'd stop goofing off, you'll actually finish."

"Maybe if you'd stop goofing off, you'll actually finish," she mimics in a nasal voice.

"You're worse than my students."

Johnny Cash starts to sing from somewhere deep inside her purse. "Good Lord, I swear that man is going to drive me nuts."

She's not referring to Johnny but rather to George, who's been hounding her since their first "date," a word she refuses to use. "We had a cup of *coffee*! It wasn't a date!" Tomorrow they're having lunch, which I've been warned is also not a date.

She digs inside her purse as I sing, "George and Clem, sitting in a tree, *K-I-S-S-I-N-G*."

"Oh you!" she snaps. "Leave me alone." She answers her phone. "What? I'm busy. Yes. I don't know what I'm wearing." She lowers her voice to a whisper. "Yes, that's fine. Okay. Good-bye."

I pucker my lips and make a loud kissing sound.

"It's just lunch! We have a lot in common. He knows a few of the folks I know from back home. Nothin' more to it!"

"Okay. No need to get defensive."

"Who says I'm being defensive? Now, will you help me with this godforsaken mirror? Maybe if the two of us work on it, I can get it in shape."

I take the mount and start grinding the higher end. Not much later my own phone rings.

"Aunt P, Mom's hurt!" It's Sophia.

"What do you mean?"

Margot now: "Mom shot Curtis!"

My heartbeat shoots straight to panic mode. I see how terrified I must look when I catch Clem staring at me with her own worried expression.

"Okay. Try to calm down for me. What's going on?"

Margot says, "Curtis hit Mom, and Mom shot him!"

"What?"

"Curtis hit Mom, and Mom shot him!"

"Are you two okay?"

"Yes."

"Where are you?"

"Mom told us to stay in our rooms. We're in Sophia's room."

"Okay. Where's your mother?"

"We don't know. We've been in my room."

"Where's Hélène?"

"Mom sent everyone home," Sophia says.

"Even Tru," Margot adds. "She started yelling and kicked everyone out."

"Listen, I want you to call 9-1-1."

"No!"

"Why not?"

Margot says, "Mom doesn't want the press to know."

"Mom says they won't go through with her show if the press finds out."

I almost blurt, *Fuck her show!* But I figure an outburst isn't needed right now.

"Mom said not to call anyone," says Sophia. "She made us promise."

"Okay." I check my watch. If I leave now, I can be in Lafayette in less than fifteen minutes. "Okay, sweeties. You guys are going to be okay. I want you to stay in Sophia's room and lock the door."

"It *is* locked."

"Good. Keep it locked. And don't let anyone inside except me or your mother, okay? I'll be there in a minute. Just sit real tight."

"Okay."

"Hurry, Auntie P."

I immediately dial 9-1-1. I explain what's going on as best I can, then ask the dispatcher to send someone to have a look. Lafayette is so small and has such a low crime rate, I imagine the cops will be at Margot's in no time; the only thing that might slow them is the curvy hill she lives on.

"Honey, what is it?" Clem asks.

"It's the girls. I have to go." I snatch off my apron.

"Is there anything I can do?"

"Clean up my work area."

"Of course. Call me if you need anything, okay?"

I don't respond. I'm already running out the door.

I have to cut my driving speed in half once I hit the windy road that leads to Margot's. She and Curtis live at the top of a hill, their humongous home nestled behind a grove of cedars and oaks. I park in between Curtis's Rolls and Margot's Mercedes. I've never seen the driveway so empty; the girls weren't exaggerating when they said Margot kicked everyone out. Friday

traffic was worse than I thought, and it's been twenty-five minutes since their phone call. Just as troubling, there's not a cop or
ambulance in sight.

I let myself in with my key. I listen closely for any sound of
violence or turmoil, but the house is eerily silent. "Margot?" My
voice echoes to the top of the living room's vaulted ceiling.
"Margot?"

A four-foot-tall oil painting of Curtis and Margot hangs
above the fireplace mantel. Curtis stands behind Margot, wearing a gold crown and long white robe opened far enough to
reveal his bare chest. Margot, also in a crown and white robe,
sits in a gold chair with a leopard reclining at her feet. I usually
roll my eyes at the painting, but now I only worry that my sister
and the girls are not okay. *"Margot?!"*

I continue to call her name as I race up the stairs. I give a
knock on Sophia's door. "Sophia?"

She opens the door, and both girls rush into my arms. "Are
you two okay?"

They nod.

"Where's your mother?"

"We don't know," says Sophia.

Margot says, "We were, like, watching a movie, and we heard
a loud noise."

"Like a gunshot."

"Mom came up and told us not to leave the room and not to
call anyone."

"Her eye looked really bad," Sophia adds.

"I want you both to stay here while I look for her. Keep the
door locked until I say it's okay to open it. Everything is going
to be okay."

I have to pry their arms from my waist, but they finally let
me go.

I call out Margot's name as I make my way through the sprawling house. It's not until I reach Curtis's office, downstairs and closer to the kitchen, that I hear voices. "Margot?" I walk cautiously toward his office door. *"Margot?"*

"I don't understand," I hear her say. "If I could make some fucking sense out of this shit, maybe then I wouldn't be so upset. But I can't. I can't make sense of it."

I step into Curtis's office without making a sound. The office is the size of a large living room, and neither Margot nor Curtis notices me. Margot stands with her back turned, her right hand pressed against her hip; in her left, she holds a gun. Curtis, clearly shaken, stands with his back pressed into the wall in between the TV and trophy shelf. The office itself is in shambles. Curtis's gold record, once framed and hanging above his trophies, is now shattered on the floor with a bullet hole in its center; a shattered crystal vase lies next to it. Furniture has been tipped over and the large engagement photo Curtis kept above his desk is also on the floor. A gunshot hole perforates his front teeth in the picture, leaving him with a creepy Howdy Doody smile.

Curtis holds his arm as if it's a separate appendage. When I step closer, I notice he's trying to stop blood oozing from a spot near his elbow.

"I thought you loved me," Margot says.

"I do love you, baby. Now put the gun down."

I take another step, feeling oddly out of body, as though I've stumbled onto a movie set. Is this part of *Margot and Me*? "Margot? You okay?"

She turns abruptly, and that's when I see the crescent-shaped bruise under her left eye, green and mucky; a lighter bruise more red in color flanks her cheek.

I turn to Curtis. *"You hit my sister?"*

"Hold on now," he says, his eyes growing wide at the thought of having to deal with two pissed-off women. "Where did you come from?"

"The girls called. *You hit my sister?*"

"I can explain. It was self-defense. I swear! Your sister came at me with a knife! She cut me!" He holds up his arm and shows me the wound, a two-inch slice down the forearm, leaking enough blood to indicate that he might need stitches but not enough to indicate he'll lose his arm—too bad. "She cut me! If this affects my game, I assure you, we are all going to pay." He looks at Margot and pleads, "What if I can't play no more, baby?"

"Who gives a shit."

"You're gonna give a shit when my paycheck is cut in half. Baby, your immaturity in this matter is startling. You could ruin us both. Think about it. Tell her, Piper."

"Tell her what?"

"Not to leave me!" He steps forward but, second-guessing himself, moves back into the wall. "Baby, I'm sorry. But we have to stay in this together. You and me. No matter what. We made a vow." He turns his head in a way that gives me a clear view of the scratches on his cheek and neck. I can't help but think, *We are a family built on dysfunction.*

"I don't know what's going on," I say, "but the cops will be here any minute, so you two had better both calm down."

"They've been here," Margot says nonchalantly. "Been here and gone." She keeps her eye on Curtis. "I told those girls not to call anyone. I can handle this asshole here. What I can't handle is bad press."

"I can't believe all you care about is the press. He hit you!"

Curtis steps forward, but when Margot raises the gun, he steps back. "Damn straight I care about the press. I need my show! And Curtis, unless you forgot, we're supposed to be representing Christian values. I can't let people know you hit me!"

"It was an accident, baby!"

Dumbfounded, I ask, "Why did the cops leave?"

"I told them there was nothing to worry about," Curtis says. "I told 'em I cut myself cooking. Gave 'em a couple of signed footballs and jerseys, and they were on their way."

I move closer to Margot. "Are you okay?"

"No. I am *not* okay."

"Are you hurt?"

"She's not hurt!" Curtis pleads. "*I'm* hurt! Hell, girl, why don't you tell Piper how you came at me with a knife? While I was sleeping! I got her in the eye, true, but it was an accident. I had no idea what I was doing. I was half asleep! And when I woke up, you would have thought she was going to slice my throat. As God is my witness."

"What about the bruise on her cheek?"

"That was also an accident. I tried to get her off me, and she started screaming all hysterical and shit and clawing at me, so I slapped her to get her to shut up—calm her down like in the movies, and that's how she got that spot on her face. Tell her, Margot."

Margot doesn't hide her boredom with his story. "What he says is true."

"Still doesn't give you the right to hit her," I snap. "You're, like, three times her size."

"I know! It was an accident!"

"Now tell her what *you* did, Curtis," says Margot. "Tell her why I came after you in the first place."

"Baby, I messed up. I'll admit it. But I keep telling you, what I did was in the past. It happened before we got engaged. We both agreed that the ceremony was our new beginning. You can't punish me for what happened before I became committed to you—the second time, I mean. That's what we agreed."

"Yeah, but you didn't tell me the whole truth. Tell Piper what you did, Curtis." She raises the gun, aiming just below his navel. "Go on."

He recoils and moves back toward the wall, using his hand to protect his groin. "I slept with Danielle," he whispers. "But I swear it was an accident!"

"An accident," Margot snorts. She looks at me askance, as if to say, *Can you believe the bull coming from this man?* "How can you stand there and tell me putting your penis inside my best friend's vagina was an accident? You must think I'm crazy."

"No, baby, but I do think you're upset, and you have a right to be, but I'm tellin' you, it didn't mean anything. I promise, all that—all that womanizing is in the past. Danni was one in many!"

"Way to go," I say. "I'm sure that makes her feel better."

"My point being, I have not cheated since the engagement party. I swear. Baby, you know me," he pleads, his eyes brimming with tears. "I have been your most humble king and you—you have been my most cherished queen. I wanted to show my love for you. I know moving the wedding date has been difficult, and I wanted to make it up to you."

His tears are working on her, I notice, and I watch as her resolve begins to tiptoe out the door. Sure enough, she lowers the gun. "But Danielle," she says weakly. "My best friend. Why her?"

"Yeah," I say, in hopes of keeping her focused. "Why Danielle? How did you find out, anyway?" I ask.

"I was going through his e-mail. I wanted to trust him, but I wanted to be sure. I went back an entire year, and then I found two pictures of her—*butt naked*. Danni!" she says, stomping her foot. "Why *Danni*?"

"It was a moment of weakness, baby. She came at me with everything she had, and you and me—we were having trouble.

You know how my game was all off during that time. It just happened."

"She's like a sister to me, Curtis. You may as well have slept with Piper."

He grimaces as though tasting something sour. "That'll never happen." He shivers.

"Never," I add, making my own disgusted face. "Never ever. Ever. *Ever.*"

I hear Margot moan softly. She's moved to the mirror next to Curtis's desk and stares at her reflection in disbelief. "Oh my God. Look what you did to my face, Curtis! Look at my face. My beautiful . . . Oh my God, look at me." She places the gun down on the edge of the desk and gingerly touches the bruise under her eye. "How can they film for the show now? The wedding is in less than three weeks, and"—she suddenly breaks into a long loud wail—"I look like fucking Frankenstein! I'm ugly!"

"So the wedding is still on?" Curtis asks.

"Shut up! Look what you did to me!"

"Baby, that bruise is not that bad. It'll heal in time. But what needs to heal more is our relationship. Now, I forgive you for coming at me with a knife—and a gun—but you have to forgive me. You are my everything. We have to stay together."

Before I know it, he rushes over and uses his good arm to turn her from the mirror and pull her into his shoulder. She breaks down as soon as he touches her and begins to cry softly as he strokes her hair. "She tempted me, baby. She's a seductress. I told you she liked me."

"Margot, don't buy it. No one forced him to sleep with her. He'll never change!" I shake my head in disgust when neither she nor Curtis pays any attention to me. "Might be nice if someone checked on the girls," I add bitterly. "Remember them?"

Curtis continues stroking Margot's hair. "Yeah, Sis. Why don't you do that. Tell 'em everything's okay. Thanks."

I grumble more than a few curse words under my breath and head upstairs. Margot opens the door with Sophia directly behind her.

"Everything is fine, girls. Your mom is okay. There was an accident, and that's why her face is bruised, but she's fine."

"What about the gunshot we heard?" Margot asks.

"It went off by accident. Your mother was upset, but no one is hurt. You two okay?"

They both nod.

I bend down and look from one to the other. "Your mom loves you very much. And I love you very much. I'm sorry all of this is happening, but none of it has anything to do with either of you."

"But where's Mom?"

"Why isn't she up here?"

"She'll be up in a second. Right now, I want you both to focus on the fact that everything is okay. And bottom line, girls? Never date or marry an idiot. I don't care how good he looks or how much money he makes. Got it?"

We hug and I return downstairs where I find Curtis and Margot still holding each other while whispering and staring into each other's eyes. *Oh brother.*

"In case you're wondering, the girls are fine."

I spot the gun on the desk. I think of using it to kidnap Margot and force her into some kind of deprogramming, but I know if she ever manages to dump Curtis, she'll only replace him with another first-rate ass.

The gun is heavier than I would've imagined, and the thought that it can take out a life is terrifying enough that I feel my hand start to tremble. "Is there somewhere you two keep this thing?" I hold it away from my face as if it's a dirty diaper.

Margot lifts her head from Curtis's chest long enough to motion toward the closet. "That box up there."

I go to the closet and take down the lockbox from the top shelf and secure the gun inside. I stare at them in their embrace, surrounded by all the chaos and mess. "I can't believe you're letting him touch you, Margot, let alone hug you. Guns? Fighting? What about the girls? You really want them growing up in this kind of madness?"

"I need my guns," Curtis barks. "All these crazies everywhere wanting a piece of me. I need them for protection. And I keep my guns safe, so you don't need to worry about that. Every last gun in this house is locked up. Tell her, Margot."

But Margot is looking around the room now as if she's getting my point. I egg her on: "He could have said no, Margot. He didn't have to sleep with your best friend. You must be so hurt."

"I am," she says, pushing Curtis away. "You and your fucking dick have ruined everything, Curtis." She begins pacing the room, occasionally kicking a piece of glass or stray pillow. "What the fuck are we going to do now?"

"Nothing has to change, baby. We'll get married on the twenty-fifth just as planned."

"Oh really." Margot continues to pace, talking to herself as though she's alone. "Anyone who sees me will think I was abused! How are they going to handle this on the show? What am I supposed to tell the producers? I ran into a wall? I'm so fucked!"

"Is that all you can think about, baby? Our show?"

"No, I can think about you putting your dick in my best friend's vagina. Should I think about that instead?"

He lowers his voice. "We'll just stay incognito until you heal. 'Cause you're right, baby. We can't afford to have you leave and people seeing you and taking your picture. One picture and the paparazzi will be on us. People will think the wrong thing and *my* career will be ruined. That's why we've got to keep this family together. Why don't you hide out here until you're better?" He points to the picture of the two of them on the cover of *Ebony*, the glass in the frame smashed. "Don't forget who we are, Margot. You and me are the golden couple, baby."

Margot stares at the photo, too. She lowers her arms, her eyes tearing. "But I can't be around you right now, Curtis. I just can't."

"But why?"

Margot and I yell in sisterly unison, *"Because you slept with Danni!"*

"I'll go to Calistoga," she says.

"No, baby. Someone will see you there. Guaranteed. All it takes is a picture, and your face will be all over the Internet."

"What about my place?" I offer.

"No," Curtis says. "You can't stay at her place. Everybody knows me in Oakland, and that means they know you."

"Okay," I say. "What about Mom's?"

"Sweetheart, think of everyone at the church. Everyone is always stopping by your mother's. You want them to see you? You want to have to explain how you came at me with a knife? Why don't you just stay here? With me. Baby, we can work this out!"

"I don't trust myself around you right now, Curtis. I swear I could kill you." She thinks for a second, her hand at her brow. "We'll just pack a few things and go away until my face heals. I'll call the director and tell him I need a few days of me time." She turns my way, her expression like when she was five years old, during that one year when she actually looked up to me. "Can you think of somewhere I can go, P? Somewhere I can take the girls?"

I think of the man before I think of the city. I think of our time together gazing at Saturn, our walk around the altars. I think of his kindness. And even if we can't find him, why not hide out in his city? I know my idea is crazy at best, but it's all I have right now.

I look at Margot. "Ever been to Livermore?"

eighteen

Margot stands several yards from the car, waving her arms as she yells into her cell phone. The wind blows the cypress trees behind her to and fro, until they look like long limbs cheering her on. The girls and I wait in the Mercedes with the windows rolled tight, staring at her as if watching a silent movie. She decided that she needed to give Danni a piece of her "fucking mind" before driving any farther and stopped halfway down the hill from her house; the only other house in sight is one hill over and just as massive. We watch as she raises a finger and lets loose another round of insults.

"Did Aunt Danni mess something up with the wedding?" Sophia asks.

Boy, did she ever.

"You can say that. Your mom has had her feelings hurt pretty bad and . . . she's a little angry."

"More than a little," Margot says.

"Are they still friends?"

"I don't know. I don't know what's going to happen between them. But that's why we're going away, so your mom can take a breather and figure things out."

"What about Curtis? Is she still marrying him?"

"Your mother should answer that question, Soph. Let's let her rest and calm down. And I want you two not to worry about all of this. Really. Everything is going to be fine."

Margot marches toward us, slamming the car door after she gets in. She sits for a second with her face frozen in a mix of hurt and rage. I try to remember how upset she must be. She and Danielle are far closer than she and I are.

"Margot?"

She takes off her sunglasses and stares down at the keys in the ignition. I'm worried that she might start the car and do something crazy, but then her eyes well over and she groans loudly before bringing her hands to her face and breaking down completely. I take her in my arms. "It's going to be okay, Margot. You're going to be fine."

"Mom?"

"Mom, are you okay?"

"She's just having a moment, girls. She'll be okay." I hold her until she goes for a tissue. Her eyes grow steely as she blows her nose.

"She was like a fucking sister to me."

"Margot," I remind her, "the *girls*?"

She glances back. "Hey, sweeties, I'm sorry. Mommy is just pissed off right now. Your aunt Danni is a fucking cunt, you know that? She's a bitch who sle—"

"Margot!"

She pokes out her lips, then puts on her sunglasses and turns the ignition.

"Uh. There's no way I'm letting you drive."

"I'm fine."

"Far from it." I try to take the keys from the ignition.

"I'm fine," she says, snatching them away.

I stare hard until she lets out a huff and opens the door. "Fine. Drive."

It's after eight p.m., but traffic is still heavy. I ease into the carpool lane. After driving my compact for so many years, I find that Margot's Mercedes feels otherworldly, as if I'm navigating a jetliner or cruise ship. I looked up the address to Livermore's city hall, and GPS handles the navigation. The only problem, really, now that we're actually on the road, is that my idea to seek out Selwyn for help feels far more quixotic than smart. I never heard from him after sending my note of apology, and what if we do find him at city hall once we get there? What am I supposed to say? *Did you get my card? Why didn't you write back? I thought you wanted to be friends.* And then there's, *Hey, I thought I'd bring my abused sister to Livermore!* I do feel I should try to find him at least. If he works for the mayor, he might know the best place to hide out. There's also a part of me that wants to see him for self-ish reasons. I still think of Selwyn from time to time, how he helped me the night of the engagement party and how we ran into each other a few months ago in San Francisco. Maybe he was right. Maybe we do have some kind of connection—a connection obviously strong enough that I'm driving to Livermore right now.

I take a deep breath and glance over at Margot. After exchanging a barrage of text messages with Curtis, she took an anxiety pill and now either stares off into space or dozes. The girls listen to music with their headphones in their ears and their iPads in their laps. I'm tempted to ask for an anxiety pill of my own, but sobriety being the slippery slope it is, I take another breath and continue driving.

Soon we're making our way into downtown Livermore, which isn't all that bad with its old-fashioned streetlamps and park benches lining the main drag. Very Mayberry, USA.

I drive to a parking lot adjacent to city hall and find a parking space.

"I'm going to see if my friend is here." Everyone ignores me. The girls are still listening to music and busy with their iPads; Margot leans against the door with her eyes closed. "Be right back."

I cross the street and walk up the steps leading to the glass doors. While the building is still open, no one is around except for a young woman chatting with the security guard.

"Would either of you know Selwyn Jones?"

The woman points to the elevator. "Fourth floor. Third door on your left."

The security guard adds, "Building closes in ten minutes."

"Thanks."

The elevator doors open to a long corridor. I read gold placards as I walk past each office: MICHAEL F. ANDREWS, MAYOR; LYNDA THOMAS, VICE MAYOR. To calm my nerves, I remind myself of how kind Selwyn was the last time I saw him. I find his placard and knock.

"Yeah?"

I open the door just enough so that I can step inside. He sits behind a huge mahogany desk that seems ready to swallow him whole. A large window offering a view of the city serves as a backdrop, along with floor-to-ceiling bookshelves filled with law books. Selwyn himself is so intent on the papers in front of him, he doesn't bother to look up.

I clear my throat.

He takes off his glasses and slowly gazes up from his work. I watch as his expression changes from irritation to curiosity to downright shock.

"*Kilowatt?* Oh my God. Kilowatt? Is it really you?"

"It's me." I feel my cheeks grow warm from embarrassment at showing up out of the blue, and I'm also surprised at how good it is to see him.

He walks over and begins squeezing my arms in the same way he did when we ran into each other in the city, as though I might be an apparition. *"Is it really you?"*

I laugh. "It's me, Selwyn."

He places his hand on his hip while using the other to scratch at the back of his head. "I can't believe it's you. I can't believe you're here."

I lock eyes with his. "It's me." I then surprise us both by bursting into tears.

"Hey, now. Do I look that bad? What's wrong? Don't cry. What's going on?"

"I'm sorry." I continue crying while he leads me to a chair. He pours water and hands me a box of tissues and waits until I'm able to pull myself together. "I don't know why I'm here. Why am I always in distress when I see you?" I cry all the harder. "You must think I'm crazy!"

"Of course not. What is it? Tell me what happened."

I blow my nose and fall into a fast-paced ramble about Margot and Curtis, the fight, the girls. After catching my breath, I look at him and add, "I don't know why I thought I should come here. I don't know what made me think of you at all, but as soon as I did, I came up with this crazy idea that you'd be able to help. I'm sorry."

"Stop apologizing. I'm happy to see you."

"Why didn't you write me back?" I blurt out.

"What?"

"I sent you a card. Did you get it?'

"I did," he says. "But since you were working things out with your husband—ex-husband—I figured I should leave things alone."

"Fair enough. I am sorry for the way I kept blowing you off. I'm sure that's what it must look like."

"No need to apologize. You were doing what you had to do. I respect that." He pulls back to take a long look at me. He then takes a tissue from the box and gently wipes a tear from my chin and another from under my eye. "It's great to see you. Come here." He stands and opens his arms. I give him a hug, briefly closing my eyes until I start to feel embarrassed by how good his arms feel.

When we move apart I say, "My sister is waiting, so I should get going, but if you'd be interested in seeing each other again, I'd like that. If you'd want to, I mean."

"Of course I want to see you again."

"Great." I start to leave but then realize I have no idea where I'm going. "Do you know of a hotel where we can stay?"

"Hotel? Kil, don't insult me. You and your sister will stay with me. I'm sorry to hear about her troubles. It's a real shame." When I open my mouth to protest, he shakes his finger. "No arguing. Not this time. You all are staying with me, and that's that. There's no need for you to drive around looking for a hotel when I have plenty of room at my place and would love to have you." He goes for his jacket, but the piles of papers on his desk catch his attention and he pauses.

"Selwyn, listen. If you have work to do, I understand. Honestly, we can go to a hotel. It's no big deal."

"Absolutely not. There's nothing here that can't wait until Monday. I can work on it over the weekend, too, if need be. It's not your worry." He grins as he sticks his keys in his pocket and straightens his tie. "My God," he murmurs. "I can't believe it's you. I never thought—" He takes a breath as his face grows flush. "I never thought I'd see you again, Kilowatt. It's good to see you."

"You, too, Selwyn."

He beams up at me a beat before opening the door. "Unbelievable."

It's dark when we walk to the parking lot. I introduce everyone briefly, but we decide it's best to get going. We follow Selwyn as he drives onto the highway for a mile or two, but then we exit and begin following him down a road that takes us inland, so far inland, I'm soon using the high beams as we leave all traces of civilization behind—no houses or signs, no traffic except for Selwyn's car leading us down a narrow two-lane road.

"Where is he taking us?" Margot gripes. "Go figure. We'll get out here in the middle of nowhere and get ourselves killed." She sits up in her seat. "How do you know this person again?"

"He's a friend."

"You don't have any friends."

I make a face. "Anyway, don't worry about it. At least no one will find you out here. Isn't that the point?"

"Might be, but I don't want to die in the process."

Little Margot says, "There aren't, like, *any* houses out here. Are we in the country?"

"I see a light over there," Sophia says. "That's probably a house."

"We can only hope," Little Margot replies.

"Okay, everyone. Let's try to be more positive. Selwyn is trying to help us."

"But what if Mom's right and he's a serial killer?" says Little Margot. "Does anyone, like, know we're here? Should we leave a trail?"

"If we don't, we'll never be found," Sophia says ominously. And again: "Never be found."

"See what you started?" I say to Margot.

"He looks familiar," she says. "Do I know him?"

"He was at your engagement party."

"My engagement party . . ." It's not so dark that I don't see the frown forming on her face. "That short guy!"

"He has a name, you know. Besides, he's not that short!"

"He's shorter than you."

"Not by much. And who cares? He's a good man."

"Are you dating him?"

"No. I told you, we're friends. And he's nice enough to let us stay in his home, so try not to be rude."

She crosses her arms and looks away. "All I know is, you two ruined my engagement party."

"Unless you forget, I left your party because I was upset. Selwyn was there to help."

"Yeah, he helped all right."

"Just be grateful for once, okay? Just once in your life? Could you do that?"

Selwyn's right-side blinker flashes, and we follow him onto a gravel road that eventually leads to a remodeled Victorian. The house has tall windows and a wraparound porch with a porch swing and wrought-iron table and chairs, perfect for drinking lemonade on a hot summer's day.

"Now, would a mass murderer live in a house like this?" I ask brightly.

"That's how he gets away with it," Little Margot says shortly.

"No one suspects him," says Sophia.

We park, and I pop the trunk. As soon as Selwyn climbs out of his car, two basset hounds, ears flopping, come bounding around the house. They're followed by a German shepherd, hunched over and slower in gait. Selwyn takes his time greeting each dog before joining us. The girls, who have always loved animals, immediately forget about serial killers and run up to the dogs even as Margot tells them to stay away. The two hounds look exactly the same with their low bellies and sad, droopy eyes. The German shepherd, although big, is gray around his nose and mouth and periodically lets out a loud wheeze that makes him sound like an old man in need of an oxygen tank.

Margot presses her back against the car and turns down her mouth as though smelling something awful. "Are they safe?"

"Are you kidding?" I say, eyeing the German shepherd, who is currently hacking up large amounts of phlegm.

"Oh yeah," Selwyn says, pointing to the German shepherd. "Dizzy there is almost fourteen and too old to do much outside of sleep. Louis and Ella would rather play than just about anything. They have their dog kennels and can sleep outside if that would make you feel more comfortable."

"That's a good idea. Thank you."

Margot notes the truck parked nearby. "You have company?"

"That's mine. Classic 1960 Chevrolet. Had her restored a few years back."

"Lucky you."

I roll my eyes and continue unloading the car. When we have everything, we follow Selwyn into the house. The kitchen and living room are all one large open space, both rooms decorated early-American style with antique tables and rockers. I catch Margot staring at the furniture derisively. When our eyes meet I mouth, *Be nice.*

We take our things upstairs, and Selwyn continues the tour. There are three bedrooms, two baths, and an office. I also glimpse an outside balcony spanning the length of each bedroom. We end up in the room that Margot will share with Little Margot. It's been decided that the girls shouldn't sleep alone. I'll sleep with Sophia in the room next door.

The girls ask if they can go downstairs and play with the

dogs. Selwyn tells them where he keeps the dog biscuits and says they can give them two biscuits each. It's nice to see the excitement on their faces.

Margot picks up a pillow and studies the embroidery before returning it to the bed. "Piper says you're an attorney. You can live out here on that kind of money?"

"Margot!" I'm tempted to explain how living off various men has done nothing to help her understand what it means to earn a living, but Selwyn takes her question in stride.

"It's okay. It was actually relatively inexpensive to buy this place. Not many people want to live out in the middle of nowhere, but it suits me fine."

"A lot of space for one person. You're not married?"

"*Margot.*"

"I was married, but we divorced three years ago."

"What happened?"

"Geez, Margot. You'll have to excuse my sister. She has a social disorder called 'too nosy for her own good.'"

"I'm just curious. He doesn't have to answer if he doesn't want to."

"It's fine," Selwyn says. "Guess you could say Charlene and I had issues that couldn't be resolved. She's in DC now. The house is too big for one person, but I can't get myself to move. I'm a country boy at heart, and this is as good as it gets without having to move out of state."

"I don't blame you," I say. "It's a beautiful place."

"Thanks." He starts toward the door. "You all must be hungry. I'll get dinner started."

"You're going to cook?" Margot asks, as though he's just told us he's about to perform a backflip.

"Yeah. I'm no four-star chef, by any means, but I'm sure I can put together something fairly edible."

"We don't want you to go to any trouble, Selwyn," I say. "We could just as easily order pizza."

"No delivery out here." He laughs. "Besides, I don't mind at all. You two make yourselves at home."

When I hear his footsteps on the stairs, I turn to Margot. "What's with all the personal questions? You'd think Mom never taught you manners."

"Oh calm down. He seemed okay with it."

She sits on the edge of the bed and takes out her phone. The bruise near her eye is already turning a deep purple and taking on the shape of a lima bean.

"He's left five messages," she says, already pressing the phone to her ear and listening intently. "He says he misses me."

"He's full of shit. Come downstairs."

She's too busy listening to her messages and doesn't respond. "Margot. *He slept with your best friend.* Why are you bothering with him?"

"I know I know. I just want to hear these messages. I'll be down in a sec."

I pause at the door, but then I think of what I'm learning in AA. I can only take care of myself. And with that in mind, I tell her I'm going downstairs to help with dinner.

Selwyn and I clean the kitchen while the girls play Scrabble. Margot ate with us but has since returned to her room to call the producers of her show and talk to Curtis. After I help Selwyn load the dishwasher, he claps his hands together. "There's something I want to show you. Will only take a second."

"What is it?"

"Follow me."

I follow him upstairs to his bedroom. "You have something to show me—in your *bedroom*?"

He raises his hands in defense. "It's not like that. If you haven't noticed, I'm a perfect gentleman."

He leads me into the bedroom where there are two oil paintings on the wall and an antique bureau and dresser. On his bureau I notice a picture of a woman I assume is his mother and a second picture taken decades ago of a young man in a football uniform, a younger, leaner version of Selwyn.

"That's Sylvester."

"You two do look alike."

"Yeah, like I said, everyone thought we were twins." He picks up the photo. "I don't know of any single person who could make me laugh so much."

I try to remember the last time I laughed with Margot. I think and think. "You were lucky you two got along so well. You have a lot of good memories you can look back on."

"Good memories are one thing I do have." He returns the photo. "This way."

He leads me to the balcony. I feel my breath catch as soon as I step outside and stare up into the night sky. I had assumed there would be low light pollution out here, and it looks like I was right. I instantly make out double the number of constellations I'd see in the city. I can even see Delta Cepheus and Antares, and just to the south, Scorpius's butterfly cluster.

"*Amazing.*" I keep my gaze on the magnificence of it all. "A sky like this makes living out here completely worth it."

"Won't argue with you there. But *this* is what I want to show you."

I turn and see him at the opposite end of the long balcony, his hand extended toward—"A Meade 280! I forgot you owned one!" I walk over and run my hand over the tubing. "Selwyn," I say, inhaling deeply, "it's gorgeous."

"I'm telling you, Kil, I've been hooked since I bought her. I've been to the Danner Observatory a few times now, too. Last winter I went to the Gheller."

The Gheller Observatory in New Mexico is supposed to have amazing views. "I've always wanted to go to the Gheller."

"It's certainly worth the trip. Well," he says, pointing the Meade farther upward, "what are you waiting for? Why don't you take a look-see? Go ahead."

I peer through the viewfinder until I find Mercury; the power of the Meade 280 is that strong. I stare briefly at the planet, but then, in a burst of sheer, unadulterated happiness, I stop stargazing altogether and give Selwyn a hug.

"Whoa! Hey, what's this for?"

"Everything," I say as I continue to hug him. "Everything."

Selwyn and I have decided to stay up late and find Neptune, named after the Greek god of the sea due to its perfectly blue coloring. It's a windy planet with thirteen moons, and since it's in conjunction with Jupiter this week, we have the opportunity to use Jupiter as our necessary starting point to chart our way to its territory. We have to wait until Jupiter comes into view at one a.m., but we don't mind; Neptune is the farthest planet from Earth, and worth the wait. I also sense we're both happy for the excuse to stay up and talk. Selwyn has made hot chocolate, and we sit at the table out on the balcony. I tell him about my childhood and Mom's exploits, about Mr. Hoffman, Spence, and AA. He in turn describes his life in Alabama, and the devastating loss of his mother to cancer three years ago, coupled with his divorce the very same year. "Worst year of my life. My mother passes, and then I have to find out my wife is having an affair. We were growing apart, but why not ask for a separation? Why cheat?"

He explains that Charlene was his college sweetheart, but over time she became more of a "city mouse" while he wanted to slow down and have a family. They bought the house together with the intention of doing just that, but she wanted more time for her career. "That's probably not the entire truth," he says. "I just don't think she wanted me."

"Don't say that. She married you."

"Yeah, she loved me, but I think she married me because that was what she thought she should do at the time. We were together for three years in college, and I think we both thought the next step was marriage. But did she love me for me? Nah."

I follow his gaze up to the blanket of stars, but I soon find myself looking over at him. I feel much like when I saw him in San Francisco, startled by how handsome he is. He's lean and muscular with nice eyes and a kissable mouth. With all the work I have to do on myself, I'm not ready for a relationship, but I can't deny the feelings I have for him. Why else would I have thought of hiding out in Livermore?

He feels me staring. "What?" He finds his napkin and begins wiping at his mouth. "Do I have a hot-chocolate mustache?"

"No. You're fine."

He pulls back, then, and stares suspiciously. "What is it?"

"Nothing."

He grins slowly. "Were you checking me out?"

I feel myself blush deeply. "No! Absolutely not."

"Yeah, you were."

"No, I wasn't."

"I think you were. It's okay if you're starting to like me, Kil. Just don't objectify me. I'm a human being, not just a piece of meat."

I know I'm busted and smile.

"I will add, however, that if you *were* checking me out, it means you're a smart woman, and I like smart women. Momma always said better to have one smart woman than a roomful of beautiful ones."

"Oh brother." Still smiling, I go back to staring at the sky.

"I can't believe what you told me about Curtis. It's a shame that one of our premier football players has to behave like . . . like an ass. But, Kil, how crazy is it that Curtis Randolph's fiancée is inside my house right now! Right now! How crazy is that?"

"Selwyn," I warn.

"Curtis Randolph's fiancée is inside my house! And she's your sister!"

"*Selwyn.*"

He leans back in his seat and brings his hot chocolate to his lips. "It's pretty remarkable."

I smile at him as he takes a swallow.

"Will you stop obsessing, please?" he teases. "I feel like you're unclothing me with your bare eyes."

"Oh my gosh, you're so conceited."

"But you know you're fallin' for me. Can't help but fall under my spell."

"Shut up."

"You know you like me."

"It would help if you weren't so cocky. Then I might tell you whether I do or not."

"I'm listening." He sits straight up and pretends to zip his lips together.

"I like you, okay? There. I said it. Maybe at some point we can go out for coffee, or dinner. If you want," I add, already feeling somewhat discomfited by my admission.

"Dinner would be great, Kil."

"When I'm ready for something like that," I say. "I'm just kind of getting my act together right now."

"Of course." He leans back and shakes his head at the stars. "It's a beautiful, beautiful night," he says with a sigh. After a moment, he reaches over and takes my hand and kisses it. I in turn take his hand and do the same. We continue holding hands as we keep our heads tilted back and our gaze toward the swath of sky where Neptune shines. I understand why we amateur stargazers get caught up in images of planets like Saturn, with its razzle-dazzle ring, and Earth, marked by its land formations, but there *is* something about Neptune, warranting its name as it does as it shines at the edge of our galaxy, some two billion–plus miles away, cloaked in perfect cerulean blue.

nineteen

Only five hours after saying good night, Selwyn and I are now making breakfast together. The girls, still in their pj's, are in the living room, continuing the game of Scrabble they started last night. Margot is asleep upstairs. A mix of Bill Evans, Art Tatum, and Chet Baker plays on the stereo.

Selwyn's property lies between two vineyards and is surrounded by oak trees. Every time I get a glimpse out a window, I'm taken aback by all the wide-open space. I'm putting water in the teakettle when Selwyn says, "Sounds like someone's here." He's in charge of making his famous biscuits, and flour covers his apron.

I didn't hear a thing. "Really?"

He tosses the towel he's holding over his shoulder and cocks his head. "Who'd show up this early?"

I follow him into the living room, and we look out the window as a white Mercedes makes its way up the long gravel driveway.

"That looks like my mother's car."

Sophia says from behind, "Granny's here already?"

"What do you mean *here already*?"

"Mom told us Granny was coming," says Margot.

I look out the window again. Sure enough. Mom.

"You knew she was coming?" I ask.

Little Margot glances up from the game board. "Yeah, Mom told us last night."

I look at Selwyn. He knows all the drama going on with my family, so I can only hope he'll forgive me for leaving him to greet Mom alone. I'm already boiling mad and have no time for manners. I haven't spoken to her since my disastrous visit when I stopped by the house two months ago. It's not as though I'm afraid of her or afraid she'll push me toward the bottle again, but I don't want her to see me right now either. Don't we have enough going on? I say to Selwyn in a pleading tone, "Would you please excuse me for a second? I need to find out what the hell is going on. I'll be right back."

"Sure."

I march directly upstairs and find my sister fast asleep. I give her a hard shake.

"Mmm?" She pulls her sleeping mask slowly from her face. Her bruises have darkened, and her hair is a mat of curls.

"Why did you tell Mom we were here?"

"Because I need her, why do you think? What time is it? Is she here?"

"Yeah. Downstairs."

She sits up and yawns. "Oh good."

"You could have told me she was coming, you know."

"Why? I assumed you'd know I'd call her. If I ever needed her, it's now."

"But it's rude to invite people without telling the host."

"I thought you'd tell him."

"Why would I tell him?"

"Because you'd know that I'd call her and that she'd be coming." I watch her put on her robe and push her feet into her slippers. "This isn't about you for once, okay? My life is in shambles right now, and I would think you'd be happy Mom is here to be with me."

She walks out, leaving me to follow. We find Mom just inside the door, talking to Selwyn. Channeling Vivian Leigh in *Gone With the Wind*, Margot takes the stairs two at a time with her arms outstretched. *"Mom!"* Mom opens her arms, and they hug as the adagietto from Mahler's Fifth swells in the background.

Mom holds Margot at arm's length. "Let me look at you. Oh, this is terrible."

"I know, Mom. What about the wedding? And my show?" Her voice rises. "Mom, look what he did to my face! The wedding is in three weeks! What am I going to do?" She breaks into her ugly cry.

Mom takes her by the arms and shakes her so that her head wobbles like a rag doll's. "Margot! Margot, listen to me. You've got to stand firm, baby. Now is the time to rely on faith. If you're not better by the wedding, you'll get a good makeup artist; that's all there is to it."

Margot lowers her eyes in an affected manner that portrays both humility and strength. "You're right."

I roll my eyes at the drama. In an attempt to focus on letting go, I haven't called or tried to contact Mom since I last saw her, and watching her with Margot feels a bit surreal. I finally realize that I need to let go of my idea that we might one day be close. I'm no longer willing to bang my head against the wall Mom has in place. Still, there's no need for me to act resentful or ugly either, so when it's clear Margot has calmed down, I walk over and tell Mom hello. She stiffens under my embrace but then hugs me back, if only briefly. She calls to the girls to come and say hello, and they leave their game long enough to give her a hug.

Knowing good and well the girls will only eavesdrop, I suggest they finish their game upstairs.

"Can we go outside?" Margot asks.

"Sure. Put some clothes on first."

They run upstairs while Mom and Margot find a seat on the couch.

Selwyn says, "May I get you anything, ma'am?"

Margot sniffles. "Is there coffee?"

"He was asking Mom," I grumble.

Mom says, "Call me Margaret, and coffee would be nice, thank you."

I follow Selwyn into the kitchen while Mom and Margot converge on the couch. "I'm sorry about this," I tell him.

"Don't apologize. There's plenty of room, plenty of food."

I glance back at them—Margot clutching a tissue and carrying on, Mom holding her and stroking her hair—and I feel somewhat jealous. I'm a new, sober Piper, yes, but jealousy is jealousy, sober or drunk. I take the plate of bacon to the table while Selwyn puts together a tray of coffee.

Margot calls out, "Shawn, would you mind if my mother joins us for breakfast?"

I practically slam the platter down. "His name is Selwyn, Margot. *Selwyn.*"

"I'm sorry! It was a slip. I apologize, Selwyn. I'm a mess right now, if you haven't noticed. Please forgive me."

"Hey, no worries. And of course everyone is welcome. We've got plenty." He leans in close to my ear. "You okay, Kil?"

"I'm fine, *Shawn.*"

Minister's wife that she is, Mom is more than pleasant as we eat and asks Selwyn questions about his job and his house and compliments his cooking. She also asks me about school and my plans for summer vacation. She's so nice, in fact, I soon feel myself relax. Maybe catastrophes like having to drive your sister to Livermore, after her loser boyfriend has practically beaten her, do bring people together. Or maybe our latest family catastrophe has helped Mom realize she needs me as much as Margot and she wants to make up. I offer to pour her more coffee; she smiles politely and raises her cup. I'm not sure what the hell is going on, but it's nice to have a family breakfast. I can't remember the last time we were all together like this.

When we're finished eating, Sophia pushes her chair back. "Can we go back outside?"

Margot stops her latest text long enough to check her watch. "We're leaving soon, so no more than fifteen minutes."

I watch the girls run off. Based on their nonreaction to the news that they're leaving, I gather the girls knew something else I didn't know. "Leaving?" I ask.

"Curtis talked to the producers and convinced them no taping until the wedding," Mom replies. "We'll get a good makeup artist in the meantime and stay low."

My gaze shifts back to my fool of a sister. "You're going back to him? Are you insane? *He slept with Danni.*"

Mom glances over at Selwyn. "Lower your voice, Piper."

"Apologies." I turn back to Margot. "Are you insane?" I say through gritted teeth. "He slept with Danni!"

"He's more than sorry, P. He knows he messed up."

Mom pulls back in her chair. "Mathew 26:41: 'Keep watch and pray, so that you will not give in to temptation. For the spirit is willing, but the body is weak.' Curtis made a mistake. But bottom line, he's a good Christian, and as Romans 8:1 says, 'There is no condemnation for those who are in Christ.'"

"So you're saying your daughter should marry a cheat?"

Margot now says, "You don't understand, P. Curtis and I had a long talk last night. He knows he was wrong. I'm not trying to excuse his behavior, but I'm not sure I was there for him last year the way he needed me to be. We realize none of this would have happened if we had kept our relationship first and everything else second. We lost our focus, and he lost his way."

Mom nods. "The man needs to be the head of the household, or it becomes a house divided. Don't you think so, Selwyn?"

Selwyn, obviously startled to be pulled into the conversation, chuckles nervously. "You're looking at a divorcé here, ma'am—Margaret. I should probably stay out of it. More coffee?"

Mom tells him she'd love more coffee, and he escapes to the kitchen. "Curtis is a good man who made a mistake," she reiterates.

"Mistake*sss*," I say, leaning on the *s*. "What are you teaching the girls, Margot? Stay with a man who beats you?"

"First of all, he didn't beat me, and don't you ever tell anyone he did. And second of all, I'm teaching the girls the importance of forgiveness."

"Please, I doubt if either of you would be so forgiving if he wasn't worth a fortune."

"That's not true. Margot knows where her riches lie."

I look over at Margot who has her phone out and is texting furiously.

The girls, dressed by now, run through the kitchen.

"Be careful of those dogs," Margot says without looking up from her phone. She holds it up so Mom can see what she's typed.

"Good for you. Do what you have to do."

Margot says to me, "I just told you know who she shouldn't expect a cent for the work she's done on the wedding, and I'm going to sue her ass something good."

"On what grounds?"

"I'll get Curtis's lawyers to figure that out. I'm going to take her for everything she has; I know that much. She should be happy I don't go over there and kick her skinny butt. Fucking two-faced bitch."

Selwyn, who has since returned with coffee, clears his throat lightly.

"I'm so sorry you have to hear all of this, Selwyn," Mom says demurely. "You must think we're the most dysfunctional family there is."

"We are," I mutter, rising from the table. "I think I'll go outside for a while."

Selwyn shoots up from his seat. "Mind if I join you?"

"Tell the girls five minutes," Mom says.

"Margot, they just left."

"I realize that, but we need to get back, and we've taken up enough of your friend's time as it is."

"His name is Selwyn," I tell her, but she and Mom both have their phones out and either don't hear me or choose to ignore me. I glare at them both until I feel Selwyn's hand on my back.

"It's okay, Kil. Let's go."

Far off in the distance, Margot pushes Sophia on a tire swing while the dogs bound around them. Selwyn and I are in no rush and walk at a languid pace. I'm seething inside, though. I thought at the very least Mom was here to help, but she only showed up to take the girls away, right when they were starting to relax and have fun. And then there's my idiotic sister.

"You okay?" Selwyn asks.

"I'm fine, except I worry that my sister is teaching my nieces that they should put up with bull." I add halfheartedly, "I'm starting to wonder if there's a way I can keep them legally. I could certainly charge on grounds of neglect and foolish parenting."

"On the bright side, considering all that's happened in the last twenty-four hours, it's nice that they can be kids right now and relax."

He has a point, of course. I also know that I need to calm down. To that end, I take a deep breath and gaze at the vineyards and sloping hills. "Hailey would have loved it here."

"It's a good place for children."

"Adults, too," I say. "I really have to apologize for my family."

"Don't worry about it. It's nice having you here, Kil."

"You're kidding, right? This has been total chaos."

"Not at all. And you're here. I still can't get over that."

"Well, thanks for having me. And thanks for being so nice to my family." I stare at him briefly. We did nothing last night except to share a couple of long hugs, but I feel myself blush, nonetheless. "It's nice being here. With you," I add cautiously.

He starts to say something but stops himself. Starts again. Stops.

"What?"

"I know your family is leaving, but if you want to stay longer, I'd love to have you. There's plenty of room, and you can start your summer vacation off right." He raises his hands. "Strictly platonic, of course."

I gaze around the property. It's a tempting offer. Very tempting. Although—"strictly platonic"?

"I'd love to take you out to dinner, but it doesn't have to mean anything other than a nice meal. Now that you're here, I don't want to ruin anything. I'd like to get to know you and take things slow. I don't want to mess this up, Kil."

"I don't either. And dinner would be nice." I look down at my clothes. Except for the T-shirt Margot loaned me, I'm wearing the same outfit I had on yesterday, which, thanks to all the drama, feels like days ago. "I can't go out to dinner like this, though."

"Not a problem. I can drive you back to your apartment so you can pack a few things, or you can borrow my car. So what do you think about the offer?"

I bring my hand to my brow and watch the girls briefly. If I stay, we can continue talking and stargazing. Watch movies and take walks. And given more time, when I'm more sure-footed in my sobriety and settled in my life, who knows? Maybe Selwyn and I can have something real together. I'd like that, actually. And I like the idea of taking things slow, starting with a few days together. "Thanks for the invite, Selwyn. I think I'll stay."

"Really?"

"Yeah, really."

"Really really?"

"Yeah, really really. I hope you're more articulate as a lawyer." I laugh.

"What can I say, Kil? You rob me of all verbal skill. I feel like a kid around you."

We smile at each other until he holds up his hand, which I take. We then walk toward the girls, hand in hand, not letting go until we're close enough that they can see us.

"Aunt P, check this out!" Margot yells. She pushes Sophia higher, and Sophia lets out a delighted scream.

"I hate to tell you, but they want you back at the house."

"Already?" Sophia asks.

"'Fraid so."

She asks Margot to help her stop the swing. "But we don't want to go, Aunt P. We've only been here, like, less than twenty-four hours." She climbs out of the tire, then bends down and strokes Ella's ear. The dog buckles at her touch.

Selwyn says, "You both will come back soon; that's all there is to it. You and your family are always welcome."

They look up at him, not believing a word. "You mean it?" Margot asks.

"Absolutely."

"Just let me know when you want to come back for a visit and we'll come back. I'll bring you." I glance at Selwyn to see if this is okay.

"Whenever you want," he says with a firm nod.

"Okay, then. Let's go, Sophia."

They walk ahead of us, but I overhear Sophia ask Margot: "You think Ingleton will be like this?"

"Like what?"

"You know, like a lot of trees and stuff."

"Guess we'll find out soon enough."

I stop short. "Girls . . . what's this *Ingleton*?"

The girls shoot each other panicked looks.

"Girls?"

"We can't say," Margot says.

"Mom made us promise not to tell you."

"Go back to the swing."

"But—"

Anything Margot is keeping the girls from telling me cannot be good. "Go back to the swing. I'll come and get you in a minute."

I don't need to explain to Selwyn that something is awry. "I'll stay with them," he says. "Give you some privacy."

"Thanks."

Mom and Margot chat as though everything is perfectly normal as they descend the stairs. "What the hell is Ingleton?"

Margot throws her head back. "They told?" she says, then tromps down the stairs and sets her suitcase on the floor. "I specifically told them to keep their mouths shut."

"They didn't tell. I overheard them. So what is it?"

"A school."

"What kind of school?"

"A good school," Mom interjects. "They'll be taught good Christian values."

"I know most of the schools around here, and I've never heard of it."

"It's in Oregon," Margot says with a sigh. "It's a boarding school, okay?"

"*Boarding school?* Have you lost your fucking mind?"

"Piper Michelle, watch your mouth," Mom chides.

"Curtis and I need time after the wedding to continue to work on the show, and you know training starts for him."

"Margot, we're talking about your children. You can't get rid of them because your schedule is busy."

"But Curtis and I want to start a family ourselves, and we need time alone. And it's a good school. We did our research."

I try to will myself to calm down, to think of AA slogans and advice from Deacon Morris, but I'm so angry, nothing comes to mind. She can't send them away. What does shipping them off to boarding school say to them except that they're not wanted? As egotistical as she is, how can she possibly kick them out of her life? *My life.* Because it comes down to that, too, I have to admit. I'm closer to those girls than I am to my sister or my mom. I can't lose them.

"Please don't do this, Margot. It's not right. Think of what you're saying to them by sending them away."

"If they don't like it, we agreed they can come back in a year. It's not a big deal, P."

"But it is. An entire year away from their family is too long. Let them stay with me."

"They may as well stay with me, if they're going to stay with you," says Mom. "It's a good school. They'll be fine."

"No they won't, Margot. They're too young to be sent away, and you know I'll look after them; they practically live with me as it is."

"No, we've already decided, P. They want to go."

"That's a lie."

"They'll like it once they get there," she quips.

"When did you decide to do this?"

"I don't know. A few months ago. Like I said, Curtis and I want to have a baby, and now that I have my show—it's the best solution."

"Don't forget Danielle," Mom interjects.

"Yes, after what happened with that slut, Curtis and I need time alone more than ever. The girls can focus on school, and my husband and I can focus on starting over again."

She's not getting it. Not hearing me at all. I step closer so that we're almost nose to nose. I need to make her understand. I fear the girls will think they're unloved if they're sent packing just because she's newly married, and they're too young to be sent away. What is she thinking?

"Don't do it, Margot, please. A year without their mother is too long. I know they act mature, but they're still little girls who need their mother." I take her hand. I slow my breath. "Margot, you have only so much time with your children. And even that's not promised."

She understands exactly what I'm saying and lowers her gaze. "I realize that, P. But I have to do what I think is best for *my* children. I know they spend a lot of time with you, but they're mine. *Mine*. And they're going."

I snatch my hand away. "How can you be so heartless? You wouldn't be sending them away if they were Curtis's children. If those kids were his, there's no way you two would be sending them away; he wouldn't let you. If and when you get pregnant, just watch how you treat the baby as opposed to those girls. And they'll see the difference, just like I saw the difference with how Mom treated you when you were born."

I hear Mom from behind. "Oh Lord, here we go! Here we go! See what I mean, Margot?"

"Let them stay with me. I'm begging you, Margot." I'm on the verge of tears now but jump when I feel Mom's hand on my arm. "Don't touch me."

"You need to calm down."

"I don't need to do anything."

The girls walk in with Selwyn in tow. The tension in the room is biting and oppressive.

"Everything okay, ladies?"

Sophia says, "Can we come back here and visit, Mom? Selwyn says we can."

"We'll see. Go get your things."

Mom turns to Selwyn as they leave. "I'd like to thank you for your hospitality. We appreciate your kindness."

"Think nothing of it."

Margot starts toward the stairs. "I'm going to help the girls."

I let my gaze follow her, unsure of what to do next. I felt neglected as a child, and I know I might be putting some of my own stuff on the girls, but I also know for a fact that they used to complain that their mom was "never around" and "ignored them" all the time. Problem is, they've grown used to it. We all have. But that doesn't make it right. I know I'm going into a panic, dangerous territory for a drunk, but for the life of me, I can't accept the spitefulness of Margot's gesture. Who sends her ten-year-olds to a boarding school because she needs time with a man? More specifically, a self-absorbed cheat? And not just any ten-year-olds—*my nieces*. I just can't let this happen. I glance over at Mom. She's the only person who can sway Margot, and if I have to beg her to use her parental powers, so be it.

"Can I talk to you for a second, Mom?"

She steals a glimpse at Selwyn in a way that only I would notice. *Now is not the time for whatever you have to say.*

Selwyn looks from my mom to me, surely feeling the tension between us. "I should get to that kitchen," he says, making a speedy exit.

Mom rests her hand on her hip after he leaves and stares me down. I'm up for the challenge, though, and refuse to break her gaze.

"Mind if we step outside? For privacy?"

"After you."

We walk out to the porch. When the sunlight catches her face, I'm reminded of how beautiful she is. When Margot grows older, she'll look exactly like her.

I come to when she says, "Selwyn is that man you left with at the engagement party, isn't he?"

"Yeah. So?"

"Are you seeing him? How many men *are* you seeing?"

"I'm not seeing anyone—not that it's your business."

"It's my business when you're taking advantage of young men at my church."

"Mom, I said I'm sorry for that. How many times do I have to apologize? And anyway, I don't want to fight. I don't. Look, I am sorry for everything I have ever done wrong, okay? I'm sorry for everything you think I've done wrong and everything I'll do wrong in the future. But let's just forget about us and focus on the twins, okay?"

"Go on."

"Is there any way you can convince Margot to let the girls stay? She'll listen to you. They can stay with you or me—I just think sending them away is wrong. I don't want them to think we don't love them. Would you talk her out of it, Mom? Please?"

"You're asking the wrong person. As I said, I think it's a good idea. Margot and Curtis need to work on their marriage, especially after what happened."

"But the girls are a part of their family, too. How is sending them away going to help?"

"You act like she's sending them to prison. They'll be fine."

I shake my head in disbelief. "I'm so stupid. Why did I think you'd help? Of course you wouldn't get it. You hardly raised me."

"Don't you ever get tired of hearing yourself complain?"

I try to think of all I've learned in all those lousy AA meetings, but none it of matters at this moment. I can't recall a word of helpful advice from Sherry or Deacon Morris or any of those stupid self-help books Sherry asked me to read either. All of it is erased by my rage. I step closer to Mom. "You were a terrible mother and you were completely selfish and now Margot is selfish."

Mom stares up at the sky and takes a long breath as if asking the heavens to give her patience and guidance. She closes her eyes and rolls her shoulders back as if she knew this moment would come and knew she'd have to steal herself for it. "Look, Piper. I know you want to blame me for how your life turned out, but it's not my fault we lost our Hailey."

"What?"

"I've been talking to Charles, and he helped me see why you're so angry with me."

"This has nothing to do with Hailey."

"It must, and I'm sorry for that. I know I can be hard on you, but you tend to make poor decisions based on her passing."

I think back to the first time I visited Clem and how

angry she became at the mention of her husband. I'm as pissed now, even more so. "Don't you dare mention my daughter. You don't know a thing about my relationship with her, or me, and you have absolutely no idea what I've been through. I'm sick of it, Mom. I've never told a soul what you were like before you met Charles, and you've never thanked me. All you do is act like Margot is Miss Perfect while you treat me like I'm the major source of all your problems. But Margot is no better than I am. She pops antidepressants like candy and picks men who treat her like shit. You raised a complete narcissist. She has no empathy and no sense of integrity—and in the same way she ignores the girls, you ignored me. And now you're going to let her take them away!"

"I'm not going to *let* her do anything. She's a grown woman. And you have to remember, Piper, *she's* their mother, not you."

"I know that," I say. "I know."

I also know I've blown it. I wanted to convince her to let the girls stay, but instead we're right back where we always end up, arguing over the same old issues. I cross my arms and stare out at the hills in the distance. I've lost. The girls are going.

"I'm sorry you're so upset, Piper, but it's for the best."

"Hardly. She's making a huge mistake."

"Even if it is, there's nothing you can do about it now." She turns toward the door. "I'm going to see if she needs any help."

"Of course you are."

She sighs before going inside.

I stare out at the hills in the distance, but then I'm crying and wiping the tears from my face. I'm more composed, at least, by the time Margot bustles out. She clicks the trunk of her car open. "Piper, you should get your purse and whatever, so we can get outta here." Mom comes out next. She has Margot's bag and ignores me as she walks to the car and places the bag inside the trunk. She calls for the twins while Margot answers her phone. "Yeah, baby, we're leaving right now."

The girls come from around the side of the house with the German shepherd cavorting at their feet until he starts wheezing uncontrollably and plops to the ground. Ella and Louis follow, and the girls get in their last moments of playtime. Selwyn trails from behind.

Margot calls, "P, get your purse. It's time to go."

"Is your offer to stay still open?" I ask Selwyn.

"Sure is."

Margot looks from Selwyn to me and back to Selwyn. *"Okaaaay,"* she sings. *"All right. I get it."* She then says to Selwyn, "Someone on the phone would like to speak to you."

"Me?"

She gives him her phone, and in an instant he's clutching his chest as though he might pass out. "Curtis? Is this some kind of joke? How you doin', man?"

I can't help but smirk. Why is he so impressed by such an asshole?

Selwyn continues. "It's no problem, man. It was a pleasure to help. You and your family are welcome back whenever you want. Okay. No, you don't have to do that! VIP? No, man, I couldn't. Seriously, man, season tickets are more than enough."

Margot smiles and calls out, "Girls, looks like Aunt P is staying here. Say good-bye."

They run up the steps and give me a hug. I hold them longer and tighter than necessary. I dig my nose into their hair and kiss the tops of their heads as if already having to say good-bye for an entire year.

"Geez, Aunt P," Sophia says, squirming away. "You'll see us next week. Mom says you're babysitting."

"Yeah, Aunt P, not so tight."

Selwyn lets out a hoot. "That was Curtis Randolph! He's

sending over a signed football and season tickets in the VIP lounge!"

Mom smiles. "You deserve it. Thanks again for helping my daughter in her time of need."

"There's no need to thank me. It was my pleasure. As I told Curtis, you all are welcome anytime."

"Well, thanks again." She shakes his hand, then says, "Girls, I know you heard what your mother said. Time to leave." They run down from the porch and to the car. "Well, are you coming?" Mom asks.

"She's staying," Margot says, in her singsong voice. "She's staying here with Shaaaaawn."

Mom gives me a look and tosses her eyes, then throws her hand as if to say she's done with me before getting to her car.

I step down from the porch as Margot gives Selwyn a hug good-bye. When she hugs me, I remain stiff. "I wish you wouldn't," I whisper.

"Decision's made, P. Try to chill out."

Mom starts for the main road. I keep my mouth shut as Margot walks to her car and climbs inside. The girls turn in their seats and wave good-bye as the Mercedes pulls away.

We continue to wave as the car heads down the long driveway and out onto the road. It's when they're no longer in sight that I burst into tears. I cry just as I had in Selwyn's office, without any warning whatsoever.

"Kilowatt? Oh, Kil," he says, taking me into his arms. "Hey now. What's wrong?"

"I can't stand my mother. I can't stand my sister. I feel like I'm just—this piece of shit."

"What? Come on now. You all will figure things out. Sometimes you have to have an argument or two to help get to the bottom of things."

"I don't think you understand, Selwyn. My fucking sister is sending the girls away. I don't get along with my mother; I don't get along with my sister. If I had any feeling of family, it was from my two nieces. And now she's sending them to boarding school?"

"Kil, you're upset because you just heard the news, but we don't know what's going to happen. She might even change her mind—or you'll visit them."

"I don't want to visit them; that's the point. I want them here. They hardly understand what real life is about as it is, and living at a boarding school surrounded by snobby rich kids will only make matters worse."

"Try to calm down, Kil. We all survive our childhoods."

"Do we?" I suck air through my teeth. "They're only ten, Selwyn. *Ten*. They're going to feel completely abandoned. And there's not a thing I can do about it."

"Kil, come on now. Calm down."

He tries to take me in his arms, but I step back and cover my face with my hands. "Just give me a second, all right?" I keep my face hidden. I feel hot tears wanting to break free again, but I hold them at bay. By this point I know I should find a meeting or call Sherry or both, but I don't want to. I'm tired of talking and crying, crying and talking. I've had it.

"Kil? You okay?"

"Yeah. I'll be all right." I take a deep breath. He tries to take my hand, but I won't let him. I slowly wipe my face and eyes. When I'm more composed I say, "Can I ask a favor?"

"Of course. Anything."

"I'd like to take a drive. You know, just to clear my head a little. Do you mind if I borrow your car? I still need to get some clothes from my place, and if it's all right with you, I'll go get my things and come back. Would that be okay?"

"Are you sure you're okay? Why don't I come with you?"

"I need to be alone. I'll go get my things and come right back."

"Okay, Kil. You do what you have to do to take care of yourself." He kisses my forehead lightly.

"Thanks, Selwyn."

twenty

I'm spinning as fast as Sophia on the tire swing that hangs from Selwyn's tree. When the beat changes, I kick my leg up high and spin again. The song is by a teenaged country-pop singer the girls love. I know every word and sing along at the top of my voice. I twirl and two-step, laugh and sing.

Another country song is playing, but this one I don't recognize. Nor do I recognize the voices I hear:

"Do you want help taking her to your car?"

"No thanks, man."

"You sure?"

"No, man, I can handle her. But thank you."

Someone shakes my shoulder, but my eyes have been glued shut.

"Piper."

I know I'm sitting upright, though, with my head smashed into what feels like my desk at school. "Gladys?"

I feel the same hand again and another shake. "Piper? *Piper!*"

I manage to lift my head. As soon as I open my eyes, the room spins and my stomach churns. "Ow." I wince.

"Come on. I'm taking you home."

I stare into Selwyn's face—all six of them. I watch as they swirl around and around one another as synchronized as Uranus's moons. "Juliet?" I mumble. Uranus's moons are named after characters from Shakespeare's plays. I continue going down the list—"Puck? Portia?"—before closing my eyes entirely.

"Oh no you don't. Wake up." This time he holds me at the shoulders until I'm sitting upright.

I try to remember what's going on and where I am as I look around the room—or, rather, the bar. Because that's where I am apparently—inside a dive bar with booths and a jukebox and a small group of patrons too busy drinking or dancing to the awful country music to pay me much mind.

Selwyn tries to lift me at the elbow, but I fight him off. "Leave me alone," I gripe. "Go away." I grab the nearest empty glass. "Barkeep! I'll have another!"

"Oh no you don't," Selwyn says again, taking the glass from my hand. "You've had more than enough."

The bartender walks over and places a cup of coffee in front of me. Selwyn thanks him.

My stomach lurches at the stench. "I'd prefer more scotch, thank you."

Selwyn pushes the cup under my nose. "You're drinking coffee here or at my place. Which is it?"

I rest on my elbow as I gaze around the bar. I try and try to remember how I ended up here, but nothing comes. I turn to Selwyn. "Remind me again? Where am I?"

"Downtown Livermore. If you're not going to drink that coffee, let's get the hell out of here." He pulls hard enough that in no time I'm off the stool and trying to find my balance on the shifting floor. I lift my foot as if stepping over a large boulder. Selwyn drags me along, but the sudden motion sends my head and stomach into a simultaneous death spin. "Bathroom," I mutter. "Quick."

Selwyn says, "Excuse me, sir. Ladies' room?"

"That way."

He pulls me by the elbow through the bar. I clutch my stomach as he practically pushes me through the bathroom door. I run to the first stall and throw up within seconds. It's as if no time has passed at all, really. No meetings, AA or otherwise. No sobriety chips. No Sherry. Here I am again, head over toilet.

When my stomach has finally emptied, I get up and wash my hands and rinse my mouth with water. It's when I'm getting a paper towel that everything starts to come back: the girls and their good-bye; the drive to my house to pick up clothes; more crying and the thought that I should call Sherry. But instead of calling, I headed back to Livermore, or more specifically, to the nearest bar in Livermore for just one drink before returning to Selwyn's.

I press my back into the wall and sink slowly to the floor. It's official. I'm a two-time loser, and my sobriety's literally down the toilet. I choke back the tears that want to come. I'll never change. I'm a total failure and alcoholic fuckup.

I find Selwyn at the end of the hall with a perturbed look on his face. I see now how disheveled and worn-out he looks. "Why didn't you call your sponsor?" he asks.

"Yeah, that would be the question, wouldn't it?"

"I'm serious. If you knew you wanted a drink, you should have called her or me. Or you could have gone to a meeting."

"Oh, suddenly you're an expert on sobriety? That's great. Just what I need right now, someone else on my fucking back."

"I'm no expert, but I know childish behavior when I see it."

"No lectures, right now. I know perfectly well that I screwed up." I try to walk past him and back into the bar, but he grabs me by the arm.

"This way." He pulls me toward the entrance. I see he already has my wallet and keys. "I paid your tab. We're out of here. Thanks again, man," he says, waving to the bartender and shoving me out the door.

I'm surprised by how dark it is. "What time is it?"

"After midnight."

I see his truck parked next to his BMW.

He opens the door to the car, and I climb inside. "How did you know where to find me?"

"Seat belt," he says, putting the key in the ignition.

I oblige. "So?"

"You called. You were so drunk I could hardly understand what you were saying, so I told you to give the phone to the bartender so he could give me the address." He shoots me a look. "If you knew you were so upset that you wanted a drink, why didn't you ask for help? You have people who want to be there for you. Besides that, I was worried sick. I had no idea where you were."

"Sorry."

"Empty word at this point, Kil."

"But I am."

"I don't think you get it. I was *worried sick.*"

I lower myself deeper into the seat. "Could you cut me some slack, please? I feel bad enough as it is. I know I messed up."

He doesn't respond, though, and he doesn't say a word during the entire drive back.

"Kil."

The smell of coffee wafts under my nose.

"Kil."

I open my eyes and stare directly into Selwyn's face. One face this time.

"I made breakfast. Get up."

I moan loudly. My head feels as though it's being smooshed by an anvil. "I hurt."

"Breakfast is getting cold. You need to eat somethin'."

I roll onto my side as slowly as possible so as not to make my head pound any more than it already is.

"Come on. You need to eat. Breakfast is waiting." He claps his hands next to my ear. "Up and at 'em!"

"Could you not do that, please?"

He claps again, louder. "You mean that?"

I moan and sit up. He hands me the mug of coffee, and I thank him.

"Breakfast is out on the balcony." With that he turns and leaves.

"Thank you," I whisper into the empty room. I have a strong feeling he's not speaking to me. Last night he forced me to drink a glass of water, and he put me to bed in the guest bedroom, where I've been sleeping, without a word. I don't blame him for giving me the silent treatment. I can't imagine what it was like for him to find me in a bar as drunk as I was. I can't believe how much I've messed up either. How do I start over? Is it even possible?

I take another sip of coffee. I can't fathom the idea of eating anything, but I also don't want to piss Selwyn off any more than I already have, so I moan softly and get out of bed.

It's already warming up outside, and the table is set. There are fruit and more coffee, bagels and cream cheese, and eggs.

"This looks great." I doubt I'll be able to eat more than a couple of strawberries but hope I sound polite.

"Dig in."

I stick to my coffee while, vampirelike, I try to duck from the sun in the event that I evaporate. Selwyn has what looks like legal documents out and basically ignores me. I want to apologize, but I know he doesn't believe I'm sincere. If memory serves, last night he called my apologies "empty." And I'm starting to agree. I feel my head pound and close my eyes. I can't believe I've fallen off the wagon. I'm not even sure what it means, except all those months of sobriety feel wasted. I'm obviously a drunk to the core, and this both shames me and terrifies me. What do I do now?

I look up at Selwyn, who continues reading.

"Sorry about last night, Selwyn."

"Yeah, you keep saying that."

"But I am."

"Kil, I've been thinking." He removes his reading glasses and sets his documents next to his plate.

"I know. Don't worry. I'll leave as soon as we're finished eating."

"It's not about you leaving. I meant it when I told you I think we have a connection, and I hope you can see how much I care for you. Thing is, Kil, I don't want to be with someone who caves every time she doesn't get her way."

I raise a brow. "Caves? I was upset. I had another fight with my mom, and Margot's sending the girls away. Yesterday was awful."

"Yeah, but that's no excuse for disappearing the way you did. Going off to some bar where God knows what could have happened to you. I don't know what I would've done with myself if you'd been hurt."

"I said I'm sorry."

"You need to do better than that. You're not the only person with troubles in this world, and troubles don't give an excuse to act poorly. And when people want to help? A person shouldn't try to push them away. You say your sister's selfish, but you've got some of that in you, too. You gotta stop acting like everybody owes you. A turnip can't be anything but a turnip, and your mother, unless she decides to change, can't be anything but who she is now. You worry about how she behaves. At what point do you worry about how *you* behave?"

He's right, and I have absolutely no retort or reply.

He says, "You told me about the teacher who was like a father to you—"

"Mr. Hoffman."

"Have you have ever tried to find him?"

"I wrote him once when I was in high school, but I never heard from him and didn't bother trying anymore." Already my lack of effort seems infantile.

"Try again, Kil. And again. That's my point. You act like life owes you something, Piper. You have so much going for yourself. When are you going to stop looking to other people to be kind to you and *you* be kind to you?"

I think of Sherry: *"Grow up. Forgive yourself. Like yourself."* "But I'm not sure it's possible to have a better relationship with myself if I keep messing up. Look what I did last night."

"Yeah, keep saying that. That's the easy way out. Excuses. What if you stop with that mess and start telling yourself how good you are? You have a lot of love inside you. I know you do. I see it when you're with the girls. And I know you still carry the love you have for your child. Think about that. Think about all the love you have, and let it help you."

Now I think of Deacon Morris. "Since when did you become so knowledgeable?"

"Since I had to go through hard times myself. When Momma passed and I had no brother, no mother. Like I told you, my dad died when I was a boy. So I was alone, and then Charlene did what she did. Yeah, I had to do a whole lotta soul-searching. Tough times, Kil. Tough times. But I came out on the other side the better for it. That's what I want for you, to come out better. No matter what happens between us, I want to know the best you. Not the so-so you, or the half-trying you, the best you. And listen, Kil, whether those girls go to that school or not, they're going to need you. They need a *role model*. Show them how to get through tough times with confidence and grace. Be a woman they can look up to."

I nod slowly. He's right. I know he's right. But just as quickly I plop my head into my arms. "But what about last night? Look what I did."

"That was last night. New day, in case you haven't heard. Isn't that what they say, one day at a time? Today is today. What are you going to do with it?" When I don't respond, he sips his coffee. "You might start with forgiving yourself."

"You make it sound easy."

He turns his gaze out toward the property. "New day, Kil."

I take my coffee and walk to the edge of the balcony. I watch a bird flutter about before speeding off over a hill. I take in the sweet smell of grass and trees; I'm relieved when I don't feel the sensation of having to throw up. I like what Selwyn said about getting to know the best me. Hell, I'd like to know the best me, too. I messed up last night, truly, but at least I was on the road to meeting that self.

Selwyn joins me. He leans over the balcony with his coffee, and we stare out at the property.

"I am sorry, Selwyn."

"I know."

"It's just hard sometimes."

"Yeah, I know. But so what? Your mother isn't the mother you want. Your sister isn't either. But so what? You have the twins, and you have your sponsor, and, Kil, you have me."

"I do?"

"Yeah, Kil. Can't you tell?" He sips his coffee and looks away.

Sherry "stumbled," as she calls it, *three* times before she started to believe in herself and stuck with the program. Where would she be now if she hadn't found it in her heart to forgive herself and start over? Where will I be if I don't?

I turn so that I can look Selwyn in the eye. When our gazes meet, I keep mine steady and focused. "I've been behaving self-ishly, and I regret drinking last night. I made a terrible choice yesterday, and I'm sorry I scared you. I'm going to call Sherry after we eat. And if you'll let me stay tonight, I'll find a meeting to go to somewhere in town later."

He searches my face to see if I'm bullshitting or not. Alcoholics are expert bullshitters. When it's apparent that I mean every word, he takes my hand and kisses it. "That's my girl."

He kisses my cheek next, and I rest my hand across the back of his shoulder and point up to the half-moon suspended in the morning sky, a big dust ball when you get down to it. "Pretty, huh?"

He begins to hum softly.

"What's that?"

"Little jazz tune from back in the day." He sings quietly. He has a nice voice, deep and rich: "'Shake down the stars. Pull down the clouds. Turn off the moon, do it soon. I can't enjoy another night without you.' I used to sing it on nights when I was thinking about you and wishing you'd call."

"Guess it worked, 'cause here I am." I bump his hip with mine and smile. "'Shake down the stars.' I like that."

"I'll have to play it for you later. Wait till you hear Sarah Vaughan's version."

We continue to stare up at the blue sky. The stargazer in me can't help but point out Venus just below the moon, shimmering faintly in all that pale blue. "We're pretty lucky, you know. Mars's sky is a yellowish brown and Jupiter's is black."

He takes my hand and gives it another kiss.

"She knew the names of the planets in our galaxy before she knew the alphabet. She was named after Halley's Comet. Her middle name was Mercury. Spencer fought me over that, but I won."

"Pretty name," he says. "You know, I was thinking. If your sister allows it, we'll bring the girls back here after the wedding while she's on her honeymoon. Have a nice visit. What do you say?"

"That would be great. And I'll keep trying to change her mind about the boarding school." I sigh loudly and toss my head back. "And I guess I owe Mom another apology for losing my temper."

He kisses me on the cheek, but I don't let him pull away. I kiss him on the mouth softly, holding my lips on his until I hear his breath quicken and feel my heart beat faster. I see a star cluster with millions of densely packed stars burst behind my closed eyes. After we kiss, we both sigh loudly at the heat we feel and the possibilities of what that heat represents.

"Wow," he says.

"Wow." I laugh.

Smiling, we go back to gazing at the blue sky. We're quiet until he reaches for my hand. "The universe," I say, "is mostly made of dark matter. It's primarily a huge void of darkness that goes on and on and on. But every now and then between those vast eternities of black, there's a galaxy filled with billions and billions of stars—and some stars, like our sun, are surrounded by planets, like our planet." I pause, my eyes fixed on the moon. "It's pretty amazing when you stop to think about it."

twenty-one

Sherry nudges my arm and nods toward the corner of the tent. "Check it out."

Clem and I follow her gaze. TV crews are filming Margot's wedding reception for a future episode of *Margot and Me*, and when a cameraman steps off to the side, we spot Curtis's mother, flanked by her daughters, Tweedledee and Tweedledum, fast asleep at her table. His sisters wear matching weaves that hang past their shoulders; their silver silk gowns have enough dips and slits to make anyone wonder why they bothered dressing at all. Mrs. Randolph, meanwhile, sits with her head bowed into her chin, eyes closed, thick legs crossed at the knee. She wears a platinum-blond weave and a silver and black sequined dress with a matching sequined hat shaped like a fried egg.

"Poor thing is worn-out," Clem says.

"She got the Holy Ghost so many times at the wedding, I'm not surprised," I say. Twice, Mrs. Randolph jumped from her seat during the wedding and started shuffling her feet and praising God. "It's not even midnight. You'd think her daughters would wake her up."

Sherry laughs. "She sure did give the cameras a show."

We raise our brows and giggle. Sherry is my plus-one tonight; Clem, my plus-two. A few weeks ago, after I called Sherry and told her what happened, there wasn't a hint of judgment or anger in her voice. She simply said, "Today is a new day, and now you get to see exactly how kind to yourself you can be."

She drove out to Selwyn's place two days later. I've pooh-poohed the idea of angels in the past, but that's what she is to me. I take a peek at her as she eyes an actress on the dance floor. She knows all the celebrities here and keeps pointing people out to me. I'm glad I was able to bring her.

There are three times the number of people here than at Margot's engagement party, and everyone is either on their feet dancing or laughing and chatting it up. The thirty-plus-member band moves effortlessly between old- and new-school grooves—with Curtis, of course, taking over the mike now and then for solos.

We're celebrating tonight at a movie producer's estate in St. Helena. The property is located on several acres of land, most of which are used for his winery. Richard Atwell, Margot's new wedding planner, found the estate after declaring the Hunting-ton, her last-minute find with Danielle, "banal at best." Cancellation fee paid, Margot moved the wedding to Napa County.

For a surprise, Curtis had the Edward Johnson Mass Choir flown in from Los Angeles to perform several songs. I notice a choir member with a pompadour and lopsided choir robe stumble and laugh out loud. As someone who knows drunk when she sees it, I can count on two hands the number of choir members who are higher on champagne than on Christ, and Pompadour is no exception.

Curtis is suddenly draping his arms around us from behind. "You ladies having a good time?"

"Great!" Sherry says, raising her flute of apple juice.

Curtis takes me by the neck and rubs his knuckles on top of my head before I can push him off.

"Can you believe how great this all is?" he exclaims. "This is a wedding!"

"*Good*," I say. "This *is* a wedding. Do you know who got married?"

Befuddled, he stares at me for a second, then grins at Clem while pointing my way with his thumb. "This one here is always full of jokes."

"That's why we love her," Clem says.

I nod toward Sleeping Beauty. "You might want to check on Mrs. Randolph."

Curtis glances in her direction but only waves his hand at his slumped-over mother and half-dressed sisters. "Aw, you know, that's just Mom. When she's tired, she's tired, and there ain't no two ways about it. She'll wake up when she's good and ready and'll be like new. You can trust me on that. 'Sides, she don't ever sleep more than thirty minutes a shot. She's like one of them rechangeable batteries."

"Rechargeable."

"That's what I said."

"No, you didn't."

"Yes, I did."

A tall, skinny man with a receding hairline interrupts us. "Curtis?"

Curtis opens his arms. "Wilcox, man! Good to see you!" Wilcox congratulates him and says something about the book Curtis is "writing," and he and Curtis wander off before an introduction is made.

"Who was that?" Sherry asks, excited.

"Hell if I know. More cake?"

We head over to the wedding cake, a seven-tiered affair with seven varieties of cake. Our goal is to taste every one.

After finding a table, we watch a TV camera close in on Margot and Richard, bride and wedding planner, who are suddenly taken over by the impulse to dance. Margot smiles into the camera just as Richard extends a hand, and she twirls into his arms.

"She's so beautiful," Sherry murmurs.

"She is," Clem says in agreement. "Just as pretty as she can be."

Margot *is* otherworldly tonight, a woman who belongs in a fairy tale, albeit a dysfunctional tale involving mistrust, cheating, and a dopey jerk of a prince. After the Danielle debacle, Margot made sure to hire a wedding planner of the male variety, and Richard is as efficient as they come, running the evening with military-like precision and an expert's eye to detail: a look-alike waitstaff in tuxedos and slicked-back hair served dinner, and it was his idea to hire dancers from Alonzo King LINES Ballet to perform two numbers, the first set to an acoustic version of one of Curtis's songs. Sparkling gold lights glow from behind the white chiffon that drapes the tent, giving the space an ethereal feel. The head chef from French Laundry presides over the kitchen, having been paid probably twice what his entire staff makes in a year.

Since Danielle is no longer in the picture, I was asked to give a toast. Initially, I worried I wouldn't have much to say except, *Let the girls stay, you spoiled bitch!* But a lot can happen in a few weeks. I found a therapist, for starters, and along with Sherry and the meetings, I'm learning on a deeper level about forgiveness and acceptance, for others and myself. In the end, I managed a quick two-minute speech that spoke to Margot's tenacity and her ability to make friends with whomever she meets. I then wished her success, ending the toast on a tone that sounded snider than I intended—"Good luck with the marriage!"

The band switches into a 1990s pop hit, and I hear Selwyn's yelp from somewhere in the crowd. I spot him near the band, dancing with Coco. Selwyn and Coco are my plus-three and -four. When I asked Margot to send Selwyn an invitation directly, she responded with, "Who?" So I told her, "Shawn," and she finally got it, although not without making one of her digs: "Who the hell are all these people you're inviting? Since when do you have friends? Space is limited!"

If Coco is a natural bowler, she's gifted on the dance floor, too, and doesn't let any of the extra pounds she carries hold her back. She shakes and shimmies and kicks her legs with ease.

Clem grabs an hors d'oeuvre from a passing waiter. "I don't know where that woman gets her energy."

The band moves into another tune, and Sherry jumps from her seat. "That's my song!" She sets her plate down and sashays out to Selwyn and Coco. Selwyn yelps again when he sees Sherry, then breaks into one of his James Brown spins, leaving Sherry and Coco laughing.

When Selwyn waves at me, suggesting I join them, I hold up the cake as evidence that my hands are full. He waves again, and I shout, "Maybe the next one!" He points and does his spin. I smile to myself as I think back to last week when he blasted old Ella Fitzgerald tunes and we danced in his kitchen after pigging out on homemade ice cream.

Clem leans close to my ear. "Selwyn and Piper sitting in a tree, *K-I-S-S-I-N-G*!"

I give her a light shove, and we laugh.

The man who congratulated Curtis earlier, Wilcox, walks over and extends his hand toward Clem. "Care to dance?"

My turn to tease: "I'm gonna tell George. You know he won't like your dancing with other men."

"Oh you," she snaps, her face immediately souring. "Leave

me alone. I'm not married to George. It's just been a few dates is all." She makes a point of taking Wilcox's hand. "I sure would like to dance. Let's do it!"

They trot off, and I watch until my attention turns to Mom and the Reverend, dancing beneath the shimmering disco ball. Mom's lightly tousled hair softens her face, and she has the moves of a professional dancer. It seems that everyone homes in on her smile. The twins dance next to them with a group of friends from the church. I've been trying to put a positive spin on the whole boarding school nightmare, but all I can think is that I'll visit and call and write and see them whenever I can. At least Margot agreed to let them stay with Selwyn and me while she's on her honeymoon. Hopefully she'll keep her promise and let them come home if they don't like prison—*school*, I mean.

I finish off my cake with a smack of the lips. Margot dances over just as I'm handing my empty plate to a waiter. "I'm tired of watching you standin' on the sidelines while everybody is having fun." She starts to drag me out to the floor, even as I protest; slow dancing in Selwyn's kitchen is one thing, but dancing to something that has an actual beat is quite another.

I try to hold back—"No! Don't make me!"

But she's on a mission. "You're dancing with me, like it or not!"

Once on the floor, she takes both my hands and lifts them in the air. "Wiggle your ass. That's all you gotta do!" I eventually lighten up, and we dance like silly schoolgirls.

We dance through two songs before Curtis taps her on the shoulder. "Wife!" he exclaims, opening his arms.

"Husband!" Margot squeals. They start dancing, and I'm thankfully forgotten.

I check my watch and go over to Sherry, Coco, and Selwyn, currently bumping the sides of their hips in a three-way groove. "It's time?" he says over the music.

"Yeah, but you keep dancing."

"Okay, I'll join you soon."

I make my way outside toward the valet parking. I'm just in front of the tent when Mom steps out, laughing and trying to catch her breath. She holds a flute of champagne and gulps it back like water. She doesn't see me, but I smile anyway and continue walking. We're doing our best to remain civil. I'm not sure what will happen between the two of us, but I'm so focused on staying sober, I don't mind whether it's distance or pleasantries.

"Piper?"

I turn. "Hey, Mom."

She walks up, exhaling loudly. "Ohhh, I don't remember the last time I danced so much. My feet are going to be so sore tomorrow."

"You look good out there."

She fans herself. "Thanks. I thought I was going to pass out for a minute there. I needed some fresh air. You having a good time?"

"I am."

She takes a sip of her champagne, then smiles and looks at me. I hold her stare and force her to keep mine in hopes of telling her everything I want to say without saying a word, *I'm sorry and I love you*, the typical things a daughter wants to tell her mother. I do not assume that she's sober enough to remember this moment tomorrow, but I don't care.

She gently touches my hand. "She was a beautiful little girl, Piper."

"Perfect."

"I miss her, you know. I wish she were here."

"I know, Mom. I do, too."

A couple falls out of the tent, laughing loudly, and our spell is broken. She gives my hand a squeeze. "I should check in on Charles."

I watch her walk back inside. Selwyn says Mom and I are a lot alike and that's why we clash so often. Maybe he's right. Mom is certainly a fighter, and I don't mind taking that from her.

I head to the makeshift parking lot and ask the valet to get my car so that I can take out my binoculars. After I retrieve them, I start the climb up the winding stone driveway that leads to the estate. The climb takes several minutes, the music and sounds from the wedding growing increasingly tinny and inaudible.

I'm perspiring by the time I reach the top. I stand at the edge of the circular driveway in front of the estate and gaze at what must be all of St. Helena down below. As expected, the light pollution is minimal, and it's easy to spot several constellations and planets. I take a moment to catch my breath. Tonight a loose star cluster, CGN108, is only twenty thousand light-years away and viewable through binoculars. When Selwyn and I read about the cluster online, we decided we'd take a break from the wedding at some point and check it out.

Most star clusters orbiting the Milky Way are packed with stars bound tightly by gravity. Not so with CGN108, whose stars are loose and not nearly as codependent. Astronomers, in fact, refer to clusters like these as "sisters" that will eventually go their separate ways. The stars aren't as dense as a regular cluster and so not nearly as magnificent, but they're special in their own right—able to fight the pull of gravity and make their own course.

It takes me a moment to find the cluster, and when I do, I whisper, "Thank you." I lower the binoculars after a minute or two and look down at the tents and people walking about the grounds. I stare out into the distance, at the dark hills and vineyards, then let my gaze wander back to the night sky. I gaze at CGN108 and all those stars inevitably separating as they make their way through space. I take in Orion's Belt and Taurus the Bull off to the left. Eventually, I take a breath and close my eyes entirely. I see the moon and fiery sun. I see all eight planets nestled in their corner of the Milky Way. I see the entire galaxy itself. I see fast-spinning pulsars with fuchsia-colored radio waves and supergiants emitting ten thousand times more light than the sun. I see the Horsehead Nebula, dark and ominous, and the Lagoon Nebula with its pool of newly developed stars. I see supernovas and dark matter and black holes. I see molecular gas and far-off galaxies. I see it all.

Todd Foster

Renee Swindle is the author of *Please Please Please*, a Blackboard bestseller. She earned her BA from UC Irvine and MFA in creative writing from San Diego State University. She lives in Oakland, California.

shake down the stars

the stars

Renee Swindle

A CONVERSATION WITH RENEE SWINDLE

Q. In Shake Down the Stars, *you take the bold step of making your protagonist an alcoholic who doesn't always behave responsibly or admirably. What inspired you to tell Piper's story, and what pitfalls were you aware of as you took on the challenge?*

A. I always start with voice when I'm writing. When I first started the novel, I saw a woman in a room by herself nursing a drink while her best friend was celebrating her wedding. I sort of let her speak to me as I played around and "listened" to what she had to say. It wasn't long before I realized her struggle dealt with the loss of her child. I then thought, "Uh-oh, this is not going to be easy or fun," but I fell in love with Piper, and since I'm a one-idea-at-a-time kind of writer, I stuck with her.

Piper started with a drink in the opening scene and continued to drink in the scenes that followed. I knew she drank a lot, but it took my writing group and early readers to help me see that she was actually an alcoholic. I fought off the idea (much like an alcoholic might!), but after I accepted the fact that she had a problem, it was another uh-oh moment. I knew another part of her journey would have to involve gaining sobriety, and I wasn't sure how I was going to pull that off either. All of her problems were exciting challenges for me as a writer, though: How will Piper ever be happy again? How am I going to write about so many life events I know nothing about? As for pitfalls, I knew I was going to have to stay away from melodrama and scenes that lagged because of the subject matter. Some of the earlier drafts were too preachy. And I knew I wanted to keep humor present as much as possible. I like giving readers, and myself, the unexpected.

Q. For me, one of the strengths of the novel is your portrait of Piper's family, especially her sister and mother. These are capable but flawed women who just can't meet Piper's needs. Can you share a bit about how you came to pair Piper with Margot and her mother, Margaret? And how you saw their relationships playing out?

A. You know, I really take things scene by scene when I write. Margot showed up in chapter one, and I figured out she wasn't Piper's best friend but rather her sister. She entered the scene the center of her own universe and stayed that way! She and Piper had a great dynamic, so I wasn't about to change her. Over time I started wondering what it would be like to grow up with everyone focused on your beauty and nothing else. This question led me to think about the mom and the type of woman she is. What kind of woman raises her daughter to focus on her beauty more than on her smarts? Why does she prefer Margot over Piper? With each draft, the mother became more and more integral to the story. Once I began working on Piper's sobriety, for instance, I knew her drinking was about more than the loss of her daughter; it also had to do with the longing she had for her mother's love.

Q. Piper tells Sherry that she believes in the sun, and when she's really feeling down, stargazing is one of the few reliable sources of emotional comfort she has. Are you also an amateur astronomer?

A. Hardly! I can find the Big Dipper, but that's about it! I don't own a telescope, although I hope to someday. I have visited Chabot Observatory here in Oakland, and that's always an incredible experience. I'm a lot like Piper when it comes to feeling amazement when I stare up at the sky or when I see images of space that the Hubble sends back. I think it's all so mind-boggling that we're out here floating in this galaxy, part of this vast universe. I'm surprised we don't all stare up at the night sky more often.

Q. *I enjoyed the juxtaposition of people from very different economic backgrounds—from superwealthy Margot and Curtis to middle-class Selwyn and Spencer to the struggling students in the Oakland school and neighborhood near where Piper teaches and lives. Why did you want to include such a spectrum of backgrounds?*

A. That's my life. I live in a neighborhood much like Piper's. There's a mix of races and socioeconomic classes. There are people in government-subsidized housing and people who own their own homes, all within the same block. I also have friends who are doing well—not as well as Margot, but who is?! I guess it's natural for me to write from a place where people have varied lives because this is what I see and it's what I'm used to.

Q. *You draw a striking contrast between two very different approaches to Christianity—the celebrity-driven evangelism of Piper's mother and stepfather and the "basement Christianity" of Deacon Morris's grief-support group. Why did you decide to describe both?*

A. I practice Buddhism, but I grew up in the church. I've seen how cruel people can be to one another and I've seen how kind people can be as well. I think any religion has the ability to harden people or make them more vulnerable and compassionate. I knew Piper would never become a Christian, because she's a devout atheist, really, but I wanted her to experience love and her own brand of spirituality; otherwise I didn't see how she'd find any sense of peace or comfort or joy.

Q. Selwyn is one of my favorite characters in the book. He's so all-out willing to give his heart to Piper even upon a short acquaintance, yet you refrain from making him a stereotypical romantic lead. Can you tell us something about what inspired Selwyn and what your intention is for him?

A. I'm so happy you like him! As I said, I had Piper alone in a room with a drink in her hand when I started the novel. I had one draft of the first chapter in which Margot walks into the room, and that was okay, but then I decided to scrap the scene because I wasn't enjoying myself. I knew someone had to walk into the scene; otherwise Piper would just be standing there with a drink. So I had a guy walk inside and—*bam!* Selwyn took over! I was like, who the heck is this guy? But I was having so much fun with him, he stayed right through the first three chapters. I don't write with an outline, so I was grateful he showed up. I wasn't sure for a long time who Piper would end up with, Spencer or Selwyn, or if she'd end up alone, but the more I continued to write, the clearer it became that Selwyn should at least return as a friend. And then I liked him as a romantic partner. I like putting twists on things and liked that he wasn't a typical romantic lead. Why does the love interest always have to be six feet tall and perfectly handsome? Why can't the nice guy get the girl?!

Q. The homemade memorials to dead youth that dot Piper's neighborhood remind us of the tragic loss of young life that has become a constant in such places—a loss that we tend to easily forget when we don't live in those neighborhoods. Can you tell us more about why you wanted to include these memorials in the novel?

A. I think people do forget. I take my dogs for long walks every day and see these memorials all the time. I also see young boys wearing T-shirts with pictures of friends and loved ones who've died, the way other kids would wear T-shirts of their favorite rock bands. It seemed only fitting that since Piper lives in the same kind of neighborhood as I do, she'd see the same memorials.

Q. I found the classroom scenes particularly fun and engaging. Have you been a teacher? Is that why you were able to write such convincing student characters?

A. I teach as an adjunct instructor at two community colleges, and years ago I worked as a substitute public schoolteacher. I didn't base any of the scenes in the novel on anyone I know or anything in particular I've done in the classroom, but I'm familiar with that world. And my students definitely make me laugh!

Q. Can you tell us something about the path that brought you to this point in your writing career? And what's your "process"? How do you go from initial idea to finished book?

A. I start with voice. I love writing in first person and hiding behind or inside a character's voice and story. I also love surprising myself and writing material that is humorous or offbeat. If I'm stuck in a scene or I'm not interested, I always throw in a wrench. I also like to take on a challenge. With my first novel, *Please Please Please*, the challenge was keeping the reader interested in a woman who would sleep with her best friend's boyfriend. As soon as I wrote the first chapter, I knew I was in trouble—the good kind of trouble. How will I make readers care about a character who would do such a thing? How do I keep the story entertaining? The same questions came up with *Shake Down the Stars*: How will Piper ever find happiness? How do I stay away from melodrama? How do I surprise myself? I write scene by scene with these types of questions in mind until I start to see the story evolve and I understand the characters and their motivations. I also make a point of learning what they want in life, and to create conflict I take what they want away.

Q. What can we expect to see from you next, and in the future?

A. My goal is to write stories I don't see out there much. I like characters who aren't perfect and who make mistakes. I'm also heavily influenced by living in a city like Oakland and feel lucky to live in a place with such diversity.

QUESTIONS
FOR DISCUSSION

1. What was your response to the novel overall? Did the story hold your attention and engage your emotions?

2. What parts of the novel made you laugh? Did any parts make you cry?

3. Did you ever lose sympathy for Piper because of her "acting out," and if so, when? Did she win you over again? What does the author do to help make you like her?

4. Have you ever before read a novel with a main character who is alcoholic? Are alcoholic women more rare in fiction than you might expect, given how many people suffer from the disease? Did you find Renee Swindle's portrait of Piper's alcoholism realistic?

5. Stargazing is one of the few reliable sources of emotional comfort for Piper. When you're feeling down, what sources of comfort do you turn to?

6. Piper comes to realize that she must accept the family she's got rather than the family she wishes she had. Is the same true for you and your family?

7. The novel includes characters from a wide range of economic backgrounds—from rich to poor, from used-to-be-poor to now-more-than-comfortably-well-off. Did you enjoy seeing rich and poor rub up against each other? How did that aspect add to the story for you?

8. Discuss the different approaches to Christianity described in the novel. Does one approach appeal more to you than the other? Does one seem more heartfelt and authentic?

9. Discuss the young people in the novel—from Piper's twin nieces, Sophia and Margot, to the students she teaches to the kids she encounters in her neighborhood. Whom did you most enjoy spending time with, and why?

10. You could say that Piper is saved by some new friends she makes. Discuss the sacrifices her friends make, and the role of friendship in the novel overall. Has a friend ever saved your life?

11. Piper is, above all, a mother grieving for her lost daughter. How central is Hailey to the novel? How does this exploration of a mother's grief compare to similar stories you might have read?